TRUE
SON

Also by J.T. Holden

Fiction
The Winter White House
Apple-polisher
Three Imaginary Boys
JB: Or The Unexpected Virtue of Being Swaggy
(also published as *The Curious Disappearance of JB*)
The Boys From Manchester

Poetry
Alice in Verse: The Lost Rhymes of Wonderland
Twilight Tales: A Collection of Chilling Poems
O the Dark Things You'll See!

AN AMERICAN TRAGEDY BASED ON ALTERNATIVE FACTS

TRUE SON

J.T. HOLDEN

A KURO BOOK

黒

ISBN 13: 978-1-937696-25-2 • ISBN 10: 1-937696-25-1

First Edition

For Devona, Kathy & Marilyn
For Becky, Sarah & Sheila
&
the rest of the 65,844,610
who voted for sanity.

Special thanks to
Bobby Cannavale,
who gave me an image to lock
onto so I could see this one through.

In Loving Memory of
Gary P. Newell
&
R. Lee Ermey

The Following takes place in the United States of America on a dark and chilly night, fraught with mystery and political intrigue.

As far as I know or can tell, half of what you are about to read is 100% accurate—based upon alternative facts, gathered from the actual people who were involved in the events depicted in this story. As for the other half, I don't know, but I heard it somewhere, so I'm pretty sure it's all true.

—JTH

JACOB LATNER WOKE TO COMPLETE DARKNESS, FROM WHICH there came a single sound: a steady ticking, like that of a large clock. His grandfather had owned such a clock; it stood against the east wall of his study, between the twin sets of French doors that opened onto the sprawling back garden of the estate where Jacob and his siblings had spent their childhood summers. As a boy, Jacob had been both fascinated and frightened by that clock. By the light of day, the movement of the gears inside the polished cabinet entranced him. But as he lay curled under the covers in the dead of night, the specter of the shiny brass pendulum, swinging deftly from side to side behind the spotless glass door, cut a vastly different image. Though his bedroom was on the second floor, he could hear the clock's hourly chimes throughout the night, and the ever-swinging pendulum hovered in his thoughts, like encroaching doom, inching closer with each fateful tick.

Jacob strained to see, but in the windowless room, no object came into focus, not even a crack of light from under a door. Nothing but pitch black all around.

Despite his growing fear, which held him nearly paralyzed, Jacob resolved to get up and feel his way around the room for a doorknob or a light switch, but his attempt to rise was immediately checked by the strap around his chest, which held him snugly in place. He tried to raise a hand to remove the strap, but both of his wrists were bound to the chair's sturdy armrests—and to his growing alarm, he discovered his ankles were secured to the chair's legs.

With his heart pounding and his breath coming in short, quick bursts, Jacob strained against his bonds. When the straps didn't budge, he became still and took a deep breath to stave off the wave of panic that threatened to drown all rational thought. He held the breath for a moment and then let it out in a long, slow stream while from the darkness, the metronomic ticking continued like a countdown.

What is happening to me? Jacob screamed in his mind, not daring to speak the words aloud for fear that he might actually receive an answer. *Am I dreaming? Is this a dream? Please, God, let me wake up right now. Right NOW!*

He expelled a shaky breath and immediately drew another. Then, with a fierce effort, he pushed forward in a vain attempt to break free from the dream. He had seen people in movies wake suddenly from nightmares with bloodcurdling screams, and he wanted nothing more than to do that right now—even if he screamed so loud that it woke not only Ilona but the kids as well. He would tuck Abby and Jake back into bed and carry baby Tom around the house for as long as it took for the little guy to drift back to sleep—anything to escape this nightmare.

But then something happened that brought Jacob's struggling to an abrupt halt and sent a wave of chills crawling over his flesh.

A voice spoke.

A surreal voice, muffled yet clear, as if the speaker was wearing a mask with a breath screen that altered his natural tone (and indeed the speaker *was* wearing such a mask, though Jacob, who could see nothing in the encompassing darkness, did not yet know this). Even more chilling than the disembodied voice was the paradoxically pleasant tone of the discourse.

"Are you comfortable, Jacob?"

Jacob stuttered. "I . . . I don't—"

"There are rules that must be observed," the voice cut in, smoothly. "Before we proceed, I will need your affirmation that you are indeed comfortable."

"I . . . I don't understand," Jacob stuttered again, his heart pounding madly now. He fought through the fear and asked, "Wha—what is this? Who are you?"

Something shifted in the darkness—a sudden movement that drew a stifled cry from Jacob.

Then the voice came again, closer this time. "You are not here to ask questions, Jacob. You are here to answer them."

In the silence that followed, Jacob shuddered.

"Please, I don't know what this is about, I—"

"The rules must be observed, Jacob," the voice said flatly, "so, I'll ask you again: Are you comfortable?"

Jacob was trembling now, and his voice came out in a choked sob. "Is this . . . is this a dream? Am I dreaming?"

Another extended silence, punctuated by the steady sound of the ticking.

Then the voice, closer still, spoke again: "No, Jacob. You are not dreaming. You are awake. And as soon as you answer my question, we can begin. Are you comfortable?"

"Begin . . . begin what?"

"I cannot answer your question until you've answered mine," the voice said calmly. "Are you—"

"Yes!" Jacob blurted out. He was trembling fiercely now, but he needed to know what was happening. "Yes, I'm comfortable. Please . . . please tell me . . . what is this? What do you . . . what do you want? *Please* just tell me, I'll give you anything, just tell me, what do you want?"

The silence that followed seemed infinite, like waiting for a coin to hit the water in a bottomless well.

When Jacob could take it no longer, he opened his

mouth, but before he could speak the voice came again—this time mere inches from his face; it came in a deathly whisper that sent a wave of shivers along Jacob's limbs.

"I want him to see me."

Jacob shook his head in confusion; his lips parted, but nothing came out. Then suddenly, a dim spotlight from above glowed into eerie life, revealing the black metal mask, with its dark glass eyes—like the eyes of a colossal insect.

And that's when Jacob began to scream. A high-pitched scream that echoed flatly in the surrounding shadows.

But this scarcely mattered to Jacob's captor, who had chosen this space specifically for its seclusion.

And besides, before the night was out, this quiet place would be filled with more than the sound of one man's screaming.

R OWAN MEADOW STRAIGHTENED THE LOOSE STACK OF PAPERS on her desk before shooting a pregnant gaze into the camera.

"Good evening, and thank you for joining us on this extremely chilly Wednesday night. We have breaking news from the White House, as you may have already heard if you've been watching my good friend Calvin Haynes's coverage of this unfolding story over the last hour. But before we get to that—before we get to that truly incredible breaking news story that's happening right now, *live*, as I speak—before we get down to all those juicy details in that stunning and frankly bizarre story—before we dive into that—before we get to the explosive breaking news that has everybody in the world literally holding their breath—before we get to that, I want to start by telling you what we *were* going to cover before this unexpected breaking news broke and turned everything upside down and helter-skelter and fifty shades of cray-cray, and sent the Oval Office into sheer panic mode—and by that, I mean full-on, all-out red alert, *cajones*-to-the-wall panic mode.

"But before we get to all that, I want to tell you about *this* guy . . . "

An inset photograph of a smiling young man appeared in the upper right corner of the screen, and after a measured beat, Rowan Meadow repeated those two words, with emphasis: "*This* guy."

She looked directly into the camera and gave a curt nod before continuing.

"Pleasant-looking guy, right? Nice smile, cute dimples, wholesome boy-next-door type that any parent would be happy to see their daughter bring home for dinner, right? But he kinda-sorta looks like those cloned butler guys on *Watchmen*, don'tcha think? I think so—maybe it's just the dimples. But he's attractive, well-groomed, tall, slender . . . I mean, he looks like the sort of guy who would be class president, star of the school play, captain of the lacrosse team—maybe the swim team as well—I mean, he *looks* like he's got it all. The sort of guy who walks between the raindrops and always ends up on the sunny side of the street; the sort of guy that even his rivals can't help but admire . . . "

Rowan tapped her pen on the desk while gazing thoughtfully into the camera.

"The sort of guy that you just *know* is going to take the world by storm and rise up victorious, no matter what obstacles are in his way. The sort of guy who was born for greatness and all the accolades and prizes and glory that come with achievement. That rare individual who seems blessed from birth. He's got the looks, he's got the brains, he's got the ambition to reach for the stars, and he's got the drive to actually *catch* them.

"This guy. The guy who kinda-sorta looks like the clones from *Watchmen* and carries himself with the confidence of someone who was born for greatness . . .

"His name is Jacob Latner, and despite his boyishly youthful appearance, he is a thirty-six-year-old real estate developer, newspaper publisher, and father of three. He comes from a wealthy family, and he married into an even wealthier one. He has a BA from Harvard and a JD and MBA from New York University. He is the husband of Ilona Kingley, brother-in-law to her five siblings—all pictured here on the cover of US Weekly—son-in-law to her mother and three stepmothers, and uncle to all of her nieces and nephews.

"But beyond all that—well above and beyond those aforementioned family ties, and imminently more conse-quential—is his connection to his father-in-law, President Royal Kingley. Because Jacob Latner not only happens to be the President's son-in-law; he is also the President's chief advisor."

Rowan paused, her lips pressed together, her eyes nar-rowed pointedly, before continuing.

"His name is Jacob Latner. He is the President's son-in-law and closest confidant, which means that at the end of the day—every day—when all the staffers and cabinet mem-bers and other miscellaneous advisors are gone, this guy, Jacob Latner, is the last person the President sees and the last person the President speaks with. He gets the last word with the President. His father-in-law. Every single night. He is the President's closest and most trusted advisor. And he's not only the President's closest and most trusted advi-sor; he's also the guy in charge of negotiating peace in the Middle East, solving America's opioid epidemic, spearhead-ing diplomacy with Mexico and China, reforming care for our veterans, reforming the criminal justice system, and, last but not least, reinventing the entire government to make it work more like a business! Yay!"

Rowan chuckled, shook her head, and straightened up.

"But beyond all that, first and foremost, Jacob Latner

is the President's main guy. Which means everything the President knows, Jacob Latner knows . . . including all of the best-kept secrets of the United States Executive Branch. All those little goodies about what's going on in our country and around the globe that the President shares with only a select few. This guy, Jacob Latner, is *the* guy who has the most influence on the President of the United States . . . "

She paused and took a deep breath.

"And as of six P.M. this evening, it has been confirmed that no one knows where Jacob Latner is. Not the Secret Service, not White House staffers, not his wife, not even the President himself . . .

"Two hours ago, White House Press Secretary Skip Spinner confirmed to the press gathered in the James S. Brady Briefing Room that Jacob Latner has disappeared."

Rowan threw her hands up with an ironic chuckle.

"That's right, the guy with the cute dimples who kinda-sorta looks like those dapper clone guys from *Watchmen*, the guy who walks between the raindrops and not only reaches for the stars but actually *catches* them, the guy who knows every little thing the President knows—possibly even more if rumors within the Kingley administration are to be believed. That guy, *the* guy—who, incidentally, has round the clock Secret Service protection—is right now . . . at this very moment . . . missing."

She made an "exploding" gesture with her hands and chuckled that ironic chuckle again.

"Poof! He's gone, just like that. And nobody knows where he is! Just gone. 'Disappeared.' White House Press Secretary Skip Spinner's exact words were—and I quote: 'Mr. Latner had a meeting with the President in the Oval Office at ten o'clock this morning. The meeting lasted approximately forty-five minutes. The President said it was a very *productive* meeting, with lots and lots of really big things covered'—I am not making that up; these are the press secretary's exact words—'and after leaving the Oval Office, Mr. Latner disappeared and hasn't been seen or heard from since.'

"No, your ears aren't deceiving you, that's what the statement says, verbatim: 'After leaving the Oval Office, Mr. Latner disappeared and hasn't been seen or heard from since.'"

Rowan shook her head and rolled her eyes before looking back into the camera.

"'Lots and lots of really big things,'" she quoted with a chuckle. Then after a measured moment, she added: "The President's chief advisor has 'disappeared.' Like a rabbit in a magic act. But there's a catch—in *this* magic act, the 'rabbit' didn't disappear from the secret back door of a magician's cabinet; he disappeared from the White House." She paused to let those last three words sink in before repeating them with a hard look into the camera: "The White House."

Another pause, punctuated by a short sigh.

"Surrounded by the Secret Service—who aren't the *easiest* group of people to pull a fast one on, if you know what I mean—Jacob Latner, one of the most high profile individuals in the President's inner circle—perhaps *the* most high profile individual in the President's inner circle—just . . . vanished. Poof! Now you see him, now you don't. That's some impressive sleight of hand."

Rowan pursed her lips and gazed into the camera with a serious expression. "Much more on this breaking news when we return. In the meantime, watch this space."

Marilyn Jacks stood at the window of her Georgetown apartment, gazing down at an odd sight: a procession of grade school kids, walking along the deserted street. This in itself wouldn't have been odd had it been seven o'clock in the morning with the kids headed in the direction of the local school. But it wasn't seven o'clock in the morning; it was nine o'clock at night, and the kids were headed in the *opposite* direction of the school. Stranger still, none of them were talking and laughing as kids usually do; they all moved silently with their heads down, like mourners in a funeral march.

Marilyn was still gazing out the window when her husband, Kyle, called out from the living room: "Hey, Mare, you gotta see this. Something's going on at the White House."

Kyle lay on the sofa with Trixie curled up on his stomach. The little dog gazed at the TV with wary eyes while her brother, Rusty, circled the coffee table restlessly and only halted when images of the President popped up on the screen. Rusty was growling at the TV when Marilyn came from the hallway, and he didn't stop growling until the still frame image of the President was replaced by a live shot of the White House, where reporters were gathered in the cold. Then he went right back to circling the coffee table.

Marilyn said, "What's going on?"

"Some crazy shit," said Kyle, his eyes focused on the TV. "Have you heard from Ilona?"

There were seven text messages on Marilyn's mobile phone; they had all come from the same number over the past few hours, and she hadn't read any of them.

"No," she said, looking at the TV with a blank expression. Kyle suspected that his wife wasn't being entirely honest, but he knew better than to get involved—especially when it concerned discord between Marilyn and her old college friend Ilona Kingley. He kept his eyes on the TV while he stroked Trixie behind her ear, and the little dog leaned into his touch.

The live shot of the White House now featured a young reporter with rosy cheeks and shining eyes, her breath hitting the air in white plumes. On the split-screen, Rowan Meadow, in the New York studio, said, "For more on this breaking news, we have Kayley Tru outside the White House. Kayley, can you hear me? This is Rowan."

"Yes, I can," said Kayley, touching her earpiece. At the sound of Kayley's voice, Trixie perked up and her little stub of a tail started wagging enthusiastically. Kyle stroked her fur and told her that Kayley wasn't really here, that she was just on TV. He pointed at the screen, but the little Norfolk terrier kept wagging her tail, expecting Kayley to appear and play with her as she always did whenever she dropped by to visit Marilyn, her best friend since high school.

"It looks cold out there," Rowan said with a chuckle.

"It is," said Kayley, smiling. "Everyone is bundled up and trying to keep as warm as possible. But we're told that they're going to be letting the press inside any minute now."

"So, have they given you guys out there any updates on the disappearance of Jacob Latner? Do they have anything new?"

"No, nothing yet. All they've told us is that we're going to be let inside soon."

"You'll let us know as soon as they do?"

Kayley touched her earpiece. "What was that?"

"You'll let us know as soon as you hear anything about Jacob Latner."

Kayley nodded with a shiver. "Absolutely."

Rowan chuckled sympathetically and said, "Kayley, I know you're cold and hoping to take shelter soon, but Leonard O'Keefe is here with me, and he'd like to ask you something."

A wider shot of the studio appeared on the left half of the screen to include a handsome man in his late sixties with neatly combed ginger hair and keen blue eyes. "Good evening, Kayley," he said with a warm smile.

"Good evening, Leonard."

"Kayley, can you tell us if there's been any update on the whereabouts of the President's phone?"

Kayley pressed her hand to her earpiece again. "I'm

sorry, Leonard, the wind just came gusting in again. What was your question?"

Leonard smiled. "I was just wondering if they've found the President's phone. We've been keeping an eye on Twitter here and haven't heard a peep from his account since this story broke—that's got to be a record for him, right?"

Kayley smiled at the joke and nodded. "Yes, I'm pretty sure this might be a record for the President. But you're not the first one to ask that, Leonard. I just ran into Charles Waller at FIX News, and he asked the same thing."

Leonard chuckled. "I'm sure that's on a lot of people's minds right now. Can you tell us what the mood is inside the West Wing? Has anyone other than the press secretary spoken with reporters?"

"No. We haven't actually heard from Press Secretary Spinner. One of the staffers came out to read that state-ment by him. We don't even know who will be giving the briefing. Will it be Skip Spinner? Secretary Payero? No one knows. There are rumors floating around that it might even be the President, or his daughter Ilona. Everything's up in the air, and no one knows exactly what's going to happen."

Leonard raised an eyebrow. "Interesting. Have they told you when the briefing will begin?"

"We don't know exactly when, but they did tell us that they'll be letting us inside any minute now."

"Well, hopefully, it's soon. It looks pretty cold out there."

"It is," said Kayley with a shiver and a smile.

"Try and stay warm."

"I will."

The screen now featured a shot of Rowan Meadow. "That was Kayley Tru, reporting from outside the White House, where any minute now someone—Skip Spinner, Secretary of State Payero, Ilona Kingley, or perhaps even the President himself, who knows?—will be giving a briefing to the press on the disappearance of the President's son-in-law and chief advisor, Jacob Latner, who went missing sometime after ten o'clock this morning, shortly after a private meeting with the President in the Oval Office. That was over eleven hours ago, and no one in the White House has seen or heard from Mr. Latner since. I'm here with Leonard O'Keefe, and we'll be covering this breaking news story for the . . . " She shook her head and chuckled. " . . . untold future, bringing you live updates as the details become available. So, stick around. Much more to come."

At the same moment the station cut to a commercial, Marilyn's phone began to ring in the kitchen. Kyle looked up at her over the back of the sofa. With Kayley's voice no longer coming from the TV, Trixie sighed and snuggled up against Kyle's chest, closing her eyes. Rusty let out a sudden bark, but when he realized that the image on the screen was just an old guy in a Cialis ad and not the President, he went right back to circling the coffee table.

Marilyn stood rigid, gazing at the TV, while her phone continued to ring in the kitchen.

C HASE GRIMLEY FISHED HIS MOBILE PHONE OUT OF THE POCKET of his suit jacket as he headed away from the table, leaving his just delivered dessert untouched. His dour expression only deepened when he looked down at the phone's screen to find a number he didn't recognize. He supposed it was one of the new interns at work with a question that couldn't wait until morning. He stopped in a quiet area by the coat check, punched ACCEPT, and put the phone to his ear.

The caller wasn't an intern, and he didn't have any questions that couldn't wait until morning. It was a kid from *The Post* who had appeared on *Fastball* a few weeks back. The kid was only a junior editorial assistant, but Chase had been impressed with his knowledge and thought he'd done a hell of a job stepping in for E.G. Hephaestus, who'd had to cancel at the last minute.

"Are you still at the studio, Mr. Grimley?"

"Nah," Chase said. "I'm having dinner at The Blue Duck. What's up?"

"This is Evan," the kid said, practically bristling with excitement. "Do you remember me, sir?"

Chase remembered him. The kid had been all agog at being on the set of *Fastball* and kept calling him "sir" and "Mr. Grimley," which had made Chase blush with embarrassment. "Sure, I remember you. The refugee piece. Good stuff."

"Yes, sir! I was hoping you'd remember me."

"'Course I remember you," said Chase with a mournful glance toward the dining room, where his dessert was waiting. "What's up, Evan?"

Evan's voice dropped to a conspiratorial tone. "You remember when I told you I had a contact at the White House—well, a contact *with* a contact at the White House—and that it was *my* contact that got me the scoop on the refugee story from *his* contact?"

Chase remembered. The kid's "scoop" had impressed him even more than the kid himself, who for a first-timer came off like a seasoned pro, dishing out facts and figures like candy on Halloween.

Evan's excitement brimmed beneath his hushed tone. "You know what's going on at the White House right now, with the disappearance of Jacob Latner, right?"

Chase knew, but he waited for the kid to turn the page.

"Well, what if I told you that my source's source knows a guy who went to school with someone *very* close to the President?"

Chase frowned, wondering how cold his apple pie was going to be when he got back to the table. "I'd tell you to skip the garnish and cut to the meat and potatoes, Evan."

The kid giggled. He liked Chase's euphemisms, especially the ones that sounded more like dysphemisms. "Well, what if I told you, my source's source's friend has a recording of this someone who's very close to the President, and *in* that recording this very close someone to the President is spilling a whole messy can of ugly that the White House is desperate to keep under wraps?"

"I'd wonder what I did to deserve the love," said Chase with a tinge of skepticism. "Why didn't you just take this straight to your guys at *The Post*?"

"I'm not with *The Post* anymore. I'm working with these guys at Sawbucks."

"Sawbucks? What's that, a new blog or something?"

"No, Mr. Grimley," Evan said with a chuckle. "It's an online currency, like Bitcoin, you know? Only without all the hassle and a better exchange rate."

Chase grunted offhandedly and mumbled, "Ah, that sounds lucrative."

The kid chuckled again; he was a big fan of Chase's under-the-breath sarcastic quips and seemed honored to have one shot in his direction. Chase wasn't nearly as cheery; he just wanted to get back to his table and sit down to his lukewarm pie.

But then the kid said something that sent a tingle up Chase's leg.

"What if I told you that this *very* close someone to the President happens to be the President's son, Merrick Kingley?" Evan paused briefly, and a little thrill rose in his voice. "And what if I told you that my source's source's friend has a recording of Merrick Kingley spilling the beans about what's *really* going on with the disappearance of Jacob Latner . . . and that I have the *file* of that recording on my phone? What would you say to that, Mr. Grimley?"

Chase looked back toward the dining room, but he was no longer concerned with his dessert. And he was no longer in a sarcastic mood. His expression was that of a hard-nosed journalist on the verge of a real scoop.

"I'd say, you got my attention, kid."

KORI-LYNNE CARPWELL DIDN'T WANT TO BE ANYWHERE NEAR a television camera tonight. She wanted to be back in the West Wing, where she could keep her finger on the pulse of the President and soothe him at the first sign of a spike. And more importantly, she wanted to keep any "stimulating" influences out of the Oval Office.

When she'd left him twenty minutes ago, the President was holding up remarkably well. For a while, he'd been sitting on one of the two chairs in front of the fireplace—the same he'd occupied during his first official meeting with the former president—quietly observing the hustle and bustle around him. But his posture and demeanor had worried Kori-Lynne. Hunched over, with his elbows resting on his knees, fingers and thumbs pressed together, lips pursed, eyes gazing in a distant, reflective manner, he'd looked like a homesick kid at a sleepover, waiting for his parents to come get him. Kori-Lynne had considered giving him his mobile phone, which always lifted his spirits, but she worried that he might be tempted to call the former president—or worse, that he would start tweeting.

In the end, she had come up with a compromise. She got the President out of the chair in front of the fireplace (where he kept glancing at the empty chair beside him as if expecting the former president to suddenly appear) and sat him behind the desk with a stack of official-looking leather-bound folders, each containing executive orders for him to peruse and sign. She laid out a long row of Sharpie Permanent Markers and surrounded the President with a group of low-level staffers to accept the markers after each signing.

In preparation of her departure from the West Wing, Kori-Lynne had strategically moved the pieces around the board to prevent the already fraught situation from escalating in her absence. Shortly before the news of Jacob's disappearance had been released to the press, Kori-Lynne placed two calls to former members of the President's staff. The first call was to Franco Scaramanga. It was true that the former Communications Director had gone sour on the President—indeed, his blistering summer-long press tour, hammering the President on everything from policy to diplomacy, had left nothing but scorched earth between the two men. But of all the people Kori-Lynne could think of to call on in a pinch, Franco was the only one who'd ever had any success calming the President's inner beast. She didn't whitewash the situation. She told him that a big story was about to break and that she, not the President, needed his help. She apologized for pulling him back in, but there was no one else she could trust to handle the President in her absence. Franco arrived at the White House in less than thirty minutes, and Kori-Lynne filled him in on the details.

The second call she'd made was to Rance Plebeius. It wasn't easy convincing the former chief of staff to help out, but in the end, Kori-Lynne, who was the only person left in the White House with strong ties to the Republican Party, was able to finesse Rance into taking on the task of keeping Stretch Biggerstaff occupied during the crisis. Though Stretch no longer possessed the credentials to get inside the White House, let alone the Oval Office, he still had friends on the inside, and with one phone call, his razor-sharp tongue could be wagging in the President's ear. And *that* was something Kori-Lynne could not allow, particularly not on this of all nights.

A small camera crew was waiting for her in the Queen's Sitting Room on the Second Floor of the East Wing. Kori-Lynne had chosen this room not only for its seclusion but for its flattering background, which she felt would help to soften what some in the administration had begun to refer to as her "blunt edges." Though none had dared to speak of this openly to her, Kori-Lynne had a sharp ear that readily picked up on the whispers in all corners of the West Wing.

She had the elegant yet practical Carver chair brought in from the Lincoln Sitting Room across the hall and instructed the staffers to position it in front of the fireplace. She sat with her head tilted back while the makeup artist touched up her face, and then she sat up straight, looking into the camera, waiting for her cue without any second thoughts. With the press at the gates, clamoring to be let in, and the President itching to speak, Kori-Lynne knew she had to make this preemptive move. She needed to get out there, ahead of the story, and try to frame it in a "softer light." She would have preferred to do this with FIX News, where the reception would be more sympathetic, but it wasn't the President's base that she needed to reach out to here.

Kori-Lynne took a deep breath and let it out slowly, confident that her preemptive move would work. She'd left one of the staffers to monitor her performance on the TV in the Cabinet Room, and instructed him to call the President in to see her the moment she established dominance over the interview. If she nailed her appearance on this broadcast, Kori-Lynne felt there was a good chance the President would send the press corps at the gates packing and deal with the situation out of the public eye.

Kori-Lynne adjusted her posture for a more casual appearance, took another breath, let it out, and looked into the camera at the exact moment the NCMSB producer began the silent countdown to airtime. When the familiar voice came through her earpiece, Kori-Lynne hit her smile on the mark and said cheerily, "Good evening, Rowan, and thanks so much for having me."

MELVILLE NOYCE PICKED UP HIS PHONE ON THE THIRD RING. It was the second call he'd received that night. The first had come about an hour earlier from an old contact in Yemen, Akram Abdi. Abdi was a cautious man who had little faith in the administration that currently occupied the White House. His call had been a courtesy to Melville, out of respect for the relationship they had built over the years

Melville had served as a CIA operative in the Middle East. Abdi assured Melville that what was going on in DC was not connected to either the AQAP or the AQIM, both of which Abdi's team had been monitoring closely over the past three years. It was possible that a US-based cell was operating on behalf, yet independently, of al-Qaeda, but Abdi doubted it. Indeed he doubted involvement by any sanctioned organization in the Middle East, as an event of this magnitude would have certainly sprouted wings by now. But nothing was coming down the pipe. Even Umm Hussain al-Britani (more commonly known as the "White Widow") hadn't posted so much as a single tweet on her prolific page about the disappearance of the President's son-in-law.

Had it not been for this call from Akram Abdi, Melville Noyce might have let the second call go straight to voicemail. Like his old friend from Yemen, Melville was a cautious man and had even less faith in the Kingley administration.

The second caller was Percival "Buzz" Hartman, Deputy and Acting Director of the CIA, who didn't sound like his usual self at all. His tone was soft, almost conciliatory, like that of an old friend calling after a long cold spell. Melville didn't make it any easier for the deputy director; he greeted him with his trademark patient silence.

"I don't suppose you've missed the news, Mel," the deputy director said wistfully as if he and Melville were sitting on a porch, watching the sunset over a couple of cold beers.

Melville didn't like being called "Mel," but only his closest friends knew this. He took a measured breath and said, "I've been watching."

Hartman waited for more. When nothing came, he released a soft sigh and spoke in the docile drawl of one who has long since traded his spurs for a rocking chair.

"Look, I don't have to tell you this, but it's been pretty thin around here lately, what with all the . . . well, the transitions and all, you know how it goes. And I guess I don't have to tell you how tight it's been among those who've stayed on. Everybody's unsure of . . . everybody. You know how it is with these things. Oh, there's still plenty of leaks at the executive level—that ship's going down faster than the RMS Lusitania. But here at the brass, the well's gone dry. Even our closest allies are afraid to share with us. Intel's like a precious commodity in the best of times, and nobody wants to go shooting his mouth off and spilling secrets and such to the wrong people, for fear of . . . well, I don't have to tell you that loose lips sink ships, but . . . well, Melville, we've got ourselves a situation here, and it's not going to fix itself, if you know what I mean, and . . . "

Melville could almost see the deputy director rubbing his eyelids, but still, he didn't speak. If the man wanted his help, he was going to have to ask for it.

Another sigh came through the phone, and then Buzz Hartman spoke softly, more to himself than to Melville this time. "Jesus, how did it all come to this? You'd think there'd be a safeguard in place, or something, right?" He uttered a short laugh that sounded more hollow than humorous. In the background over the phone line, Melville could hear the neck of a bottle touching the rim of a glass, followed by a long steady flow of liquid courage.

"Christ, Mel, I've been on the horn with more foreign agents and dignitaries over the past few months than I can begin to count on ten fingers and ten toes. I even got a call from Guðni Thorlacius Jóhannesson, if that's how you pro-nounce his name, I don't know, but he's the President of Iceland—nicest guy you'd ever have the pleasure of speak-ing with—and I probably don't have to tell you that he's a little worried, Iceland not having any armed forces of their own to speak of and all. And he's not alone, this Icelandic fellow. There are a lot of other scared people out there too."

Hartman paused to take a drink. Melville waited.

"These are difficult times we're living in right now,

kemosabe. We got a whole lot of questions, and not enough answers, bouncing around the globe, and people are looking to us for a signal—hell, right about now, I'd bet they'd settle for a candle in an open window on a stormy night." The humorless laugh came again. "But I'll tell you what they sure as hell don't need," he continued in that same calm southern tone. "They don't need the media feeding frenzy that's about to hit the fan. And whatever our differences, old buddy, I'm pretty sure you agree with me on that one."

Melville remained silent, but Buzz Hartman didn't have to ask if he was still there; he just went right into his final pitch with a soft sigh of resignation.

"Christ, Mel. You want me to tell you that the President of the United States doesn't know his asshole from his elbow? You want me to tell you that the West Wing is loaded up with a bunch of pinballs bouncing off the bumpers just to hear 'em go ding-ding and see the pretty lights flash?" Another sigh. "I don't need to tell you what we both already know, kemosabe. And I don't need to tell you what's gonna happen when this rocket lights up." Another sigh. "If you're in the know, as I suspect you are, I take it you've heard about that little shitbag's phone call to his buddy, Stiverson."

Melville acknowledged that he knew about the recorded phone call between Merrick Kingley and his former schoolmate, Benjamin Stiverson.

"Jesus," Hartman sighed. "Four sons—and I won't cast any aspersions on the two younger boys, as they've yet to reach manhood—but the daughter, the one that's married to Latner, she's more man than either of those two older boys could ever hope to be."

Melville could not disagree with the deputy director's assessment of the President's older sons.

Hartman continued, "I'm amazed that little dirtbag Stiverson's recording isn't all over the Internet by now—thank the good Lord for small miracles, and knock on wood—but I suppose it won't be long before someone turns that stone. Either way, the fuse is burning and time is not on our side, kemosabe. We need to find Latner, dead or alive— hopefully, the latter—and shut this thing down before the curtain goes up at the late-night picture show."

Hartman released one last sigh, the sigh of a man who has reached the fallen bridge and needs someone to throw him a line from across the divide. Melville patiently waited.

"I don't have a leg to stand on here," Hartman said wearily, "so I'm asking for your help, Melville. I'm asking on behalf of this great country that we both love and would hate to see torn asunder by this shitshow. What do you say, old buddy? Will you help us find the prince and get him back inside the castle before the gate comes down and the drawbridge goes up?"

D AYTON HAMMERSMITH HAD WALKED THE CAPITOL BEAT since the Carter Administration, and over the years he'd seen just about every manner of demonstration, from "The Longest Walk," in which thousands of Native Americans walked all the way from San Francisco to rally at the National Mall, to the "Tractorcade," in which six thousand family farmers drove their tractors to DC to protest American farm policy—and that was just in the late '70s. Since then, there had been countless marches on the Capitol—women's rights, gay rights, black rights, peace sit-ins, environmental movements, Tea Party rallies, you name it. But never in all his time on the beat had Dayton seen anything quite like what he was seeing right now.

The procession making its way up Constitution Avenue was odd in more ways than one—not the least of which was that it happened to be taking place at half past nine on a bitterly cold Wednesday night. There were no signs, no slogans or chants to rally the crowd and draw attention to the cause—indeed, the participants of this march were inexplicably silent as they walked in orderly rows of four with their heads down.

And odder still, all of them appeared to be kids.

At first, Dayton thought he must be mistaken. But as the seemingly endless line passed by, he scanned the solemn faces and could not find one that looked older than high school age. Some of the bigger kids had lifted the smaller ones onto their shoulders, and even these smaller kids were eerily silent with downcast eyes.

Dayton stood frozen, a dumbfounded expression on his sober face, as they passed. When he finally shook himself out of his stupor and cleared his throat, one of the approaching kids—a handsome boy with rosy cheeks and shiny dark locks that rippled in the breeze—looked up with piercing eyes that halted Dayton before he could speak. The boy couldn't have been any older than sixteen, but he was tall and broad-shouldered, and the look in his eyes was as fearless as it was determined. Up on this boy's shoulders was a little guy of no more than seven, who looked at Dayton with the grave gaze of a soldier on his way into battle.

As the procession continued on toward the Capitol, Dayton took the handset mic from his shoulder and called it in. The dispatcher, a gung-ho young officer named Katie Dell, asked him how many intruders there were in total. When Dayton gave her his estimate, she said, "Six. Got it."

"No," Dayton said, "not six—six *hundred*." He looked out along Constitution Avenue, where the line of marchers stretched back as far as he could see, and spoke into his radio again: "Maybe more . . . a lot more."

Katie Dell said, "Is this a joke?"

"I wish it were, honey," Dayton said, his eyes still focused on the long line of kids.

"I'm calling in CERT now—"

"Hold up there," Dayton said firmly. CERT, which stood for Containment & Emergency Response Team, was the last thing this situation needed. "You get me the chief on the horn before you do anything."

"That's not protocol—"

"I don't give a damn about protocol, sweetheart. You get me the chief, pronto. And put me through to González in the meantime."

"If the intruders are—"

"The intruders are *kids*."

"Come again, you broke up."

"The intruders are *children*. You got that, Dell? *Kids*, the youngest among them *kindergartners*. You got that? Come back."

"Copy that."

"Now, get the chief on the horn and put me through to González."

"Stand by."

Dayton would have been lying if he told himself that the trembling sensation he felt at that moment was solely due to the chilly wind that swept across the mall. "I'm standing by," he said, working to keep his voice steady as he looked into the near distance, where the Capitol stood tall and silent against the crisp night sky.

L EONARD O'KEEFE SAT JUST OFF-CAMERA, IN THE SEAT NEXT to Rowan Meadow, quietly watching Monitor 3, which featured a moderately flattering medium shot of Kori-Lynne Carpwell up in the East Wing of the White House. Considering the circumstances, Kori-Lynne looked remarkably composed, like a woman in charge. The Queen's Room provided a disarmingly quaint backdrop for the interview, and the addition of the Carver chair from the Lincoln bedroom was a nice touch, one that brought a small smile of admiration to Leonard's lips. Kori-Lynne was easily the sharpest knife in the drawer of the Kingley cutlery. But given the extreme gravity of the situation at the White

House, Leonard doubted that even *she* would be able to spin this latest turn of the screw into the proverbial "nothing burger" that the Kingley administration had been success-fully feeding its hungry base over the past three years. Still, he waited, like a patient cat in the tall grass, as Kori-Lynne pivoted away from Rowan's every attempt to pin her down on the Latner disappearance.

The moment presented itself when Kori-Lynne opened a side door by taking an oblique shot at former President Boyega. Leonard waited for a break in the back-and-forth between Rowan and Kori-Lynne before cutting in with a pleasant smile and a cordial tone.

"Good evening, Kori-Lynne. It's Leonard here."

The startled look in her eyes told Leonard that she hadn't expected to be speaking with anyone but Rowan. The two of them had had what Kori-Lynne thought of as a successful solo interview a couple of months into the Kingley presi-dency, and Kori-Lynne looked flustered—perhaps even a bit betrayed—to discover that Rowan had brought Leonard on board. She recovered quickly and pushed out a smile as if the interjection were a pleasant distraction.

"Good evening Leonard, and how are you tonight?"

"I'm very well, thank you," said Leonard with an unmistakable lilt in his tone—a coyly pleasant lilt that never failed to make Kori-Lynne's jaw tense. "But I'm curious. You just told Rowan that the President, and I quote, 'doesn't need to validate his every decision with protocol set by his pre-decessors'—which I presume is in reference to his decision not to treat the disappearance of his son-in-law as a pos-sible threat to national security, despite the fact that Jacob Latner has the highest level of security clearance, giving him what would be considered extremely valuable intel to any number of international organizations who might seek to harm the United States."

"Well, that's a bit dramatic," said Kori-Lynne with a practiced smile. "Are you implying that one of the

President's top advisors is giving state secrets to a foreign enemy? Because that would be a very irresponsible thing of you to say."

Leonard smiled pleasantly. "Nothing of the kind, Kori-Lynne."

"Well, I certainly hope not," said Kori-Lynne, brushing back one side of her hair as she shifted in her seat. "Because that's precisely the sort of thing that's turned so many people off of the media—the wild speculation and constant innuendo—and it's precisely the reason that the American people voted for Royal Kingley. *President* Kingley. Because, frankly, they're sick and tired of the false narrative that the mainstream media has been generating just to boost its ratings. You want to know what the American people really care about? They care about jobs and the economy—both of which President Kingley has done so much to revive—that's what the American people care about. You go out there to the Rust Belt and talk to the coal miners and factory workers who lost their jobs under the Boyega administration—they'll tell you. They're not concerned with the latest 'Washington intrigue' story that the media has cooked up. They're only concerned about all those jobs that went overseas due to the heavy burden of restrictions and regulations placed on the job creators by the previous administration."

"*There's* the point I was getting at," said Leonard with a deceptively cheery chuckle.

"What point is that?"

"When defending his actions, President Kingley and his surrogates often cite the actions of his predecessor, President Boyega. Is the President worried that, in doing so, he may be viewed as using President Boyega as a crutch? That his own actions can only be validated in comparison to those of his predecessor?"

Kori-Lynne halted and gave the camera a pointed look. "I don't know what you're getting at. What actions do you mean?"

"Well, all of the executive orders, for one," Leonard said with an amiable smile. "President Kingley has stated, on more than one occasion, that his abundance of executive orders is justified because President Boyega did so many of them."

"But that's just the truth, Leonard. President Boyega signed more executive orders than any other president before him. Why doesn't the media report on that instead of attacking President Kingley for *his* executive orders? Executive orders, which, by the way, President Kingley only signed to undo all the unfair and unconstitutional executive orders of President Boyega—orders that have hurt the American people, like BoyegaCare, which has been a complete disaster, as the President—President Kingley—has said time and again, throughout his campaign and continues to say in his presidency."

"Actually, Kori-Lynne," said Leonard with that same amiable smile, "the Affordable Care Act was not done by executive order, as you well know. It was a bill. Passed by both the House and the Senate. And only after months of revisions and open debate was that bill then signed into law by President Boyega."

"But it was *his* plan, is my point, Leonard, and it was a disaster that's hurt American taxpayers and driven up the cost of health care for everyone."

"As we both know, Kori-Lynne, enrollment numbers for what you disparagingly refer to as 'BoyegaCare' have spiked dramatically since the election of President Kingley—hitting a record high of 6.4 million. And public support for the ACA has only grown stronger with each failed attempt President Kingley and the Republicans have made to repeal it. But I'm not going to debate that with you, because I know you're smarter than all those nonsense peddlers who fly in the face of facts, Kori-Lynne."

"Thank you, Leonard."

"You're welcome. But what I *will* do is address the

incorrect statement you made about President Boyega's executive orders." He held up a sheet of paper and put on his glasses. "According to Pew Research, and I quote, 'President Boyega issued fewer executive orders on average than any president since Grover Cleveland.' In fact, 'during his eight years in office, President Boyega issued a total of two hundred and seventy-seven executive orders, or thirty-five per year.'" Leonard took off his glasses and looked into the camera. "That's slightly more than Grover Cleveland's thirty-two per year during his eight nonconsecutive years in office."

"So, what's your point?"

"My point, Kori-Lynne," said Leonard with a pleasant smile and a keen eye, "is that you were incorrect when you said just a moment ago that President Boyega had issued more executive orders than any president before him. In fact, President Boyega ranks *sixteenth* among presidents in the total number of executive orders issued—and *twenty-first* in the average number issued per year. By contrast, in his first nine months in office, Royal Kingley had already issued *forty-nine* executive orders, which far exceeds President Boyega's *yearly* average. And the number has only grown since then."

"I don't know about that, you may be right, you'd have to ask President Kingley. I can't speak for the President."

"No, Kori-Lynne," Leonard said, chuckling, though not unkindly, "I don't *need* to ask the President. Because I have the numbers right here in front of me. Would you like me to read President Kingley's individual orders to you."

"No, I trust you, Leonard. If you say President Kingley issued those executive orders, I believe you."

"It's not *me* saying it, Kori-Lynne. It's fact."

"OK. It's fact. What can I say . . . ? I mean, what do you want me to say? The President issues a lot of executive orders . . . that's his style of governing. I can't change that, it's not my job. I'm his counselor . . . I don't make decisions,

I counsel him—you know that, Leonard, from your time working with Senator Halloran. I serve at the pleasure of the President. That's all I . . . that's all I do, and you want . . . it's like you want to make it seem like I'm calling the shots . . . which I'm not . . . the President is. And you make it seem like it's some . . . some conspiracy or something, and that's just not . . . that's just not fair, you know?"

"I apologize if that's how I made you feel," said Leonard. "It certainly wasn't my intention."

Kori-Lynne shifted in her seat. "It's just not very . . . it's just not very nice, you know? If you want to talk about the facts, then let's talk about the facts and not be throwing around baseless accusations, because that's what I'm here for . . . to talk about the facts, which is what the American people deserve to hear."

Leonard nodded. In the seat next to him, Rowan Meadow watched and waited. In the Queen's Room at the White House, Kori-Lynne whisked her hair back from her face once again.

"The facts are all we should be talking about, anyway."

"Fair enough," Leonard said kindly. "Let's do that then."

F RANCO SCARAMANGA GOT UP THE MOMENT HE SAW THE TWO young interns step through the doorway of the Oval Office with the large flat-screen TV. But before Franco could shoo the interns out, the President pointed toward the fireplace and said, "Set it up over there, guys."

Franco said, "Sir, I think—"

The President ignored him and addressed the interns, who were lowering the TV onto the coffee table. "No, over there. Move those couches back. We need room for the press . . . " And with a sad smile, he added, "The dishonest media needs to be treated with respect. Sad, sad people, but we'll show them respect, won't we, guys?"

"Yes, sir," the interns said in unison.

Franco said, "Mr. President, the press secretary already has this covered. He's going to do the briefing in the Brady Room. And it might not even have to happen. Kori-Lynne is on TV right now. She might be able to kill the story before it grows legs."

The President waved him off. "The only thing getting killed over there is her."

He lifted the phone in his hand and showed it to Franco, who, for the life of him, couldn't figure out how the President had gotten hold of a phone, especially after Kori-Lynne had given specific instructions to all staffers *not* to enter the Oval Office with their phones.

"Look at her," said the President as he gazed down at the tiny screen, shaking his head sadly.

Kori-Lynne was featured on a split-screen with that pinko bastard O'Keefe. The sound was on mute because the President couldn't bear to listen to anymore, but by the look on Kori-Lynne's face, things weren't going very well.

"She always gets that haggard look when she's going down," the President said in a mournful tone, "like an old Lhasa Apso—you know those dogs with the long hair that look so beautiful when you brush them and put those pretty ribbons on their heads? My first wife, Iliana, loved that breed, begged me to get her one, but I knew she'd never keep up with all the brushing and grooming—lazy woman, very slothful, believe me—so I told her no. Now she's got like a ton of dogs, all little ones, yipping away all the time— cute little things, but I'm not into dogs, who needs all that fur all over your clothes, and all that yipping, am I right? I saw her like ten years ago, I was over at her place—dogs everywhere, and I say to her, the minute I get to the door, I say, 'I gotta tell you, Iliana, if one of those mutts bites me, I'm gonna kick it.' It's true. Vicious little things, constantly yipping and nipping. They're cute if you're into that sort of thing—which I'm not, believe me—but they're vicious."

Franco remained silent. The President looked down at

the phone's screen and shook his head at the image of Kori-Lynne going at it with the media sharks.

"Just like an old haggard Lhasa Apso," he said sadly, "clinging to any piece of debris she can sink her claws into after the ship has sunk. It's too pathetic to watch. Look at her with the sharks circling, and she keeps paddling away to stay afloat. Sad. Very sad. But she's a scrapper—just like all those little dogs yip yip yipping away and nipping at your ankles—I'll give her that much." He grunted and released a doleful little chuckle. "They're not gonna come away without a few scratches on 'em, let me tell you, but eventually they'll drag her under. Look at this . . . "

He pointed to the phone, which now featured Chase Grimley on a three-way split-screen, along with Kori-Lynne and Rowan Meadow. Franco looked but said nothing.

"Look at that Meadow bitch," the President said with a grimace, "chomping away at the bit—she's almost as disgusting as that smug prick O'Keefe. They're like the tag team of the lyin' media, both of 'em sitting there like a couple of grinning hyenas, just waiting for the old lion Grimley to finish poor Kori-Lynne off. And he'll do it, trust me. He's old, but he's still got his teeth, believe me."

Franco said, "We can still let the press secretary do the briefing."

The President made a face as if Franco had just farted. "Who? Skippy?"

"It's his job," said Franco, hoping against hope that reason would prevail.

"No, that's no good," said the President with a distant look in his eyes. "No, that's not gonna work at all." And before Franco could protest any further, the President shifted his attention back to the interns and asked, "Am I right, guys?" Both young men looked uncertain, but they nodded in agreement. The President sighed with a sad smile. "No, the lyin' media has to be fed, we have to feed the jackals, those are the rules, right guys?"

"Yes, sir."

"We're gonna set them up here," said the President with a gesture to the area opposite his desk.

"They won't all fit in here, Mr. President," Franco countered softly. "There's more room in the—"

"There's plenty of room in here, plenty. All are welcome. Even the most disingenuous." To the interns, he added, "We gotta make room for the deceitful, guys, the deceitful have to be heard too." Then, to Franco, he said, "Make sure that Little Kayley gets a front-row view—don't stick her in the back—she's tiny! Right up front is where she belongs. She's been extra specially dishonest, telling such lies about me—such a liar, she is—terrible, terrible lies, she tells—but she's still Little Kayley, and I respect her the same as I do all my enemies. She's a special girl, that Kayley, and we wouldn't want her to miss anything, OK?"

Franco attempted to talk him down again, and the President listened and nodded while giving further instructions to the interns on the placement of the huge TV and the rearrangement of the furniture.

Standing in the open doorway, a tall and slender fifteen-year-old boy watched the machinations in the Oval Office with the casual eye of one who has seen it all before and could scarcely care less. He was a handsome boy with raven-dark hair that overhung his intense grey eyes. He stood there, looking out of place in his baggy jeans, pinned-striped hooded pullover, and industrial Doc Martens. When he caught the President's eye, there was no mistaking the chill between the two of them.

The President said, "If you're going to be in here, change into something appropriate and comb your hair. You look like a thug. Honestly, who dresses you like that, your mother?" The President turned to Franco. "Tell the truth, does he look like a thug, or what? I don't dress like that. His brothers don't dress like that—not even his younger brother. Does he look like he's my son?" He shrugged, and with a humorless chuckle muttered, "I don't know, maybe he's the pool boy's kid, who knows?"

The boy in the doorway gave no reaction. He just continued to stare at his father through the veil of his long, dark locks, which hung carelessly over his eyes.

The President shook his head with a sour expression. "Any time you want to go back and live with your mother, you know where the door is. See how that works out for you." He croaked out a clipped laugh and shook his head while rolling his eyes. Aside to Franco but audible to all, he said, "That woman was a piece of work, believe me." Then, to the boy in the doorway, he said, "But in the meantime, you start dressing like a civilized young man—what're you, sixteen now?"

"Fifteen," said Franco.

"Fifteen," said the President with another eye-roll. "You know where I was when I was fifteen? In military school. That's right, military school. And I had that same tough-guy look you have right now, and those sergeants and colonels, they knocked that tough-guy look right out of me, and whipped me into shape—boy, did they ever, let me tell you, believe me, and they made me a *real* tough guy."

The boy held his gaze, waiting for more; he'd been through this before.

The President shook his head with disgust and said to Franco, "He has no respect, absolutely none. The only one he cares about is himself. So selfish, can you believe it? Like the world revolves around him, and the rest of us are just peons. Unbelievably self-centered, I don't know where he gets it from, I really don't. I've got the weight of the free world on my shoulders here, I make foreign dictators tremble, absolutely tremble with fear—'cause I could drop the bomb on them at any time, and they know it—I've got the codes right here, I'm telling you, I could do it. I've got more power than anyone on the face of the planet, right here at my fingertips, right Franco?"

"Yes, Mr. President."

"But I can't get this kid," said the President, pointing a rigid finger at his son, "to dress like a civilized person. Now, tell me how fucked up that is? Tell me why the most powerful man in the world, who could nuke the entire fuckin' planet out of orbit any time he pleases—I'm totally serious, ask anyone—tell me why a man with that kind of power at his fingertips can't get his own fuckin' kid to comb his hair and put on a decent suit. Tell me that, Franco."

"I don't know, Mr. President."

The President shook his head and pulled his lips into a crooked line while shooting a hard gaze at the boy in the doorway.

"I named him Dane," the President said to Franco, "because I thought it stood for 'strength,' you know? I heard that somewhere—on the internet or the TV or someplace—so I thought it was true, right? *Wrong.* Turns out it comes from Denmark, where the people are all so depressed all they do is kill themselves. They just keep killing themselves. Every day. It's true, they wake up, realize what a shitty life they have and kill themselves—their population has literally been cut in half because they can't stop killing themselves, they're so depressed. It's like their national pastime over there—killing themselves. I'm serious, somebody oughta do something about it before there's nobody left. It's true, you know?"

Franco didn't know how or if to respond. But it didn't matter, the President had already shifted gears again.

"So, it turns out 'Dane' doesn't stand for 'strength' at all—it stands for 'depression and suicide.' It's crazy. I looked it up on Wikipedia, and it says 'Dane' means 'dweller in the valley.'" He hooked a thumb at the boy in the doorway. "That's this one, all right—to a tee—moping his way through the valley, like he's lost his milk money or something. Unbelievable, I'm telling you. Seriously. Can you believe it?"

Franco, who was looking at Dane with scarcely concealed compassion, remained silent.

The President released a sigh, and suddenly his ire was gone. He addressed his son in a gentle tone as if the verbal assault he'd subjected the boy to only moments before hadn't occurred at all. "Where's your little brother? Where's Barret?"

Dane held his gaze on his father but said nothing.

The President's tone became gentler still. "You're a good brother. Barret looks up to you. Go find him and play some video games, OK? He likes that. He shouldn't be alone right now. He needs his big brother, OK? Go find your brother. I've got to work now."

Dane stood motionless in the doorway, gazing at his father. Franco held his breath, hoping the President would not take up the challenge.

The moment lasted long enough for Franco to reposition himself so that he would be able to block any sudden advance on the boy from the President.

The tension broke when the President said softly, "Go on, find your little brother. You're a good brother. He loves you. Go take care of him."

A tense moment of silence passed, in which Franco held his breath as both father and son held their gazes. Then, much to Franco's relief, Dane Kingley turned and left the Oval Office without a word.

Looking at the empty doorway now, the President mused, "He's a good brother."

Stan Schnetzer sat at the long glass table on the set of *Fastball* in the DC studio, along with presidential historian Delores Knox Greenwood, Pulitzer Prize-winning journalist Elwood Robertson, and *Fastball* host Chase Grimley. Though they had only just joined the conversation between Rowan Meadow and Leonard O'Keefe in the New York studio and Kori-Lynne Carpwell in the White House, Stan had jumped right into the conversation with the one question Kori-Lynne was most eager to dodge: "When can we expect a statement from the President on the disappearance of Jacob Latner?"

Normally, the presence of a fellow Republican strategist at the table would have eased Kori-Lynne's anxiety. But the current situation was anything but normal. And Stan Schnetzer wasn't what Kori-Lynne would call "a fellow Republican strategist."

Throughout the campaign, Stan had displayed open disdain for his party's "unorthodox" nominee—indeed his contempt had culminated in a searing and emotional rebuttal to Candidate Kingley's declaration during the final presidential debate that he "might not accept the outcome of the election" if he felt it was rigged against him. Kori-Lynne still couldn't understand why Stan's reaction to Kingley's admittedly stunning statement had been so vehement. If the election had been rigged, wouldn't any candidate have the right to stand up and call out the other side for cheating?

Kori-Lynne felt that Stan had blown the whole thing out of proportion and that he had come off more like a crybaby Liberal than a conscientious Conservative—particularly when he'd called her candidate's statement at the debate a "disqualifying moment" that represented a "clear and present danger to our constitutional order."

Kori-Lynne still bristled when she thought of the fallout from that debate. She recalled the smug way Nichelle Willis, who'd co-managed the failed McQueen-Parish campaign with Schnetzer back in '08, had prematurely proclaimed Royal Kingley's political demise that night: "He may as well have laid down in his own coffin with a hammer and nail and pounded it in himself."

But as the numbers had come rolling in on election night, state after state, including those that nobody could have predicted would fall into the Kingley column,

Kori-Lynne found that she could not resist the allure of what the German's called *schadenfreude*—that intoxicating elixir of joy derived at the suffering of others—and she had treated herself to her own little smug smile of satisfaction: *Now who's lying down in their coffin with a hammer and nail?*

Of course, here in front of the camera in the East Wing of the White House on this chilly night, Kori-Lynne was feeling neither smug nor satisfied—not with so many of her adversaries circling.

She was still trying to come up with a delicate dodge to Stan's question about the President's impending press briefing when a quip by Chase Grimley to the pundits seated at the table in the DC studio came through her earpiece: "What is she *doing* there in the East Wing? Sitting there in front of the fireplace in the Queen's Room like she's Lady Bird Johnson or something."

"I can hear you, Chase," Kori-Lynne said with a frown.

"I know," Chase muttered. Then he looked into the camera. "What the heck's goin' on over there, Kori-Lynne? Why aren't you in the West Wing with the President?"

"Because I'm sitting here with you," Kori-Lynne replied with a cheery smile that didn't quite reach her eyes.

"Yeah," said Chase distantly.

"Do you want me to leave?" Kori-Lynne asked with a wide-eyed expression that almost looked sincere.

Chase smiled bashfully. "Nah, stick around."

"If you don't want me, just say the word."

Chase blushed, but his smile deepened. "Ah, cut it out, you're loved here."

"Why, thank you, Chase," said Kori-Lynne with that cheery non-eye-smiling smile again.

"You're welcome," said Chase, waving her off. Then, on a dime, he shifted. "So, tell me, what's going on with this Latner kid? You're as close to the President as anyone, so if anyone knows, it'd be you. What's the deal?"

"Well, first off, Jacob Latner isn't a *kid*, as you well know,

Chase. He's an accomplished businessman, a loving husband, and a wonderful father of three beautiful children—not to mention, one of the President's most valued advisors."

"He's a kid to me—"

"How can you say that, Chase? How can you sit there and diminish the accomplishments of this . . . of this highly accomplished man? Does that seem fair to you?"

"At my age, you're all kids to me. But fair enough. He's the President's closest advisor—or at least *one* of them—and now he's gone missing for, what is it now, ten, eleven hours?"

"I'm not exactly sure . . . or even that we've established that he *is* in fact missing," Kori-Lynne countered, prompting an eye-roll from Chase, who sensed another diversionary speech coming on.

"Whatever," said Chase, more concerned with getting down to the brass tacks. "Nobody's heard from him since this morning after his meeting with the President. He walks out of the President's office, and he's gone. That's it, right?"

Kori-Lynne's features seemed frozen for a moment. Then she said, "Well, if you put it that way—but that's not the point, really, is it?"

"That *is* the point, Kori-Lynne," Chase barked. "That's *exactly* the point. The point is that one of the President's closest advisors—perhaps *the* closest—is missing."

Kori-Lynne closed her mouth and waited.

Chase said, "Are you still there?"

"I'm here."

Chase grunted. "I thought we lost you for a second there."

"I'm still here."

Chase grunted again and then picked up the thread. "So, we've got this guy—not a *kid*—who's probably the closest advisor to the President . . . certainly, at the end of the day, he's got the President's ear, after all the rest of you guys are gone—Secretary Payero, Mort McElhinney, you, and that other one—" Chase turned to Elwood Robertson, who was sitting between Delores Knox Greenwood and Stan Schnetzer. "Who's the guy with the fiery attitude—or 'addy-TOOD,' as they say in Philly—the guy who's always sweating bullets and talks in the hard cadence? You know who I'm talking about, that 'The President will not be questioned' guy."

Elwood suppressed a laugh. "Mahler."

"That's it," said Chase. "Mahler. What is it? Stuart?"

"Spencer," said Elwood.

"That's it, Spencer Mahler," Chase said, and then with a chuckle, he added, "He's no Spencer Tracy, I can tell you that much, 'cause *that* Spencer didn't break a sweat! Tremendous actor, one of the all-time greats. Remember *Inherit the Wind* with Tracy as Clarence Darrow and Frederick March as William Jennings Bryant? They didn't call them by those names in the movie, but we all knew who they were playing. The Scopes Monkey Trial, with Dick York—underrated actor, great guy—teaching the kids Darwin's Theory of Evolution, remember? Great stuff. *March* broke a sweat—and in the end, it killed him—but Tracy never breaks a sweat throughout the whole trial. It's like a hundred and ten in the shade, and Tracy's as cool as a cucumber, remember? Great stuff. Classic movie."

The members of the panel all nodded, some of them smiling at Chase's digression.

Chase turned back to the camera and picked up right where he'd left off with Kori-Lynne. "So it's you, Payero, McElhinney, and a handful of others, and this guy with the waterworks, Spencer Mahler. And when you're all gone, Latner's right there, because he's family, and no matter what anyone says, family means something—especially for *this* president. I mean it. Say what you want, but when it comes down to the clutch, this guy—the President—he isn't banking on advice from any of his generals or cabinet secretaries. He's not even banking on *you*, Kori-Lynne—no offense—"

"None taken," said Kori-Lynne with a measured smile.

"—and he sure as heck ain't taking any . . . *advice* from these federal judges who keep slapping him down every time he takes a pen to another one of those goddamn executive orders he's been shooting off like dime novels—"

"I think you're misrepresenting the facts," Kori-Lynne interjected, "to complement your own narrative, Chase. The fact of the matter is that the President listens to a lot of advice, and he's always open to the advice of any of his—"

"No," Chase cut in, "I'm not gonna let you spin this one. I'm asking you a direct question here, and I'd appreciate a direct answer—"

"I would love to give you a direct answer, if you'd let me speak, please—"

"That's all you've been *doing* here tonight, Kori-Lynne. You've been talking and talking, and nothing's coming out. All of it keeps going in circles, and we're still at square one." Chase rolled his eyes and barked a laugh. "Jeez, what is it with you guys in this administration? Everything is a dodge and weave act. Anything that comes your way, you serpentine."

"That's just not true, Chase—"

"All right, then answer the question."

"I will if you'll repeat it."

Chase looked across the table at his panel. Elwood and Delores were both trying not to laugh. Stan was suppressing a small smile, but his eyes looked serious. Chase gave them a crooked grin, rolled his eyes, and muttered, "It's like pulling teeth." Then he turned back to the camera to address Kori-Lynne: "I want you to tell me, is this Latner kid, who is arguably one of the President's closest advisors, missing or not? Simple question."

"Would you answer a question for me first?"

Chase dropped his head and muttered, "Oh my god, this is unbelievable." He rubbed his eyelids and then looked up with a lopsided grin while Elwood chuckled across the table from him. "Sure," Chase said. "Why not?"

"Don't be upset with me, I'm serious."

"I know you are, Kori-Lynne," Chase said with a pained smile. "Go ahead, ask your question."

"OK, then answer me this," said Kori-Lynne, "and I'll be more than happy to answer your question. Is that fair to you?"

"Fair enough. Ask your question."

"OK," she said with a straight face. "Define 'missing.'"

Chase's pained smile spread, and he shot a look at Elwood, whose shoulders were shaking with silent laughter now. "She's not kidding," Chase said.

"I know," Elwood said, laughing out loud.

Chase looked off, shook his head, and then spoke to the camera. "Gone. Vanished. Absconded. Absent. Lost. Not there. *Missing*. Take your pick." He sighed.

Kori-Lynne blinked in a confused manner.

From his side of the split-screen in New York, Leonard O'Keefe said, "Kori-Lynne, it's Leonard again."

"Yes, Leonard," she said, grateful for the timely rescue, despite the obvious irony of it coming from someone she would normally consider infinitely more adversarial than Chase Grimley.

"Are we correct in assuming that there has been no contact between Jacob Latner and his wife, Ilona Kingley, since before Jacob's meeting with the President this morning?"

"Yes, Leonard, to the best of my knowledge, that is correct. Of course, I haven't spoken to Ilona since seven o'clock this evening when we spoke briefly on the phone. But the last I heard, there hasn't been any contact between the two of them, Mr. Latner and his wife, since earlier this morning."

Leonard nodded with a kind smile. "And do you know if anyone else in the family or at the White House has heard from Jacob since that meeting this morning with his father-in-law in the Oval Office?"

"I can only speak for the people I've had contact with today, and none of them have told me they've heard from Mr. Latner today."

"Thank you, Kori-Lynne."

"You're welcome, Leonard."

Chase's gaze was still on the monitor that featured Kori-Lynne in the Queen's room, and by the look in his eyes, he wasn't finished. Not by a long shot.

"Yeah, Kori-Lynne, it's me again. You still there?"

"I'm here, Chase," said Kori-Lynne.

"Yeah," Chase said, "not to make you feel like Jimmy Stewart in *Anatomy of a Murder*, with us firing at you from all sides here—"

"I can take it," she said with a chipper smile.

"I know you can."

"I'm a big girl."

Chase smiled thinly. "I know you are. But getting back to this Latner kid—or man, I know he's a grown-up—but getting back to him, and his . . . 'absence,' we'll call it."

"Fair enough."

"Yeah. So, as far as you know, the President's son-in-law could be anywhere—maybe he gave the slip to his secret service detail, took off for a drive to clear his head, just to have some alone time, whatever."

"But you're assuming that Mr. Latner *has* a secret service detail, Chase."

"Well, does he?"

"I don't know." On Chase's chuckle, she said, "I'm serious. I honestly don't know if he has a secret service detail or not, Chase. I know that it's been offered to all of the members of the President's immediate family, but I don't really know who's accepted it and who hasn't."

Rowan Meadow chimed in: "Kori-Lynne, it's Rowan. I have confirmation here that Ilona and Jacob and their three children all have secret service protection."

Kori-Lynne smiled. "OK. Well, there you have your answer, Chase. I don't know where Rowan's information comes from, but I trust her that it's factual."

"The information comes from the White House Press Secretary's office," said Rowan, holding up the letter with the White House seal on it.

"Oh, well, if anyone would know, it would certainly be them."

"So," Chase went on, "if Jacob Latner has Secret Service protection, why haven't they been contacted?"

Kori-Lynne's features froze. Chase didn't wait for the thaw.

"I mean, he's got this detail, this protection—so, why hasn't anyone in the administration contacted these Secret Service guys to find out where Latner is? Seems to me that it would be the logical first step, don't you think?"

"I . . . I don't know, Chase," said Kori-Lynne, whisking her hair back from her cheek and tilting her head slightly to the right. "I just heard about it for the first time, just like you, that Mr. Latner *has* a Secret Service detail. But just because he has a Secret Service detail doesn't mean that he didn't dismiss them for the day."

Chase blinked. "Well, don't they have to report something like that? I mean, the Secret Service guys. Don't they check in with somebody at the White House—'Hey, we're Latner's detail, and he just told us to take the day off.' Isn't there some protocol in place for something like that? You think?"

"Honestly, I have no idea, Chase. You'd have to check with somebody at the White House."

Chase released an incredulous laugh. "You're *in* the White House, Kori-Lynne! You're sitting right there in the Queen's Study, across the hall from the Lincoln Bedroom, for Pete's sake!"

"Exactly, I'm sitting here in the *East* Wing, giving you

my valuable time while the President's son-in-law is missing—"

"Ha!" Chase barked with a laugh. "You finally said he's missing! Congratulations."

Kori-Lynne's smile faltered. "You know what I meant. I only said it that way because it's the only way you're willing to accept it. It doesn't mean that I—"

"OK," Chase cut in, "let's take a look at this from another angle for a second. Bear with me. Is it possible that there's some *other* reason for Jacob Latner not to be . . . *present* at this time. Could there be another reason that Jacob Latner has been out of contact with his family and the White House for the past eleven hours? Has he ever done anything like this before? To the best of your knowledge, has something like this ever happened—Jacob just up and taking off on his own, without a word to anyone, not so much as a phone call to say 'I'm out for a drive, I'll be back when I'm back,' anything like that? To the best of *your* knowledge, Kori-Lynne. You work with this guy, he's one of the President's advisors, just like you. Tell me that. Tell me that, and I'll lay off."

For a moment, Kori-Lynne looked at a loss for words; then color rose to her cheeks. "Are you asking if something . . . *nefarious* has happened to Mr. Latner?"

"That's *your* word, Kori-Lynne, not mine, but it's a good one. Nefarious. Yes. Do you have any reason to believe that something nefarious might have happened to the President's son-in-law and personal advisor Jacob Latner?"

Kori-Lynne flared her eyes and shook her head with a confused smile and a nervous laugh. "Where is this coming from? Is there something . . . is there something you know that I don't?"

Chase shrugged. "I dunno, maybe. Tell me what you know, and I'll tell you what I know."

Kori-Lynne stuttered. "Because it sounds like you're trying to . . . trying to . . . entrap me or something . . . "

"I'm *trying* to have a dialogue with you, Kori-Lynne. I'm trying to get you to give me an honest answer to a simple question about this . . . *situation* that's going on at the White House right now."

Kori-Lynne made a sour face and whisked her hair from her cheek. "Well, it feels like you're attacking me. I mean, I come here . . . in good faith . . . with a crisis going on—"

"Crisis? Now it's a crisis?"

"That's what you're trying to make it out to be, right?"

"I'm not trying to make it *anything*, Kori-Lynne—"

"Yes, you are."

Chase rubbed his eyelids again. "No, I'm not. I'm trying to—"

"Yes, you are," Kori-Lynne snapped. "You're trying to make this whole thing seem like news when there's nothing here to . . . there's no news to be found. It's just something you're blowing way out of proportion because that's what you people in the media do. You don't want to report on the facts, you don't want to report on how this country was hemorrhaging jobs at an alarming rate when the President— President Kingley—took office, and how he's saving jobs and bringing all those good-paying coal and steel jobs that were lost under the previous administration right back here to America—just look at all those jobs he saved from going to Mexico before he was even inaugurated! You want to talk about something, you want to make news, let's talk about those jobs, because that's what the American people care about—not all this . . . nonsense—they care about *jobs!* And this booming economy we have under President Kingley."

Chase shook his head with a dumbfounded smile.

Kori-Lynne frowned. "I'm glad you find this so amusing, Chase. I'll bet you the hardworking American people whose jobs were saved by President Kingley don't share your cavalier attitude about it." She raised her chin defiantly and stared down her nose as if daring Chase to try and pivot back to the Latner disappearance.

Chase looked into the camera with a contemplative expression, as if sizing up a player who'd just pushed a substantial amount of her chips into the pot, fully expecting him to fold what she'd assumed was a marginal hand. The only problem was, Chase happened to be holding an inside straight flush, and he had more than enough chips to not only call with but to raise and put her all-in.

"OK," he said, in the casual tone of a pro taking one last peek at his cards to make sure that he did indeed have the stone-cold nuts. "Let's see if the American people are interested in this 'nonsense.'" He paused briefly before shoving all of his chips into the pot. "I've got a recording here of a phone conversation that took place earlier today, and I'd like your opinion on it—see if you recognize the voice of one of the speakers on this call—"

"I don't know anything about any phone calls," said Kori-Lynne, instantly bristling.

"I'm not saying that you do, Kori-Lynne—who said anything about that? I'm just saying, let's listen to this recording, and then you can tell me if you recognize either of the voices on it. That's all."

Kori-Lynne gazed into the camera for a hard second. Then she whisked the hair from her cheek and said, "You know, I come on here, like I said, out of the kindness of my heart, to have a frank and open discussion about this—and if you want to talk about the disappearance of Jacob Latner, I'm more than happy to do that, if that's what makes you happy, if you think it will help your *ratings*, or whatever. But suddenly, out of the blue, you throw this 'gotcha moment' at me, and I'm only here out of the goodness of my . . . my heart, to keep the press informed. It seems odd then that you'd want to hit me with a gotcha moment . . . " She shook her head. "That's just the sort of thing that makes the President mistrust the media, because it isn't fair. And here's a *real* fact: every time we try to . . . every time he tries to reach out to you people—"

"'You people?'" Chase laughed. "What's that supposed to mean, 'you people?'"

"*You* people," Kori-Lynne continued without taking a breath, "you in the elite media—"

"Oh, right," Chase grunted with a short eye roll.

"That's right, you're darn right, it's right. You in the elite media take every chance you get to turn everything Royal Kingley—*President* Royal Kingley—and he's your president too, even if you didn't vote for him—you just want to turn everything the President says into a gotcha moment."

Chase shrugged with the ghost of a sheepish smile. "Well, it's not really a *gotcha* moment . . . unless, of course, I got you with it. Did I?"

Kori-Lynne's eyes iced over, even as she pushed out a razor-thin smile. But the words weren't coming anymore.

Chase waited, just in case, before adding, "Would you like to hear this recording. I think you'll find it . . . enlightening." Chase squinted and with a grimace said, "Let's roll the tape."

DAVIS FROME NEVER SLEPT DEEPLY IN ANY BED OTHER THAN his own, regardless of the location or accommodations, and on this particular night, in his favorite suite at his favorite hotel in the city he had once called home, things hadn't changed.

He woke at once to the soft buzzing of his mobile phone on the bedside table; looking tired and a bit disheveled, he stepped into his slippers and pulled on his robe. He went out to the sitting room before answering the call, so as not to disturb his sleeping wife. The caller was Mason Logue, an associate editor at *The Pacific*, and he sounded excited.

"Are you watching the news?"

"No," said Davis in his soft yet direct manner, "I was sleeping. I have an early call."

"On Morning Jay?" Mason didn't wait for a response,

and he didn't apologize for disturbing Davis's sleep. "Well, your call might have just got a little earlier. Turn on NCMSB."

Davis didn't bother to sigh; it wasn't his style. Nor did he waste his breath to ask what had prompted this call; he'd find out soon enough. He padded across the room and turned on the TV. The glow from the screen lit his drawn face in a ghostly hue, highlighting the stubble on his cheeks and chin while deepening the hollows of his sad-looking eyes.

"Are you seeing it?" Mason asked.

"I'm seeing it," Davis said softly.

"I mean, are you *seeing* it?"

"Yes."

On-screen, the President's chief counselor, Kori-Lynne Carpwell, was in the middle of a tense debate with Chase Grimley over the right to privacy of public figures. But this wasn't the reason Mason Logue had disturbed Davis's sleep. The real story was scrolling as "breaking news" on the chyron at the bottom of the screen—and unlike most breaking news stories, this one actually *was* breaking news . . .

. . . SECRET RECORDING OF A PHONE CONVERSATION BETWEEN THE PRESIDENT'S SON, MERRICK KINGLEY, AND A FORMER SCHOOLMATE, BENJAMIN STIVERSON, REVEALS THAT PRESIDENT KINGLEY'S SENIOR ADVISOR AND SON-IN-LAW, JACOB LATNER, HAS BEEN ABDUCTED BY AN UNIDENTIFIED TERRORIST DEMANDING AN AUDIENCE WITH THE PRESIDENT ON LIVE TV . . .

"Are you *seeing* this?"

"I'm seeing it," Davis said calmly, even as his pulse quickened. "Has it been confirmed? Is it Merrick Kingley's voice on the recording?"

"It's him," said Mason. "They just played it, and Carpwell hasn't denied it."

Davis appraised Kori-Lynne with dispassionate eyes. There had been a time when he might have felt a little sorry for her. But she'd sown her fate when she'd hitched her trolley to Kingley's wildly out of control steam engine, and no amount of pity was going to save her now that the train was careening into the final stretch, where the rickety track abruptly ended over a gaping chasm.

Davis stood in silence for a moment longer, studying the scroll at the bottom of the screen—*terrorist demanding an audience with the President on live TV*—with only one question on his mind.

"Has he agreed to do it?"

"No official word yet," Mason replied in a tone of scarcely contained exhilaration that did not jibe with Davis's sensibilities. "But the rumor is, he's going to hold a press conference *inside* the Oval Office. Can you believe that?" Mason barely took a breath before getting to the point of his call. "Jonathan wants somebody from *The Pacific* covering this one on-air, and he wants something for the a.m. online edition, as well as a follow-up in print. I've put in a call to FIX News—"

"No," Davis said softly yet pointedly, his eyes still focused on the TV screen. "Call O'Keefe's producer at NCMSB."

"Jonathan wants somebody there live. He doesn't want this phoned in—"

"I understand," Davis said in that same calm tone. "I'm in New York. I'm a five-minute cab ride away. Call O'Keefe's producer."

Davis didn't wait for Mason to get back to him; he already knew that he would be more than welcome to join Leonard O'Keefe and Rowan Meadow. He dressed quietly and left a note for his wife on the bedside table. Then he headed down to the street to hail a cab.

NERO GONZÁLEZ WAS NOT A TOWERING MAN, BUT WHAT HE lacked in physical stature was more than made up for by the depth and intensity of his dark brown eyes. He had worked as a corrections screw at a detention center in Lubbock, Texas, before relocating to DC and joining the Capitol Police Force. During his time down in Lubbock, he'd stared down his share of violent offenders, many of them twice his size, and subdued all but a few without having to resort to physical force. But in all his years of law enforcement, he had never come across a situation quite like this.

Nero stood on the steps of the Capitol, along with a line of officers, to prevent unlawful entry—at least in theory. In truth, Nero doubted the entire force wouldn't have much effect if the crowd presently gathered on the sprawling West Lawn of the Capitol decided to storm the steps. But there was no sign that any such thing was going to happen. Though massive in numbers—easily close to a thousand strong—the crowd was remarkably docile. If the faces up front were indicative of the group as a whole, all of these protesters were kids. Hundreds upon hundreds of kids gathered on the lawn, all the way back to the reflecting pool and beyond, all of them gazing up at the Capitol Building in solemn expectation. Even the youngest among them—who appeared to be no older than kindergarten age—wore sober expressions and showed no signs of fussing as little ones often do.

"What'd I tell you?" Dayton Hammersmith said in a low tone to Nero. "Sorta creepy, eh?"

A younger officer close by croaked, "Sort of?"

Another said, "They look like those demon kids in that movie."

The younger officer emitted a shaky laugh. "Better bust out the riot guns and machetes, Sarge."

"Stow that shit," Dayton barked in a hushed tone. He turned to Nero and dropped his voice even lower. "We're not gonna do anything . . . rash here, right?"

Nero was still surveying the crowd with a solemn expression when something odd happened—even odder than several hundred kids storming the Mall on a chilly Wednesday night.

Tiny lights began to pop up across the expanse of the West Lawn, illuminating the young faces in an eerie glow.

It took a moment for Dayton to understand what was happening. Nero knew at once. The lights were coming from mobile devices. But the kids weren't holding their phones up over their heads to illuminate the darkness as they would at a concert; they were staring at the glowing screens with transfixed expressions on their angelic faces.

Dayton shook his head. "What the—"

Suddenly, a wave of sound began to ripple through the masses as the kids turned up the volume on their phones. At first, it was indistinct, but as more and more kids turned up the volume, the sound gained in strength and clarity.

Nero acted swiftly. He took his phone from the pocket of his jacket and turned it on. As he listened with a keen ear, he navigated the tiny screen with his thumb—more deftly than Dayton would have expected—until the sound coming from his phone matched that of the wave drifting up the steps of the Capitol.

Dayton raised an eyebrow as he looked at the screen of Nero's phone, where a live newscast was streaming.

"What the hell—?"

Just then, Dayton's radio squawked. It was Dell, the young hotshot dispatcher.

"I have the chief."

"Yeah, patch him through."

A burst of static, and then the chief's voice came through. "Lieutenant González?"

"No, Chief, it's Hammersmith."

The line went silent for a moment. Then the chief said, "I hear you have a situation there at the Capitol."

"Yeah, you could say that, sir."

"What are the numbers?"

Dayton's eyes shifted from Nero's phone to the crowd. "Eight hundred, maybe a thousand."

"Come again," the chief said. "I lost you."

"Eight-hundred to a thousand, sir."

"That's a lot."

"Uh, yes, sir, it is."

"Are we talking docile or aggressive here?"

Dayton scanned the crowd. "They appear to be docile, sir."

The chief paused for a moment and then said, "Well, what do they want?"

Dayton sighed softly. "I couldn't say, sir."

The chief said, "Well, take a look at their signs. What do they say?"

"Would that they had any, but they don't, sir."

Another pause, longer this time. Then the chief said, "You're telling me there's close to a thousand people on the Mall, and none of them have any signs?"

"That's correct, sir."

Dayton waited while the chief pondered.

"Well, what the heck kind of protesters are they if they don't have any signs? Are they indigent?"

"No, sir," Dayton said.

"Well, who the heck are they, and what do they want?"

"I can't rightly say what they want, sir. But they're kids."

"They've got kids? You mean as hostages?"

"No," Dayton said. "They *are* kids. Children. All of them—at least as far as I can tell. Most of 'em high schoolers, by their looks."

The chief's voice faded as he spoke to someone on his end, muttering something about "bedtime" and "curfew" and it being a school night and all. Then his voice came clearly through the radio again, and he asked to speak to Nero.

Dayton passed the radio to Nero, and Nero gave his

mobile phone to Dayton. The small screen displayed that feisty gal from New York, talking about the abduction of the President's son-in-law. Dayton didn't care much for the President, or his family, for that matter—a bunch of lying hypocrites, in his opinion. But he liked that Rowan Meadow gal. She had pluck, and she wasn't afraid to stick her neck out for stories that a lot of other news shows seemed to miss. He liked her spitfire commentary and her biting wit. He also liked it when she had one of those Washington hotshots in the crosshairs, as she did right now with that motor-mouthed little blonde piece of damage from the White House who wouldn't know the truth if it came up and bit her on the ass.

Dayton watched *The Rowan Meadow Show* whenever he wasn't working the night shift—it was certainly a fast way to pass an hour alone in his apartment. But as good as her show was, for the life of him, he couldn't imagine that it would hold much interest for kids, even with the "breaking news" about the abduction of the President's son-in-law. Kids weren't interested in that sort of thing. Kids should be doing their homework, hanging out on the Internet, playing computer games, watching TV shows, like *The Flash*, or the one with all the teenage vampires or werewolves or whatever. But they sure as hell shouldn't be gathering on the National Mall in the dead of night to watch a news program on their phones.

Dayton looked up and scanned the crowd again—all of them gazing at the glowing phone screens that stretched out across the West Lawn of the Capitol like a luminescent blanket; even the little ones, up on the older kids' shoulders, appeared to be transfixed by the news program. Dayton shook his head in disbelief, and a shiver passed through him as he recalled an old passage from Scripture that he wasn't sure he'd ever fully understood.

Then were there brought unto him little children, that he should put his hands on them, and pray: and the disciples rebuked them. But Jesus said, Suffer little children, and forbid them not, to come unto me.

Dayton was still gazing at the crowd when he heard Nero speaking to the chief. Nero was recommending that they "wait and observe." He felt confident that the kids would eventually disperse of their own accord.

Dayton suddenly wanted to believe that his old friend Nero was correct, that the kids would tire of the cold and eventually seek the warmth and comfort of their beds. More than anything, he wanted to believe this. But the longer he looked out at the sea of glowing lights, the harder it was to shake the needling feeling that something more was happening here; that, crazy as it seemed, these children had been summoned to this spot . . . and, crazier still, that they were waiting for hands to be laid on them.

R OY KINGLEY JR. STOOD AT THE TALL AND WIDE WINDOW OF THE lavish suite in Tower K, from which he ran the family empire. With his mobile phone pressed to one ear and his stoical gaze fixed on the cold night skyline, he listened with flagging patience to his brother, Merrick, on the other end of the line. Roy Jr. was not pleased with his younger brother right now—indeed his poised chin, raised a few inches higher than usual, and the hard line of his mouth, slightly down-turned at the corners, were clear indicators that Roy Jr. was doing all he could to contain his anger at Merrick's colossal screw-up.

With a silent sigh, Roy Jr. shook his head in disbelief. Jacob's life was in the hands of the enemy (most likely a radical Islamic nutjob who wouldn't think twice about cutting off Jake's head on live TV), Ilona was beside herself with fear and desperation (though, like Roy Jr., she contained emotion well), Kori-Lynne was sinking fast in her ill-advised impromptu interview with the sanctimonious vultures over at NCMSB, and the old man was about to capitulate to a terrorist. And with all that going on, here was Roy Jr., playing nursemaid to his thirty-one-year-old brother, who'd caused this shitstorm with his loose lips.

Un-fucking-believable, Roy Jr. thought. But he bit his tongue. As the oldest, it was his job to protect his younger siblings—even when one of them screwed up big league.

"I'm sorry," Merrick said in a weepy tone that grated against Roy Jr.'s ear. "I swear it, I had no idea Benjy was recording the call. I would have hung up right away, I swear it. I only told him about what happened to Jake because . . . because I needed to talk to someone about it, you know? And I couldn't talk to you, because you were on a call with Dad, and I couldn't get through to Ilona, because she wasn't picking up, and I didn't have anybody to talk to . . . "

Roy Jr. held his tongue. Merrick took a shaky breath.

"I can't believe Benjy would *do* something like this to me," Merrick whined. "We were like really close in college. I mean, we didn't hang out or anything, but he lent me his notes whenever I missed a lecture, and I saw him at parties, and he was always so nice, smiling and all, you know, like he was a friend . . . or at least friendly. He dated that one girl, Penny—you remember her, right?"

Roy Jr. didn't know who the hell Penny was, but he didn't tell Merrick this, because he didn't want to get into a drawn-out and pointless conversation about Merrick's social life in college, which he knew nothing about, anyway.

"She was the redhead with the little tattoo of a clover on her ankle—she came down to Largo Morta with Bethany and Brittany and Clarissa that one year. Remember?"

"I remember," said Roy Jr., hoping that Merrick would drop the trip down memory lane and just cut to the chase.

"She was like *so* trustworthy, you could tell her anything. I used to just sit in her room and tell her everything that was going on, and she'd just listen and never tell anyone—"

There was a sudden hitch in Merrick's voice, and Roy Jr.

closed his eyes, hoping that the waterworks weren't about to start—like his father, Roy Jr. had zero tolerance for displays of emotion from grown men.

Merrick collected himself and went on. "Penny was just really cool that way, and I just can't believe Benjy would do this, you know? He *dated* Penny, and she would never have been with a guy who'd do something like that, you know? It *had* to be someone else. Someone who has it out for us. The CIA hates us—they've had it out for dad since the beginning, they've probably been tapping our phones since we won the election, just waiting for one of us to slip up, you know, so they could give the tapes to the press, you know?"

Merrick sniffed back snot, and Roy Jr. pictured him wiping the tears from his eyes as he gained confidence in his theory. Roy Jr. didn't believe the CIA was behind the leak of the recorded call any more than he believed some guy who'd let his brother crib off of his lecture notes back in college was trustworthy. But he could deal with a misfiring fired-up Merrick a lot easier than a whiny crybaby.

"They *hate* Dad," Merrick said with sudden vehemence. "They hate him *so* much, and they'd do anything to stop him from making America great again, the fuckers. I think that's what happened here. They set this whole thing up. They've probably got something on Benjy's dad—he's a banker, and he's got tons of investments in foreign companies all over the world. They probably set him up, like they're trying to do with Dad and Jake and Uncle Dodger— just because he tweeted about Pascale's emails and Hannah being done by Wednesday? Everyone knew she was gonna be done! She's crooked! Everyone already *knew* that before Pikileaks dropped that story! I'm telling you, they set Benjy up just like they did with Finch and Mangold—they've been tapping our lines all along, they think *everyone's* in on it, you know?"

"Yeah, that's probably it," said Roy Jr. distantly.

"Yeah," said Merrick, sniffling, "they probably *forced*

Benjy to record the call—threatened to expose his dad, if he didn't cooperate. They'd do that, I know it. They'd do anything to hurt Dad. They hate him so—"

Merrick's voice cut off so abruptly that for a second Roy Jr. thought the call had been dropped. Then a groan came through the phone, followed by a whimper.

"Are you—are you watching the news?"

Roy Jr. had turned off the TV shortly after that crafty old prick Grimley had played the recording of the phone conversation between Merrick and that rat bastard Ben Stiverson. He couldn't watch the feeding frenzy that followed. Poor Kori-Lynne had tried bravely to hold her own against the Liberal Elites, but there were just too many of them, all coming at her from every angle, including that traitor Stan Schnetzer, who had the gall to still call himself a Republican! Roy Jr. just couldn't watch it anymore.

That changed when Merrick said, "Dad's on right now."

Roy Jr. was floored. The last he'd heard, his father was still debating going on air, and Franco had promised to call him the moment his father had made a decision.

"Jesus," Roy Jr. muttered as he stepped away from the window and turned on the TV. Both of his sisters were nearby. Ilona was in the outer office on her phone, and Tabby was sitting on the sofa, texting with a friend. As Roy Jr. turned up the volume, he called out, "Ilona, you'd better come see this."

Ilona ended her phone conversation abruptly when Roy Jr. called out again with urgency: "Ilona, get in here."

Roy Jr. was staring at the screen and shaking his head when Ilona joined him. "Jesus," he muttered again. "What the hell does he think he's doing?"

Ilona didn't respond. She just stood next to her brother and watched as their father spoke to the press corps gathered in the Oval Office. It didn't look like a typical presidential address with a single camera focused on the commander in chief at his desk or behind a podium. It was a multi-camera shoot that cut back and forth between the President and the press.

And there was something else odd about it.

A widescreen TV had been mounted to the wall above the fireplace. At present, this TV's screen was dark, but it gave Ilona a foreboding feeling.

Roy Jr. shook his head again and muttered, "What is he *doing?*"

As if in response to his eldest son's question, the President turned to the main camera in the Oval Office and said, "I've called the dishonest media here not only to explain what's going on to the American people but also to give them the unvarnished truth that the deceitful, hypocritical, lying media so often denies them with their disingenuous reporting, outright lies, and fake news stories—all aimed at destroying the faith that the American people entrusted me with by giving me the landslide victory I received back in '16—one of the biggest victories in the history of the presidency, believe me, folks, it's undeniable."

The President paused as if waiting for a round of applause that only he could hear to taper off. Then he made a sweeping gesture to the front row of reporters and smiled a sad smile.

"As you can see, I have assembled all of the networks and newspapers—we got 'em all, folks, none have been left out, because that's not the way we do things here. We are an all-inclusive administration." His smile brightened a bit, but his eyes still looked sad, almost weary. "We welcome all because we have nothing to hide, do we fellas? No, nothing to hide. Total transparency here, all-inclusive, believe me, folks. We got 'em all. The big liars as well as the little liars—they tell the little lies that lead to the big ones—and all are welcome to create their fake news stories, which they do so well and so often, they really do, such lies, you wouldn't believe, folks, believe me. But I'm a big fan of the First Amendment, and I will defend the right of any of these despicable vultures to make up whatever lies they want—it's in the Constitution, folks: the liars have equal protection, and I support their right to lie."

A brief cutaway shot featured the reporters gathered in the Oval Office. Some looked stunned; others, unmoved; a few even smiled incredulously; none responded. Then back to the President, nodding and smiling sadly.

"It's true," he continued. "I hold no ill will against any of you." His solemn eyes fell upon Kayley Tru, and his sad smile exuded something close to pathos. "Even you, Little Kayley. Kayley Tru—such an ironic name. Lil Kayley—I call her that 'cause she's lil, folks, I mean tiny, just look at her." He sighed. "You were always special to me, even when you told such lies—such lies, folks, believe me, oy oy oy—such deceitful lies that wounded me more than you could ever know. Of all the disgusting and dishonest media vultures, I always respected you the most." He pressed his lips together and shook his head with a painful gleam of nostalgia in his eyes. "It's true, Lil Kayley, very true."

The camera crew picked up a shot of Kayley Tru, attempting to suppress a nervous smile. Though she'd written a detailed account of his campaign and probably knew him better than any other reporter in the room, it was still difficult to tell when he was joking.

"It's OK," the President said, nodding with his sad smile once again. "I like it when you smile, it makes you look prettier." To the other reporters, he said, "Doesn't she look pretty when she smiles?" He waved them off absently and turned his attention back to Kayley. "She's a pretty girl, all right," he said softly. Then his voice rose a few octaves. "Kayley." And a few octaves more, with gusto. "*Lil* Kayley." Then back down again. "She's all right. Kayley and I go way back, don't we, Kayley?"

Not knowing how to respond, or *if* to respond, Kayley nodded with an awkward smile.

"Sure we do," said the President with a fatherly gleam

in his eye, and his voice trailed off in an almost musical manner, "Lil Kayley . . . Lil Kayley and me . . . we go way back . . . way, way back . . . yes we do, folks, yes we do. She's all right, that one . . . she lies—terrible lies, believe me—but she's all right, my Lil Kayley . . . she's a good girl, she is . . . "

Roy Jr. pushed a short breath out of his nose. "What was Kori-Lynne *thinking*, leaving him alone to run off and do an interview? What the *hell* was she thinking?"

Ilona didn't respond. She just continued to stare at the TV in silence. On the sofa behind them, Tabby was no longer texting but watching her father's address from the Oval Office with a slack-jawed expression.

Merrick's timid voice came through the phone in a weak attempt to sound encouraging. "He's doing OK so far . . . he's putting those bastards in their place, at least . . . "

Roy Jr.'s jaw tensed at the sound of his brother's voice in his ear. In the Oval Office, his father was getting down to the crux of the matter, and as Roy Jr. gazed at the TV, the knot in the pit of his stomach twisted tighter, and he braced himself for the worst.

"And so, to the reason I've called you all here—the dishonest media inside the Oval Office with me, as well as the decent, hardworking *real* American people watching at home—so there will be no confusion, no spin, and, above all, no lies." The President sniffed loudly and raised his chin. "The deception and corruption of so many past administrations that have lied to the American people—both Democrat and Republican—stops here."

Roy Jr. relaxed a little when he realized that his father was reading a speech from the Teleprompter—but the reassuring feeling swiftly faded when it became clear that his father had written the speech himself.

"As I promised throughout my campaign," the President continued, "and well into my presidency, I, Royal T. Kingley, pledge never to lie to the American people. Or to any of the foreign nations around the world that show this great, great country of ours the respect it not only *deserves* but *demands*. And I am here tonight to make good on that pledge of transparency, and to let *you*, the wonderful, hardworking, decent, and honest people of this great, great nation know that I—have—your—back."

He raised his chin and, after a beat, continued.

"So, it is in the good faith of the pledge that I made—and continue to make—to always be totally transparent and totally honest with the American people—it's true, I will always be honest and transparent, believe me, folks, no matter what you hear from these very dishonest and, frankly, terrible people here in the press—the fake news, I call them, and believe me, the stuff they say about me is as fake as it gets, unbelievably fake, lies, it's disgusting, they oughta be ashamed, really, so dishonest . . . "

The President shook his head with a grim smile while some two hundred miles northeast, in the lavish office suite of Tower K, Roy Jr. unconsciously mirrored the expression, though for a very different reason.

" . . . and so," the President went on, "it is in that good faith that I am here to tell you that the tape of the conversation between my son, Merrick Kingley, who I am very proud of—you're a good man, Merrick, and I'm very proud of you—that tape you've heard, all over the news, of Merrick and his deceitful friend—false friend, really, terrible person, really-really bad guy, his parents should be ashamed, maybe they are, who knows?—Benjamin Stiverson, who is both gutless and spineless, and probably should be locked up, I don't know, seems like a criminal to me, recording conversations and selling them to the highest bidder in the dishonest media . . . that—tape—is—real."

The President paused to let his audience absorb the bombshell he'd just dropped. And after a measured moment, he nodded with raised brows as if to confirm that this bombshell was, in fact, the truth and not fake news. Then he looked back to the Teleprompter.

"Completely distraught over the abduction of his brother-in-law—Jacob Latner, who also happens to be my closest advisor and son-in-law, and an all-round great guy—my son Merrick sought comfort and solace in what he thought to be his good friend, Ben Stiverson, who turned out to be a back-stabbing opportunist and lowbrow Benedict Arnold, who was more willing—and more than only willing—to sell out my son for a quick buck. It's treason, a real act of treason, and he should be jailed, I don't know, maybe he will be, who knows, am I right? . . . "

Either the Teleprompter had malfunctioned, or the written part of his father's speech had ended. Roy Jr. suspected the latter, though it hardly mattered, either way. His father was already off on another tangent, asking the press and viewers if they could believe that a friend ("any friend, even an enemy that you only *thought* was your friend") could be so unfaithful and stab a friend in the back like that.

It took a while for his father to get back to the actual point of the press conference, but by then Roy Jr. had already started to feel the same sinking sensation that had made him switch off the TV a half-hour earlier when Kori-Lynne was under the full assault of the Liberal jackals.

Had it really been only a half-hour ago? Roy Jr. thought, shaking his head in disbelief. Of course, he of all people knew that once his father got going on a rant, it could feel like ages had passed in a matter of mere seconds.

Roy Jr. lowered his head and rubbed his eyelids with the tips of his fingers and only looked back at the TV when the sudden sound of Merrick's gasp came through the phone.

In the Oval Office now, his father stood in profile, looking up at the widescreen monitor above the fireplace. The huge screen that had been dark only moments before was now lit up, and the image displayed there sent a wave of chilly tendrils racing up Roy Jr.'s spine . . .

A nondescript room whose surrounding shadows appeared to fade into infinity. At the center of this room, under the soft glow of a spotlight, a slender man sat with his wrists and ankles bound to the arms and legs of a solid wooden chair; about his upper body was lashed a sturdy strap that pinned him securely to the back of the chair.

Roy Jr. studied the image on the screen, but it was difficult to tell for certain if it was Jake because the guy's head was bowed as if he'd fallen asleep . . . or passed out. The shock of dark hair, hanging damp and loose over the face, looked familiar, but still, Roy Jr. wasn't sure. He spoke through clenched teeth without turning to look at his sister beside him. "Is it him?"

Ilona stood rigid and silent, gazing at the TV.

"Is it him or not?" hissed Roy Jr.

Ilona took a short breath, and a single tear spilled down her cheek. She whisked it away and collected herself before whispering, "Yes."

Roy Jr.'s features hardened, his gaze locked on the TV screen. "Are you sure? Are you positive?"

"Yes," she replied, whisking away another tear.

"*Fuck*," Roy Jr. said softly yet forcefully. "Son of a *bitch*."

Through the phone, Merrick whimpered, "Is it Jake? Did she say it's Jake?"

Roy Jr. released an even breath. "It's him." A low keening sound escaped Merrick, and Roy Jr. immediately cut him off. "Get a grip."

"I'm trying—"

Roy Jr. cut him off again, his voice tight and low. "I said, get a grip. Man up, don't panic. Do you hear me?"

Merrick's voice came in a breathless whimper. "Yes."

"Yes, what?"

"Yes, I hear you."

Merrick's voice was choked with emotion, but he held back the waterworks, which was all that mattered to Roy Jr.

On the TV screen above the mantel in the Oval Office, a tall figure, clad entirely in black, stepped into frame. His face was concealed by a black metal mask whose darkened glass eyes reflected the minimal light in eerie replication of dispassionate menace. The mask, which covered his entire head, looked vaguely familiar to Roy Jr., like something out of a movie he'd seen but couldn't recall.

The masked figure stood silent for what seemed an eternity. Then a voice came clearly through the black metal breath screen. The tone was calm, controlled, and decisive: "I am True Son, Second to the Last, Diviner of Secrets, Destroyer of Demagogues. I seek not to corrupt that which is pure and innocent but to drag that which is soiled and profane out from the shadows and into the light—kicking and screaming, if necessary . . .

"I call to the Father of Division and Duplicity and challenge him to face me before the eyes of the world. Man to man. If he acquiesces, the life of his faithful soldier will be spared."

With a black-gloved hand, the masked figure gestured to the young man bound to the chair.

"If not . . . "

The masked figure pressed a button on the small black device in his left hand. Instantly the young man in the chair, who'd appeared to be unconscious only seconds before, threw back his head and cried out in pain. As his body twisted with violent spasms, the black mask pivoted smoothly to view his agony.

Merrick released a sudden high-pitched shriek that shot through Roy Jr.'s ear like a knife. Ilona's hands flew up to her mouth. Tabby's eyes grew wide with shock.

There was no longer any doubt in any of their minds. The guy bound to the chair under the soft and eerie glow of the spotlight was indeed Jacob Latner.

The masked figure released the button on the device, and Jacob's convulsion stopped at once. But he sat there panting and sweating, his chest rising and falling with each gasping breath as the aftershock of the assault passed through his body.

The black mask pivoted back to the camera. "If the Father of the Wounded Nation is the man he claims to be— if he does not wish to sacrifice his loyal knight—he will face me by the zero hour. I will accept no second. He must face me himself, as a man and a leader, or be proven a coward. I await your response."

The TV screen above the mantel went dark, and the news camera cut back to the President, who appeared to be reading from the Teleprompter once again. The scripted material was basically an assault on the intelligence agencies whose "Gestapo tactics" had led to "yet another complete and total breakdown in the chain of command," and whose failure to immediately bring the video to the attention of their commander in chief had "wasted many-many valuable hours." (In fact, Acting CIA Director Hartman had phoned President Kingley within minutes of viewing the video, and had personally brought it to the White House in under thirty minutes.)

While his father went off on an impromptu rant (which included everything from the "complete and total incompetence of the CIA" to the "unbelievable courage and strength of Jacob, suffering so bravely for his country in the face of such evil terror—very sad"), Roy Jr. stood rigid, his eyes shining hard and dark under the ambient lighting of his Manhattan office. But he wasn't really listening anymore. His mind had already skipped past the present moment of his father's most recent string of tangents and was laser-focused on what would come next. Would his father actually accept the masked terrorist's challenge and speak with him on live TV with all the world watching?

As unthinkable as that was, the alternative could actually be worse. Roy Jr. could not shake the image of Jake, tied to the chair in the dark room, and as much as he tried to steel his nerves, the reality that Jake's life was now in his father's hands made his knees feel weak.

Roy Jr. was still working to push back against the knot

of dread creeping up from his core when Merrick's voice came through the phone in a weepy tenor.

"What did he do to Jake's eyes? What did he *do* to them? Did he blind Jake? Did he *blind* him?"

Merrick was referring to the circular pads that had covered Jacob's eyelids in the video they'd just seen. Each of the pads had been fixed with tiny red indicator lights that had flashed in a strobe-like manner when the button on the remote control device was depressed. More pads had been affixed to Jacob's body—on his temples, his chest, the backs of his hands, the tops of his bare feet. And in addition to all that, Jacob had been fitted with a pair of odd-looking headphones. Roy Jr. didn't know what any of this accoutrement was or precisely how it worked; all he knew was that, whatever it was, it had caused Jake severe pain when the guy in the mask pressed the button on the remote control.

Roy Jr. gnashed his teeth, wishing he could be inside that room right now. He'd shove that little black remote control straight up that masked freak's ass.

Merrick's weepy voice came again, choking down tears. "Is Jake going to . . . is Jake going to die?"

Roy Jr. flinched and said forcefully, "No, he isn't."

"But that guy is *hurting* him," Merrick whined pitifully. "And he's going to do something bad if Dad doesn't do what he says. He said he's going to . . . he's going to . . . do something to . . . to Jake if Dad doesn't do what he—"

"Nobody's doing nothing to Jake."

A heavy sob came from Merrick's end of the call, and Roy Jr. flinched again.

"Are you crying?"

"N-n-n-no," Merrick said in a shaky voice. Then came the sobbing; he couldn't help himself.

Roy Jr. took a tense breath and said, "I can't deal with this. You either stop crying right now, or I'll hand you off."

A heavy sob came over the line, followed by high-pitched keening, like a tea kettle nearing full boil.

"That's it," said Roy Jr., "I'm handing you off."

"Lona," Merrick sobbed like he used to when he was little and needed security. But Ilona was no longer standing next to Roy Jr. She'd left the room after the video in the Oval Office had cut to the black screen. Roy Jr. could see her through the open doorway, blowing her nose. He turned to the couch and handed his phone to Tabby.

"I can't anymore," he said. "You deal with it."

Tabby put the phone to her ear and spoke gently. "Merrick? I'm here."

"Lona?" Merrick sniffled.

"No," she said soothingly. "It's me. Tabby."

The heavy sob returned, and Merrick whined, "I want *Lona*."

The compassionate expression dropped from Tabby's face at once. She got up and took the phone to her older sister. Ilona wiped tears from her eyes and spoke into the phone as if one of her own children were on the other end of the line. "I'm here."

"Lona?" said Merrick in a tiny voice.

"Yes," said Ilona gently, pulling herself together. "It's me." And that was all it took to open the floodgate. Merrick sobbed heavily as he begged his older sister to forgive him for his phone call with Ben Stiverson and swore to her that he'd had no idea he was being recorded.

Ilona soothed him, whispering, "Shhhhh, it's OK, everything is going to be all right. Daddy is going to get Jake back home safe and sound. Everything is going to be all right . . . "

In the office, Roy Jr.'s eyes were on the TV, where his father was now taking questions from the media. As Roy Jr. listened to both his father and sister assuring their respective audiences that all was going to be well, he shook his head with a clenched jaw, knowing that all was about as far from "well" as it could get.

Thackery Ansara shifted gears on his Aston Martin One-77 Superbike as he sped into the curved half wall at the south end of the indoor track, clearing the generous turn in 2.7 seconds, according to the Motorsport data logging system built into the bike's handlebars. The track wrapped around the circumference of the vast loft that served as headquarters for HiroBot LLC.

HiroBot was Thackery's first venture located outside of California. His parents, Marwan, a podiatrist, and Navi, a nurse, had immigrated to the US, along with Thackery's three older sisters, Parva, Rima, and Sara, back in the early 80s and settled in Fresno, where Thackery was born and raised. By the age of nineteen, Thackery was pulling down triple the amount of his parents' combined income from his first business venture, a dotcom that manufactured a security software called *Bulletproof*. After the exclusive rights to *Bulletproof* were purchased by the US Department of Defense, Thackery went on to create several other successful companies, including his latest venture right here in Annapolis, a gaming group, under the umbrella of HiroBot, called *Bizzazzazz!* Among the top-selling items *Bizzazzazz* manufactured was a virtual reality headset, along with software that could be fine-tuned to the user's specific level of intensity for an experience so realistic *Wired* magazine dubbed it "Mind-crushing!" The ESRB initially gave the game unit an "AO" rating (due to the "extreme intensity" and "graphic sensations" of the virtual experience), but after a long battle with Thackery's lawyers, they bumped it down to an "M" rating.

Thackery came out of the curve so fast that he was a full half-lap around the track before he noticed the tall black man in the dark suit and overcoat at the east entrance.

"Burn the intel and flush the files," Thackery called out in a tone that sounded anything but urgent. "The dark ops are here!"

The tall man stood motionless, a sober expression on

his face, as Thackery cut across the main floor and sped to a stop inches from him.

"Melville Noyce, CIA, UAE, SRSI, L-M-N-O-P," Thackery exclaimed, extending a hand in greeting, "what can I do for you that has everything to do with the 'unsettle in the metal' at the White House? And by 'metal,' I mean the man in the mask, the descendant of Darth, the nadir of Vader, the poison pill with the chill: Kylo Ren."

Melville remained expressionless.

"Come on, yo," Thackery nearly cried with an exasperated smile. "Kylo Ren! The dude in the black metal mask with the jagged red lightsaber from *Star Wars, Episodes VII, VIII, and IX*—that's what everyone's calling your boy! Catch up with the times, Retro."

"Is this relevant?"

"Nah, I guess not," said Thackery. "But your boy's *dope*, M. He's even got a fan page on The Mirror, and his digits are out of the stratosphere!"

Melville raised an eyebrow.

"The *Mirror*, homey! They used to call it The Black Mirror, but then that show came out on the BBC, and now they just call it The Mirror—which is tighter, anyway. It's like Facebook for cool people. Your boy's profile has been active since November, but up until about a half-hour ago, he had a scant nine hundred followers. Now he's up to like nine million, and counting. *Nine million* in a half-hour—you can't *buy* that kind of press, G. The age of innovation, a TV on every phone, and anybody can be a celebrity."

Melville's eyes narrowed. Thackery grinned.

"I know where that big brain of yours is headed," said Thackery, "but you're not gonna track him through The Mirror. That's the dark web, bro. What happens in the dark web stays in the dark web. Onionland guards its secrets jealously, Cochise. There ain't no light in that forest."

Melville looked nonplussed. Thackery rolled his eyes.

"Don't tell me you don't know *that* one, homey! *The Light in the Forest*. Standard seventh-grade reading by Conrad Richter. It's like a classic. White boy raised by Indians. They call him 'True Son.' Everything's all kosher until the whites and natives make a treaty and True Son has to go back with his white family—but he ends up hating it, and all sorts of messed up shit happens when his Indian cousin comes to bust him out of Whitebread Land, and in the end True Son can't go with the whites or the natives, and he's left on his own. A lone wolf. Just like your boy in the Kylo Ren mask. That book was dope, yo! You should be readin'."

Melville recalled the book from his boyhood, but other than the terrorist adopting the name of the central character, True Son, he couldn't see any connection. He gave Thackery a measured look and said, "So, I take it, you've been watching the news."

"Don't have to, my brother," said Thackery, tapping the device in his right ear, which looked like a modified Bluetooth. "I get it all from my boy Jimmy John, uncut, in real time."

"Jimmy John" wasn't a person; it was a network of geeks who hacked government emails, phone calls, and texts, both foreign and domestic, to share with others in the network and occasionally "pass for cash" to the press. Thackery used Jimmy John mostly to keep up with new R&D at the DARPA programs in the US, Asia, and Europe.

Thackery stepped on one pedal of his bike, kicked off, and coasted over to one of the glass-topped tables at the center of the loft, where his laptop computer sat open.

Melville followed but stopped short when he saw the cat sprawled across the table. Melville had nothing against cats—he regularly put food and water on his porch for neighborhood strays—but this was no ordinary cat. Stretched out lengthwise, the cat was over three feet long, and it had the markings of a leopard.

"That's just my boy Simba," Thackery said as he dismounted his bike and propped it against one end of the table. "He's a Savannah, huge but harmless—looks like a Cheetah, purrs like a kitten, don't you, buddy?"

Thackery petted the cat's huge head, and it began to purr, but it didn't sound like a kitten to Melville.

"I got him from a breeder in San Diego, cost me like twenty K, as in Gs, yo. He's supposed to have a lot of energy because he's half-serval—which means he's technically part wild—but he's actually pretty lazy most of the time, just chillin' and whatnot . . . until you get him on that crazy wheel over there." Thackery nodded at the massive purple exercise wheel at the far end of the loft. "He gets on that thing, and he's like a maniac—at it all night, like a hamster on steroids, aren't you, Simba? You're just like a big crazy hamster on the Anabolic Express, aren't you?"

The cat blinked languidly at Thackery while continuing to purr like the motor of a small automobile. Melville still looked apprehensive.

"You can pet him, yo. He's down with the brown." He shot a grin at Melville. "But he's not always kosher with the pale face—I don't know why, but white people piss him off." He turned and called out, "Klaus Maria, come here, bro."

A paled skinned guy in his mid-twenties came from the table where he was working, and even as the big cat continued to lean into Thackery's touch, it's purr became more like a growl. Klaus Maria appeared unmoved by the display of ferocity. He stepped right in and stroked the growling cat under the chin while speaking to it in German.

Thackery laughed. "I don't know. Maybe he just doesn't like German talk. Klaus Maria, this is my buddy Melville. He's old school, but he's cool, so show him some respect."

The young German extended a hand to Melville and shook firmly. Melville gave him a nod, but it was difficult to keep his eyes off the big cat for long.

Thackery laughed again. "Take him over to the wheel, Klaus Maria, see if he'll run. He loves that crazy wheel."

The German scooped the large cat into his arms like a

baby, and the cat protested by gnawing gently at his chin while growling. Klaus Maria took no offense and continued to coo in German as if soothing a fussy child.

Thackery called after him, "And when you get him settled, could you get me a large cherry fizz fro-yo float?" He turned to Melville. "We got a machine, makes any flavor you can think of. You want one?"

Melville shook his head.

Thackery called out, "Klaus Maria, just one."

Klaus Maria called back over his shoulder, "*Welche größe?*"

"Large."

"*Was?*"

Thackery shook his head. "The guy understands what a cherry fizz fro-yo is, but he doesn't know what 'large' is." He called out to Klaus Maria again, "The big one. Tall."

"*Was?*"

Thackery sighed. "How do you say 'large' in German?"

Melville said, "*Groß.*"

"Gross," Thackery called out and shook his head again. He turned back to Melville. "What have you got?"

Melville took a memory stick out of his pocket and handed it to Thackery, who plugged it into his computer.

"Interesting," Thackery mused with narrowed eyes. "Is this thing live?"

Melville nodded.

Thackery uttered a soundless laugh with a thin smile of admiration. "Brother Kylo's got some serious stones— daring the spooks to come and get him, taunting you with his mad skills. That's some hard-core-Johnny-Lee-Miller-Angelina Jolie-*Hackers* shit, yo."

"If only it were that simple," Melville said. "ELINT's been on it since the transmission came through, but every time they get close, the signal vanishes."

Thackery's eyes gleamed now as he took a seat and scanned the screen. "That's because they're moving on her with too much aggression. Daisy's a sweet and sensitive girl—you gotta *romance* her. She's smart too. You can't just knock on the back door and slip in—she'll already be out the side window and gone before you make it to the hallway, let alone the bedroom, homey."

"You're familiar with this code?"

"Intimately," said Thackery with an arched brow as his fingers machine-gunned over the keyboard. "I wrote it."

Melville's eyes narrowed.

"Don't bust out the cuffs and the Miranda on me just yet, Danno," said Thackery with a chuckle. "I'm a lover, not a fighter—you know that, boo." He took a breath and let it out as he continued: "But . . . your boy is *definitely* using my Daisy to cloak his ten-twenty."

"How did he get your code?"

Thackery raised his eyebrows. "Good question, the answer to which I can only guess at . . .

"A: He's someone in my tight network—don't get excited, yo. My tight network is tighter than tight, and if one of those guys is Kylo Ren, I'll eat whatever that mega nasty is that's wafting from Simba's litter box." Without taking his eyes off the computer screen, he called out, "Klaus Maria, do me a solid, yo, and check that litter. I think Simba just dropped a deuce bomb." To Melville, he said, "For some reason, that cat doesn't cover his poop. My buddy Ricky Glenn brings his female Siamese, Chantal, over to play, and she's always back there covering up Simba's poop—I think that bitch spoiled him."

Klaus Maria brought Thackery his float.

"Thanks, man. Make sure you Febreze after you scoop that box. Whew!"

He turned his attention back to Melville.

"Or B: He's someone who exploited a weakness in one of my boys' firewalls." As if reading Melville's mind, Thackery shook his head. "It won't help. Even if one of my boys had a leak, we wouldn't be able to trace it back to Kylo Ren . . . *per se.* If he knows what he's doing—and with you guys running in circles all night to find him, it looks like he *might* know what he's doing—he's already stripped my signature and replaced it with his own. Personalized, Double-O-Seven, it's the only way to go."

Melville waited for the but.

"*But*," Thackery said, "unless he's a full-fledged, bona fide evil genius, such as myself, it's a safe bet he hasn't discovered Daisy's chain . . . "

"What is Daisy's chain?"

"Just a little innocuous bit of decoration woven skillfully through her coding that prevents her from wandering too far away from her true love," said Thackery with a small smile of satisfaction. "I am a jealous god, yo."

The computer chimed. Melville leaned in closer to the screen. "What's that?"

"That, my friend," said Thackery, "is what we're looking for."

"That's Daisy?"

"The one and only," Thackery said with a nod. "Or, more accurately, one of the *many* ones and only."

Melville's brow knit.

Thackery turned in his ergonomic swivel chair. "OK, here's the skinny: Your average cloaked transmission typically uses a relay to avoid the signal being traced back to its source. So you're sitting in your safe place, transmitting your evil plans of world domination and destruction while the Five-O is racing to some empty warehouse loaded up with explosives that are triggered seconds after they arrive—at least, that's the way it always happens in the movies, right?

"*But*," he added with a wise gleam in his eyes, "*Daisy* doesn't work like that. Daisy's constantly on the move—or at least, she *appears* to be—so, instead of being in a warehouse someplace with explosives, she's out on the prowl. Any active mobile device—smartphones, blackberries, tablets, netbooks, ultra-mobile PCs, even crap PDAs—she just keeps bouncing off of all their signals, like a pinball, so just when you think you've got her . . . whoops, it's just some chick at Starbucks on Facebook, or some kid calling Mom from the mall when his older brother doesn't show up to get him after the movie lets out, or some old douche in the Oval, tweeting a little cray-cray at three A.M.—no offense to your boss."

Melville didn't bother to remind Thackery that he was retired from the CIA and no longer beholden to the chief executive. He simply replied, "But you can track Daisy with the chain you embedded in the code."

Thackery winced. "The trouble is, I designed her *not* to be caught . . . by anyone . . . including me." Before Melville could respond, Thackery added: "That's not to say that I *can't* catch her. It's just gonna take time."

"How much time?"

Thackery contemplated the screen thoughtfully. "I'm not gonna lie to you, brother. I don't know."

Melville was silent for a moment. Thackery sipped his cherry fizz fro-yo float.

Melville said, "You're sure this is Daisy?"

Thackery stopped sipping and gave Melville a pointed look. "I know my girl, yo."

Melville was silent for a moment longer. Then he said: "This has to be your top priority."

"I'm on it, Jeeves."

"Will you need backup?"

"Nah, I got Klaus Maria."

Melville looked at the German, who was spraying air freshener at the far corner of the loft while the Savannah cat raced on the big wheel nearby. Then he turned back to Thackery and said, "Call me the second you have anything." He took an ivory card out of his wallet and placed it on the glass table beside the computer. "Use this number, not the usual one."

Thackery nodded.

Melville looked at the screen. "Anything at all, call me."

"You know it, brother." Thackery took another sip of his float and said, "You sure you don't want one of these?"

M YCROFT MCTORY, SENATE MAJORITY LEADER FROM THE great state of Kentucky, stood in the parlor of his DC residence, dressed in his housecoat and slippers. The TV was on, but the sound was muted because Mycroft was presently on the phone with the White House—or more accurately, he was on hold, waiting for someone to pick up at the White House. Though it was going on eleven P.M., which was well past his bedtime and certainly not an hour he would be entertaining company, especially not on a weeknight, Mycroft's parlor was occupied by an odd assortment of guests. From the Left side of the aisle, there was Senate Minority Leader Caleb Sherman, Speaker of the House Noreen Pascarelli, and House Intelligence Chair Aaron Straight; from the Right side of the aisle, Senators Sharon Callow of Maine, Ritt Monterey of Utah, and Llewellyn Granville of the Palmetto State. While the participants, as well as the venue, appeared almost comically out of place, the matter at hand was indisputably grave enough to warrant such a gathering.

All stood with somber expressions as they waited for Mycroft to reach his party at the White House—all, save for Llewellyn Granville, who sat in a chair by the fireplace, elbows on his knees, fingers laced beneath his chin, looking more like a schoolboy who'd been summoned to the principal's office than the Chair of the Senate Judiciary Committee. Senators Monterey and Callow looked like stern parents, waiting to hear what mischief their child has been up to, while the House Intelligence Chair and Senate Minority Leader gazed down their noses like teachers who'd been pushed to their limits by a particularly disruptive pupil. But it was the inscrutable gaze of House Speaker Noreen Pascarelli that drew a nervous half-smile from Llewellyn

Granville, who said defensively, "What did *I* do?" His smile vanished when he caught the stony glare of Senator Monterey, who was in no mood for humor.

An awkward silence followed.

Then Mycroft suddenly spoke into the phone. "Yes, Skippy? Mycroft McTory here . . . Well, I'm doing all right, but I suppose the real question is, how are *you* folks doing over there at the White House . . . ? Well, that's good to hear, but I'll be honest with you, I've been watching the TV over here with some friends, and I'd be gilding the lily if I told you we weren't a little bit concerned about what's going on over there in your neck of the woods . . . Well, Ritt Monterey is here with me, along with Sharon Callow. And Speaker Pascarelli and Minority Leader Sherman are here too, along with Chairman Straight, and they're a tad concerned, understandably so . . . Well, I don't doubt that you haven't heard from Llewellen, as he's here with us too, sitting by the fire, as we speak, all warm and toasty . . . Yes, it certainly is a cold one out there. I believe the weather report said we might be in for some snow by morning . . . Yes, I miss Maria too; she was quite a gal and a fine meteorologist . . . Yes, he's a hellava brave man, that husband of hers, chasing down those storms the way he does, that's a hellava way to earn a living, I'll say . . . Well, the good Lord willing, I'm sure he'll keep safe and not make our little Maria a widow. But, you know, Skippy, the reason I called you is because of this foofaraw going on over there at the White House. Can you . . . ? Well, yes, I can imagine as much. From what I've been seeing here on the news, I can imagine there's a touch of pandemonium over at the Pentagon as well, phones ringing off the hook and whatnot. But what would really be helpful just about now would be to have some insight on the President's thoughts, to know where his mind is at, so to speak, and how he intends to proceed on this, uh, situation . . . Yes, I fully understand your position, Skippy, and I respect your discretion, as I'm sure you respect mine—as well as the discretion of my distinguished colleagues here with me at this late hour. So, anything you might see fit to divulge would be received as a professional courtesy and held in the strictest of confidence, of course . . . "

Mycroft glanced at Caleb Sherman, who could not conceal the glint of admiration in his eyes. Across the room, Llewellyn Granville offered a thin smile, but it was difficult to tell whether this smile was out of appreciation for Mycroft's skillful smooth-talking or the tasty cup of hot cocoa and cookies Mycroft's wife, Erika, had just brought in on a tray from the kitchen.

The phone conversation continued for several more minutes, with Press Secretary Skip Spinner doing most of the talking and Mycroft throwing in an occasional "I see . . . " and "You don't say . . . ?" along the way. It ended with Mycroft saying, "Well, I certainly do appreciate your candor, Skippy—as do all of my colleagues here, I'm sure— and you have my word that our lips are sealed, of course . . . Yes, the same to you, and please feel free to contact me at this number if anything else should arise that you feel might warrant my attention. I'll be more than happy to take your call anytime."

After he hung up, Mycroft stood for a moment with his profile to the others. All of them looked anxious. Caleb Sherman spoke first.

"What did he say? What's going on?"

"It would appear," Mycroft said in a lugubrious tone, "that the President is leaning toward accepting the terms of engagement."

Ritt Monterey pursed his lips and released a labored breath through his nose. Sharon Callow stood stone-faced. Caleb Sherman shook his head in disbelief.

Aaron Straight said, "Who's counseling him?"

Mycroft blinked. "No one."

Monterey's jaw tensed. Callow shook her head.

"There has to be *someone* there with him," said Caleb.

"One of the Joint Chiefs, someone from NSA—he has to at least be in contact with someone . . . "

Mycroft shook his head. "According to Skippy, the President is holed up by himself in the dining room."

"Which one?" Llewellyn asked.

"I don't know," Mycroft said softly. "The little one, I suppose. Skippy says the President has been in there since he left the press in the Oval Office, and the only person that's been allowed entry is Franco Scaramanga—and that was only so Franco could bring him a Napoleon and a glass of milk from the kitchen . . . apparently he has a sweet tooth."

"This is ridiculous," Caleb snapped with a look of disgust. "Enough is enough. This has got to stop right here."

Monterey cleared his throat but said nothing. Noreen Pascarelli stood stoically, but thoughts were moving at an accelerated pace behind her eyes.

Llewellyn shook his head with a smile that didn't look nearly as confident as he hoped it would. "I think y'all're blowing this way out of proportion. We need to just calm down and let the President do his . . . thing . . . and see how it goes."

Caleb Sherman glared at him. "I think we've seen enough of how it goes when this president does 'his thing.'"

Llewellyn held up a hand in a gesture of peace. "Look, we all need to take a breath here, OK? All I'm saying is . . . he's the President, and it's . . . his call. It's a tough call, but it's *his* to make. Presidents make tough calls all the time . . . and sometimes they make the right call, and sometimes they . . . But all I'm saying is, it would be prudent for us to wait and let him . . . be the decider. That's all I'm saying."

Caleb looked coolly astonished. "Are you still trying to sell us on him, Llew? Are you still holding your nose and toeing the party line against everything your party supposedly stands for? Are you still willing to sell your soul for a few more judicial appointments? Do you really not get the big picture of what's happening to our democratic republic here? Do you not understand that the world is watching this right now and that they are making decisions of their own? Decisions that will have far-reaching implications for the future of the United States of America, such as where we fit in the grand scheme of the world order. Decisions based on what our president is doing right now, and what he's *been* doing—what he's been *allowed* to do under the auspices of your party. Do you really not get that?"

Llewellyn chuckled. "That's a bit dramatic, Caleb."

"You bet your ass it is, Twinkle Toes."

Llewellyn's grin faded, and his eyes became dark. Caleb Sherman's eyes lit up with a tightly controlled fire. The others watched with contained interest.

"This isn't a game," Caleb went on, his sharp gaze fixed on the Senator from South Carolina, "and it isn't a 'reality' TV show, either. There aren't any roses, or million-dollar prizes, or all-expenses-paid vacations to be handed out at the end. This is *actual* reality—with very real consequences. You want to sit there with that smug look while playing footsie with a man who has trampled all over the United States Constitution, besmirched Federal and State Judiciaries, accused a former president of wiretapping him—without a shred of evidence beyond a 'report' he read online by some alt-Right nutjob—a man who has made outrageous lies and insane tweets a daily presidential activity, and I won't even get into his shakedown of an ally for dirt on his political opponent or his unilateral decision to take this country into yet another war in the Middle East—you want to hitch your little red wagon to that train-wreck, be my guest. But those of us who still have our dignity—or whatever passes for dignity in a time like this—we're out. No more. This is the end of the line."

Llewellyn gazed up at the Senate Minority Leader with scarcely concealed contempt. For a moment, it looked like he might wage a counterstrike, but he held it in and waited for one of the cooler heads from his side of the aisle to speak up in his defense.

In short order, someone did speak up, but not in Llewellyn Granville's defense.

It was Mycroft McTory, standing there in his housecoat and slippers with a pensive expression on his long face. "Normally," said Mycroft in his usual measured cadence, "prudence would presuppose cautious observation. But, given the manifest mercurial tendencies of the President when vexed, this might be a good time to ponder a course correction."

Caleb Sherman, Aaron Straight, and Sharon Callow all nodded. Ritt Monterey and Noreen Pascarelli remained motionless. Llewellyn was floored.

"Jesus, I can't believe you," he said with a nervous chuckle. "Mycroft, what's wrong with waiting? Who *knows* what's going to happen? Anything could happen. We can't just . . . cut and run. Who knows what the hell is going to happen? Kori-Lynne is still in there. She could turn this whole thing around on a dime—you've seen her in action, you know how good she is. And the President *loves* her. He's watching her right now on *live* TV. You know he eats that sort of thing up, it's his bread and butter! He believes anything he sees on TV—for Pete's sake, that's how he makes ninety-five percent of his decisions! If Kori-Lynne nails it over there, this whole thing could be shut down before it even gets started."

"*Before* it gets started?" Caleb Sherman cried with an incredulous laugh.

Llewellyn ignored the interjection and looked up at Mycroft with hopeful eyes. "Come on, at least give her a chance, at least give her that much. She could spin this whole thing around, that's her job. Let her do her job."

Mycroft glanced at the TV. Even with the sound off, it was fairly clear which direction the back and forth between

Kori-Lynne Carpwell and the pundits was headed, and no amount of spin was going to change that.

Mycroft sighed like a tired turtle in search of a shady spot to rest and said, "Well, I'd say she's doing about as well as a one-legged man in an ass-kickin' contest."

Llewellyn threw up his hands and laughed again without humor. "Come on, Mycroft," he said, "Senator Sherman—all due respect, Caleb—is just spouting bullshit, hoping we'll blink."

Speaker of the House Noreen Pascarelli spoke for the first time. Her tone was soft but serious. She said, "All due respect, Llewellyn, but as your old friend Senator McQueen would say if he were here, 'Shut the fuck up.'"

Llewellyn froze, his mouth agape, his eyes locked on the Speaker. The moment between the two lasted all of a few seconds before Llewellyn collapsed back into the arm-chair and turned to the fireplace with a hand on his chin and his cheeks burning red.

Noreen turned to the Senate Majority Leader and said, "My mother used to say, 'You'll learn more listening than you will talking.' All right, Mycroft. I'm listening."

Caleb Sherman nodded. "We all are."

Mycroft stole a slow glance at the TV, where Kori-Lynne Carpwell looked like Dan Quayle being slapped around by Lloyd Bentsen at the '88 debate in Omaha. Then he turned back to his colleagues, took a short breath, and said carefully, "It may be time to cut loose the lifeboats . . . and row out far enough that we don't get sucked under in the wake."

THE PRESIDENT SAT AT THE TABLE IN THE SMALL DINING ROOM adjacent to the Oval Office with his lips puckered into a pout and his eyes narrowed nearly to a squint. His gaze shifted between the empty glass and pastry plate before him as if the dried swirls of milk in the former or scattered crumbs on the latter might contain some secret meaning in their random patterns. Or perhaps his scrutiny of the empty glass and plate was due to the fact that he was still hungry and wished he'd told Franco to bring him *two* servings instead of one. Whatever the case, the President continued his examination, unabated. He was in no hurry to get back to the jackals in the Oval Office, and he had more than enough time to respond to the demand of that arrogant little terrorist punk True Son.

If the Father of the Wounded Nation is the man he claims to be . . . he will face me by the zero hour.

"More than enough time," the President muttered under his breath. "Plenty of time, believe me. Plenty."

I will accept no second.

He must face me himself, as a man and a leader, or be proven a coward.

"Filthy little arrogant prick," the President grumbled, as if *he*, the President of the United States, the most powerful man in the world, would even *think* about sending someone in to fight his battles for him. "Boyega, maybe," the President croaked with a humorless grin, "*he'd* send in one of his little minions. Probably that nasty woman—such a deceitful liar—Shady Hannah."

The President chuckled, this time with genuine humor—though there was a bitter edge to it, as if some hidden wound still stung.

"What a bitch," he spat under his breath. "We showed her, though, didn't we . . . showed her right to the fucking door, that's what we did, you bet your ass, we did. Her and that arrogant prick husband of hers. Criminals, the both of them. They should be locked up." His eyes took on a momentary nostalgic gleam. "'Lock her up,' remember that one? Good times, good times. Solid glass ceiling, *very* solid. Bulletproof and bitchproof. No second chances for the crooked lyin' loser. And she *is* the loser. Five million dead people, plus all those illegals, voting for her! Dead people and illegals, that's all she had. I beat her by a land-slide—biggest landslide in history—and she knows it. Nasty woman. Very nasty, very deceitful. But we showed her, didn't we, yes we did. We *saved* that glass ceiling . . . saved it from raining down on America and cutting everyone to ribbons—they oughta pin a medal on me! I'm the *real* war hero. I won this war. I saved this country from complete and total disaster . . . complete and total disaster . . . big time, believe me. Bigly . . . *bigly* . . . bigly, that's right, bigly—don't tell *me* what's not a word—it's *bigly*, look it up, it's there . . . it's there, all right . . . "

The President unclenched his white-knuckled fists and spread his hands flat against the tabletop. He didn't like looking at his hands. Not anymore. Not since that smart-ass, Rojas, made that crack during the primaries, the sweaty little bastard. The President shook his head. The last thing he needed circling his thoughts right now was Mini Mateo Rojas—or any of the others—stomping around up there in the attic.

Mini Mateo. Lyin' Tad. Lethargic Judd. Shady Hannah. Crazy Benny. Horse-face Corly. And of course the Bride of Dances With Wolves, Evelyn Herring. All of them losers and liars and frauds. So jealous of him, so spiteful, so jealous, every last fucking one of them.

Too many memories, way too many memories, all swirling and colliding up in the attic. A complete mess.

The President took a short breath and concentrated on the table instead of his hands.

He had replaced Boyega's square table, which was far too big for such a small area, with a more suitable round table, like the kind Reagan had back in the '80s. A nice solid mahogany top, stained in a deep shade of cherry, with a high gloss finish that you could see your reflection in.

For a moment, the President was tempted to lean for-ward, but he didn't want to see his reflection any more than he wanted to see his hands. He grimaced at the thought of that sweaty little Cuban prick making that nasty crack about his hands.

Who the fuck attacks somebody's hands, anyway?

He sniffed deeply. He needed to keep all distractions at bay, so he just sat and admired the smooth polished surface of the beautifully crafted table. He had insisted it be identical to Reagan's table, or he would take a fire ax to it. The designer had laughed at the joke, and the President had smiled, though, in truth, he hadn't been joking.

Reagan. That guy had taste. Impeccable man. Very presidential man. Boyega, on the other hand, had terrible taste. The red curtains in the Oval Office were atrocious and were the first thing to go. The President had them replaced with beautiful gold curtains, and everyone agreed that these looked far more appealing—and presidential—than Boyega's brothel colors.

"What an eyesore those red curtains were, am I right, guys?" The President had asked this of a small gathering of reporters shortly after the new curtains had been hung, and none of them had disagreed—not even the ones who were totally in the tank for Boyega and had cried when Hannah lost the election.

"She lost," he muttered in a distant and oddly small voice. "She did . . . that's the way it happened."

He tried to picture her all alone in her glass-ceilinged room, crying over her devastating surprise loss. But the image wouldn't come.

Instead, a very different image rose in his mind—a memory he'd never lost: Hannah Crichton as a guest at his wedding reception—long before she had become his rival for the presidency.

Back then, things had been different. Very different.

Barret hadn't even been born yet, and Dane couldn't have been more than three or four and had yet to develop that willful gaze and obstinate attitude that made the President see red. The older kids—Roy Jr., Ilona, and Merrick—had all been in their twenties, and Tabby had been eleven or something and showed no signs of the weight problem that would plague her by the time she hit her teens.

But it wasn't his kids that he saw now in his mind's eye.

It was Hannah.

Not Shady Hannah, the lying, conniving, nasty woman who'd attacked him so viciously and unfairly on the campaign trail. Not that bitch.

Just Hannah.

Hannah at the reception, dancing with her husband, so easy and carefree. But ladylike. Elegant and ladylike. Always a lady. She wasn't born to it—he knew that much about her. She'd worked her way up from nothing, earned everything she had—and took by force what was freely given to most men. She was a scrapper, and he liked that about her. He admired it.

But on that night at his wedding reception, she was a lady. A true lady. She wore a gold dress that complemented her figure and a simple pearl choker with a tasteful silver pendant. Her hair was short—shorter than he preferred on a woman (or at least on his own women)—but it suited her. He remembered how pretty she had looked, how that smile of hers had lit up the room. And her laughter—he had never heard such infectious laughter in all his life . . .

People often accused her of being a phony and made fun of her laugh, but they didn't know her like he did. They'd never spent time with her—*real* time—away from the political scene, at a party, or a dinner. She was nothing like the way they portrayed her in the press. She was funny and vivacious and smart—*really* smart. She studied things, right down to the last detail, and her knowledge was as varied as it was vast. She could hold her own in a conversation on just about any topic you could think of.

It was fascinating how much knowledge she had in that head of hers. Love her or hate her, you had to respect that. She worked harder than any man he knew, and she could stand toe to toe against the toughest of them, himself included. She was a strong woman, a good mother, and a better wife than that philandering husband of hers deserved, that was for sure . . .

The President blinked like he suddenly hadn't a clue where he was. The music from the reception and the dim lights over the dance floor at Largo Morta filled his senses. He could hear someone telling the punch line of a joke, followed by that infectious laughter, and then he could see himself joining the group and putting an arm around Hannah's shoulder, smiling and asking, "Is this where the real party is? I think the real party is here. Screw the rest of these people—I don't know half of 'em, anyway—I'm sticking with you guys." And that got all of them laughing.

He remembered leaning in close to Hannah's ear and speaking over the noise. "You're the life of the party, and you'd better be running in '08, 'cause I got a big check for you, and a big mouth to match it, and I'm gonna be shooting it off, telling everyone I know to support you, or I'll make life miserable for them! I mean it. You're a special lady, and this country needs you. We need a woman—the guys just keep fucking everything up. It's time for a woman, and I'm gonna be there for you. You're the best. I mean that. I really-really mean it. You're gonna be the first woman president, believe me."

But he had been wrong about that one. Dead wrong.

That uppity Harvard prick with the smug grin had swept in out of Africa and stolen the nomination from her. She had the votes, but he had the delegates. It was disgraceful, the way her little cronies in the Democratic Party had turned on her, totally and completely disgraceful—disgusting, really, total sham of an election. She should've sued the

DNC for cheating her out of the nomination and then gone after that illegal son of a bitch with his phony Hawaiian birth certificate and sent him packing back to Nigeria or wherever he really came from, the miserable cheating prick.

The President took a deep noisy breath and exhaled, pushing all thoughts of his predecessor out of his mind.

But the memory of Hannah at his wedding wouldn't budge. Indeed, the harder he pushed against it, the more entrenched it became. He just kept seeing her in that gold dress, out on the floor, beneath the sparkling lights, dancing with her husband, Blake, the two of them smiling, carefree and happy.

He supposed that another man—a lesser man than he—might have been envious, perhaps even jealous, of the former president dancing with the future first female president as if it were *their* special night and not his. But Royal Kingley had harbored no such feelings. Not on that night. Not ever. He envied no man and didn't have a jealous bone in his body.

I'm the president now, a small yet vehement voice at the back of his mind cried out.

But the part of his mind that guided the flow of memories to the forefront wasn't finished. It just kept rolling the image of the former First Lady in that gold dress and the elegant pearl choker, so close to her throat, dancing and smiling and laughing the night away.

She was by no means *his* type—not physically, anyway. But her style and her acumen—not to mention her competitive strength and fierce determination—were undeniably appealing. And if she were a few years younger, a few pounds lighter, a few inches taller . . .

The President sniffed back another breath and let it out slowly through his nostrils, like an aging dragon who has lost the ability to produce flame and therefore must rely solely upon his talons and cunning.

In a flash, the image of Hannah Crichton vanished and was replaced by the black-masked figure with the subhuman voice in the video message . . .

Face me by the zero hour . . . I will accept no second . . . face me as a man and a leader, or be proven a coward.

The President lifted his chin and looked down his nose at the crumbs on the dessert plate.

"Crumbs," he muttered to himself, "all of them, just crumbs on my plate . . . "

The terrorist could wait. There was more than enough time to deal with him. More than enough.

The President called Franco to the door and told him to bring up another Napoleon and a fresh glass of milk. Cold. Not lukewarm, like the last one.

"Franco, how do I want it?"

"Cold, Mr. President."

As the door swung shut behind Franco, the President spoke under his breath in a singsong tone: "That's right. Good man. Make it cold. Nice and cold. It's a dish best served cold."

The President examined the crumbs on his plate at length, searching the patterns of their seemingly random trails because nothing was ever random; everything was deliberate and done with purpose.

When the patterns began to make sense, he pressed his fingers to the plate and then proceeded to lick the sticky scraps from each fingertip slowly and deliberately. He had more than enough time to respond to that arrogant little terrorist dirtbag. Let the prick wait. He didn't take orders from anyone. *He* was the president now. *He* called the shots.

And he had more than enough time.

Plenty of it.

DELORES KNOX GREENWOOD SAT AT THE GLASS TABLE ON THE set of *Fastball,* quietly listening to the heated exchange between Kori-Lynne Carpwell and former Communications Director for the Crichton campaign Jemma Paganini. With the way the rivals were going at it, Delores figured the two-hundred-mile distance between them was a good thing. Across the table, Chase Grimley wore the expression of a moderator at a high school debate that has gotten a bit out of hand. Looking at Chase, Delores was reminded of a photo of Churchill at the Tehran Conference with Roosevelt and Stalin back in '43. Like Church, Chase was a good listener—right up until the moment he was done listening.

Kori-Lynne was in the middle of a fiery attack, accusing Jemma and her "Liberal elite cronies" of being "sore losers" who would "embrace any means necessary to tear down President Kingley," when Chase cut in.

"Hang on a second there, Kori-Lynne," Chase said sharply. "Are you saying that this . . . *mishegas*, this insanity at the White House, this abduction of the President's son-in-law by a terrorist—a *terrorist*, Kori-Lynne—are you saying that this whole thing is some sort of *plot*? Some devious calculation, a Machiavellian *scheme* by the Democratic Party—the 'Liberal elites,' as you so coyly call them—to publicly discredit the sitting president of the United States? Are you saying that the Liberals all got together and said, 'Here's what we're gonna do: We'll kidnap the President's son-in-law, and under the guise of terrorism, we'll take him down on live TV in front of the whole world.' Is that what you're saying? That this whole thing is some elaborate Liberal plot to bring down this president?"

"You can make any inference you like, Chase. I'm not saying—"

"*I'm* not making an inference, Kori-Lynne. *You're* the one using cutesy phrases like 'Liberal elites embracing any means necessary' to bring down this presidency. I'm just asking you a straight question, and I want a straight answer. Do you believe that what's going on right now—this abduction of the President's son-in-law—is in any way connected to anyone in the Democratic Party? Do *you*, Kori-Lynne—*personally*—believe that this is a liberal plot to take down your boss? Don't give me any double talk, don't get cutesy with words, don't get clever with cryptic innuendo, just give me a straight answer. Let's make some breaking news right here. Do you believe that what's going on at the White House right now is in any way, shape or form connected to any individual in the Democratic Party? Give it to me straight, because this'll be a real bombshell, and I'm sure the FBI and CIA will love to hear what you've got. Are you saying that the Democrats are behind this terrorist attack on the United States?"

Kori-Lynne stuttered. "Don't you think you're being a bit dramatic, Chase?"

"No, I don't. This is damned serious business here. You're one of the President's chief advisors, and if you have information as to who's behind this mess, you need to come out and say it right now—not in hyperbole, with a wink and a grin, but in plain English."

"I wasn't speaking in hyperbole, Chase. I honestly have no idea who is behind this. It could be anybody—"

"Nah, you're not getting around this one," Chase said abruptly. "You said the 'Liberal elites' would 'embrace any means necessary' to bring down this president. Now answer the question. Are you accusing the Democratic Party, or anyone in the Democratic Party, of an act of terrorism?"

"Absolutely not. I was just saying—"

"So, to get this straight, you do *not* believe that the abduction of Jacob Latner is some plot by the Dems to discredit the President."

Kori-Lynne blinked, and her lips parted, but nothing came out.

Chase released a humorless laugh. "I'm serious, Kori-Lynne. This is a serious situation, and the last thing anyone needs is baseless accusations being lobbed around—by either side. This is the *real* news, not the fake news your boss keeps piping off about. This is the *real* news, and you're making it right here. Do you understand that? This isn't a game of political footsie anymore—we're well past that point. Do you get that? Well, do you?"

"Yes, I get it."

"Because sometimes I don't think you do. You're a smart lady—too smart for your own good sometimes, I think. You're like the White House's Baghdad Bob—or Baghdad Babette—the tanks are rolling in right behind you, and you're smiling in our faces and telling us there's no invasion going on. I'm talking metaphorically here, but you get the point, you know who Baghdad Bob was. And that's what you're like, Kori-Lynne. All hell is breaking loose around you, and you're smiling away, like 'there's nothing to see here, folks.' Well, there *is* something to see here—and we don't need a recording of the President's son spilling the beans to his friend to prove it. We just got it straight from the horse's mouth, right from the top, up there in the White House, and the whole world has seen it. This thing has gone global, the toothpaste is out of the tube, and no amount of finessing is going to get it back in there, you understand?"

Kori-Lynne sat stone-faced and pale. Chase continued with a hard expression.

"We just saw a video message from a terrorist who has abducted the President's son-in-law. We saw this terrorist *torture* the President's son-in-law—the entire world saw it. We listened to this terrorist make a demand that the President face him on live TV—*or else* . . . and I think we all know what *that* means. And now the President is holed up in his private dining room—at least, that is, according to Josh Tanner at NCN, who overheard Skip Spinner on the phone in the hallway outside the Oval Office talking with God only knows who—and now we got the President of the United States holed up in his private dining room there next to the Oval Office, all by himself, drinking milk and eating pastries. *Napoleons!* How's *that* for irony?"

Chase shot a side-glance at the panel across the table, and with a pained half-smile said, "You can't write this stuff! They'd laugh you right out of Hollywood—ask Leonard, he'll tell you, he knows those Hollywood guys, he worked with them on *The West Wing* with Sorkin. I'm not kidding. This is like something out of the wacko annals of a bygone era. Like Nero saving his tears in little glass vials—remember that one? *Quo Vadis.* Peter Ustinov as Nero—what a performance! He should've got the Oscar for that one—I don't know, maybe he did; he's got like two Oscars, I think. Or maybe it's more like Marie Antoinette: 'Let them eat cake!' Or, in this case, 'Let them eat Napoleons!' Either way, you can't make this stuff up. You just can't. No one would believe it—ask Leonard, he'll tell you. But it's happening. This is real, and it's happening right now . . . "

He turned his focus back to the camera and continued speaking directly to Kori-Lynne, who tilted her head slightly to one side and readjusted her seating, bracing for the assault.

" . . . And as much as I'm sure you'd like to deny that, Kori-Lynne, and fluff over all the messy parts, and shift blame to your political opponents—or 'enemies,' as the President likes to call them—you know that it just isn't true. This is *serious* stuff here. You've got a real crisis going on over there at the White House, and your boss—the President of the United States—is holed up in there, all by himself, eating pastry, for Christ's sake! I mean, what the hell is *that* all about? Where are his people? Where are his advisors? And I'm not talking about that gaggle of loosey-goosies who don't know the first thing about running an effective government—Mack "We-Do-Quid-Pro-Quos-All-The-Time-So-Get-Over-It" Moroney, or the President's daughter Ilona, or that Spencer Mahler character, who barks like a Rottweiler trapped inside the body of a Shih Tzu—you know the lineup, I don't have to tell you. I'm talking about the smart ones, the ones who know their asses from their elbows—pardon my French—the generals, the intelligence guys and gals. Where are those people, and why aren't they in there with the President right now, figuring this mess out? I'm serious, Kori-Lynne. I want to know this. The American people want to know this."

"Know what?" Kori-Lynne asked defensively. "They already know the sensitive information that you so carelessly leaked just for . . . for ratings—a leak that could very well hamper President Kingley's efforts to safely resolve the situation. They already know that."

Chase rolled his eyes. "Are you kidding me? This has gone way beyond that, Kori-Lynne. This isn't some secret mission with dark ops sneaking in by moonlight."

Kori-Lynne shook her head with a bitter smile. "You're never going to let that one go, are you?"

"Let *what* one go?"

"Don't act so innocent, Chase. You in the media—"

"You mean the dishonest media? The Fake News?"

"You're damn straight, the dishonest media," Kori-Lynne shot back. "You guys have been hammering that story about the moonlight raid from the start when you've known all along that raid was already set in place by the Boyega Administration, long before President Kingley took office, and you jump at every chance you get to blame it on this president—President Kingley—who wasn't even to blame for it. You want to blame somebody, go blame all those generals who were so gung-ho for the raid. Go blame them for dragging the President into that mess. And you wonder why he isn't calling on those same generals right now?"

"What? Are you talking about the Yemen raid?"

"Yes, I am. The raid that *your* president—"

"*My* president? What's that supposed to mean, *my* president?"

"You know exactly what it means—I know who you voted for, and it certainly wasn't Royal Kingley—"

"Well, you got me there," Chase muttered with an impish smile.

"You bet, I do," Kori-Lynne snapped. "And that raid was approved by *your* president—President Boyega—*before* he left office. The same raid that would have been handled the same way—with probably even greater loss of life—if Hannah Crichton had won the election. Why don't you tell the American people about that?"

Rowan Meadow chimed in from the New York studio. "Uh, Kori-Lynne, according to officials in the Boyega Administration, the raid carried out by President Kingley was never specifically discussed in the White House when President Boyega was in office."

"Well, they *would* say that, wouldn't they?" Kori-Lynne scoffed with a smugly raised chin. "So, why don't we get to what the American people *really* want to know, Chase? Because there's a lot more here than is being discussed in the media, a lot more, and you know it."

"What I *know*, Kori-Lynne," Chase said pointedly, "is that the American people—in this critical moment, right here, right now—the American people want to know that their president isn't sitting there in the White House, holed up like some hermit in his private dining room, scarfing down pastries with his thumb up his ass."

Kori-Lynne's shoulders tightened. "Well, that's a crude way to put it."

"Take it as you will," said Chase, "and pardon my further crudeness, but this is a goddamn serious situation. We've got a guy here—*your* guy, Kori-Lynne, a card-carrying member of the club—Jacob, the President's son-in-law, a chief confidant and advisor, who has a lot of information, perhaps some of our most prized secrets, I don't know, you might know that—"

"I have no idea what Mr. Latner knows—"

"—and he's now in the hands of a terrorist. An enemy combatant—one of those 'bad hombres' your boss is always going on about. Only, *this* hombre really *is* a bad guy, and not someone just looking for a better life north of the border. And your guy, Jacob, who may or may not know some top-secret intel that in the wrong hands could harm us, he's now in the hands of this terrorist—who, by the way, is not above using 'enhanced interrogation techniques' to get what he wants. So forgive me for being blunt, but where are all the generals and intelligence experts? Why aren't they in there with the President right now, hashing this thing out and coming up with a plan? Look into that camera you're sitting in front of up there in the Queen's Room in the East Wing of the White House and tell the American people that. Because that's what they want to know. They want to know who's advising the President during this crisis, and they want to know what the President is going to do about it. So look straight into that camera and tell the American people that."

Kori-Lynne forced the muscles in her face to relax as she gazed into the camera's lens. "I can't tell you what I don't know, Chase. The President has a battery of resources at his disposal, as I'm sure you know, and I'm sure he'll call upon them as the need arises . . . as he sees fit . . . He *is* the president, after all, you know."

Chase looked at the panel across the table with the ghost of a pained smile and said, "Anybody else want to take a crack at this? I got nothin'. It's like the merry-go-round at Coney Island—it just keeps going round and round in circles. I'm getting dizzy . . . literally." He shot a wary side glance into the camera as if debating whether to go back in for another round, but before he could make a decision, Rowan Meadow chimed in again from New York.

"Hold that thought, Chase," she said. "We have break-ing news from outside the Capitol building, where our own Andromeda Mitchum is reporting live on a developing situation . . . Andromeda, it's Rowan Meadow here. What can you tell us about what's going on out there?"

"Good evening, Rowan," Andromeda said. She was on

the north end of the West Lawn, bundled in a warm over-coat, her cheeks rosy and her eyes shining in the chilly night air. "I'm not sure if you can see the full scope of what's happening behind me, but there is a gathering of sorts over here on the West Lawn of the Capitol. It started sometime earlier this evening when Capitol police spotted a group of marchers making its way up Constitution Avenue. I'm not sure whether you can call them protesters—they've been very peaceful, almost eerily silent, one might say—but their sheer numbers are absolutely stunning . . . " She looked over her shoulder and motioned to the West Lawn. "Can we get a shot of this? I'm not sure if you can see this, Rowan, but it's a breathtaking sight from here on the Capitol grounds . . . "

The cameraman at the Capitol pulled back to bring the West Lawn into frame. Row after row of the silent demonstrators stretched back as far as the eye could see.

"We can see it, Andromeda," said Rowan. "Do you have any idea how many protesters or demonstrators are gathered there?"

The camera panned back to Andromeda, who shook her head. "I can only guess. Well into the hundreds. And as you could see from that shot, it's an orderly gathering. No signs, no chanting, or any indication of what this is all about, or what these demonstrators want. No one . . . no one really knows what's going on at this point."

"Andromeda," Leonard interjected, "have you spoken with the Capitol Police? Do they believe this has anything to do with what's happening over at the White House right now? Is this possibly a protest aimed at the President? Or is it something else altogether?"

"That's just it, Leonard," said Andromeda, shaking her head, "no one knows. The police haven't spoken to any of the demonstrators. They've been holding a line, the police have, across the steps leading up to the Capitol Building, barring entrance to the Capitol itself. But so far, the demonstrators haven't made a move. They're just standing on the West Lawn, as if . . . as if they're waiting for something. More like a vigil than a protest, really. I suppose that would be the best way to describe this . . . gathering. A rather stark and eerie scene, like something out of a movie. Honestly, I've never seen anything quite like it. And there's . . . and there's one other thing that sets this apart from other demonstrations. All of the—"

Andromeda stopped in mid-sentence and looked off-camera. A young bearded man in a parka leaned in and spoke to her briefly, and she nodded and turned back to the camera.

"I'm sorry," she said. "That was my producer, Jayce—"

"Hi, Jayce," Rowan called out.

Andromeda said, "We've just been told that Sergeant Dayton Hammersmith of the Capitol Police has agreed to speak with us. I think this is him coming over right now. If you'll bear with me for just a second here . . . "

"No worries, Andromeda," said Rowan. "We're staying right here with you."

Dayton stepped into frame and stood beside Andromeda. He looked a bit uncomfortable being on camera, but he carried himself well. He had a kind face and somewhat sad eyes that belied the keen intellect behind them.

"Sergeant Hammersmith," said Andromeda, "can you tell us what you know about this . . . gathering? Does anyone know what this is about? Is it an organized movement? Do they have a spokesperson? If so, has there been any communication between your department and that spokesperson?"

"Uh, no, ma'am," said Dayton. "We haven't had any contact with the demonstrators—so far. Right now, our instructions are to hold the line on the steps and prevent unlawful entry to the Capitol Building—that order came straight from the chief . . . Chief Brody, that is. So far, the demonstrators have shown no sign of aggressive behavior—as you've observed, they're just standing out there on the lawn . . . But we have, uh . . . unusual, uh, extenuating circumstances here, in that, uh . . . all of the demonstrators appear to be . . . they appear to be kids. High school age on down . . . "

Andromeda nodded. "You were the officer on the scene when the demonstrators were first spotted on the Mall, is that correct?"

"Uh, yes ma'am, I was. They came from up that way, along Constitution Avenue, and headed up here toward the Capitol."

"And that was at what time?"

"That would have been about half past twenty-one hundred hours—nine twenty-six P.M."

"And you were close enough to identify the marchers as children."

"Not quite as close as I am to you right now, but close enough, yes, ma'am. They passed right by me, a whole line of them, right down there, as they rounded the bend to make their way up here."

"And they saw you in your uniform, and kept on going? They weren't intimidated by the sight of a police officer?"

Dayton smiled, but there was little humor in it. "This was a procession upward of six hundred strong at that point, and, kids or not, I'm pretty sure they weren't likely to be spooked by one old uniform on his lonesome. One of the older boys looked me right in the eye as he passed . . . " Dayton shook his head as the eerie moment played back in his mind and said, "These kids aren't easily spooked . . . "

Andromeda waited a moment before continuing. "Is there a plan in place? Will there be an attempt by the police to . . . disperse the crowd? How would you even go about something like that in a delicate situation like this? Is there even a protocol for this sort of situation?"

Dayton shook his head again and spoke honestly. "At present, ma'am, we have no plan for dispersal. We've never faced anything quite like this before. Our primary concern is the safety of these kids." He didn't add, "particularly the little ones," but in his mind, Dayton was picturing the little guy up on the shoulders of the older boy who'd stared directly into his eyes back on Constitution Avenue. If he lived to be a hundred, Dayton Hammersmith doubted he would ever forget the image of that little guy's eyes gazing back at him as the procession headed up toward the Capitol.

Dayton blinked as if waking from a dream. Andromeda had asked a question, but for the life of him, he hadn't a clue what it was.

"Pardon me?" he said apologetically.

Andromeda repeated the question. "Some of these children look pretty young, don't you think?"

"Uh, yes," Dayton said, "yes, ma'am, they do. And considering how young all of these kids are, we don't want to take any action that might, uh . . . escalate the situation. Things are peaceful now, and we're going to continue monitoring the crowd. Our primary goal is to keep everyone safe until . . . until we can get this situation worked out and get all these kids home, safe and sound in their beds."

"Well, you heard it there," said Andromeda, looking back into the camera. "Police are going to continue monitoring the situation out here on the West Lawn of the Capitol, where hundreds of kids, high school age on down, have gathered in what might best be described as a vigil—a vigil that, so far, has been without incident. For what purpose or cause, we don't yet know. But we'll be here throughout the night, and we'll keep you updated on any development."

"Thank you, Andromeda," said Rowan, "for that very informative report. We'll be checking back with you to see how it's going. Try to stay warm out there."

"I will," said Andromeda with a smile. "Thank you."

Rowan turned to Leonard and Davis Frome, who'd recently joined them at the table. "Wow," she said, shaking her head. "Just . . . wow." She chuckled. "Is there a full moon out tonight, by any chance?"

Both men smiled, but their eyes looked thoughtful.

In the Washington studio, Chase Grimley said, "That Andromeda, she's a tough lady. She's not going anywhere, I can tell you that much. She'll stick it out all night in the cold if that's what it takes. Something's going on here—and it isn't a coincidence, that's for sure. Did you see all those kids? Did you see them out there in the cold? It looked like something out of that old George Sanders movie, *The Village of the Damned*, with all the kids standing there, preternaturally patient, waiting." He pointed a finger at Stan Schnetzer and grinned. "I see the way you're looking at me, Stan. You're too young to remember that old movie, but Delores and Elwood know what I'm talking about, and Leonard does too, he's an old movie buff—"

"I've seen that movie," said Stan with a small grin.

Chase waved him off with an amiable laugh. "Ah, you're from that *Children of the Corn* generation. These kids aren't out there with sickles and scythes. This is serious. Did you see those faces? This has something to do with something. This didn't just happen spontaneously. There's a reason those kids are out there on the Mall. Something triggered this movement. I don't know what it's all about, but these kids are out there for a reason. They're waiting for something. This is something. It's eerie as hell, and it means something." He turned back to the camera. "Stick around. We'll be right back, see if we can't figure all of this out. This is happening right now on NCMSB. The politics stop here."

SPECIAL AGENT MATT HASNEY STOOD IN THE DOORWAY OF THE East Room at the far end of the silent and deserted Cross Hall. Like every other agent on the Presidential Protection Detail, Agent Hasney was fully aware of the crises currently unfolding in the West Wing—from the abduction of the President's senior advisor by the masked terrorist known as True Son to the multiple conflicts brewing between the

President's inner circle and the Joint Chiefs. But these were neither his concern nor his responsibility. Indeed Agent Hasney's sole responsibility was the intensely focused ten-year-old boy standing before the model of the National Mall at the north end of the East Room.

The boy was the President's youngest son, Barret Kingley. The model, which spanned the entire length of the vast room and stood in some places as tall as the boy himself, was comprised of over four hundred thousand white tumbling tiles and had taken more than two weeks to construct. Though his older brother, Dane, had helped out with some of the trickier parts—most crucially, the dome on the Capitol Building and the ornate South Front of the White House—Barret, who was the most cannily self-possessed kid Hasney had ever met, had done most of the work himself, tirelessly placing each tile, from the parquet floor up, with a steady hand and a critical eye.

As the boy walked around the model, checking for any final adjustments, Hasney looked on in silence, recalling their first meeting.

At the age of twenty-two, Agent Hasney had been the youngest of President Boyega's protective detail. He had come on board at the beginning of President Boyega's last year in office and had fully expected to continue on in the Crichton administration. But after the surprising result of the election, Hasney put in for reassignment to the investigation division. Though his request had been approved, he never made it to his new assignment.

Three days before the inauguration, Agent Hasney received an invitation from incoming Chief of Staff Rance Plebeius for a face-to-face with President-elect Kingley. The meeting took place in the Blue Room of the White House, where the two of them spoke privately, or "man-to-man," as the President-elect put it. Through the short hallway that connected the Blue Room to the Red Room, Hasney could see Barret Kingley sitting alone on a chair against the north wall of the smaller room. The boy was playing a game on his mobile phone. Hasney doubted he would ever forget the solemn look in the boy's eyes when he looked up from the game and glanced down the hall at him. The moment had been brief, but the effect had been lasting, and Hasney couldn't help feeling that the President-elect had staged their little "man-to-man" talk so that just such a moment could occur.

"Look," the President-elect had said in a confidential tone of voice. "I'll be straight with you because I think you're a very bright young guy—I wouldn't be talking to you right now if I thought otherwise, OK? So, I'm gonna skip the bullshit and get straight down to the bottom line . . .

"I know that you would never take a bullet for me. And I appreciate that. You've got integrity. Your soul isn't for sale to the highest bidder—which is more than I can say for most people, believe me—so, I've got no problem with you asking to be reassigned. None whatsoever. But I also know your history. I know that you graduated top of your class. I know that your reflexes are off the charts and that your marksmanship scores are perfect. I know that your nickname is 'Deadshot' because you never miss. And I know what happened to your little brother—terrible tragedy, senseless, really. Terrible, terrible tragedy—to see your kid brother killed by a stray bullet right there in your living room. I heard how you jumped on top of him to shield him with your own body—and what were you, like twelve, thirteen, at the time? That's the stuff of heroes, let me tell you, unbelievable. You were a hero that day, even though your brother died, you were a hero, believe me, kid. A true American hero, we need more like you, let me tell you . . . "

It had felt like the man had thrust his fist inside Hasney's chest and yanked out his beating heart—and it had taken every ounce of Hasney's considerable resolve to keep from putting the older man up against the wall and jamming a forearm into his throat.

The President-elect, however, seemed oblivious to the overstep and appeared to take the young agent's well-contained emotion as a sign that his words had offered some level of comfort.

While Hasney continued to gaze through the short hall into the Red Room, where the boy sat quietly playing the video game, the President-elect said, "He's about the same age your brother was . . . only the bullet coming for him won't be a mistake. The bullet coming for him will have his name on it."

The President-elect paused to let that sink in, and Special Agent Hasney absorbed it without taking his eyes off the boy in the Red Room.

"I know you wouldn't take a bullet for me," the President-elect repeated in an oddly casual tone. "One look in your eye tells me that much. And I respect you for it." He paused deliberately before tipping a nod toward the boy in the Red Room. "But as sure as I'm breathing, I know that you'd take a bullet for *him*. I know that you'd sacrifice your life in a New York minute before you'd let any harm come to another kid. And that's all that matters."

Standing in the doorway of the East Room now, watching Barret Kingley scrutinize the impressive model of the National Mall, Agent Hasney recalled the final moment of his meeting with then-President-elect Kingley in the Blue Room on that chilly afternoon. He recalled the sunlight streaming through the windows, the short shadowy hallway between the Blue Room and the Red Room, where the boy sat silently waiting, preternaturally patient. He recalled the burning sensation in his cheeks when the President-elect had placed a hand on his shoulder and squeezed the way a coach would before the big game. And he recalled the man's parting words: "I'll let you two get acquainted."

It had been the most humiliating moment of his life, to be so blatantly manipulated by a man who treated people like an endless supply of pawns on a chessboard. But on that January day, Agent Hasney had found it impossible to tear his eyes away from the boy; he couldn't unring the alarm that the President-elect had triggered inside his mind with such calculated ease.

There had been speculation among some staffers that the selection of Agent Hasney had been based less on his qualifications and more on his striking resemblance to the President's youngest son—the theory being that, when in public, the young man and the boy would be mistaken for brothers and not recognized as a Secret Service agent and the President's son. Others posited that Hasney simply fit the "Kingley criteria" (at six-foot-three, with blond hair, blue eyes, handsome features, and an exceptional physique, the junior agent certainly looked like he'd come straight out of central casting).

Only Hasney knew the real reason he'd been selected for this duty, and as he watched the boy with the intensely focused eyes make tiny incremental adjustments to the model of the Lincoln Memorial across the room, he could not deny that the man who had scored a surprising victory in the electoral college had been correct about one thing on that sunny afternoon in the Blue Room. While he would not take a bullet for President Kingley, Agent Hasney would do anything necessary, including sacrificing his own life, to protect the President's ten-year-old son.

And he would do this as the man himself had put it: in a New York minute.

ILONA KINGLEY LIFTED HER FACE TO THE CHILLY NIGHT WIND as she strode across the roof of Tower K at a brisk pace. The rush of cold air, heightened by the blur of the massive propeller atop the waiting helicopter, not only soothed her flushed cheeks, it strengthened her resolve. She was, after all, her father's daughter, and tenacity—particularly in the face of adversity—was her brand. She reminded herself of this as she settled into the plush leather seat at the back of the Sikorsky S-76 chopper. But it was difficult to maintain her trademark resolve when she was on her way to apologize to a friend who was no longer taking her calls.

Ilona had promised herself that she wouldn't grovel. She would stand by her number one principle: never show weakness—even to a friend. Apologize, by all means; ask forgiveness, if necessary. But never grovel; never beg. And above all, never show weakness—nothing was worth exposing yourself to that sort of scrutiny and humiliation.

There were, however, *some* forms of weakness that were acceptable, and depending on the individual and the circumstance, these weaknesses could even be endearing. Back when they were dating, Jacob had sliced open his hand while trying to impress her with his culinary skills in the kitchen. She'd rinsed the wound under the faucet and applied pressure to it with a clean towel, but by the time they'd pulled up to the emergency entrance of the hospital, Jake was bathed in sweat and gazing at her through dazed and glassy eyes from the passenger seat.

It hadn't been a serious injury—it had only taken five stitches to seal the wound—but later that night, as they lay in bed, Jake, with his injured hand wrapped in gauze, had looked into her eyes and told her that she was his hero. She'd laughed, but only because he'd sounded so sincere, more like a boy than a man. She'd stopped laughing when she saw the hurt look in his eyes and told him that she was just being silly and hadn't meant anything by it. Then she'd pressed her naked body against his and peppered his neck with slow kisses.

"I'll always be there to rescue you," she whispered as she traced the frown line above his brow with her fingertips. "I'm Wonder Woman, and you're my Steve What's-his-name."

"Trevor," Jake said, smiling now because she was kissing his neck.

"Oh yeah," she said, moving down to his chest, "Steve Trevor. He's like the hot guy ambassador to the Amazonians, right? Oh my god, you're such a geek."

She laughed again, but this time Jacob didn't look hurt. He smiled, and she smiled too—but something more was smoldering beneath her smile.

"I think you might need some more rescuing . . . "

Jake's lips had parted, and he drew a staggered breath as her hand moved under the covers. Then his eyes had taken on that dreamy-dazed look that had engulfed him in the car on the way to the hospital—that helpless look that had made her feel powerful and in control.

As she gazed out the window of the Sikorsky S-76, Ilona wanted more than anything to draw strength from Jake's helplessness, the way she had on that night he'd cut his hand in the kitchen. But every time she pictured him bound to the chair in that dark room—at the mercy of the masked terrorist with that frighteningly dispassionate voice—it took everything she had just to keep from breaking down in a fit of tears and screaming at the top of her lungs. She could not allow that sort of emotion to leak out, for fear that the first scream to escape her lips would lead to an agonizing outburst that would continue long after they'd stuck her in a padded cell and bolted the door.

She could not—*would* not—allow that to happen.

What she needed was to be with a friend. A good friend who genuinely cared about her. A friend who would forgive all the terrible things that had been said in the heat of passion. Because friends forgive. No matter what, friends forgive.

As the Sikorsky lifted off the roof, Ilona closed her eyes and took a breath. She would be strong now. She would be in control. She would keep it together. For Jake. She would *will* herself to keep it together and not fold under the pressure of this crisis. Many women still looked up to her as an example of what a woman can achieve when she is strong and in control of her own destiny, when she is willing to take responsibility and atone for her actions.

Marilyn would respect her for that, and she would forgive her. Ilona had to believe this. She had to believe there could be redemption for her, and that it would be found in the consoling embrace of a true friend.

Redemption, she thought as the helicopter sped toward DC, where an unexpected fate awaited her. *That's what I need. That's what we all need.*

M ELANIE SOUTHERHOLM HAD SEARCHED THE ENTIRE West Wing, and most of the private residence, before finding the President in the darkened Solarium on the Third Floor. He had somehow disappeared from his private dining room on the State Floor and found his way up here without anyone noticing. Melanie had tried to reach him on his mobile phone several times and was in the process of trying again when one of the staffers reminded her that Kori-Lynne had taken the President's phone from him before heading off to the East Wing to do "a little damage control." Melanie respected Kori-Lynne and would have never presumed to tell her how to do her job. Still, with all that was going on, she couldn't help thinking that Kori-Lynne's considerable skills were being wasted trading barbs with the pundits on TV, especially when real damage control was needed right now in the West Wing.

Melanie took a breath, tapped lightly on the open door of the Solarium, and called out in a tentative voice, "Mr. President . . . ?"

The President stood in silent silhouette at the wide center window, gazing out at the Washington Monument, which, from this vantage point, looked at once both grand and diminished.

Moments of silence passed before the President shifted and released a soft sigh. From where Melanie stood, it was difficult to tell whether the President was still looking at the Monument or if his gaze had shifted to his shadowy reflection in the dark window. She was working up the courage to call out to him again when the President spoke in an uncharacteristically temperate tone of voice.

"Do you smoke, Melanie?"

For a second, she thought she'd misheard him, but before she could respond, he spoke again.

"Kennedy smoked," he said in that same oddly measured tone. "He smoked those thin cigars, like Tyrone Power in *Zorro*. Ford smoked a pipe—made him look like somebody's grandfather. Johnson smoked cigars *and* cigarettes—looked like a thug, either way. But he rolled his own—cigarettes, I mean . . . " His eyes took on a sudden nostalgic gleam. "FDR—now, *that* guy knew how to smoke one. Did it with real class, had that long black cigarette holder, and it didn't make him look like The Penguin, either. You remember The Penguin on that old TV show?" He waved it off. "That's before your time, but believe me, FDR didn't look nothing like The Penguin. FDR had style, he was a class act, through and through, and boy did he know how to smoke—he'd fire one up right there in public, and nobody said boo."

Melanie stood speechless. The President turned from the window and shot a sidelong glance at her.

"I saw him once . . . at Andrews in Maryland—beautiful golf course, not what I'd expected, tight security, very tight. I was there with General Finch, and I saw him, plain as day, large as life . . . "

It took Melanie a moment to realize that the President was not referring to an encounter on the golf course with President Roosevelt (which, she thought with no small measure of relief, was a good thing, considering that President Roosevelt had died before President Kingley had even been born). At times it was difficult to keep up with his tangents, which flowed freely and often shifted in mid-speech, but Melanie was reasonably certain that the encounter the

President was currently recollecting had been with his predecessor, President Boyega.

"He was there with the Speaker," the President continued in a reflective tone. "Not Nasty Noreen, or Pee Wee Reaper—that shifty-eyed rat was just a congressman back then, still digging shit out of his diapers and wiping it on his face." He shook his head. "He was there with the *real* Speaker—Brainerd. Good guy—total lush, but a good guy. And a decent Speaker—a *real* Speaker. The two of them were in the rough, just off the fairway on the thirteenth hole, both of 'em catching a smoke like a couple of kids hiding out from the school proctor. Brainerd looked like a monkey— like one of those chimps they teach to smoke. But Boyega . . . he looked natural, really smooth, you know? Like he was Bogart in *Casablanca* or something. He made it look cool and easy . . . the way he held it, like . . . "

The President tried to mimic holding an imaginary cigarette between his fingers but waved it off and shook his head again with a queer smile. Melanie remained still and silent in the doorway.

"I can't do it," he said with a soundless sigh. "I don't smoke, but you know what I mean. It was like . . . it was like . . . effortless. Like he wasn't even thinking about it. I guess that's what makes it look cool . . . when it doesn't look like you're thinking about it." He twisted his neck, producing a popping sound, and grimaced again. "He probably practices in front of the mirror like twenty times a day to get it right—he's not good at anything off the cuff. His speechwriters probably script every move he makes, so he doesn't look like a goon . . . but still, you can't deny that he looks cool when he smokes . . . "

The President's voice suddenly dropped to a near whisper, and Melanie had to strain to hear him.

"Walking between the raindrops . . . that's what he does . . . he just keeps walking between the raindrops . . . "

The whisper trailed off in a sing-song rhythm ("*raindrops,*

raindrops . . . all those raindrops . . . raining down . . . ") as the President turned his gaze back to the window.

Melanie waited, unsure of what to say or do.

Her paralysis broke when her phone vibrated with a message from Franco, which read: ANY LUCK?

She sent back a text, saying that she'd found the President and that they would be down shortly. She didn't mention anything about the President's odd demeanor or statements—she wouldn't have known where to begin, anyway. And she didn't see any reason to alarm Franco, who was already alarmed enough as it was. She would handle this. It was her job.

She took a breath and steeled her nerves, just as Kori-Lynne would do if she were here. "Mr. President," she called out in what she hoped sounded like an official tone with just the right hint of authority. "They're waiting for you in the West Wing. In the Oval Office. It's almost midnight, sir. They need you to take command, sir . . . they need your strength . . . they need the president . . . "

Melanie couldn't say for sure, but she suspected that last nudge had done the trick. The President's eyes narrowed as he took a breath and raised his chin. In the darkened window, his face looked superimposed over the Washington Monument—like the visage of a god, looming over a distant tower. He turned from the window and straightened his tie. He was ready. He was the president, and he was ready to take command.

They took the Grand Staircase down to the State Floor— the President in the lead; Melanie following a few paces behind. They could have just taken the private elevator to the Ground Floor and reached the Oval Office in half the time. But the President liked making an entrance. He liked walking down the red carpet of the Cross Hall with the ornate pillars off to his side and the high ceiling above him, even if it meant going out of his way.

When they passed the Secret Service detail under the

high eaves of the West Colonnade, one of the agent's lifted the cuff of his jacket to his lips and spoke softly into the concealed microphone: "Golden Eagle is approaching the Nest."

An unexpected sound greeted them as they entered the north corridor of the West Wing. It came in the low-thrumming chords of a piano, joined shortly by a simmering undercurrent of violins—an ominous orchestration, which rose as if from the bowels of a cavernous chamber in some old horror picture the President had seen at the Liberty Theatre on West 42nd Street, back in that simpler time when the flashlight under his pillow was the only weapon needed to ward off the creatures that encroached in the night.

The chords struck again, reverberating, and the President froze in his tracks with a narrow-eyed expression. The hallway was lined with staffers, most of them young, their eyes filled with uncertainty, looking for a sign of authority. It took a second for the President to realize that they were looking to him to take charge. In response, he took a deep breath through his nostrils, raised his chin, and gave them a nod.

The music swelled, and the President's feet were moving again, in dreamlike step with the driving beat that filled the hallway and only grew louder the closer he got to his destination—the oval room at the end of the hall, from whence the eerie chords came.

He stopped at the open doorway and looked inside, where the throng of reporters waited in silent anticipation. But it wasn't the reporters that concerned him. He reached into the pocket of his suit jacket and fished out the mobile phone he'd borrowed from one of the staffers after Kori-Lynne had confiscated his phone earlier that evening. He turned the phone on and swiped through the screens until he found the TuneSleuth app. It took only seconds for the app to identify the piece of music coming from the speakers on either side of the widescreen TV above the fireplace inside the Oval Office. The mobile phone's tiny screen displayed two familiar symbols as one: the silhouette of a bat embraced by a broad red "S." The print below this image read: *Batman v Superman: Dawn of Justice*. The track was entitled *The Red Capes Are Coming*.

The President felt a tingle ascend his spine as he gazed down at the title. The tingle was followed by a single thought—one that the President voiced in a cold whisper: "You bet your ass, Batman. The Red Cape is right here."

As if on cue, the music shifted smoothly to another track on the same album—this one entitled *Day of the Dead*. A subtler piece of music, which featured a mournful blend of the titular superheroes' themes, it drew a bitter-sweet smile from the President, who could not disguise his appreciation for his opponent's theatrical flair.

The press remained silent as the President entered the Oval Office to the passionate swell of the music. With his shoulders pushed back and his head held high, the President took another deep breath through his nose and hit his mark at the center of the carpet. Beneath his polished wingtip shoes lay the image of the eagle, proudly clutching the olive branch in his right talon and the thirteen arrows in his left talon—the symbol that projected the credo of the United States: the desire for peace and the readiness for war. And yet, it was difficult to tell which of these talons the President intended to extend to the masked terrorist who had forced this encounter by abducting Jacob Latner and demanding a publicly broadcast "face-to-face" audience with the Leader of the Free World.

At first glance, the widescreen TV above the mantel appeared to be completely dark. But as the music emanating from the side speakers shifted from the valiant theme of the Man of Steel to the mournful nocturne of the Dark Knight, a faint shaft of light broke at the center of the TV screen, revealing a dense cloud of swirling fog.

The atmosphere of the Oval Office was thick with

anticipation; all eyes were fixed on the TV. And momentarily, they were rewarded.

From the fog, there emerged a tall figure, clad in black from head to foot. It may have been just an optical illusion—produced by the lighting and the angle of the lens rather than the actual distance between the camera and the subject—but the black-clad figure appeared to grow in stature as it moved from the background to the foreground at a gait that was at once both casual and decisive. Either way, the effect was stunning, and the President could not deny that his enemy knew how to make an entrance.

The dim glow of an overhead spotlight glanced off the polished helmet, highlighting the facing of the mask whose black metal breath screen protruded in a prominent triangle without appearing ostentatious. The figure stood tall and silent, waiting patiently for the music to fade, as the dark glass eyes of the mask peered into the camera's lens with pitiless conviction. The voice that emanated from the breath screen sounded at once both reasonable and devoid of humanity.

"I am True Son. Second to the Last, Diviner of Secrets, Destroyer of Demagogues." A brief pause. "And you are?"

The President stood motionless, still overcome by the magnificent entrance. His lips parted, but no words came out. Like a stargazer on the precipice of the universe, he stood humbled and speechless.

True Son spoke again. "You are the Father, are you not?"

The President's brow furrowed in confusion; then he found his voice. "I am a father, yes. I have six children, four boys, two girls, all of them—"

"The details of your domesticity have no relevance," the passionless voice behind the mask said. "I am only interested in your status to the State. So, I'll ask you once more: You are the Father of this nation—the shining city on the hill—most supreme and powerful Leader of the Free World, are you not?"

The President looked bewildered for a second. Then his chest swelled as he drew a deep breath through his nose and hoisted his chin. "Yes," he responded with a steady eye. "I am the Father."

"And this man is your Lieutenant?" He pronounced it "Lef-tenant," like a British actor would in a movie.

A soft spotlight rose on Jacob, bound to the chair, slightly back and to the left of the masked figure, and a swell of pride rose in the President's chest. Though drenched in sweat and barely conscious, Jake was holding up remarkably well.

The President breathed a secret sigh of relief that the terrorist had chosen to snatch Jake, instead of one of his sons. Roy Jr. would have held up for a while but eventually folded, and Merrick—the President didn't even want to *think* about what a train wreck *that* would be. The only one of his boys who might have given this masked prick a run for his money would be Dane. You could shove bamboo shoots under that kid's fingernails, and he'd just give you his best "fuck you" look without so much as a whimper. Unbelievably stubborn, just like his mother—after a few hours with Dane, any terrorist in his right mind would be offering to pay *you* just to take the hardass little punk back.

But Jake was doing well. He was holding up like a champion, and the President couldn't have been more proud.

With his gaze still on Jacob, the President said, "He's my son—he's my son-in-law. He's a good man. You'll never break him."

"It is not my intention to break him."

The President's features froze at the unexpected statement from the man in the mask. Then, slowly, a smile began to curl at one corner of his mouth. A sly smile, fraught with understanding.

"You got your eye on the big guns, eh?" He nodded with approval, and his smile deepened. "Good for you. You're not the first to come for a piece of me, and you won't be the last."

True Son offered a scarcely perceptible nod, and the dark glass eyes of his mask appeared to shimmer in both acknowledgment and acceptance of the challenge.

With a probing look and a pleasant smile, the President said, "The music was a good touch. I like it—setting the mood of the scene. Good stuff. *Dawn of Justice.* You and me. Batman versus Superman. A clash of titans. Very, very good . . . but you know that Superman always wins, right?"

True Son offered no response. The President continued with guarded confidence.

"I mean, no offense, Batman is cool and all, but he's a night-fighter. A vigilante. No better than the criminals he goes after, really . . . because deep down, he's just like them, operating outside of the law." The President drew a pious breath. "But the Man of Steel . . . he's a real American . . . fighting for truth, justice, and the American way. He bends steel bars, leaps skyscrapers, and all that good stuff. He could break Batman in two without even breaking a sweat. You don't want to mess with the Man of Steel, believe me. It would be a disaster, total disaster, a complete and total disaster . . . "

True Son remained still and silent.

The President drew another breath, deeper this time, and squared his shoulders, feeling more in control, more like a president, ready to take charge of the situation.

"So," the President said, "here's what I'm gonna do for you—and there are people here who will tell you that this is a very good deal I'm about to offer—generals, admirals, all kinds of highly trained experts with the most sophisticated weapons imaginable—I mean, they've got it all, nuclear missiles, drones, warships, you name it—believe me, there's nowhere you could hide from guys like these—wherever you can think of to hide, they've already thought of it, and they can take you out in two seconds flat, OK? We can take anybody out—annihilate entire nations—we've got the fire-power. The whole world is trembling at our power to take them out, which we could do at a moment's notice—I got the codes right here in my pocket, always got 'em on me, never without 'em. One word from me, and it's lights out for everybody. I can do it, just like that, and nobody here would even blink. I'm god here—not *the* God, but *a* god . . . the only one that counts on this planet, anyway. I can do it. I got the power of life and death, and I can use it however I choose. Real simple, very quick, I could do it . . . but I *choose* not to, see? Because we're like the good guys here, OK? And we don't just go around annihilating people, OK?"

The President paused to let the gravity of his words sink in. True Son continued to gaze at the image of the President on the massive screen behind the camera in the darkened room, from which his transmission issued.

"So, I'm gonna make you a deal," the President said, "and you really want to listen up because this is a very good deal. A limited, one-time-only offer—a very generous offer because I'm a generous guy, and I don't want to see anybody get hurt here, OK? But also because I'm a negotiator—that's like my thing. I negotiate. I'm an unbelievable negotiator. They say 'never negotiate with terrorists,' but it's not really a rule, more like a guideline, but I don't care, because I don't do guidelines, they're meaningless, and they get in the way of negotiations, and I'm a negotiator, that's what I do, OK? I do unbelievable negotiations all the time—I even negotiate with Democrats. *Democrats.* It's true—pisses off my base, but I do it anyway because I'm a negotiator. I wrote the book on negotiations, number one bestseller for many-many months, probably more like years, it's never gone out of print, sells like hotcakes, even today, it's still selling like crazy—but the point is, I negotiate. That's like my thing, OK? And I've got a deal for you that's unbelievable—you're not gonna see a better deal in all your life, believe me, this is a big one, best offer you'll ever get, the very-very best . . . "

The President licked his lips and dropped a wink at the

camera with a sly grin as if he was about to impart a juicy secret. The reporters in the Oval Office stood frozen. The room was deathly silent. Then something shifted, and the President's gaze suddenly became hard and dark.

"So, here's my offer—and it's the only one you're gonna get, so prick up those bat ears.

"You release my son-in-law immediately—unharmed, and in a location of my choosing—and in return, I won't unleash the full hellfire of the United States military on your people. I don't know who you are or where you come from, but you gotta have people somewhere, and sooner or later, I'll get to them. I'll just pick a spot on the map— doesn't really matter where—and start dropping payloads until I see you flinch. And believe me, you'll flinch—they all flinch, believe me, do they flinch! But by then, my more than generous offer will be off the table. I'll just bomb the shit out of your country, and I'll keep on bombing it until the whole place is one big, black, lifeless crater." He paused briefly and leaned in close to the camera's lens. "And then, Batman, I'll come for you. I'll crawl into that little rat hole where you're hiding and stick the knife into your heart myself."

Moments of silence passed. The press corps looked on with stunned expressions. True Son stood as still as a statue. The President nodded with an eerie smile.

"Now that I've made my position crystal clear, what do you say? Are we cutting a deal here, or what? Clock's ticking, and my bombers are cocked and loaded. Time to put up or shut up. The Man of Steel is waiting. Your move, Dark Knight."

The President held his gaze on the camera for a hard beat; then he looked up at the TV screen above the mantel.

A brief flicker of light glinted off the eyes of True Son's mask. Then, without averting his gaze from the camera before him, he pressed one of the buttons on the small, black remote control in his left hand.

Though the response was immediate, there was no sudden jolt, no cry of agony from the young man bound to the chair—indeed, at first, there was no sound at all.

But as Jacob's body twisted and strained against the straps that pinned him down, his hands balled into white-knuckled fists, and his toes curled into clawlike arches. Veins stood out on his forearms and neck. His chest swelled, and his stomach tensed as his face turned an ugly shade of red, and his mouth opened in a silent scream.

Time spun in a seemingly endless series of seconds, and as Jacob's twitching and squirming continued, a low keening sound escaped his lips—a pitiful pleading that pierced the President's ears like a blade. The President looked into the soulless black eyes on the monitor and could almost swear that the face behind the mask was grinning at him—a sly "fuck you" grin.

As Jacob continued to writhe and plead in that low keening tone, True Son's passionless voice came through the metal breath screen of his mask: "He doesn't like it when they crawl on him."

The President looked confused. His gaze shifted to Jake, who did indeed look like he was squirming against something crawling on his skin. But there was nothing *on* his skin, save for the circular white pads with the tiny flashing red lights.

The President's confusion gave way to uncertainty, and instinctively, his lips parted. But before he could speak, True Son pressed another button on the remote, and at once Jacob's twitching and moaning ceased.

While Jacob sat panting and sweating in the chair, True Son looked into the camera and said calmly, "We'll try this again after the interlude."

And without another word, he pointed the remote at the camera, pressed a button, and the screen above the mantel in the Oval Office went dark.

The President and the press corps stood in stunned

silence, like figures in a tableau, all of them gazing up at the blank screen as a very different sound from the previous selections of music drifted down from the speakers. The filtered intro quickly gave way to a crisp, poppy dance beat that seemed at once both incongruous and apposite to the President's ear.

The tableau of onlookers in the Oval Office broke when the President fished the mobile phone out of his pocket to identify the new piece of music.

S TRETCH BIGGERSTAFF WASN'T DRUNK YET, BUT HE WAS well on his way to getting there. He had been ringing the President's mobile phone for over an hour, and the fucking thing kept going to voicemail. If he had to listen to that infuriating recorded greeting telling him to leave a message one more time, he'd throw his Galaxy S7 right into the huge mirror that kept mocking him every time he looked across the bar.

"The *motherfucker*," Stretch muttered under his breath as he scrolled through his contacts list and tapped the bar top for a refill. The bartender poured a finger and was retracting the bottle when Stretch held up two fingers, without looking up from his phone's glowing screen. He stopped scrolling near the bottom of the Fs and tapped Franco Scaramanga's name.

Stretch took a swig of his drink, clapped the glass down on the bar, and let out a wheezing sigh as he waited for Franco to pick up. His tablet, which was propped up on the bar, displayed four different newscasts: FIX, NCN, NCMSB, and a live stream from the FreedomCave with A.C. Janus, who was currently on a full-blown power rant, with his bulging eyes leaping out of their sockets, his round face as red as a side of beef, and his pudgy fists punching at the air. Right now, all four broadcasts were on mute, but Stretch didn't need the sound to know what A.C. was bitching about.

Anyone with access to a television, smartphone, or tablet couldn't have missed what the masked terrorist had done to Jacob Latner. And the diehard freedom faction, of which A.C. was the grand guru and chief mouthpiece, wanted the masked terrorist's head . . . and they wanted the President of the United States to serve it up to them on a stick.

Stretch couldn't care less what happened to that primped-up little cuck Latner. All that concerned him was the optics. The President needed to be seen as a strong nationalist leader, fighting to protect his people from the clear and present danger posed by a foreign entity. This abduction of the cuck was actually a gift straight from God, right when they needed it most, and Stretch didn't want to see the President muck it up. This thing was bigger than all the rallies put together—bigger than the election itself!

If the President could scratch a notch in the win column on this one, all the messy rumors and innuendo about his presidency being illegit would die on the vine. Nobody would give two shits about the FBI's investigation into collusion, *or* the sacking of their sanctimonious leader, that Lurch-looking freak Jonas Brushing.

If this Latner abduction could be turned into a referendum on national security against foreign terrorism, nobody would give a flying rat's ass about collusion, or any of that other crap about Constitutional rights—as if terrorist-refugees had any protection under the United States Constitution!

But this needed to be handled properly. It needed to be *finessed*. And that meant somebody needed to be *in* there, up close and personal, guiding the President through it. Reining him in, when necessary, and letting him loose at just the right hot spots . . . to facilitate maximum "damage gain" results. Not that Stretch wished the Latner punk any harm, but the right amount of torture could go a long way in shaping public opinion and driving up the President's sagging numbers. And if that cocky little cuck Latner happened to become a casualty . . . well, that would be a small price to pay for the greater good. This was war, and in war, there were always casualties. Anybody leaving the field without at least a few stains on his jersey wasn't in the game, to begin with.

Nobody had held a gun to the little preppy prince's head, Stretch thought, as he downed the second finger of his scotch and tapped the bar top for another hit. *He knew what he was getting into, same as the rest of us. Sometimes sacrifices have to be made.*

As he watched the bartender refill his glass with a generous two fingers, Stretch reasoned that he would do everything in his power to get the cuck out of this alive. But he didn't make himself any promises, because there was no way to be sure of the outcome, and he didn't like going back on his promises. Unlike some people, Stretch Biggerstaff's word was as solid as his conviction, and no one had ever dared to question his conviction. With Stretch, you always knew where you stood, and if you were foolish enough to stand in his way, God help you.

Stretch took another sip of scotch and glanced at his wristwatch while he waited for Franco to pick up. His nerve endings felt like they were on fire; blood pumped through his veins rapidly and pounded at his temples. Everything depended on him getting back inside the West Wing and close enough to the top dog's ear to work some magic. Maybe the cuck would only lose a finger—terrorists loved cutting off fingers to send a message, and it would make a great visual for any Americans still on the fence about immigration and the ban on Muslims. This was a win waiting to happen . . . if he could just get through to someone in the West Wing.

Of course, he couldn't help thinking as the phone continued to ring in his ear, *if all else fails . . . there's always plan B.*

But he'd need to have a hell of a lot more drinks before he'd even *consider* plan B . . .

When the ringing suddenly stopped, and Franco's voicemail greeting came on, the blotches on Stretch's face grew redder. He didn't bother to leave a message. He just went back to his contacts list, and as he scrolled through the long list of names, he tapped the bar top for another two fingers, thinking, *Two fingers of scotch, one finger of Pretty Prince Cuck, sounds about right.*

The thought lifted his spirits enough that by the time that little mealy-mouthed worm, Rance Plebeius, got back from the toilet and took his seat at the bar, Stretch was smiling amiably and offering to buy the next round.

The former chief of staff allowed a small awkward smile in return, hoping this sudden change in Biggerstaff's demeanor was a sign that things were finally calming down.

Stretch clapped Rance on the shoulder and gave him a wink, along with a friendly chuckle, as if he'd read the smaller man's mind. And as he sipped his scotch, a single thought ran through his own mind, *Oh, it's far from over—in fact, it's only just beginning . . .*

B ART BENEDICT WAS THE SORT OF YOUNG MAN THAT EVERY father—at least every responsible father—dreamed of when it came time to marry off his daughter. He didn't come from wealth and had no blood ties to anybody who was anybody, but he was upwardly mobile and eager without coming off as solicitous. The President liked his clean-cut appearance and wholesome good looks. To a degree, Bart reminded the President of Jacob back when Jacob and Ilona were dating—a sharp kid with keen senses, and a good listener who never interrupted. But there was something that Bart possessed that Jacob did not: killer instinct. The President could see it in his eyes, and he admired it. The kid was only twenty-one, or twenty-two, or whatever, and yet he'd already developed what the President called "the edge"—the ability to cut through an opponent's defenses with a single unflinching glance. The edge wasn't some-thing that could be taught; you either had it or you didn't. Some people had it, but never put it to use; they spent their whole lives wasting the gift that others—lesser men—would kill for.

Bart Benedict wasn't one of those people.

He wasn't the sort who abused the edge, either. He was patient and disciplined, which was more than the President could say for most in his administration. The kid knew his place and understood that his time would eventually come. And in the meantime, he was more than willing to pay his dues.

Bart had been one of Finch's hires; Monty had plucked him straight out of college to be the President's "body man," unaware that the position had already been filled. Still, the President had taken a liking to the kid and kept him on as a "second," warning his body man, James McFarland, that his "understudy" was waiting in the wings and ready to take the stage at the first sign of a fuck-up. The President had smiled when he told McFarland this, but the edge in his gaze had implied that he was only half-joking.

The President found Bart, along with Franco and Spencer Mahler, in the crowded hallway outside the Oval Office. Most of the staffers avoided the President's gaze—whether out of embarrassment for him or fear of him, he couldn't say. But still, the sight of their downturned faces stung a little. Sure, things hadn't gone quite as he'd planned, but it wasn't like he had botched the whole deal. Who could have possibly known the dirty little terrorist prick would be so remorseless in the face of authority?

Unlike the other staffers, Bart greeted the President with the respect his station commanded.

"How am I doing, guys?" the President asked.

"Outstanding, Mr. President!" Mahler beamed. But the President wasn't interested in what the resident "yes man" thought. He had just taken one up the kazoo on national TV, and the last thing he needed was Spencer Mahler poking his nose up the old Hershey Highway to soothe the burn. And besides, Mahler was still on his shit list over that whole border fiasco—putting babies in cages! How in hell he let that beady-eyed little prick talk him into *that* one was well beyond the President's comprehension. It made him look like a monster with the good illegals—the ones that worked hard and didn't steal jobs from real Americans. And come November, he was going to need to swing some of those good illegals into his column—particularly in the Southwest—and those people didn't like it when you put the babies in cages, even when it wasn't *their* babies. Unbelievable.

"He got round one," said Bart, his deep hazel eyes steady and sure under the ambient lighting of the hall. "Don't sweat it, sir. You'll take him down—a clean knock-out—before the final bell."

The President peered into the edge of Bart's gaze. Then a smooth, almost dreamy smile broke across his lips, and he patted Bart's cheek—a fatherly gesture, which did not go unnoticed by Mahler, who looked like a dwarf among giants alongside the three taller men.

"This is my guy," the President said with a gleam of pride. "This kid has more metal than most guys twice his age. Look at him. He's like a matinee idol, this kid. Reminds me of me, back in the day." He dropped a wink at Franco. "He's after my job, Franco, I'm telling you . . . "

"He might be, sir," said Franco with a smile that did little to conceal the concern in his eyes.

"I'm not worried," said the President, still smiling proudly. "I'm not worried at all. He's a good kid, he's got my vote, I'd be proud to call him my president." He squeezed Bart's shoulder and gazed at him with the fondness of a coach for his star player. "He's my guy, all right. I'm gonna need him after tonight, I think. Maybe? This thing . . . " He tipped a nod back at the Oval Office with a heavy sigh. " . . . it doesn't look so good in there, not so good at all . . . I dunno, maybe, who knows, nobody knows, am I right?" He chuckled softly and shook his head. "I mean, this psycho terrorist . . . I think he means business. This guy isn't fuckin' around here. I mean, I love Jake, but this thing, it looks . . . bleak . . . I mean, who knew it would be this tough? Am I right? Boyega never had to deal with anything like this— I'm not saying he couldn't have handled it, he was a smooth son of a bitch, nobody's gonna argue with that. I dunno, maybe he would have folded, who knows? With a nutjob like that, who knows? I doubt it. Boyega was a hawk—they all thought he was a dove, but he turned out to be a real hawk . . . shot that bastard bin Khalashifra right in the eye—right in the fucking eye, can you believe that? Didn't even blink. Nobody saw *that* one coming. Nobody. Doesn't matter that *I* took out Salahuddin—the highest-ranking terrorist in the history of the Iranian military, guy was *yuge*, I'm tellin' you, spooky-looking fuck, and in his prime, not like that broken-down used mule bin Khalashifra, let me tell you. But still, bin Khalashifra was famous, got all the press, nobody'd ever heard of Salahuddin before I bombed his ass into oblivion. But you gotta give it to Boyega, he's a stone-cold son of a bitch—you wanna fuck with Boyega, you'd better be wearing a shitload of Kevlar, let me tell you—the guy was a monster hawk, an absolute monster with huge fuckin' wings. Tepes—and don't get me wrong, Tepes is a cunning leader, who commands the respect of more than just his own people over there in Russia—but, let me tell you—because I know the guy, like personally, OK, we've had many-many talks—but Tepes, he would have never fucked with a Boyega election, that's for sure. Bank on it. Boyega was nobody's dove. He was a stone-cold hawk who'd drone your ass back to the stone ages, sooner than look at you. Aloof prick—cold as ice, warm smile, very ingratiating, smooth talker, so-so golfer—but the terrorists feared him, believe me, Boyega was a merciless bastard, and nobody fucked with him . . . "

The President released another sigh. Franco gazed at him with a mixture of apprehension and incredulity. Mahler's pale eyes shimmered under the dim light of the hallway as he geared up for his moment to jump back in. Only Bart, the twenty-one-year-old kid with the chiseled features and cool eyes, seemed unaffected by the President's sudden downshift into despondency.

"I mean, can anyone believe this?" said the President. "Can you believe this fuckin' guy with the mask and the music and that little zapper thing—what the hell is that thing, anyway? Does anyone know? What the hell happened to waterboarding and normal torture? Doesn't he know the rules? There's gotta be like something in the Geneva Convention about it, like the rules of torture, you know, don't you think? I mean, what the *hell* is that zapper thing? I thought it was like an electric shocker or something. Like when he used it on Jake in that video message, I figured he was just shocking him—which, I suppose, is an acceptable torture, I don't know, but at least it's like that's a thing, a real thing, you know, and I could get with something like that . . . that wouldn't be so bad, right? It's not like it tickles—I'm not saying that—probably stings like a bitch—but you could at least get with it, as a real thing, like a normal torture, you know? You'd expect something like that: zap a guy with a few volts of electricity, and that's it, right?"

The three men stood silent while the President shook his head, trying to make sense of it all.

"But this zapper thing . . . " the President continued in a confidential tone of voice, " . . . the way it made Jake squirm like that—and did you hear that whimper coming out of him—like a little kid, it was pathetic, heartbreaking, really. And a little creepy too, don't you think? I mean, that's some crazy shit—like something out of a horrorshow." He said it just like that, all one word—*horrorshow*—and shuddered as if the mere thought of it gave him the willies. "That shit ain't normal. Nobody pushes a button on a zapper box, and it makes you squirm and whimper like that, no way—that's some fucked up shit. You hear what he said to me? 'He doesn't like it when they crawl on him.' What the fuck is that supposed to mean?" He shot a quick breath out of his nostrils and flared his eyes at the three men before him. "This terrorist isn't normal. There's something seriously wrong with him, like his wires are crossed upstairs, like he's mentally unstable—believe me, I *know* crazy, and this guy is batshit certifiable nuts. He reminds me of that creepy guy from that movie, What's-his-name?"

"Kylo Ren," said Mahler, bright-eyed.

The President made a sour face. "No. What? Who the fuck is that?"

"From the new *Star Wars* movies," Mahler explained. "Kylo Ren. Darth Vader's grandson."

The President rolled his eyes as if he'd never heard anything more stupid in his entire life. "Fuck that. I *know* Darth Vader, and this punk ain't no Darth Vader. Get your fuckin' head in the game, Spencer—I'm serious, I'll bench your ass."

Mahler flushed. Franco looked nervous. Bart remained calm.

"Hannibal Lecter," said Bart.

The President snapped his fingers. "That's it. Hannibal. He reminds me of that creepy prick. Real cool and smooth, like he ain't got a care in the world, the crazy fuck." He shot a distasteful look at Mahler, and muttered, "Darth Vader—yeah, right, he *wishes* he was Darth Vader." The President shook his head and turned his gaze back to Franco and Bart; he just couldn't look at Mahler anymore. "So, what the hell *is* that zapper thing," he said, "and what the hell are all those white pads with the flashy red lights stuck to Jake?"

Franco shook his head.

Bart said, "Virtual reality."

The President raised a curious brow.

Mahler jumped in to regain the President's faith. "It's a gaming system that—"

"I know what it is, Spencer," said the President with a sour look. "It's that thing with the goggles—my kids play it all the time—but it doesn't make them moan and squirm like they got bugs crawling on them, and it sure as shit doesn't zap them with electric shocks."

"It's a new form of virtual reality, sir," Bart said. "For a more . . . heightened experience."

"Heightened?" said the President with an incredulous expression. "Is that what they call what that nutjob was doing to Jake in there? A 'heightened' experience?"

Bart understood the question was rhetorical and waited for the President to continue.

"That's some pretty sick shit," the President said with a grimace. "So, what's the deal? Is this . . . virtual thing, I mean, can this thing actually hurt Jake? Is it hurting him? I mean, for real, is it having a real effect on him, or is it just a game, like he thinks it hurts but it really doesn't?"

Bart took a brief moment to ponder the best way to present the answer to the President, who looked cautiously hopeful. "It depends on the individual, sir. I read an article on it in *Wired*. They called it the most intensely realistic virtual game ever. It's marketed by *Bizzazzazz!*"

"What the hell is that?"

"It's a gaming company."

"And they made this virtual reality thing that the terrorist is using to torture Jake? They market this thing as a *toy*? For *kids*?"

Bart said, "I don't know much beyond the article I read, but the unit the terrorist is using looks like it may have been modified."

The President's eyes narrowed.

Bart explained, "In a normal VR setup, the subject using the device is a willing participant. He puts on the goggles that come with the game and enters a virtual world of his own free will. If at any point the experience becomes too intense for the player, all he has to do is close his eyes or remove the goggles. This particular game also includes a set of headphones, and multiple 'pulse pads,' which the player affixes to parts of his body—these give the sensation of *feeling* the game, as well as viewing and hearing it . . . "

Bart paused. The President was eager but displayed remarkable patience. Franco and Mahler remained silent.

"But, in *this* situation," Bart went on, "the goggles aren't being used. Instead, the terrorist has affixed pulse pads to the subject's eyelids . . . which, given Jake's responses, would indicate that the terrorist has figured out a way to . . . force an unwilling subject to experience the virtual world of his creation . . . with no way to exit the game when things get too . . . intense."

The President looked down the hallway and released another heavy sigh. "Jesus Fucking H. Christ. This is *unbelievable!*" He rubbed his eyelids with his thumb and forefinger and drew a deep breath. "Is there any way we can find out if this thing could cause permanent damage or, God forbid, kill Jake? Has anybody ever been killed by something like this? Is that even possible? I mean, I know it's not real and all, but is it like, you know, I'm just saying, like if you die in a dream, you die in real life? Is it something like that?"

Mahler cleared his throat and said, "Well, that's actually an urban legend; nobody has ever actually died in a dream and died in real life, Mr. Pres—"

Without turning his gaze from Bart, the President snapped his fingers at Mahler, who immediately shut his mouth. And in a confidential tone, the President asked, "Could this thing do any real damage? I mean, like, could it give Jake permanent brain damage?"

Bart did not avert his gaze, which pleased the President. "I don't know, sir." Before the President could sigh again, Bart added, "But there *is* someone we could talk to who might know. The company that manufactures this particular game—"

"*Bizzazz,*" the President said.

"*Bizzazzazz!*" Mahler corrected.

The President snapped his fingers again, and Mahler's mouth clamped shut again.

"The company," Bart continued, "is under the umbrella of HiroBot, LLC, which is located in Annapolis. If anyone would have answers, it would be them."

The President absorbed the info and nodded. "OK. Good deal. Spencer, you're on this. Wake up whoever you have to. Do it in person. Take a couple of Secret Service guys with you—give these *Bizzazzer* guys a show of force. I want to know everything about this zappy virtual game thing, and I want it ASAP."

"I'm on it, Mr. President," Mahler said with vigor.

When Mahler was gone, the President turned to Franco. "OK. We're done here. Let me know when this freak comes back on TV."

Franco nodded. "Yes, Mr. President."

Bart turned to go with Franco but stopped when he felt the President's hand on his arm. The President had retrieved the mobile phone from his pocket and was scrolling down the TuneSleuth screen. When he found what he was looking for, he spoke without taking his eyes off the phone. "Do you know what FIYM is?"

Bart said, "No sir."

"I mean, I know it's the name of a band," the President said, still focused on the album cover displayed on the TuneSleuth screen, "but I don't know what it stands for, you know? FIYM. You know what that stands for?"

"No sir."

The President nodded and said distantly, "That's OK. Thanks, anyway."

"You're welcome, sir."

Alone in the hallway now, the President pressed his lips together and pushed a soft breath through his nose. He was still vexing over the acronym when out of the corner of his eye, he caught sight of his press secretary, Skip Spinner. The President had replaced Skippy as White House Communications Director halfway through his first year in office when the need for a more aggressive presence at the press secretary's podium arose. There hadn't been any bad blood between the two men; in fact, the President had openly supported Skippy's fairly long run on *Diva Dance*. But after the disastrous midterms, Skippy's replacement had retired, and shortly, the replacement's replacement had left too. And by the time the whole partisan witch hunt and phony impeachment, led by that foul she-devil, Nervous Noreen, got fired up, the President, feeling lonely and a bit nostalgic, called Skippy and asked if he would like to come back. Skippy was so delighted at the offer that he didn't even mind that the job wouldn't entail holding any live press conferences, which the President had done away with after Skippy's replacement had stepped down.

Skippy stood in an open doorway a short distance down the hall with a nervous yet hopeful look in his eyes that reminded the President of one of those faithful dogs, the kind that waits patiently at the door for his master to come home. The President felt an odd sensation, like a pinprick at his heart, and he arched an inviting eyebrow at the stout man with the sad eyes.

Skippy cleared his throat and with a bit of trepidation said, "It's Forever In Your Mind . . . FIYM . . . that's what it stands for. It's a boy band. Emory, Ricky, and Liam—they used to be Emory, Ricky, and Jon, but then Jon left, and Liam replaced him . . . " He cleared his throat again. "They're very good . . . That song, *Enough About Me* . . . that's one of their biggest hits . . . "

The President held his gaze on Skippy for a moment. Then he nodded and looked back at the phone. "Yeah," he said softly, "it's a catchy tune. Got a nice beat."

Skippy's shoulders relaxed, and he smiled sheepishly. "Yeah, I like it too."

The President nodded again. Then he tapped the PLAY arrow on the phone's screen and turned up the volume. While the song played, the President and Skippy nodded their heads to the beat, sharing the moment, despite the physical distance between them.

Just before the money-line hit, Skippy found the courage to announce, "Here it comes—wait for it—coming up right here, this is Liam . . . "

The President didn't get mad at Skippy for speaking during the song. He just raised the phone to his ear and listened as Liam hit the money-line in a spine-tingling falsetto:

"I play with fire just to get to you . . . "

Skippy squealed with scarcely contained delight, "I love that part!"

The President smiled and nodded, concurring with Skippy's assessment. But his body was racing with goose-flesh because in that singular heart-stopping moment, in the depths of his mind's eye, he could see that black metal helmet pivoting smoothly toward the camera's lens and filling the frame as if the eyes behind that mask were peering straight into his soul.

KYLE JACKS SHIFTED ON THE SOFA TO MAKE ROOM FOR Rusty. The little Norfolk Terrier had tired of waiting for the President to come back on TV, and with one last go around the coffee table and a wary glance at the screen, he leapt up to join his sister Trixie, who lay curled into a comfortable ball on Kyle's chest. After a complicated ritual of circling and pawing, Rusty finally settled into the cushion beneath the low arch of Kyle's bent knees, where he closed his eyes and blew a short breath out of his nose before drifting off to sleep.

On TV, Chase Grimley was engaged in a debate with

Kori-Lynne Carpwell over the President's first "face-to-face" encounter with the terrorist. Chase laid it out in boxing parlance, awarding "round one" to the "upstart challenger—a definitive knockdown" in which the President was "saved by the bell." Kori-Lynne countered that the President had maintained "measured control of the situation."

"Whatever that means," said Chase with a casually dismissive shrug. "But from where I'm sitting, the President just got his bell rung—" He shot a glance at Elwood Robertson, who was chuckling softly. "I'm not kidding here. The whole country, along with the rest of the free world—and a handful of the not so free parts, as well, I suppose—just watched the President of the United States get his lunch handed to him." He looked directly into the monitor that featured Kori-Lynne sitting in the East Wing of the White House. "*Our* president, just like you said, Kori-Lynne—and they watched him get knocked on his ass by this terrorist in the Batman getup, or the Star Wars getup, or whatever it is he's wearing—looks pretty ominous to me—and they're thinking, and this is true, count on it, they're thinking: Is this the same guy who stood up at all those rallies—during *and* after the election—and told us how easy it was gonna be to handle the terrorists, how easy it was gonna be to take them out? Is this the guy who was going to end terrorism and end it quickly? Is this that guy? The guy who just got his bell rung by a single terrorist in a Halloween costume!"

Kori-Lynne whisked her hair back and shifted in her seat but offered no rebut.

"I'm completely serious," said Chase. "This was like the Tyson-Douglas match back in the '90s. Remember that one? They billed it as 'Tyson is Back!' Yeah, he was back, all right— but not for the belt. He got knocked out in the tenth by the forty to one underdog, James Buster Douglas. Remember that? Tyson crawling around the mat, dazed, his mouth guard hanging half out of his mouth. That's what the President just looked like here on national—*international*—TV!" Chase barked a laugh. "I'm not kidding, that's what he looked like. I just saw it. He looked like Tyson crawling around the mat, looking for his mouth guard that was hanging out of the wrong side of his mouth. Say what you want, but this was a real beating. And your guy, Kori-Lynne, got trounced in the first round—and then got saved by the bell."

Kori-Lynne remained uncomfortably silent. Chase released a sigh.

"The gloves are off," said Chase, shaking his head. "I'm telling you, this is bare-knuckled action, a real street fight, and the President better get his dancing shoes on because this terrorist ain't pussyfooting around here." Chase turned to another monitor and said, "Davis Frome, what are your thoughts on this? Tell me something I don't know. Is the President out of his depth here, or am I completely off base on this one?"

At the desk of *The Rowan Meadow Show* in the New York studio, Davis Frome looked into the camera and said, "I don't think you're completely off base. There's certainly reason for concern—specifically for Mr. Latner, under the immediate circumstances, and in general for the country— if the President doesn't figure out how to handle this particular adversary and contain the situation, which is fraught with catastrophe, to say the least. But I would disagree with you on one point. Actually, it's not so much a disagreement, more of a disparate observation, I suppose, and it's this: Despite his customary bluster and bravado, I was particularly struck by the relative coherence of the President's first salvo, however misguided it was. And make no mistake, it was certainly misguided on every conceivable level—from the bullish delivery to the insane threats of retribution, which sounded more like the rant of a high school bully off his meds than a measured response from the Leader of the Free World. But, putting that aside, I was struck by the clarity of the President's delivery—eschewing his usual heaping helping of digression with a side of apoplectic word salad, the President spoke in complete sentences, for the most part, and was remarkably focused. For what it's worth."

Chase gave a short chuckle. "For what it's worth, eh?"

"Well, it backfired, of course," said Davis with a sheepish smile, "as do most of this president's attempts at brute force when appealing to anyone outside of his rapidly diminishing base." He took a quick breath and resumed with aplomb. "This is the point that I, and many others on the reasonable Right—or the 'sane Right'—have been warning about, and it's no longer speculation. We've arrived. We're not at the gate, ringing the bell; we're inside the arena, where the 'chaos president' has finally come face to face with the harsh reality of an opponent that he can neither bully nor ignore. And we're discovering just how woefully unprepared this president is to deal with an equally adept 'agent of chaos.'"

The pundits at both the DC and New York studios sat in thoughtful silence.

Davis continued. "It may seem like a simplified understatement, but this is not the time for the President to be acting on his own. This is the time—above and beyond all other times—that the President needs to seek the wise counsel of advisors, and, better still, to hand this situation off to someone who is experienced in hostage negotiations. In the beginning, there were people in the Kingley Administration that were trying to 'go legit,' and to that end, they worked to hem the President in. But the question was—and still is—*can* you hem a president in? Can you remove a president's authority and agency?" He paused and took another quick breath. "I don't expect that Ms. Carpwell will confirm this, but once upon a time, there was a group within the administration—chief among them, the generals, Defense Secretary Maddox and National Security Advisor McManus, along with others outside of the administration, most notably FBI Director McCullough and Acting CIA Director Hartman— and this group tried to encourage the President to golf more, watch more television, and let them run the government.

Under normal circumstances, that might seem a rather sinister thing, but in the present climate, even the most staunch Constitutionalist would agree it's beginning to look like the only sane option."

Chase Grimley chewed thoughtfully at the corner of his mouth for a second and then shook his head. "Lots of luck with *that* one. They'd have to drag him out of there, kicking and screaming. Kingley smells blood in the water—not his enemy's blood; his *son-in-law's* blood, but it's blood just the same—and he's circling now. It's gonna take more than one barrel to drag him down. Like Roy Scheider said to Robert Shaw in *Jaws*, 'You're gonna need a bigger boat.'" He shot a pained grin at the panel around his table. "And in case anyone missed the analogy, the *President* is the shark here. This is some scary stuff. I'm not kidding . . . "

Marilyn stood under the dim light above the kitchen sink, only half-listening to the sound of the TV coming from the living room. She was smoking one of Kyle's cigarettes with the window cracked. The chilly night breeze soothed her burning cheeks as it pulled the smoke out of the kitchen. She wasn't really a smoker; she only had one when her stress levels were maxed out. The last time she'd lit up was the night of the election. The sight of that emptying glass-ceilinged hall had been more than she could take. She'd stood in this same spot in the kitchen, listening to Tom Petretto telling everyone to go home, that votes were still coming in, and that there would be more to say in the morning. She'd wanted to hold out hope, but in her heart, she'd known it was over.

There had been no call or text from Ilona on election night. They'd had an argument a few weeks earlier when the *Tinsel Town Insider* video broke. Ilona had called her in tears, hoping to find a sympathetic ear, but Marilyn, who had not spoken a word against her old friend's father throughout the entire campaign, could no longer contain herself.

"This is it, Ilona," she'd said. "If ever there was a time

for you to step up and call him out, this is it. I listened to all the hate-baiting rhetoric, the cheap shots at his opponents, the name-calling and nasty innuendo, and I suppose that's all fair game in politics. I didn't *like* any of it, but I kept my mouth shut. I did that for you, Ilona, because we're friends, and he's your father. I know you love him—but this? This is where I draw the line. This is where you should be drawing the line too. Those things he said on that video—about women . . . girls—that goes *way* beyond the pale. It's sick, and it's criminal."

Ilona had tried to explain that it was just "guy talk," that her father hadn't actually *done* the things he'd claimed to have done on the video, that he'd just been trying to impress *Tinsel Town Insider* host Bobby Brent. She'd drawn a shocked chuckle out of Marilyn when she added, "He didn't even *know* his mic was live! He never would have said any of those things on a live mic; you know that, Mare. You know him."

"No, Ilona," Marilyn had said, "I *don't* know him. I'm not even sure I know *you*. Not anymore. Not if you're telling me that you're OK with what you heard on that video."

The line had gone silent. Then Ilona's voice had come through in a desperate whisper. "He's my *father*. What would you do if it was *your* father?"

Marilyn had been moved but not swayed. "I would be disgusted. And I wouldn't be standing there at his side, smiling like everything was normal."

"You say that, but you don't know what it's like—"

"No, Ilona," Marilyn had said flatly, "I don't know what it's like. I don't know, because my father is a decent man. He may not have all the advantages and privileges yours does, but he's a decent man who would never walk in on a group of young girls changing in a dressing room. Or make up dirty stories to impress some guy half his age. And he most certainly would never grab a woman by her pussy."

"That's ugly."

"Yes, Ilona," Marilyn had said in that same flat tone. "It *is* ugly."

That was the last time she'd heard from Ilona . . . until the texts and calls started pouring in earlier tonight, shortly before the news of Jacob's disappearance broke.

Marilyn took a drag off the cigarette as she gazed out the back window. She didn't know what she would do if the situation were reversed and it was Kyle being tortured on live TV by a masked terrorist. She supposed she would be half out of her mind by now, and in desperate need of a trusted friend.

She took one last drag off the cigarette, doused it under the faucet, and pitched the wet butt into the trash bin in the cabinet under the sink. On the TV in the living room, the pundits were still going at it. Marilyn closed her eyes, took a deep breath, and let it out slowly. For a second, she actually felt calmer. But then Kori-Lynne's little baby voice came from the TV like nails on a chalkboard.

Marilyn pressed her fingertips to her temples and rubbed. She was about to call out to Kyle, ask him to turn down the volume when the doorbell rang.

She went to answer it without thinking who it might be, but when she opened the door, she wasn't surprised.

Ilona stood there in a fashionable overcoat that looked like something from her Spring Collection, completely unsuited for the current chilly conditions. Her eyes looked glassy and weary, but her emotions were in check. Ilona rarely took the plunge without first making certain that someone was there to catch her.

Marilyn wasn't sure she was ready to be Ilona's safety net again, but she stepped aside and let her in.

MERRICK KINGLEY SAT ON THE SOFA IN BEN STIVERSON'S apartment. He didn't want to be here. He wanted to be with his family—with Ilona, to comfort her in this terrible time—but he couldn't bring himself to show his face at Tower K. Not after he'd let the truth slip about Jacob's disappearance. It had taken every ounce of his courage just to phone Roy Jr. earlier this evening. But to look his older brother in the eye, to see the disdain and disappointment in that hard gaze—Merrick didn't believe he could muster the courage needed for that. Roy Jr. hated weakness almost as much as their father did. And he hated leakers even more.

Stupid, stupid, stupid, Merrick thought, rapping his forehead with the heel of his hand. *Don't leak, no leaks, keep your mouth shut, and don't speak to anyone about anything.*

Roy Jr. had drilled that into his head, time and again, and still, Merrick had gone and leaked.

Merrick rocked to and fro on the sofa now, wishing he'd just listened and not leaked, wishing he could go to Tower K and be with his family, wishing that they could all be together during this crisis. But the more he thought about it, the more distant the possibility seemed. He could take anything but the cold silence he was certain to receive from Roy Jr. An hour-long lecture, like the sort their father often subjected them to (complete with the crazy ranting and outrageously over-the-top threats) would be preferable to one of Roy Jr.'s protracted icy silences. Merrick knew that he wouldn't be able to hold up under that sort of pressure. Eventually, he would crack, and the tears would begin to flow, and *that* would send Roy Jr. over the edge.

Merrick's childhood memories were still vivid. He could see himself and his sister and brother, all huddled in the upstairs hallway, while their father and mother went at it down in the living room. He could hear the glass smashing against a wall, and their father applauding and calling out, "That's it, Iliana, smash them all, you loony hot-blooded cooze. Smash them all, you disgusting animal—you're so disgusting when you're like this, so unattractive, you should see yourself, take a look in the mirror, really, it's disgusting . . . "

The sound of the mirror shattering ("There you go, that'll get you another seven years!") had made little Merrick flinch, but he'd fought back the tears bravely because Roy Jr. was looking into his eyes and whispering through tightly clenched teeth, "Don't cry. Do you hear me? Don't cry. Suck it up. Do you hear me?" And when Ilona had reached for Merrick's hand, Roy Jr. hissed, "Don't baby him!" But then suddenly Roy Jr.'s arms were wrapped around Merrick's skinny shoulders, and he was holding him tightly, and Merrick was hugging him back, and even as Roy Jr. repeated the harshly whispered command, "Don't cry," Merrick could tell that his older brother was crying too.

But things weren't like that anymore. They were grown-ups now, and Roy Jr. had zero tolerance for tears, so Merrick had gone to the only other place he could. It was true that Benjy had betrayed his trust by secretly recording their private conversation and leaking it to the press. But it was also true that Benjy had a sympathetic ear and an infinite threshold for melancholia—which was why Merrick had trusted his old college friend with the story of Jake's disappearance in the first place; if you couldn't trust a sympathetic friend, who could you trust?

Of course, none of that mattered anymore. Even Merrick's father didn't blame him—in fact, he'd just stood up on live TV and told the entire world that he was proud of Merrick and that he loved him and didn't blame him for the leak, and Merrick believed him because his father would never tell a lie on TV. All that mattered now was Jake; getting him out of the hands of the terrorist and back home, safe and sound.

But would Jake *be* sound? Even if they got to him in time and brought him home safe, would he still be the same old Jake? Would he ever be able to get over what the terrorist had already done to him? Would the torture he'd been put through be too much for his mind to take? Would he be permanently scarred?

Merrick didn't like thinking about this. But he couldn't keep the thoughts from coming. He couldn't drive out that horrifying image of Jake strapped to the chair in the dark room with those pads stuck to his body . . .

And his eyes. Why were those pads on his eyes?

Merrick drew a clipped breath when the sound from the TV suddenly came back on. With the remote control in hand, Benjy offered a small apologetic smile for startling Merrick and tipped a nod at the TV.

The pundits were gone, and the live shot in the Oval Office had resumed. Merrick's father stood on the presidential seal at the center of the oval carpet, gazing up at the terrorist on the widescreen TV above the fireplace. As Merrick watched, he pulled his knees up close to his chest, curling himself into a protective ball at his end of the sofa.

His father's attitude had changed dramatically since the first exchange with the terrorist. Though neither man had spoken a single word since their "face-to-face" had resumed, Merrick could tell that his father was no longer in attack mode. He wasn't in retreat, either. He had shifted to his comfort zone: campaign mode. To Merrick, the old man looked like one of those aging lions at the zoo, past its prime but still capable of a sudden strike, and wise enough to wait until the moment to leap presented itself.

The dirty liars in the media often underestimated his father, calling him "rash" and "clumsy" and "foolish," and as both a candidate and president, the old man had shoved those words right back down their throats every time. Merrick hoped this terrorist scum would make the same mistake of taking the old man for a fool instead of a king because nothing would please him more than to see his father shove the creepy prick's words right back down his throat—on live TV, in front of the entire world.

"Get him, Dad," Merrick whispered, clenching his jaw in unconscious imitation of Roy Jr.

The silence in the Oval Office lasted a full minute longer

before the President sniffed back a breath and said, "So, how does this go? Do you make a demand, or a list, or something? I don't know how it works. I've never done it before. How do we do this thing?"

True Son's chest rose and fell in an even rhythm while the darkened glass eyes of his mask pierced the President with cool conviction.

"I'm serious," said the President. "I've never done anything like this before—I've seen it in movies and on TV, but who knows how accurate that is, right? So you're gonna have to tell me how it works."

True Son remained silent.

The President uttered a light chuckle and shrugged as if in commiseration with his enemy. "I dunno, maybe you're new at this too, eh? Maybe they put you up to it—whoever you represent—ISIS, or Al Qaeda, or China, or France, or whatever—I dunno. Maybe you're just as new to this stuff as me. Who knows? I dunno. So, why don't you tell me what you want, and I'll see what I can do about it? I'm a very smart guy, I'm like really smart, ask anyone. I can make things happen. You see what I did in Pennsylvania? They said it couldn't be done—'No Republican can win in Pennsylvania,' they said, and boy did I prove them wrong. Just like *Moneyball*. You see that movie? Great movie, my son-in-law showed it to me, unbelievable movie, true story. That's how I won the election. I moneyballed it. It's true."

The President paused briefly before continuing.

"I could have taken all the states, of course—California, New York, Minnesota, which I almost took, anyway, by the way—that was a close one, very-very close—but I didn't need to, because I moneyballed the electoral map. That's what it's really all about, see? The electoral map—what a beautiful thing the electoral map is, let me tell you. I used to hate it, but now I see how it works, and boy does it work, believe me, it works. Like NATO. I used to think that NATO was obsolete, but it's not obsolete, not anymore. I know that now. *Now* I know it—before, I didn't, but I do now—very-very important thing to have, NATO, and it works once you understand what it does and how it works, you know? And now I've got this new thing going. It's called NATO-ME—I made it up myself, it's like NATO plus, only NATO with the Middle East. I'm really smart like that—making things up, you know?"

He released a sigh and shot a glance toward the mullioned glass door of the Oval Office, half expecting to find a familiar face looking in. But there was no one outside on the patio; the face looking back at him was merely his reflection in the darkened pane of glass. For a moment, he looked lost. Then he blinked as if waking from a dream.

"This is a tough job," he said with another sigh, "a lot tougher than I thought it would be—a *lot*. They make it look so easy on TV—*The West Wing*, *Commander in Chief*, *Scandal*—but believe me, it's a lot tougher than that. I *wish* it was like that, but the truth is, it's more like *24*. You know that show? With Kiefer Sutherland and all those nutjob terrorists—no offense, but your people are pretty nutty with all the plots and bombings and all that crazy crap they're always pulling . . . not that I'm saying *you're* a nutjob. You seem like you got it together, at least you have some style, with the music and the mask and all . . . I dunno, maybe you're a wacko too, but you seem pretty organized, focused, like you know what you're doing and not just killing people just to get your name in the news, you know?" He sighed again. "Too many fame-seekers out there, am I right? Oy oy oy, everybody wants attention. Too many grandstanders and showboats, am I right?"

There followed an awkward silence, in which the President drummed his fingers on his thighs while looking aimlessly about the Oval Office.

On the sofa in Ben Stiverson's apartment, Merrick's eyes narrowed, and his mouth pinched into a tight frown. He didn't like seeing his father weakened; he wanted the old man to let the bastard have it. But at the same time, he didn't want the terrorist to become agitated and retaliate with another assault on Jake, so he just watched and waited in excruciating anticipation for his father's next move. But it wasn't his father who spoke next. It was the terrorist, and the cool voice, modulated by the breath screen of the mask, sent a wave of chilly tendrils racing up Merrick's spine.

On the big screen above the mantel in the Oval Office, True Son finally spoke. "You don't approve of showboats."

It wasn't a question, but the President responded as if it were. "No, I do not."

"Like former FBI Director Brushing," True Son offered. "He was a showboat."

The President raised a brow. "Who? Lurch? Damn straight, he was. Total showboat. That's why I fired him."

"But there were other reasons—" True Son prompted, "—extenuating circumstances—for his abrupt dismissal."

"Look," the President said, an edge creeping into his voice, "Jonas Brushing was incompetent, totally incompetent, and he had to go, OK? You see the way he botched the Crichton email thing? He didn't even bother to make a simple phone call to verify that memo—from the Russians! And then it turns out to be the Ukrainians who were behind the whole deal, and Lurch, who's supposed to be this amazing FBI investigator, knows nothing! Or maybe he does, and he just wanted to pin it on the Russians. Who knows, am I right? In any case, *he's* the one who should be investigated! Hands down, *the* most incompetent FBI director ever. Total nutjob. Did you see him testifying? Oy oy oy, what a mess, an absolute mess. Like a lunatic up there before the Commission. The guy is dirty and completely incompetent. I was right to fire him, and the way he handled that fake memo proves it."

Another moment of silence passed. Then True Son spoke in that same calm tone again. "In an interview with Calvin Haynes, Douglas Day Jamison cited a scarcely noticed article back in March of that year which claimed you might have had another reason to get rid of Director Brushing."

The President snorted indignantly. "Look, Douglas Day Jamison is a lying Liberal hack and a terrible writer—you see that so-called biography he wrote about me? Filled with lies, disgusting lies. He attacked my kids—my kids! He did it on live TV. Said my kids hate me! Can you believe that? My kids love me! Believe me, my kids love me, they love me like a father, believe me. I should sue that fat bastard—I don't know, maybe I will."

True Son wasn't swayed off course. "The article stated, that to expand your real estate developments over the years, you've repeatedly turned to wealthy Russians and oligarchs from former Soviet republics—several of them allegedly connected to organized crime. One, in particular, a man by the name of Fedor Sheferovsky, was a managing director of the Covestone Group LLC, and he also happened to be one of your senior advisors—"

"I wouldn't know that guy if he bit me in the ass," the President interjected hotly.

True Son continued as if he hadn't been interrupted. "The article went on to postulate that you sacked Director Brushing for fear that, in the course of his investigation into your campaign's alleged collusion with the Russians, he would uncover certain business arrangements you've formed with less than savory actors."

"That's a complete load of crap," the President shot back. "I fired Brushing because he was a nutjob showboat, period."

"In your interview with Lemar Holmes on NCMSB, you cited the director's mishandling of the Russia investigation as your reason for dismissal—"

"He *did* mishandle it—the whole thing was a complete mess. You see that fake memo? A total mess, believe me."

"And yet," True Son countered, "that was weeks before the news broke on the fake memo regarding then Attorney

General Lenore Lydon's alleged involvement in a plot to sweep the Crichton emails under the rug."

"I knew about it," said the President, waving a dismissive hand. "I knew all about it, believe me. This thing was common knowledge, very common knowledge, everyone knew it. And Brushing should have known it too. If anybody's a Russian puppet, *he* is. He played right into their hands—*if* it even was the Russians who put out that fake memo. Could've been China, could've been a lot of people. Hannah Crichton has a lot of enemies, many-many enemies. She should sue—I'd back her up."

The President's gaze locked onto the impenetrable dark eyes of True Son's mask. The merciless bastard wasn't about to give an inch. Not one damn inch, the stubborn prick. No worries. He'd cracked tougher nuts. Many, many tougher nuts; sooner or later, they all cracked. *He* was in control here.

"Common knowledge," the President repeated, "I was fully within my rights to fire him, the guy is a total loser, and a terrible FBI director—another Boyega disaster! Huge mistake, terrible pick. It's amazing Boyega lasted two full terms, they should have impeached him—he wasn't even eligible to be president, you know? Nobody's ever even seen his papers—his *real* papers, his real birth certificate, not that phony one they showed on the fake news, but the real one, from Zimbabwe or wherever he's really from. I dunno, could be Libya, who knows?"

The black mask tilted in a subtle gesture of mild curiosity. "And yet, it was you they impeached."

"*Tried* to impeach—but my Senate showed them. They got their little House majority—just barely—but they couldn't get my Senate. They even *lost* seats, can you believe that?" The President shook his head in disgust. "And they called it a 'blue wave'—didn't look very blue from where I was sitting. Oh, Little Nasty Nervous Noreen got her little gavel back, and she rolled out her standard bag of deceitful tricks—very tricky woman, very deceitful, see how she held onto those articles, tryin' to sweat out my guy Mycroft? It was like the tortoise and the hare. There's old Nervous Noreen, racing all over the place, tryin' to rig her phony little impeachment scam against me—tryin' to nullify the will of the people—there she is, racing around and trying to collect all the carrots, like the greedy little hare that she is, and my guy Mycroft is just slowly slugging along like the clever tortoise, and he beats her to the finish line without even breaking a sweat. Old Mycroft whipped those votes and got all the Republicans in line—even those two wavering weak women, Callow and Mihulski. Mycroft led those two little sheep right back into the flock."

"But not Senator Monterey," True Son added.

The President's features froze, and his eyes shone cold and dark, even as he forced a thin smile. "Who, Righteous Ritt?"

"He voted with the Democrats to convict and remove you from office."

"Yeah, and where did that get him? Nowhere. Look, Ritt Monterey is a sanctimonious, two-faced, dishrag traitor who should be ridden out of the party on a rail."

"Some have called him a patriot," said True Son. "A man of conviction, true to his faith, regardless of the consequences to himself or his political future."

"That weepy-eyed dirtbag doesn't have a political future, not in *my* party. He's a loser, OK? Total loser, who turned his back on his party and his country to vote with the losing team. He took his shot at me, and I grabbed him by his magic underwear and gave him a wedgy, right up his withered old crack, OK? His vote doesn't even count, anyway, OK? Null and void, that's what his vote is, and that's what *he* is—null and void—because I was acquitted of *all* charges. You see the Failing New York Times headline: 'Kingley Acquitted!' Innocent. Totally exonerated of all the phony and completely made up articles of impeachment that weren't even worth the paper they were printed on. Case

closed. End of the totally manufactured fake news story."
The President shot a heavy breath through his nose and grimaced. "They should have gone after Boyega instead. They
would've had a better shot at taking him out. Easy target.
Could have impeached him on countless crimes, many-
many crimes, he's like a criminal mastermind! They'd
have run out of paper to print the articles on, believe me,
they'd've had to cut down whole forests just to get half the
articles printed on that crooked son of a bitch. The guy was
a total criminal, shadier than even Shady Hannah, who's as
shady as they come, don't even get me started . . . "

True Son was silent for a moment. Then he said, "You
harbor animus toward President Boyega."

"I know who my friends are," the President said stubbornly.

"And you count him as one of your enemies."

The President's gaze shone darkly. "I don't know whose
side he's on, but it's definitely not mine, that's for sure."

"You consider him your rival."

The President pondered briefly. "Maybe."

"But not your equal."

The President snorted. "Definitely not my equal. He
wishes he was my equal. In some ways, maybe, I guess he
is. He's cunning, I'll give him that much. And he knows
his stuff, he knows how to manipulate the system—very
manipulative, *master* manipulator—comes into office promising he's going to end all the wars in the Middle East, and
what does he do? Accelerates the whole thing, starts dron-
ing innocent women and children. *Children,* can you believe
that? And he leaves *me* to clean up *his* mess. Total mess,
believe me. And how does he do it? He manipulates the
system by twisting some resolution Congress never should
have given him in the first place. And now we have a complete and total mess in the Middle East—ISIS and Al Qaeda
are loving it, believe me. What a total mess . . . "

The President shook his head in disbelief. A long silence

followed. When it became clear that the President had nothing further to add, True Son spoke again.

"The congressional resolution you refer to—the one you've never been loath to point out that Hannah Crichton supported—granted the President the power to use military force against any entity that 'planned, authorized, committed, or aided the terrorist attacks that occurred on September 11, 2001.' President Boyega's predecessor used that resolution to attack Al Qaeda's base in Afghanistan, and when Al Qaeda fled, that same authorization was used to pursue them into Pakistan, Somalia, and Yemen. President Boyega stretched the authorization beyond recognition when he used it to justify his war against ISIL, a coalition which I'm sure even you would agree has no love for Al Qaeda."

"You got that right," said the President. "Boyega's flagrant abuse of power was disgraceful. And Hannah Crichton would have been even worse—she'd have started World War Three! Believe me, that woman is a total hawk, a real killer, she'd have been bombing every country on the map—total war hawk, believe me."

"And yet you exploited that same authorization to justify your own use of force against Dekel Attar's Syrian regime, which is at war with both ISIL and Al Qaeda—"

"Attar is a complete and total maniac," the President interjected. "Don't even get me started on that animal. Did you see what he did to those people? *Babies!* Beautiful babies, fighting for breath after that filthy animal used chemical weapons on them—which are illegal, by the way. Very-very illegal, goes against the Geneva Convention and all kinds of other laws of war—you just don't go around bombing people with chemicals, OK? There are rules. You fight like a man. Chemicals, poisons—those are a woman's method. Men use real weapons—tomahawks, nukes, IBMs—we know how to get the job done, we're not into all that suffering and watching innocent children struggling for breath. We get the job done quickly, and nobody suffers—lights out, that's it. No pain, no suffering, we put you out of your misery humanely, we don't drag it out. Believe me, men don't want to see any unnecessary suffering."

The President paused. True Son tilted his head, causing the dim light in the shadowed room to reflect mordantly off the dark eyes of his mask. The subtle irony eluded the President, who continued with vigor.

"Me, I do these strikes—and I'm getting very good at this—with surgical precision. Just ask my Secretary of Housing and Urban Development, he's a *brilliant* guy, brilliant brain surgeon—very surgical, steady hands, very-very steady hands, he knows this stuff. He separated Siamese twins, can you believe that? Siamese twins! And they both lived, God bless 'em. I'm telling you, this guy is a serious genius, very surgical man, very precise. Like me, I'm very surgical, and my strikes are very precise, very-very precise, ask anybody, they'll tell you."

True Son contemplated the image of the President on the massive screen behind the camera in the long, dark room where he stood. Then he spoke in a calm and reasonable tone. "And your move against ISIL in Yemen—was that too, a surgical strike, guided by your precise hand?"

The President's features went slack and then instantly hardened. True Son continued, unfazed by the President's glare. "I only inquire to establish the criterion upon which your claim of 'surgical precision' is predicated."

The President's eyes narrowed in confusion while the smoldering embers within began to kick up sparks.

True Son poked at the embers with a temperate touch. "An American soldier and twenty-four civilians, nine of them children, were killed in that operation, were they not?"

"I don't know numbers," said the President dismissively. "Nobody knows—could have been twenty, could have been four, could have been nobody was killed and they made up the whole thing to get sympathy. Who knows? We're dealing with some very sick and dishonest people over there, and our lying media isn't helping by pulling fake numbers out of there asses to rile up the Liberal base."

"So there were no casualties?"

The President faltered but recovered quickly. "Who knows? Could have been hundreds, nobody knows—it's a very messy situation over there, we never should have been there in the first place, and if I had been president back then, we never would have gone in, period—I said that all through my campaign. It's not our fight, it's theirs, let them deal with it. America has no business in the Middle East."

"With the exception of protecting Saudi oil fields from northern encroachment, which doubtless factored into your decision to pull US troops out of Syria in October."

"I promised to bring those troops home, and unlike my predecessor, I keep my promises."

"But they didn't go home," said True Son in a casually conversational tone. "They were sent to Iraq to continue the campaign against the Islamic State militants. And you sent an additional three thousand troops to Iran after your ill-advised assassination of General Salahuddin."

The slight edge in True Son's voice on the words "ill-advised assassination" did not go unnoticed by the members of the press inside the Oval Office, but the President appeared oblivious.

"General Salahuddin was a terrorist, OK? A terrorist. Killed many-many people, OK? And I was right to put him down. Like a dog, I put him done. Great percentages of people don't have legs right now and arms because of this son of a bitch, OK? And the Democrats should be outraged by his evil crimes and not my decision to end him. He was a two-bit thug, and I bombed his thug ass straight into oblivion, OK? And I'd do it again, believe me. He was a thug, and I'm a thug-crusher, and I crushed him like a thug bug. End of story. But let me tell you, they had thousands of soldiers—not protesters, they were soldiers, OK? And they were surrounding our embassy in Baghdad, and suddenly they see our beautiful, very expensive, brand new Apache helicopters . . . he was plotting new attacks on U.S. embassies and military bases—this is a very unstable guy we're talking about here, this Salahuddin character, very unstable, not a good guy—a very bad guy, in fact."

"Some see him as a great man—a patriot, defending his country, just like you."

"Salahuddin wasn't anything like me, OK? This guy was a complete and total nut job. I'm stable. He was a terrorist. And these protests—you see 'em?—weren't really protests, OK? Believe me. They were part of a covert campaign. But it backfired. You see those Tehran students refusing to walk over an American flag? They were the *real* protesters, and they were protesting *Iran!* They love America! They love our country! That's called progress, you get that? Progress."

True Son contemplated the President briefly. "Then, your decision to assassinate the general was a success."

"You bet your ass, it was."

"And the deaths of the one hundred and seventy-six passengers aboard the Ukrainian jetliner was a small price to pay for your victory."

The President eyed the black-masked figure on the TV screen and drew a deep, noisy breath through his nose. "Look, Iran says it was an accident—human error—and I have no reason to question them, OK? Accidents happen all the time, planes crash, OK?" He shot a heavy breath through his nose. "You've been listening to that fruit loop Munchkin Mayor, who doesn't know the first thing about what's going on with Iran. He was a lousy mayor, and he's a lousy presidential candidate, OK? And he's out there spouting off crap about me, along with the rest of the Liberal loonies—none of which stand a bat's chance in hell of beating me—so they make up these lies, terrible lies, disgusting, really, to get even with me for stealing the last election."

True Son's mask tilted in a questioning manner.

"I'm completely serious," said the President, "That's

how they see it. I must have stolen the election and worked with the Russians, or the Crimeans, or whatever, because the whining Liberal liars have to lie to themselves because they can't take it, they can't take it that I beat her. But everyone knows that I won—bigly, trust me, it was a *yuge* win, total landslide. Did you see those crowds at my inauguration? Unbelievable—just wait till you see them at my next inauguration, it'll be off the charts, totally. And I won the popular vote too because you know that she cheated with all those votes from all those illegals and dead people and people registered in two states—that's why we gotta do something about the census, we gotta get these illegals and dead people off the rolls, believe me. *Two* states, these people were registered in, can you believe that? Don't even get me started on that one. They're like, 'Vote in Chicago, OK, done, now let's head to New York or L.A.'—probably L.A., 'cause it's like Chicago out there, you can get away with anything out there, totally lawless, totally rigged in her favor. That ex-governor, Johnny Black, he's a commie pinko from way back—did you see him stumping for her at the convention? Unbelievable! He *hated* her and her husband back in the '90s when they screwed him out of the Democrat nomination— what a number Shady Hannah's cheating perv husband pulled on that poor sap, and now he *supports* her? Against me? What a phony!

"And Shady Hannah's a cheat too—not a perv, like her husband, but an incredible cheater—don't even get me started on that woman. She cheats as much as she lies, and believe me, she lies a lot, and I mean like a *lot*. She's like . . . she can't stop herself from lying, you know? So Boyega, who's like this with her—" He crossed his middle and index fingers. "—I mean like two bugs in a rug, these two are, unbelievable—and sneaky—nasty. It's totally disgusting. These are two very dishonest people, and they failed at defeating me, so Boyega sets me up by laying the groundwork for this Salahuddin thing—he could have taken that

Iranian prick out like that!" The President snapped his fingers. "A *terrorist*—responsible for the murder of countless American soldiers, innocent men and women just serving their country, and Boyega has the chance to take him out, and he does nothing. Why? Because he didn't have the guts. Either that or he set me up to take the fall—he's a very vindictive man, believe me, he's still angry that I shocked the system and beat her. Badly, very-very badly, it was a very bad beating, believe me, and that's why Boyega didn't move on Salahuddin when he had the shot back in his first term—can you believe a guy like that actually got two terms? Whatever. Total loser. And he leaves *me* to take out this crazy Iranian general because he's pissed that I beat her. He was so sure she'd win, and when I toppled her little applecart, he got pissed and took his revenge, he took it all right, and I got left with the blame. Who knew this crazy terrorist general was so popular? A complete and total setup, that's what it was."

The President shook his head like he could scarcely believe the lengths his opponents would go to just to get even with him for winning the election. True Son waited, and shortly, his patience paid off.

"Complete and total setup," the President repeated. "Just like that invasion, wherever it was in the Middle East—"

"Yemen," said True Son, the light glinting darkly off the eyes of his mask.

"The original setup," the President agreed. "Boyega's first little mousetrap in his maze of mousetraps—you remember that game, with the ladder and tub and the basket that comes down? Mousetrap. Very ingenious game, hard to get through it without getting caught in one of those traps. That's what Boyega did to me. He set up his life-size Mousetrap game here in the White House. It's true, you can ask people, all over the internet, they know, believe me, boy, do they know—Boyega set me up in his own little Mousetrap game, and he's personally responsible for the deaths of all those good people. Children, can you believe? Oy oy oy, this guy, I'm telling you—unbelievable. Worst president ever. Trust me, you can't make this stuff up."

"The National Security Advisor to the former vice president says differently."

"Who? Kanin?"

"He was in the meeting you spoke of on January 6th. He told Rowan Meadow at NCMSB that there was a discussion about AQAP at the sublevel, but that no specific target was ever briefed at the Pentagon."

"First off," the President said heatedly, "Rowan Meadow is a lying Liberal agitator—a four, at best—she's got some leg, if she'd ever wear a skirt, but her personality's disgusting. I'm honestly thinking about having her and her entire little fake news organization put under surveillance; there's something very fishy going on over there at NCMSB—very-very fishy—don't even get me started on those people. Such a dishonest organization, very-very dishonest, totally disingenuous, horrible, nasty, hateful people—they really hate me, they'll do anything to get me—they should all be jailed. And their ratings are terrible, just terrible—FIX News beats them in every time slot, I'm not kidding, NCMSB is a disaster, total disaster."

"And Mr. Kanin? Is he a liar too?"

"Look, Conrad Kanin is a bagman. He'll do whatever Boyega tells him to do, OK? These Boyega guys are very loyal, thick as thieves, tremendous liars, all of them, that's why I had to get rid of them—I had to fire them all—Deep State operatives, every last one of 'em. Boyega can't stand that he's not president anymore, OK? He'd do anything to undermine my presidency. Very deceitful man, tapped my wires at Tower K during the election. I can't prove it, of course, because Boyega's got half the intelligence agencies in his hip pocket—probably more than half, actually—but it's true. Kevin Lúñez, my guy on the House Intelligence

Committee—unbelievably reliable guy, highly respected, very trustworthy, great guy—he brought me all sorts of information on that sneaky little minion of Boyega's, Sharon Rains, who is a very deceitful woman, unmasking all those names of good people who had nothing to do with nothing. Total witch-hunt, ended up costing Monty Finch his job— very sad—a *three-star general* and a true patriot, and he loses his job because of all this totally illegal and totally partisan unmasking. And what'd it get them? Nothing. That Rains woman is a disgrace—I wouldn't appoint her dog catcher, let alone National Security Advisor—and so is Boyega for putting her up to it. Very deceitful and vindictive man . . . very-very vindictive . . . "

The President shook his head. True Son waited a moment before giving him a nudge.

"On *The O'Riordan Factoid*, you told Bing O'Riordan that you and the former president shared a mutual admiration."

The President blinked. "We do—him more than me, of course. He's a great guy, very knowledgeable, in certain areas, but he's also a very secretive guy—not at all transparent, like me—and more vindictive than he lets on, trust me."

"You believe he's out to get you."

"I *know* he's out to get me. If I succeed, his whole presidency is nullified. He never should have been allowed to run for president, to begin with."

"Like Hannah Crichton."

"Don't even get me started on that nasty woman—I'll take Boyega over her any day of the week."

"But, as you said of President Boyega, you believe that Hannah Crichton also shouldn't have been allowed to run for president. Is that correct?"

"It's totally correct. She's a crook and a liar."

"Like Senator Cross."

The President briefly considered the deceitful Texas Senator who'd nearly stolen the nomination from him back in 2016 Republican primaries and replied, "He's all right."

"But he's a liar. 'Lyin' Tad.'"

The President snorted. "He's told his share of lies, believe me."

"And Senator Herring."

"Who? Sacheen Littlefeather?" He shook his head. "*She's* a piece of work. Serial liar."

"Senator McQueen?"

"The gimp?" The President rolled his eyes. "I don't speak ill of the dead, but he should've been ashamed. Traitor to his party *and* his country."

"Because he supported the investigation into your campaign's ties with Russia."

"The completely bogus and *failed* investigation. The 'collusion delusion,' I call it. And McQueen knew it, and he didn't have the guts to stand up against Boyega and the deep state shadow government he's running to undermine my presidency. Disgraceful, completely and totally disgraceful. McQueen should've been kicked out of the Republican Party. Weak-weak man, very weak. Zero vision. He stood in the face of history and couldn't even see it. Couldn't even see how I was bringing the country together and healing wounds."

"Like you did with your speech in Phoenix."

"Don't give me that crap," the President barked. "Those people were carrying on a peaceful protest of the unlawful destruction of historical monuments. The vicious alt-Left Antifa radicals were just as responsible for the violence, if not more, probably more. There was enough blame to go around on both sides, believe me—many-many sides. I'm not a racist, OK? That's not my thing, that's not what I'm about, OK? That's why I gave that speech in Phoenix—a hundred and ten in the shade, and people were lined up for six blocks to hear me speak out against violence and hate. Six blocks, maybe more, probably more, they were lined up. Because they know that I'm the only one who can solve this racial divide—you see all those signs people were holding up—BLACKS FOR KINGLEY! You think they'd be holding up signs like that for Boyega? But they know who I am. They know I'm building a stronger America here, and they know that the alt-Left is blind to it, all of them. They can't see through their hatred, OK? I'm building a movement here, and they can't see it. I'm trying to make America great again."

True Son stood silent for a moment. Then he said, "'It is a law of history that contemporaries are denied a recognition of the early beginnings of the great movements which determine their times.'"

The President's eyes narrowed.

"It's a quote. From *The World of Yesterday.*"

"Never saw it."

"It's a book."

The President shrugged.

"A memoir by Stefan Zweig."

"Never heard of him."

The glossy black eyes of True Son's mask appeared to glint with disdain, but the President didn't seem to notice.

After a moment, True Son continued. "Zweig wrote his memoir so that future generations—those tasked with rebuilding from the ruins of what was once a society in search of greatness—would understand how the reign of terror that had brought about their collapse had become possible—and how he, and so many others, had been blind to the beginnings of such a reign."

The President snorted. "This Swyke guy sounds like a real loser."

True Son said, "He was one of Europe's most prominent humanist-pacifists. He wrote forty novels, sixteen biographies and historical texts, three plays, and a memoir that is considered one of the greatest historical documents of the Twentieth Century."

The President snorted again. "Loser."

"He promoted solidarity among European nations and

called for the founding of an international university with an exchange program to expose young people to other communities, ethnicities, and religions."

The President rolled his eyes. "Yeah, and what did that get him?"

"Ultimately? A handful of sleeping pills in the forested hills of Petrópolis—the City of Peter. But his ideology gave birth to the International European Movement, and later to the European Union."

"Which is a total and complete failure, believe me, OK? Ever hear of Brexit? Trust me, this Swyke guy was a weak loser."

"Many regard him as a hero."

"Yeah, and many are wrong. Let me tell you something, he was a loser, all right? And he was weak because he took a bunch of pills, which is the loser's way out, and, truthfully, a woman's way out—women take pills; a real man wants out, he uses a gun, blam, one shot and it's over. I know these things, OK? And if this Swyke guy really believed in all that crap he wrote, he would have stood up and fought whoever it was that he was against, OK? I know these things, I'm like a really smart guy, I have an amazing IQ—unbelievably high, off the charts—and I know things. If you're right, you stay and fight. Doesn't matter who it is you're fighting, you stay in there and fight, OK? So, who was this Swyke guy fighting against?"

"The Third Reich."

The President blinked. "Hitler? Swyke was going up against Hitler? Well, there you go. You're not gonna beat Hitler by writing a bunch of books. Who's got the time to read when you're conquering the world? Hitler didn't care about any of that crap in books. The only thing that loony son of a bitch understood was bombing—and did we bomb the hell out of him, let me tell you. We hit him with everything we had. You see what we did at Normandy? We stormed that beach and lit it up like the Fourth of July.

And we did it all by ourselves because the Europeans didn't know what the hell they were doing—the French and British troops were a disaster, complete disaster, they didn't know what the hell they were doing. The whole war was won by us because we had great Generals, like Patton, who knew what they were doing. Believe me, without Patton, those beaches at Normandy would've never been taken."

"Didn't General Patton and his troops arrive after the invasion of Normandy?"

The President made a face and waved him off. "Patton planned the whole deal, believe me. Those guys didn't know what the hell they were doing until Patton took control. They were like a bunch of bush leaguers, believe me. Patton knew things, OK? Patton knew he was the only one who could take out Hitler—who, by the way, was terrified of Patton. It's true! Hitler was in like constant fear of Patton, he had nightmares about Patton, OK? Nightmares, unbelievable nightmares, like a horror movie playing up in his head all night, every night . . .

"Hitler . . . he had like these little tiny army men—you know, like those little army men that used to come in a plastic bag when you were a kid? Maybe that's before your time, but whatever. They used to make these little green army men—you could pick up a bag of them at any five-and-dime for like a buck, and they were always green. Some of them had tiny little rifles with tiny little bayonets on the ends, some just had pistols, but they were always green 'cause they were American army men, and American army men always wear green.

"So, anyway, Hitler had these tiny little green army men all marching in his brain while he was sleeping—he dreamed about this all the time, constantly—it's true, you can look it up—and they were all coming at him in his dreams, OK? These little green plastic army men with their tiny little bayonets, they were all stabbing at Hitler's brain in his dreams. It was a total nightmare, drove Hitler half nuts . . .

these little green army men—all of them with Patton's face—coming at him every night! He couldn't escape it, hardly got a wink of sleep, he was so terrified . . . "

On the sofa in his friend's apartment, Merrick Kingley sat in dazed silence (sometimes even *he* had trouble following his father's labyrinthine tangents) while one of the cameras in the Oval Office slowly tracked in for a close-up of the Commander in Chief. There was a gleam of nostalgia in the old man's eyes, but it was difficult to tell whether this had been brought on by the memory of the little green army men themselves or the vision the old man had conjured of them moving in on a sleeping Hitler and stabbing at his brain with their tiny plastic bayonets.

Merrick sat frozen, his eyes glued to the TV, like a boy watching a high-wire act at the circus, fearful that the slightest movement might pitch the balance and send the aging acrobat plunging to his certain death.

KLAUS MARIA XYLANDER MADE BRIEF EYE CONTACT WITH ONE of the Secret Service agents as he collected a stack of papers from the glass table where Thackery Ansara sat casually reclined with his legs up. It wasn't the presence of the agents that made Klaus Maria anxious—agents from various branches of the government occasionally stopped by the loft to consult with Thackery. It was the short, balding man with the lazy gaze and haughty stance who stood between the agents that set off Klaus Maria's internal alarms. The short man shot a wary glance at the young German from across the table but didn't question what he was doing with the stack of papers, and as Klaus Maria headed toward the opposite end of the loft, the short man turned his attention back to Thackery.

"All right, let's go over this again," he said with an air of import. "Tell me everything you know about this . . . game thing." The word 'game' rolled off his tongue like something he'd sooner spit than swallow. "And when I say 'everything,' I mean *everything*."

Thackery blinked. "I'm sorry. Who are you again?"

"Who I am doesn't concern you," the short man said irritably. "Who I *work* for is all that matters, and I work for the President of the United States of America, and this . . . is a matter of national security, so I'll ask you again—"

"Yeah," Thackery said casually, "but do you have any ID—no offense, yo, but anybody could walk in here and say they work for the president, you know what I mean?"

The little balding man's lazy eyes flared. "How about I take you in for obstruction of justice and aiding and abetting a hostile foreign entity? How about I do that, and we'll see if I'm just *anybody*?" He reached into the pocket of his coat and thrust his credentials into Thackery's face. "I'm Senior Policy Advisor to the President Spencer Mahler, that's who I am . . . *yo*. That good enough for you?"

Thackery held up his hands. "Take it easy, bro, I come in peace. Can't be too careful, you know?" He glanced down at Mahler's shoes and nodded with approval. "Nice dogs, Jeeves—G. Stefano Bemers. Stylin'. I got a couple pair myself."

Mahler's gaze remained icy.

At the back of the loft, Klaus Maria surreptitiously removed an ivory card from the stack of papers he'd scooped off of the glass table. It was the calling card Melville Noyce had left earlier that evening. With a cautious eye on the government agents, Klaus Maria quietly typed the number on the card into the address block of a new message on his mobile phone. Below that, he typed a brief message in German and hit the SEND key. Then, like a skilled magician, he made both his phone and the calling card disappear into his hip pocket.

Back at the table, Thackery was in the middle of a lightning-fast round of incomprehensible exposition to distract Mahler and his Secret Service detail from Klaus

Maria's texting. He stopped in mid-sentence when Mahler suddenly jumped and took a clumsy step backward. To his credit, Mahler didn't scream, but his eyes bulged, and his face looked ashen as he hissed, "What the hell is that?"

Thackery leapt up from his seat and got between the Secret Service agents and the large cat that had padded up to the table seemingly out of nowhere. "Take it easy, boys, take it easy. It's just Simba, my cat. He's just a big pussycat; he's not gonna hurt anybody."

Both agents looked wary. Thackery held up a cautionary hand while stroking Simba under the chin with the other, and in no time, the cat flopped onto his side and rolled over, paws up.

"See?" said Thackery with an anxious smile as he stroked the cat's belly. "He's just a big baby. He's not a threat to anyone. See?"

With a mixture of apprehension and revulsion, Mahler watched as the cat lolled on his back and purred loudly. The Secret Service guys relaxed their posture; one of them even cracked a small smile.

Still stroking Simba's belly, Thackery turned his attention back to Mahler. "So, what do you want to know? I can't tell you much more than I already have. It looks like your boy Kylo Ren took one of our older models—probably the Gen 13, by the looks of it—and did some of his own modifications. None of our units work without the goggles, but he must have found a way around that—don't ask me how. Beyond that, I can't tell you much more . . . "

Mahler was still eyeing the cat with trepidation, but he managed to press on. "Yeah, we got that part. What we need to know is . . . is there any danger?" Mahler took another step back when the cat opened its mouth and made a sound that came off more like a muted roar than a meow. Then, with an edge in his voice, Mahler said, "Could this virtual game—modified as it is—could it cause any real harm to the subject? Like brain damage, or nerve damage, or . . . death?"

Confusion flashed over Thackery's eyes; then, a tentative smile broke at one corner of his mouth. "It's just a game, yo."

"A *reality* game," said Mahler forcefully.

"*Virtual* reality," Thackery countered with a curt nod. Then he tapped his temple. "It's all in his head. When the game stops, the experience stops."

"So, there won't be any lasting effects?"

"There shouldn't be. It's just tricking your mind into believing that you're experiencing something you're not. It's like watching a 3D movie—you take off the glasses and you're back in the real world. It's scary, but it's not real."

For a moment, it looked like Mahler was ready to accept Thackery's assessment and leave—if for no other reason than to get away from the huge cat that was presently holding Thackery's arm between its thick paws and gnawing on it like a baby with a teething ring.

But then something happened.

The computer on the glass table chimed, and Mahler turned to look at the complex grid displayed on the screen. For a second, he looked perplexed; then his eyes narrowed.

"What is this?" Mahler asked with an edge of suspicion creeping into his voice.

"That's Daisy," said Thackery amiably.

Mahler's eyes were still on the screen, and it didn't take long for him to realize that he was looking at a map, upon which thousands of thin multicolored lines were all converging on a single point: Washington, DC. "And whom or what is 'Daisy?'"

"'Who,'" Thackery corrected.

Mahler raised a brow.

"You mean '*who* or what is Daisy?' 'Who' is the subject of the verb; 'whom' is the object of the verb, or the preposition. '*Who* is Daisy? *She* is Daisy.' Like that, you know?"

Mahler turned from the screen and gazed at Thackery for an uncomfortably long moment.

"Who are you?" Mahler asked.

"Excuse me?"

"Where are you from?"

Thackery blinked. "California."

"No," Mahler said. "What *country* are you from? Where were you born?"

"America," Thackery said simply. "I was born in California. Fresno."

Mahler looked dubious. His next question came out slowly and deliberately. "Where are your *parents* from?"

Thackery smiled. "Are you serious, bro?"

Mahler said, "I'm dead serious . . . *bro*."

"Ah, man, and I just thought we were getting to be friends," Thackery said, rolling his eyes. "And now I'm gonna have to feed you and your boys to my cat Simba here."

Mahler's eyes widened, but neither of the Secret Service agents reacted.

"I'm *kidding*," Thackery squealed with a broad grin.

Mahler glared at him. "I could have you deported."

"To Fresno?"

One of the agents laughed. Mahler's face went red. He was about to say something when the phone in his pocket began to ring. No name appeared on the screen; just a number—but it was a DOD number. Mahler sneered at Thackery; maybe this would wipe that smarmy grin off his face. Mahler answered the call and put it on speaker.

"Hello, who's calling?" he said, eyeing Thackery with a thin smile and smug gleam in his beady eyes.

"This is Deputy Director of the CIA Percival Hartman," the stern voice boomed through the speaker of Mahler's phone. "Who am I speaking to?"

Mahler's chest swelled with confidence as he leered at Thackery and spoke into the phone. "Good evening, sir. This is Senior Policy Advisor to the President Spencer Mahler. I believe I've discovered something the DOD will find quite interesting—"

"Never mind the fancy talk, son," Buzz Hartman snapped. "What you've discovered is one of our operatives who's currently working on a time-sensitive matter for the DOD and doesn't have time to be playing footsie with the President's second string."

The smug look vanished from Mahler's face. "All due respect, sir, I'm here to acquire information vital to—"

"Well, shit, son," Hartman interjected, "you must have me confused with somebody who gives a flyin' fart. In case you haven't heard, we're in the middle of an international crisis here, and the last time I checked, I outrank pencil-pushing policy advisors—no offense—when it comes to matters of international crises. So, unless you can get someone on the horn that outranks me, I suggest you hightail it back to the White House and let the big boys handle this one."

Mahler snorted indignantly. "I am here on the direct orders of the President of the United States."

"Well, that'd definitely be someone who outranks me," said Hartman agreeably enough. "But, given that the President's currently enmeshed in his own little crisis on TV, I'd say your chances of getting him on the horn to confirm your story are pretty slim, son."

Mahler was still glaring at Thackery as he spoke into the phone with deadly precision. "I'm going to tell the President everything that's happened here."

"You do that, kemosabe," said Hartman in that same agreeable tone, "and give him my regards. He knows where to reach me."

"Oh, he'll be reaching you. Bank on it."

"I'm sure he will," said Hartman with a light sigh. "But in the meantime, there's a detail of my boys waiting for you and yours down on the street. They'll provide you with an escort to make sure you get back to DC without getting lost along the way."

Mahler drew the phone close to his lips. "This isn't over."

"From your lips to the President's ears, I'm sure it isn't. Now move along, son. You hear me?"

Mahler seethed in silence.

Hartman said, "I'm gonna need a verbal response, son, so I know we're on the same page here."

The color had drained from Mahler's face. The humiliation was nearly unbearable. He closed his eyes and swallowed hard. "Yes."

"Yes, what?"

Mahler gnashed his teeth and forced out the response: "Yes, sir."

"Good deal," said Hartman. "I'll look forward to hearing from your boss after you've reported to him."

Mahler started to say something, but the line went dead before he could get out a word. He stared at the phone for a protracted moment. Then he looked back at Thackery, who stood now with Simba at his side. For a second, it looked as if Mahler might approach Thackery. But with the Savannah cat standing at full height and looking directly at him, Mahler simply shot one final icy glance at Thackery, and without looking at the Secret Service agents, he barked, "Let's go." And as they left the loft, Mahler muttered to the agents, "This isn't over, not by a long shot . . . "

TABITHA KINGLEY SAT WITH HER LEGS CURLED UNDER HER ON the plush sofa in the executive suite of Tower K, unable to tear her wide-staring eyes from the image of her father on live TV. Her older brother, Roy Jr., was in the adjacent office—he had left in the middle of their dad's "little green army men" rant and was presently trying to get through to someone in authority at the White House. Tabby could hear him shouting at a staffer on the phone, but the scene unfolding on TV held her in a trancelike state of thrall, as if it were the season finale of a show too harrowing to watch yet too compelling to turn away from.

In the Oval Office, the President was silent, pensive, still lost in nostalgia for a war that had ended before he was even born.

After a respectful moment, True Son broke the silence. "You admire General Patton."

The President came out of his reverie and looked up at the monitor. "Big league," he said with a gleam of pride in his eyes.

"He was a man of decisive action," said True Son.

The President nodded in agreement. "Very decisive."

"Fearless in the face of the enemy."

"Totally fearless."

"Much like yourself."

The President raised his chin, but in a rare display of humility, he did not respond.

"Like your counterpart in the Kremlin," True Son prompted. "Vitaly Tepes."

The President's eyes hardened. "He's a strong leader."

"An ally."

The President's eyes narrowed. "He could be . . . if he's handled correctly."

"By you."

"Who else?" said the President as if stating the obvious.

"To form an equitable union."

The President scrutinized the image of True Son on the screen above the mantel for a protracted moment. Then the ghost of a smirk slowly curled at one side of his mouth. "You want to talk about Russian money laundering? Is that what this is about?"

"I have no interest in your financial dealings."

The President looked wary for a second. Then he sniffed deeply and said, "Look, I have a lot of interests, OK? I got interests *all* over the world—I don't tell these people how to spend their money, and they don't tell me how to spend mine. If they want to pay eighteen million instead of five per mile to build a road, that's *their* business. If some guy's willing to give me a hundred million for a piece of property I picked up for forty, I don't ask questions. That's business. That's what I do. I'm not in business to ask questions. I'm in business to make money—and I make a lot of it, many-many billions. I don't care if you're white, black, red, brown, yellow, or Russian—whatever—as long as your check clears, we're good.

"I'm a deal maker, OK? That's what I do. I make deals that make money for me, and a lot of other people too. I've built an unbelievable company, tremendous cash, tremendous company, with some of the greatest assets in the world. I don't know Russians—I make deals with them, that's what I do, I make deals, but I don't know them. Maybe we meet, over dinner—I conduct a lot of business over dinner, many-many business dinners—and somebody says something . . . or somebody I know—could be somebody who works for me, could be anybody, I know a lot of people—and somebody says something—totally unrelated to anything—that doesn't mean I know what's being said, or who said it, or that I get anything out of it, you get me?"

True Son stood silent, and the President continued as if the silence was confirmation enough that the man behind the mask indeed got him.

"My point is, there's all sorts of people saying all sorts of things out there. I can't police everything that everybody's saying—no one could, OK? It would be impossible to follow every conversation that's going on in the world. But if somebody says something at a dinner, or over the phone—and maybe they're just talking, they're probably just talking because people do that . . . they talk—and if they happen to be talking about me or my business or my campaign, whatever, and they're saying nice things, I'm not gonna be rude. It's not my style. I'm a very polite person, ask anybody. I'm not gonna question what's being said, or who said it, because who knows? Nobody knows. That's where everything gets mixed up, OK? And before you know it, everybody's slinging around accusations—totally false and baseless accusations—accusing people of collusion and all sorts of things. I don't need to collude, OK? That's not my style, I'm not a colluder—and I don't do quid pro quos, OK? Maybe somebody who knows someone who knows me says something, or has a conversation, and all of the sudden, it's like *I* said it, or I put them up to it. Unbelievable! Let me tell you something, when I'm gunning for somebody, I pull the trigger myself. I get right up there, point the gun in your face, and pull the trigger, OK? I don't send other people out to do my dirty work. If there *was* collusion—and I'm not saying there was—but if there was, *I'd* be the one doing it. *I* hold the gun. *I* pull the trigger—nobody does that for me, I don't hand the gun off. I aim right between your eyes and pull the trigger myself, believe me."

"Like you did with Hannah Crichton."

The President's brow furrowed.

"When you called upon Russia to find her missing emails."

"You bet your ass, I called on them to find her emails! I'd collude with whoever I had to—Russia, Tepes, Koslivek, whoever—to nail that bitch. I know people. I have connections, OK? I know how to get things done. I know how to win without winning. Even when I lose, I win. Believe me, I've done it. I'm a winner. And I'd do it again. In a New York minute, I'd do it again."

"I'm sure you would," True Son responded in that maddeningly calm tone.

The President's features froze. Then his eyes became stormy. "Look, Hannah Crichton is a crook, all right? A lying, deceitful nasty woman who should be jailed for what she's done."

"And what has she done?"

The President blinked, and his eyes grew wide as if he could scarcely credit the question. True Son waited patiently, which only seemed to fuel the President's passion.

"What has she *done?* I'll tell you what she's done. She's a dirty little crook, along with that perv husband of hers—the guy can't keep his hands to himself, I'm totally serious, ask anyone, they'll tell you, they don't call him Black Blake for nothing, the guy's a total perv."

True Son remained silent. The President rolled his eyes.

"Look, the Crichtons had their chance, OK? They had their shot, and they ran this country right into the ground, left that poor Texas yokel a complete mess—he was no prize, either, let me tell you, but they set him up cold. I'm not kidding you. The Crichtons are, without exception, *the* most dishonest criminal couple to have ever occupied the White House—worse than Nixon, *far* worse, believe me, Nixon had nothing on those two. They were like monarchs, the crooked Crichtons, deceitful, conniving, horrible people. They killed that guy who worked for them, Vic Forrester, what a poor sad son of a bitch he was, and they killed him. Just ask A.C. Janus, he'll tell you, he's done countless reports on the whole thing on his FreedomCave podcast—tremendous investigative reporting, very well researched, very accurate, unlike the fake news of the mainstream media. Janus tells the unvarnished truth. That was no suicide—Forrester knew too much about the Crichtons and their dirty deals, and they took him out. They had to! He was gonna expose them!"

The President rolled his eyes, shook his head sadly, and waved it off. True Son calmly waited for more, and shortly, it came.

"The whole story was in the Enquirer, back in the '90s, every sordid little detail," the President went on. "They were like the king and queen, lopping off heads, totally crazy medieval shit—it's a miracle the country survived their reign. Thank God we had our Second Amendment rights . . . which, by the way, they tried—unsuccessfully, thank God—to take away from us. Nasty people, both of them, really, the pervy king and his frigid enabler queen—and they wanted to double-dip, but I stopped them . . . without any help from Russia, or whatever. Russia—gimme a break! Russia! Can you believe that? The lyin' media's just pissed because I beat the king and queen at their own game. I tore down their little castle, brick by brick, and fed it to 'em. I should get a medal, I'm serious."

True Son contemplated the President for a moment before offering a smooth rejoinder. "The same has been said of you."

The President looked confused.

"That your presidency is tantamount to a monarchy."

"Bull."

"They call you and your family 'the Romanovs.'"

The President rolled his eyes. "Again with the Russians! So what's their story? They rig an election too?"

"They brought down an empire by placing their faith in a madman."

"Well, good for them."

"Not really."

"Yeah, why's that?"

"The Bolsheviks took the entire family down to the cellar and shot them."

The President's eyes narrowed, and he snapped his fingers. "I know that one, I know that story . . . they killed them all, except for the little girl, What's-her-name, Anna-something."

"Anastasia."

"Ingrid Bergman," the President said, nodding with a nostalgic smile. "They shot her, but she survived. Tough little girl. Nobody believed it was her, but in the end, the old lady knew—Helen Hayes, great old dame—she says it *was* her, and Bergman takes off with Yul Brynner."

"That was a movie," True Son said. "In reality, the princess was killed, along with the rest of the Royal family."

"You sure about that? I'm pretty sure they gave Bergman the Oscar for that one. Unbelievable performance. What a beauty she was. They don't make 'em like her anymore, let me tell you—tremendous talent, unbelievable beauty. All we got today are hags, like Streep and Sarandon and Cher. Oy oy oy, I wouldn't give you a plugged nickel for those old crones—you can have 'em. I mean, maybe Sarandon, back in the day, but who is she kidding now?" He shook his head with a sour expression and muttered, "Nasty women, all of them . . . "

In the background of the shadowed room where he was being held captive, Jacob Latner moaned softly. But the President, still lost in his thoughts of the three actresses who'd all publicly opposed him, didn't seem to notice.

"Nasty, *nasty* women," he muttered as he gazed off to some distant corner of the Oval Office that only he could see. Then, abruptly, he snapped out of it, like a sleepwalker suddenly awakening. His gaze shot back to the widescreen TV above the mantel, where the portrait of George Washington had hung up until a few hours ago, and he added with force, "And Hannah Crichton is their ringleader—a dirty little crook, who bleached her emails and took a hammer to her cell phone."

Jacob moaned again, but the President either didn't hear him or was too ensconced in his next tangent to respond.

"Then Shady Hannah went and orchestrated millions of illegals and dead people to vote for her, so it would look like she beat me in the popular vote—she knew she was dead in the electoral college, which is the only thing that matters, by the way. The electoral college. Pure genius. I used to think it was a cheat, but now I understand it—very-very ingenious of the founders, coming up with the electoral college to stop a dirty little crooked liar like Shady Hannah Crichton from destroying not only the country but the world—this is a very sick and twisted woman we're talking about here. Did you see that report in the Times? Two million dead people and another three million registered in different states voted for her! And that's from a Liberal paper!"

True Son said, "The report you're referring to was originally posted by Pew, and reprinted in the Times. It stated that nearly two million deceased individuals are currently listed as voters, and approximately three million people are registered in more than one state. Though the report shows that voter rolls are susceptible to fraud, it made no claim that this was evidence of fraud, either."

"Whatever," said the President dismissively. Then suddenly, he made a sour face. "Whose side are you on, anyway? If somebody's registered in multiple states, you can bet your ass they voted more than once. Bank on it."

True Son paused to consider before responding. "Then, I take it," he said in a measured cadence, "that you believe your treasury secretary Mr. Cahulain, your former chief strategist Mr. Biggerstaff, your press secretary Mr. Spinner, and your former chief of staff Mr. Plebeius—along with your daughter Tabitha and your son-in-law Jacob—all voted for you multiple times, as each of them is currently registered in more than one state."

On the sofa in Tower K, Tabby froze. There were certain triggers that set off her father—more and more each day, and with a ferocity that many in the White House found increasingly alarming—and using his own words against him was at the top of the list.

A few weeks back, Tabby had gone to the White House for a visit and ended up cutting her stay short, due in part to the extreme tension of the atmosphere, but mostly due to her father's sudden and aggressive mood swings. Growing up, she'd thought she'd heard it all—the angry proclamations and wild threats that everyone knew he'd never act upon. But this had been different. There had been a conviction in her father's eyes that she'd never seen before—the frightening look of a man who might *actually* follow through on his wild threats.

He had taken to fits of unbridled rage, often without warning, ranting about strangling this person or shooting that person ("I could get away with it too, they'd probably give me a medal or something, I'm totally serious."). And when the few with enough courage to engage him would say something like "You don't mean that, Mr. President," he would get even angrier and start rambling about "second amendment" and "capital punishment" remedies. It had gotten so crazy that even Nikolina had left for New York—she'd wanted to take Barret with her, but the old man had put his foot down.

"You want to turn tail and run for cover," he'd said flatly, "that's your business, sweetheart—don't let the door hit you in the ass on your way out. But the kid stays."

Tabby had tried to talk him down, to get him to let her take Barret back to New York to be with his mother, but he wouldn't budge. He'd just stood at the French doors in the Oval Office with his back to her and said, "If the ship goes down, the men go down with it . . . "

Then his voice had dropped to a mutter, but Tabby had heard him clearly.

"*No* woman emasculates me . . . *I* won, *she* lost . . . *I'm* in control here . . . "

Tabby would never forget the way her father had looked as he'd stood at the French doors, gazing out at the garden. She'd wanted to give him a hug and kiss goodbye, but he'd just stood there with that distant yet focused look, as if he could watch the world burn without compunction.

He had that same look now as he gazed at the image of the terrorist on the TV screen above the mantel in the Oval Office.

Tabby held her breath, fully expecting the fire within to penetrate the icy surface of her father's gaze and burst forward with the full force of his wrath. But to her surprise, the initial salvo came with remarkable restraint.

"You're a smart-mouthed little punk, aren't you," said the President with an ugly grin. "You think I don't know your game? You think you got me in your eye? I got *you* in *my* eye. I got *you*, you smooth-talkin' smart-mouthed little punk. I got *you*, tough guy. I got you."

True Son contemplated the President for a brief moment before replying, "I'm sure you do."

The President's gaze darkened. Something about that calm and reasonable voice coming from the mask—the poised timbre, the measured flow of the words—cut like a blade. Not a stab—that would have been easy to take; the President was used to getting stabbed by his opponents, and he had the scars to prove it. It was the little cuts that got to him. Little cuts, slice after slice, picking away, pulling out tiny chunks of flesh each time. It was that insinuating, lofty, *arrogant* voice coming through that provoking metal breath screen of the mask—*who the fuck wears a mask to a fight, anyway?* It was that smooth-talking, insufferable little bastard with his smarmy comebacks . . .

I'm sure you do.

I'm sure you would.

What the fuck was *that* supposed to mean? Huh? What was he supposed to say? That if given the chance, he *wouldn't* call upon the Russians to find that crooked lyin' bitch's emails? Why the hell not? What did it matter *who* found the emails? She was dirty—and guilty as hell—so what would it matter *who* found her emails? And here this dirty little terrorist prick was daring to challenge *him*? Daring to sit up on his high horse, shooting clever comebacks, prodding and poking, as if he knew exactly which buttons to push to get the desired response—as if *he* were a better man than the *President of the United Fucking States of America?*

The rational part of his brain (where the chorus of lawyers and cabinet members and so-called family and friends conspired to silence his true voice—or at least to water it down to a pathetic whisper) called out to him now, warning him not to lose his temper, warning him to wait until Spencer returned with the information on the virtual reality unit. But as he gazed at the tall figure in the black mask, he was overcome with a single image: his hands wrapped around that throat, squeezing the life out of the cocky fucker.

But there was something else. Something that almost frightened the President. Not because it was real—he knew the difference between reality and delusion, and he was most certainly *not* delusional. But for a second, it was as if the masked figure on the TV screen was no longer the terrorist . . . at least not precisely—sometimes it was difficult to get a handle on things when they played out in his mind at intense speeds. But for that odd second, it was as if the terrorist had somehow morphed into the President's predecessor. The *former* president—that smart-mouthed smooth-talker, always looking down from on high, laughing at him, mocking him like he'd done at the Correspondents' Dinner.

The President could still hear the laughter from that night as Boyega mocked his reality show, mocked *him*. And all of those people gathered at that dinner, laughing at him. At *him*. Laughing and laughing and laughing . . .

Well, who's got the last laugh now, you cocky Arugula-eating prick? Who's laughing now, you smooth-talking jumped-up pantry boy?

But that was just it. Even though he'd beaten his predecessor—and beaten him badly, make no mistake—the President still didn't *feel* like the victor. He didn't feel like the loser, either. He felt worse. He felt like the man who would always be racing to catch up. And no matter how close he got, he would never be able to surpass his predecessor . . . at least not until every last executive order, every last law that illegitimate son of a bitch had put into place was torn down. Only then would that laughter from the Correspondents' Dinner cease to echo in his mind.

The President took several noisy breaths through his nose until the blurred image on the widescreen TV above the mantel cleared and he was certain that he was looking at the terrorist, True Son, once again.

"I got you, tough guy," he repeated. "I got your number, and I'm gonna take your little pinko ass out. You think you got me? I got *you!*"

He stabbed a finger at the TV to punctuate the statement. True Son appeared unmoved.

"You think you're so tough, hiding behind that mask, standing there with your little zapper box, torturing an innocent man—" He tilted his head back and called out to Jacob in the background of the frame: "How you holding up there, Jake?"

Jacob groaned softly.

The President sneered at True Son. "You'll never break him. He's more man than you could ever hope to be, you filthy little punk."

True Son's helmet pivoted ever so slightly.

"Go ahead," the President taunted, "give him another zap, he can take it, he can take anything you dish out." He tilted his head back again and called out: "Can't you, Jake? You're not afraid of this terrorist dirtbag, are you?"

Jacob's chest began to rise and fall rapidly, and a fresh sheen of sweat broke out over his body as he gritted his teeth and braced himself for another jolt.

But True Son's thumb made no move for any of the buttons on the slender black remote control in his left hand. The dark glass eyes of his mask remained focused, preternaturally patient.

The President sneered again and released a shaky breath. "Yeah, just like I thought. You're a loser, True Son. All talk, no action. You know you can't break my guy Jake, and you know exactly why. Because you're weak. You're a disgrace to your people, whoever the hell they are—probably a bunch of weak, spineless losers just like you."

"You're overwrought," True Son said calmly. "We should take another break."

"I'm just gettin' started, little man."

"You may well be, but we should take a break."

The President's lips curled into a mocking pout. "Oh, is it past your bedtime, True Son? Will your mommy and daddy be waiting up for you? What're you, like nineteen, twenty? Your people like getting the young ones to do their dirty work for them, don't they? They promise you the forty virgins and all that jazz? You think you're going to see Allah up in Terrorist Heaven?"

True Son remained still and focused.

"You talk like a college kid, with all that Liberal idealism flowing out of that yap of yours. You in college? Did they recruit you out of college? Fill your head with all their religious bullshit, tell you it'll be an honorable sacrifice, dying for the cause? They tell you you'll become a great martyr?"

The President peered at the TV as if trying to find a way inside the black metal mask. True Son stood stoic.

"Maybe you weren't recruited at all. Maybe this is a family thing, and you're doing it for your old man, or his honor, or whatever passes for honor with you people. They say the apple doesn't fall far from the tree. You're probably just like him, your old man. What was he? A goat herder? A tinker?"

A flicker of light reflected off the shiny black mask, and the President's expression became sly.

"I touched a nerve there, didn't I? I'm very good at reading people. Even when I can't see their face, even when they aren't talking, because silence speaks volumes. My mother used to say that. She'd say, 'Silence speaks volumes.' I used to think she could read minds—swear to God, the woman was like one of those gypsy fortune tellers or something, I swear to God, she was. And it didn't matter if she could see you, either. She could be on the phone with you, and you could be dead silent, and she'd know exactly what you were up to, without you ever saying a word. It used to freak me out when I was a kid, but when I got older, she told me the secret. She was listening to the silence, and the silence spoke volumes."

The President paused. True Son waited. Then the President's sly grin returned.

"I'm listening to your silence right now, and you know what I'm hearing, tough guy? I'm hearing that I'm onto something here . . . I'm hearing that this is about your old man, the goat herder. I'm hearing that he came to this country to give his son a better life, that he filled your head with tales of the American dream—how everything in America's free, you just come over and we give it to you. No worries, no work, just free. I think he sold you on that load of crap ever since you were yay high. But then as you grew up and realized that Daddy was wrong, that there aren't any handouts, that life is just as hard over here as it is over there in Pakistan or Syria or Chechnya, or whatever rat hole you crawled out of, and you started to get pissed—not at Daddy for telling you the fairy tale, but at *us* for telling you the *truth*."

True Son remained motionless. The President tilted his head and put a hand to his ear.

"What's that I hear? Ah, yeah. Your silence is speaking volumes, True Son." He dropped a wink, along with an ugly grin. "Then when you figured out that you'd actually have to *work* to become a *real* American, you turned to the Noble Qur'an and found a reason—not a good reason, but a reason—to fight back, to justify all those terrible things you were thinking about how America screwed you and your poor deluded old man, who didn't realize how good he had it herding those goats or sheep or whatever back in your own country."

True Son's thumb twitched—or at least, so the President thought, and he nodded with a chuckle.

"Go for it, tough guy," he taunted, his dark eyes filled with malice. "Hit him with everything you've got." He called out to Jacob, "Knuckle under, Jake, we're gonna show this terrorist pussy what a real man is." Then he turned back to True Son and shouted, "Go for it! Hit him with all you got, tough guy. Do it, you miserable little bastard. Do it for Daddy. You know you want to. Do it! Hit him. Zap the shit out of him. Go for it, balls to the wall, don't hold back. *Do it, you goat herding, camel jockey, sand crawling piece of shit! Do it, you pansy-ass little Daddy's boy! DO IT!"*

Veins stood out on Jacob's neck, and his breath came in rapid little bursts like a tea kettle reaching full boil. His entire body tensed as he braced against the oncoming shock.

But True Son made no move to use the remote control. He simply continued to gaze at the image of the President on the big screen behind the camera in the darkened room where he held Jacob Latner hostage.

Red-faced and breathing heavily, the President shook his head with a disgusted smile. "Just like I thought," he muttered. "All talk, no action." He drew a tremulous breath through his nose and hoisted his chin. "You wanna mess with the big boys, you'd better have the balls to man up and follow through on your threats, son . . . because it's a big bad world out there, and I'm the big bad wolf, and I'll huff, and I'll puff, and I'll blow your little house down. You got that, you little moolie bastard, you little rag-headed loser—"

The President's tirade came to an abrupt halt when True Son pressed one of the buttons on his little black remote control, and instantly, music spilled from the speakers.

It took only a few seconds for the President to recover from the shock of being interrupted. Then, with remarkable speed, he thrust his hand into the pocket of his suit jacket and pulled out the mobile phone. The TuneSleuth graphic swirled briefly on the phone's screen before identifying the music. It was a song from that Broadway show, the one that his running mate, Milt Prevaricott, had attended after the election. He seethed just thinking about that viral video of the cast members coming out on stage at the end of the show to wage a public assault on his VP.

The President's blood boiled even more as he stared at the title of the song that now flooded the Oval Office: *History*

Has Its Eyes On You. He clenched his teeth, ready to shout over the music and unleash his fury on the terrorist, full throttle. But when he looked up at the monitor, it wasn't True Son he saw in that darkened room. It was the man he'd met face-to-face in this very office back on that brisk day in November, shortly after the election.

Now that man—the President's predecessor—stood there under a spotlight, dressed in a dark suit and smartly knotted blue tie—tall, handsome, elegant, *presidential*. He stood there, looking down at his successor. And he was singing in the most beautiful voice the President had ever heard. He was singing: *History has its eyes on you*. And as those six words spilled in a seemingly endless flow, from his lips to the President's ears, the President felt a conflict brewing within—sorrow, trepidation, longing, rage, all swirling about his thundering heart at once.

Rage won the battle when the image of the former president faded, along with the song, and once again the President was gazing into the black eyes of True Son's mask.

He was about to speak when a new song from the *Hamilton* soundtrack rose from the speakers. It started innocuously enough, with a beat that you could tap your toe to. But then it turned and lashed out at him like an accusation, assaulting him with words that came so rapidly he could only parse but a few lines—*sinners and saints . . . we rise and we fall . . . my father commanded respect . . . he takes and he takes and he takes . . . keeps winning anyway . . . changes the game . . . raises the stakes . . . I am inimitable . . . I am an original . . .*

When the money-line hit—*I am the one thing in life I can control*—True Son took a sudden step forward, and reflexively, the President took a step back and stood transfixed as the chorus swelled with the force of a command: *Wait for it, wait for it, wait for it . . .*

The President might not have done what he did next, had True Son only stayed there like a man until the song had played out. Even that challenging step forward, which had forced the President to step back—which, in turn, had embarrassed him in front of the press—even *that* could have been forgiven. But True Son had chosen to add insult to injury by slapping the President—if only metaphorically— while the whole world was watching on live TV.

True Son raised his little black remote control and pointed it directly at the President, like a weapon. He paused briefly to tilt his head in a gesture that the President could only read as open defiance. Then, without a single parting word, he pressed a button on the remote control, and the widescreen TV above the fireplace in the Oval Office went dark . . . right at the point in the song when the chorus was screaming: *Wait for it, wait for it, wait for it . . .*

But the music didn't stop. It kept coming from the independent speakers mounted to the wall on either side of the dark screen.

For a moment, the President stared at the blank TV screen in disbelief. It was the first time anyone had ever cut him off. The press corps held its breath, watching, waiting, anticipating.

When the President's paralysis finally broke, his face contorted into a mask of rage, and the members of the press that stood closest to him stepped back. The Steadicam operator moved to one side, framing a perfect shot, as the President approached the darkened TV, drew back a tightly clenched fist, and punched the center of the screen with all of his might. It cracked in a wide spidery pattern, but the President's rage wasn't spent. With a ferocious grunt, he ripped the TV down from the wall and smashed it repeatedly against the mantelpiece, until there was nothing left but two splintered pieces of the plastic frame. The President held these for a moment, and then with a grimace, he pitched them into the cold fireplace.

Then, as the music coming from the speakers faded out— *wait for it, wait for it, wait for it*—the President straightened his suit jacket, swept his tousled hair back into place, and without a word, he left the Oval Office.

Franco and Melanie were waiting for him in the hallway. While Melanie tended to the bloody knuckles of the President's right hand, Franco held up a mobile phone.

"It's Spencer Mahler, Mr. President."

The President took the phone and listened while Mahler began to rattle off what he'd learned about the virtual reality game unit. He didn't get far before the President cut him off.

"Yeah, forget all that. This guy's a limp dick, he ain't killin' nobody."

Mahler attempted to tell the President about his conversation with Deputy Director Hartman of the CIA, but the President cut him off again.

"Yeah, I don't have time for that shit. Just get back here."

The President hit the red button at the bottom of the screen and handed the phone back to Franco, who was staring at his injured hand.

"Is anything broken, Mr. President?"

"I'll let you know when I can feel it again."

"Maybe we should call a doctor—or at least the HUD secretary—to take a look at it."

The President waved him off with his free hand. "Yeah, forget that. Just get those guys back in here to hook up another TV. I got this fucker on the ropes, and I don't want to miss him when he comes back on. You see how I backed him into the ropes, Franco?"

"Yes, Mr. President."

"Right into the fucking ropes, I did. Put that little cocksucker in the corner, that's what I did. He wants to fuck with *me?* I'll show him. I've been fighting filthy animals like him my entire life, and none of them have taken me down yet. Nobody takes me down, right, Franco?"

"No sir, they don't."

"Better be wearing some serious armor, if they want a piece of me, eh, Franco?"

"Yes, Mr. President."

The President inhaled noisily through his nose.

"That's one round for each of us, it's a dead heat. And he's going down in round three. I'm not fuckin' around here, Franco, he's going down in three." He thrust three fingers at Franco's face. "Three, Franco, count 'em." He spat a dangerous half-laugh, and his eyes shined darkly. "Oh, I got this little prick. I got him all right. He's mine . . . all mine . . . bing, bong, bang . . . *mine.*"

M ARTIN BECKLOW WAS STUMPED. HE HAD WRITTEN CONCISE biographies on every US president, from Washington to Boyega, as well as numerous chronicles of past president's conflicts with leaders of hostile foreign nations. But never in all his years as a presidential historian had he come across anything remotely like what he had witnessed so far this evening. It was, in his opinion, terrifying—and he was not a man given to hyperbole. The only comfort Martin Becklow could find—and it was indeed a small one—was that he was not alone in his assessment of the situation currently playing out in the West Wing of the White House. He looked across the table at Rowan Meadow and simply shook his head. "I think it's safe to say that none of us have ever witnessed anything quite like this, Rowan."

The other pundits gathered around the table in the New York studio sat in silent reflection, like mourners at a gravesite.

The solemn moment was broken when, from the Washington studio, Chase Grimley chimed in. "Well, that's an understatement . . . considering that we just watched the President of the United States throw a violent temper tantrum in the Oval Office on live TV. I'm mean, that's about the craziest thing *I've* ever seen a president do."

Davis Frome couldn't help smiling at Chase's blunt candor; even Martin Becklow allowed a small, sad smile.

Chase shook his head. "I mean, can anybody tell me what the *hell* is going on here? I don't expect an answer out of you on this one, Kori-Lynne, even though this *is* your guy—you backed him, you've been there defending him every step of the way, pretty much from the get-go. But can anyone else tell me what the hell is going on here? I'm serious. This is real. We've got the President of the United States smashing TVs like he's the Incredible Hulk on a 'roid rage or something—right there in the Oval Office, for Christ's sake. This isn't normal."

The panels at both studios remained silent.

Chase shook his head again and shot a weary glance at Monitor 3, which featured a stout salt-and-pepper-haired man whose small, dark eyes appeared deceptively calm. "All right, Lybender," said Chase, "you're the GOP's political guru. Give us your take on this one."

Ron Lybender chuckled innocently. "I don't know what you've been hearing about me, Chase. I'm just an observer, like you—"

"Yeah, spare me the garnish, Lybender," Chase sighed with a thin smile. "Just cut to the meat and potatoes and give me the spin. You're there in PA with those guys who take a shower *after* they get off work—the real gung-ho Kingley crowd, the ones who still want to believe this guy's gonna bring back the coal mining jobs. How do you package this mess so your guy Kingley comes out of it smelling like a basket of freshly cut roses—or at least not a barrel of week-old fish left out in the sun? How do you twist this turd into an edible pretzel for mass consumption? I'm not talking about the twenty-five percent out there who'll swallow whatever crap this president feeds them. I'm talking about the *majority* now—the forgotten majority that we somehow keep ignoring whenever we talk about this. They voted for *her*, not your guy—forty-eight to forty-six percent—and they're starting to get pissed. And your guy's losing numbers . . . 'bigly.' He's holding onto his stubborn base with that sticky twenty-five percent, along with an extra twelve percent, give or take—the 'normal Republicans,' we'll call 'em—that are hanging in there for the perks. They don't like him, they don't like the way he talks about women and blacks and Hispanics, they don't like the crazy he spews on Twitter—but they like the goodies that come with the crazy: the federal court appointments, the Supreme Court justices, the hard-line stance on immigration, that whole 'America First' crap he's sold them on. But they're the soft support, the ones that could turn on him when they realize that the bow is dipping and the watertight compartments ain't so watertight anymore. So, how do you spin this . . . insanity going on right now in the Oval Office? How do you spin this mess into something positive to keep that soft twelve percent from jumping ship? I'm asking here. I'm serious. Because this is a big 'effing' deal, as the former vice president would say. How do you do it, Lybender?"

Ron Lybender chuckled again. "You're looking at this all wrong, Chase."

"How's that? I'm serious here. How am I looking at it all wrong? Your guy's tanking in the polls. Thirty-seven percent ain't gonna cut it; we both know that. Even the electoral college doesn't have enough magic to pull a victory out of its ass for him, not at thirty-seven percent. Hell, serious questions are being asked about his emotional fitness to serve as Commander in Chief by twenty percent of the people who *voted* for him, not just the forgotten majority who didn't. So, you tell me, where have I got this all wrong?"

Lybender sighed, still smiling. "Look, Ronald Reagan had an approval rating of thirty-five percent—"

"When was that?"

"I don't recall exactly when it was—"

"Yeah, well, I've got somebody here who *does* recall," Chase interjected, and he looked across the table. "Delores Knox Greenwood, when did Reagan drop to thirty-five percent?"

Delores said, "January of '83."

"And what was his average?"

"Fifty point three in his first term; fifty-five point three in his second term."

Lybender chuckled. "That just proves my point, Chase. Reagan was at about the same place Kingley is now—"

Chase barked laughter. "The same? Reagan was two years out from reelection, Lybender! Your guy has months. *Months*—and not many of them—to drive his numbers up, and the only direction he's been driving them is *down*. And now he's got this . . . madness going on in the Oval Office, trashing TVs and debating Zweig with a terrorist—who apparently knows a lot more about history than our president does. I'm not kidding. You just saw it!"

"Look, Chase, the President is handling the situation with strength and conviction, just like Reagan would—"

"HA!" Chase barked. "You're telling me that Reagan would respond to a terrorist by throwing a hissy fit and trashing the Oval Office?"

"That's just this president's style, Chase. You can't fault him for that. Every president has his own *style*, and you can't fault him for that—you're trying to make him out as if he's crazy or something—"

"Lybender," said Chase, leaning into the camera, "he's in the Oval Office talking about *little green men*, for Christ's sake! Little green men stabbing at Hitler's brain with plastic knives! This is some scary stuff. We're through the looking-glass here, and it ain't pretty." He turned to address another monitor. "Mick Wilton, you're a Republican. Are you with Lybender on this one? Is it just a matter of 'presidential style' we're dealing with here?"

Mick Wilton smiled wryly and said, "Well, I'm not *that* kind of Republican." He didn't bother to add a "no offense" to Lybender; he was fairly fed up with the far-Right faction of his party and their dogged defense of the man he openly referred to as the "clown president," and he wasn't about to apologize or pull any punches to spare the feelings of anyone stupid or crazy enough to still be on the Kingley wagon as it headed off the cliff.

"I hear you," Chase chuckled. "And I suppose I hardly have to ask the question, but since you're here, what's your take on all of this? What can we expect before we put the lid on this mess?"

In his standard laid-back yet pointed manner, Mick Wilton said, "The President is in full 'Costanza mode' now, and what we're seeing in real time is a complete and total meltdown. But none of this should come as a surprise to anyone who's been watching the shitshow from the beginning. This is simply the culmination of the Shakespearian tragedy that Royal Kingley promised at the start of his campaign when he descended on that golden escalator in Tower K. And now the Oval Office has become his theatre in the round, with all of his rabid fans gathered—from the edge of the stage, all the way back to the nosebleed seats—munching on their buckets of popcorn and watching with bated breath to see what batshit crazy thing happens next. All that's left is for the Senate to storm the Oval Office and start stabbing the buffoonish dictator to death with those Sharpie markers he hands out like Halloween candy at those ridiculously over-the-top signing ceremonies."

"HA!" Chase barked, laughing. "Don't hold back, Mick. Tell us what you really think."

Mick allowed a modest smile. "We've reached a whole new level of Kingley's little wacko world sideshow, with the Carnival Barker in Chief giving us the indelible image of thousands of tiny little General Pattons invading Hitler's dreams. I'm not sure how he'll top that one."

"What the *hell* was *that* all about?" Chase nearly shrieked with laughter while the other pundits attempted to suppress smiles. Still laughing, Chase turned to the monitor featuring the New York studio group and said, "Davis Frome, my good friend from *The Pacific*, what are we *doing* here? Have we gone through the looking-glass, or what? This is the stuff of epic movies! The President of the United States is engaged in an existential dialogue with a terrorist on everything from the merits of dictators, past and present, to Stefan Zweig! He's talking about little green men invading Hitler's brain with plastic knives or swords, or whatever you call 'em—"

"Bayonets, Chase," said Leonard with a smile.

"Bayonets—thank you, Leonard," said Chase with a short laugh. "For Pete's sake, the President of the United States, the Leader of the Free World—though, I guess that's debatable if you happen to live in France or Germany or Canada—but in any case, the President is standing there in the Oval Office on live TV, carrying on like he's Colonel Kurtz in *Apocalypse Now!* You can't make this stuff up!"

Davis Frome shook his head with a small smile and said, "The thing that's rather remarkable is that, to a certain extent, the President of the United States is being given a world history lesson by a terrorist, a lesson for which the President is woefully unprepared—and this is frightening on multiple levels—while, simultaneously, as he's been wont to do on countless other occasions, the President is unwittingly exposing himself. Whether out of brazen hubris or blatant ignorance—or, more than likely, a combination of both—the President can't seem to stop himself revealing things that his attorneys would surely advise him against exposing. His rapid-fire tangent on Russian money laundering—bizarre as it was—comes dangerously close to a confession . . . particularly when he forcefully asserts that if there *had* been collusion, *he* would have been the one doing the colluding. Of course, he then reasserts his mantra that there wasn't any collusion at all."

Lybender chuckled: "Because there isn't any *evidence* of collusion!"

Chase ignored the interjection. "This is madness. Is there any way the President can spin this mess to his advantage?

I can't see it. The Teflon coating is wearing away, and things are starting to stick. Stan Schnetzer, what're your thoughts? Can the President unstick himself from this mess?"

"As I've already stated," said Stan, "there's no one around the President who possesses the fortitude to restrain any of his impulses, on any issue, for any reason. There's no 'What the eff' chorus. And without that buffer of advisors— left to his own devices and erratic impulses—the President's odds of successfully resolving this crisis, or any other crisis, are nonexistent. He lacks the basic criteria that even the greenest presidents have all had: discipline, control, humility, and at least a modicum of knowledge on basic civics. Like Davis said, this terrorist is far more knowledgeable than the President of the United States—and infinitely more self-possessed. After losing his cool like that in front of the entire world on live TV, any other president would be facing serious consideration of being removed from office by his cabinet under the provisions of the 25th Amendment of the Constitution."

Lybender raised a brow. "On what grounds?"

"On the grounds," Stan said evenly, "that the President is unfit to carry out the duties of his office."

Lybender scoffed. "Are you kidding me? Are you saying that the President of the United States is mentally ill?"

"I'm saying that given the actions of the President here tonight—including but not limited to the violent temper tantrum, in which he first punched and then smashed a television to pieces against the fireplace in the Oval Office—the members of his cabinet have sufficient grounds to invoke the 25th Amendment of the United States Constitution. Is that clear enough for you, Ron?"

Lybender squinted as if debating whether to press the issue further, but before he could come to a decision, Leonard O'Keefe cut in.

"Stan, I know this may be a bit off base, but is there any chance this could go beyond the 25th Amendment? As

Davis stated, the President came dangerously close to hinting at the possibility that he himself might have colluded directly with the Russians in their efforts to hack the 2016 election when he said—and I'm quoting here:

"President Kingley: 'Let me tell you something, when I'm gunning for somebody, I pull the trigger myself. I get right up there, point the gun in your face, and pull the trigger, OK? I don't send other people out to do my dirty work. If there *was* collusion—and I'm not saying there was—but if there was, *I'd* be the one doing it. *I* hold the gun. *I* pull the trigger—nobody does that for me, I don't hand the gun off. I aim right between your eyes and pull the trigger myself, believe me.'

"True Son: 'Like you did with Hannah Crichton? When you called upon Russia to find her missing emails?'

"President Kingley: 'You bet your ass, I called on them to find her emails! I'd collude with whoever I had to—Russia, Tepes, Koslivek, whoever—to nail that bitch. I know people. I have connections, OK? I know how to get things done. I know how to win without winning. Even when I lose, I win. Believe me, I've done it. I'm a winner. And I'd do it again. In a New York minute, I'd do it again.'"

Leonard removed his glasses and looked up from the transcript. "How damning to the President is that statement? 'I'd collude with whoever I had to. I have connections. I know how to win without winning. Even when I lose, I win. I've done it. And I'd do it again. In a New York minute, I'd do it again.' How damning might that prove to be, and will the House Committees have anything to say about it? Are we in uncharted waters here? Are we possibly looking at something beyond impeachment or the 25th Amendment?"

"First off," said Stan, "I can guarantee you that the Chairs of the House Committees, particularly Intelligence and Judiciary, are watching every second of this drama unfold and that they're taking detailed notes to rival those of former FBI Director Jonas Brushing. No question, you can count on them to parse every word that's coming out of the President's mouth right now.

"Second, to borrow a phrase from Chase, I suspect that Secretary Crichton felt a 'tingle up her leg' when the President said he knows how to 'get things done' and how to 'win without winning' and that he'd collude with whomever he had to—specifically citing President Tepes and Ambassador Koslivek among those he'd be willing to collude with—to 'nail her,' as he put it. I can only imagine the phone calls that will be flooding Secretary Crichton's phone if the President chooses to provide the terrorist with details on his methods of 'winning without winning.'

"Barring that, it's difficult to tell what it will amount to. Was it just more of the incoherent stream of consciousness that we've grown used to hearing from this president, or was it a subliminal confession? Did we just hear the Leader of the Free World unwittingly implicate himself in an act of espionage against the United States of America? It all depends on where it fits into the puzzle. It could very well end up being a key piece."

Ron Lybender regained his backbone. "Even if your wild hypothesis were true, you're way off base on the outcome. Secretary Crichton lost the election—"

"She lost the *electoral college*," Chase cut in. "She won the popular vote—by three million."

Lybender conceded Chase's point with a nod and moved on to the greater issue as he saw it. "Even so, I just can't see how any of this could possibly benefit the loser of the race. She lost—the electoral college, which is how we decide elections here in our republic—so, I don't see how any of this could possibly benefit her. Even in the wildly extreme event of the President being removed from office for colluding with a foreign government, the only person who would benefit from a scenario such as that would be Vice President Prevaricott, who would then become President Prevaricott."

Stan Schnetzer shook his head. "There's where your mouth's getting ahead of your brain again, Ron. If the President persists on this track, and in the course of his ramblings on live TV confesses that he, then *Candidate* Kingley, conspired with the Russian government in an attempt to secure his victory in the election, that would be a crime, plain and simple. A crime of such magnitude that, in and of itself, would be more than enough to remove the President from office. And your suggestion that, in an event of such monumental proportions—the likes of which we have never seen in the entire history of the United States of America—that in such an event, the presidency would simply be handed over to the vice president is completely erroneous."

"It would *have* to go to the vice president," Lybender snapped. "That's the order of succession!"

"Under normal circumstances, you would be correct," said Stan, his tone remarkably calm. "But if we're dealing with a president who committed a crime to gain the office which he now holds, we've entered uncharted territory, and *that* would put us in a Constitutional crisis, Ron."

Lybender shook his head, but Stan continued, unabated.

"And if that ends up being the case, I can guarantee you that Secretary Crichton's battery of lawyers will argue, and with real cause, that by virtue of the President's illegitimacy—due to such criminal actions which brought him to the presidency—his running mate and vice president, Milton Prevaricott, must also be deemed illegitimate."

"And how do you come to that conclusion?"

"I come to that conclusion, Ron," said Stan with an edge creeping into his tone, "because the law clearly states that no individual, regardless of his or her innocence, or lack of knowledge of a crime, can benefit from said crime. To put it in simple words that even you can understand: If the President were to rob a bank and give the money to his vice president, the law would not allow Vice President Prevaricott to keep that money, regardless of his innocence in the commission of the crime itself. Is that clear enough for you, Ron, or do you need me to color in the lines for you?"

Lybender clamped his mouth shut—and this time he didn't need Chase Grimley to tell him to keep it shut.

Stan held his piercing blue gaze on the monitor that featured Ron Lybender for a moment longer. Then he turned his attention back to the others in the DC studio.

"Whether or not the President will pick up on the thread of his ill-advised remarks about 'winning without winning,' there's surely more red meat to come if the President intends on stepping back inside the Oval Office to continue his little back and forth with the terrorist—which, if I were a ranking member of his staff, I would strongly advise against."

In the Queen's Room in the East Wing of the White House, Kori-Lynne shifted uncomfortably in her seat, hoping that the NCMSB director wouldn't cut to her for a reaction shot.

In the New York studio, Leonard O'Keefe nodded with a smile. "I'm not sure even *you* could manage to persuade the President to back off at this point, Stan."

Stan returned the smile, but his eyes looked serious.

A moment of silence followed. Then Chase Grimley picked up the ball.

"Elwood Robertson, you're a Pulitzer Prize-winning journalist. Tell us what we're missing here. You know the terrain, you've been around the block."

"Well, not *this* particular block," Elwood chuckled softly, "or at least not since the gentrification."

Chase barked a laugh. "HA! The gentrification! Good grief, it's that bleak, isn't it." He pointed across the table. "I know you're trying not to laugh over there, Delores, but this whole thing is like a David Lynch picture—*Blue Velvet*, or *Wild at Heart*, or *Twin Peaks*—if you don't laugh, you'll end up screaming at the sheer horror of it. I'm serious." He turned back to Elwood. "I mean, what do you make of this? I've got some thoughts, but I want to hear what you think first."

Elwood pondered for a moment. "I think it's safe to say that the terrorist has the pulse of this president. He's remarkably adept—anticipating the President's moves and laying traps, like a shrewd chess player. But there's also the 'dangling shiny object' factor. From the start of his campaign, Royal Kingley has displayed a canny ability to drive the narrative by dangling shiny objects for the press to chase after—a diversionary tactic that, much to the chagrin of his opponents, has worked remarkably well."

There was silent agreement around the tables in both the New York and DC studios, as none could deny that they had pursued their fair share of the President's 'dangling shiny objects.'

"But," Elwood went on, "what we're witnessing now is a reversal. It's the *President* who's chasing after the shiny objects that the terrorist is dangling out there."

"Exactly," Chase said. "This guy is inside the President's head—he knows what buttons to push, and he's not afraid to push them. I've interviewed Royal Kingley at least a dozen times over the past twenty years or so—long before he ever thought of running, back when he was positive he'd *never* run for political office, let alone the presidency—and I thought I had a pretty good grasp on him. But this guy—this terrorist—he's got a *real* read on him. And you're right about the 'dangling shiny object' factor. Take one look at the President's eyes; you can see that he's practically mesmerized by this terrorist. I'm not saying he's enjoying all of this—though, I suspect a part of him is . . . at least the theatrics of it, being in the spotlight and all that jazz. But there's something more . . . it's like he's enthralled . . . "

"Like a cat with a laser pointer," said Rowan.

"Exactly," Chase laughed. "I know it's not funny—it's damned serious, in fact—but that's what it's like. It's like this terrorist has one of those laser pointers, and he's flashing it around, and the President is like a big cat, bounding all over the place, pouncing wildly, trying to catch that red dot of light; not realizing that he *can't* catch it. There's something surreal about it—I mean, even more surreal than usual with this president." Chase shot a glance across the table. "Delores Knox Greenwood, you've got that look in your eye. Tell me what I'm missing here."

Delores said, "I suppose the elephant in the room would be obvious, if not for the surrounding fog of chaos. As a mother of three boys, you learn pretty quickly how to cut through the fog and identify what's missing."

Chase nodded. "And what's missing?"

Delores said simply, "The terrorist hasn't made any demand in exchange for the hostage."

"*Exactly*," said Chase, pointing at Delores. "We're all watching this, every one of us just as enthralled as the President, and none of us has bothered to ask: what does this guy want? What's his endgame? I mean, what is he doing here, this terrorist, why'd he kidnap the President's son-in-law? What does he want out of all of this? I mean, you go to all the trouble of setting up an elaborate scenario like this, you want something, for Christ's sake! What the hell does this guy want?"

A palpable silence followed as Chase's eyes passed over his colleagues. Then he went on.

"Here's what I see—and correct me if anyone thinks I'm off base on this. I'm seeing the President getting schooled by this terrorist, just like Davis said. This guy in the mask— call him what you like, Batman, Darth Vader, whatever—I personally think he looks a bit like the ghost of Hamlet's dad in that old Olivier movie—how's that for adumbration? Kingley as the twenty-first century Hamlet—it doesn't get any more Shakespearean than that . . . I mean, unless you go with King Lear, I suppose—he was the one who went crazy and gave control to those devious daughters of his, wasn't he?

"But, whatever, this terrorist, the guy in the mask, whatever you think of him, good or bad, right or wrong, he knows his stuff. He took the time to study for this test, and he's not pussyfooting around. He's well educated, he's articulate, and you can bet your ass he has a plan. He's building a maze here, and the President is following him deeper and deeper into that maze, step by step—he's boxing the President in. He's a sharp son of a bitch, and he knows what he's doing, and the President has neither the intellectual wherewithal nor the verbal arsenal to hold his own against a guy like this. I'm telling you, this guy showed up prepared for a championship chess match, and the President isn't even qualified to play checkers.

"You want to know what he wants? I'll tell you what he wants—and it ain't arms for hostages or the release of his fellow 'freedom fighters' or any of that. He's here to make a statement, and he wants the President's undivided attention—which, no one can dispute, he's got. This isn't an attack on the country. This isn't about our Western culture or democracy or any of that other good stuff. This is personal. Something's going on here—call it gut instinct, a hunch, whatever, but wait and see if I'm wrong about this one, and I don't think I am. This is something personal. It's a personal and strategic attack—not on our way of life, or even the presidency. This terrorist has it out for the President. He's locked and loaded for bear, and his sight is squarely focused on the President. I got a feeling about this—a bad feeling—and I don't think this is going to end well. Mark my words. You heard it here first. If you're looking for a happy ending, you're in the wrong theatre."

Vᴵᴄᴇ Pʀᴇsɪᴅᴇɴᴛ Mɪʟᴛᴏɴ Pʀᴇᴠᴀʀɪᴄᴏᴛᴛ sᴀᴛ ɪɴ ᴛʜᴇ ꜰʀᴏɴᴛ ᴘᴇᴡ of St. Patrick's Cathedral with his head bowed, though not in prayer. He was looking down at his mobile phone, which displayed the friendly faces of FIX News hosts Step Dancy, Emberly Bristlebeck, and Brentley Hummer. All heck had broken loose after the President's "Russian revelation" and subsequent blowup on live TV. Over the past half-hour, Republicans across the board had been scrambling to get in front of cameras and publicly distance themselves from the Kingley Administration in general, and, specifically, from the President himself.

The first wave had hit even before the President had torn the TV down from the wall above the fireplace and smashed it to smithereens against the mantel. It had come from a bipartisan gang, led by Senate Majority Leader Mycroft McTory, who'd skillfully framed his argument around the faltering competency of the President while extolling the admirable "restrained resistance" of the Administration. Senate Minority Leader Caleb Sherman had followed up with a statement of his own, in which he concurred, for the most part, with his distinguished colleague from across the aisle. But he'd added that "certain members" of the Kingley administration were, at the very least, complicit in enabling the President's disastrous and criminal actions.

"I'm not going to name names at this time," Senator Sherman had said, "but they know who they are, and they know what they've done. And soon, the American people will know too." The Senate Minority Leader had paused here and looked directly into the camera before closing with an over-the-top yet effectively ominous statement: "And to those culpable and complicit individuals, I have one thing to say: You can run, but you can't hide."

The Vice President looked up from his phone, and his gaze fell upon the sculpture of the Virgin Mother, which stood in humble prominence on the altar. It had been nearly thirty years since he'd set foot in a Catholic church, but St. Patrick's was not only the most accessible house of worship available on short notice, it also happened to be under renovation, which made it the easiest place for his Secret Service detail to secure—and with the current state of the nation, the security of the Vice President was of paramount concern.

The house of the Lord isn't built of brick and mortar, but of flesh and blood, as the Lord can only truly live and thrive in the hearts of his devoted flock.

Pastor Frank had told him that when he'd first visited University Commons Evangelical, looking for an alternative to the church of his upbringing. That had been back in the days when the future vice president still considered himself a "Reagan Democrat" and had yet to receive the Lord's greater message. It was during one of Pastor Mark's sermons (which, unlike the staid sermons of the Catholics, were rousing and full of life) that the Lord had spoken clearly to young Milton Prevaricott and given him the mantra that he would repeat whenever asked about his views: "I am a Christian, a Conservative, and a Republican—in that order."

During the election, of course, this mantra had come in quite handy, as party affiliation carried little weight for the voters—particularly the sort of voters that he and Royal Kingley needed to win: good people with strong values who were fed up with the rusted machinery of Washington and hungered for real change. Those good people wanted the broken system torn down, brick by brick, and reconstructed in the *true* vision of the Founding Fathers—those wise and devoted men who had been guided by the beneficent hand of the Lord, God Almighty Himself, back in those trying days of revolution against a tyrannical monarchy.

Milton Prevaricott hadn't been sure of the messenger the good citizens of the United States of America had chosen to take on the corrupt environment of DC and bring about the much-needed change—at least not early on, he hadn't. He hadn't been sure that he could stand beside a man who so freely and publicly spoke in such a profane manner that one looked at him in stupefied wonder that the good Lord did not strike him dead where he stood. Milton hadn't been sure that he could compromise his values—not to mention his faith—by taking up with a man whose moral compass appeared to perpetually point south and whose self-aggrandizing antics reached meteoric heights of narcissism.

But, as always, the Lord provided the answer to Milton Prevaricott through scripture.

It was Psalms 1:1 that the Vice President was thinking of now, the very passage that had led him from the darkness of conflict and indecision to the light of the Lord's chosen path . . .

> "Blessed is the man that walketh not in the counsel of the ungodly, nor standeth in the way of sinners, nor sitteth in the seat of the scornful.
>
> "But his delight is in the law of the LORD; and in his law doth he meditate day and night.
>
> "And he shall be like a tree planted by the rivers of water, that bringeth forth his fruit in his season; his leaf also shall not wither; and whatsoever he doeth shall prosper.
>
> "The ungodly are not so: but are like the chaff which the wind driveth away."

Milton Prevaricott had pondered this passage countless times during those dark yet hopeful days of waiting. And when the call from Royal Kingley's people had finally come, he knew the answer. He knew it because the Lord had spoken to him through the Holy Scripture, and He had told Milton Prevaricott in no uncertain terms what to do.

And now, in the silence of the deserted cathedral, the Vice President closed his eyes and whispered the Lord's command . . .

"Though I stand in the shadow of the sinner, I do not walk in his counsel, nor stand in his way, nor sit at his table of scorn. I am the tree by the water. I will not wither. I will wait for the chaff to be driven away by the mighty wind of Your breath. And then, most Heavenly Father, I will bring forth the fruit of my season. I will do it in Jesus' name. Amen."

When the Vice President opened his eyes, the friendly faces of the FIX News hosts were still there on the tiny screen of his mobile phone—Step, Emberly, and Brentley, God bless them. Wonderful folks, good decent folks. They were just wrapping up a lively discussion on the crisis at the White House with their guest, former Representative from The Peach State's first district, Zach Princeton, a staunch advocate for the Conservative cause and all-around heck of a guy. The former congressman was assuring the pundits that there was nothing to worry about; that no matter what the outcome of the night's events, a solid leader was waiting in the wings, should the need for his service arise.

The Vice President allowed himself a small smile of pride at his good fortune. He was indeed a solid leader, ready to steward the flock at a moment's notice.

He was still smiling that dreamy-eyed smile when Step Dancy turned to the camera with a big friendly smile of his own and said, "We'll be right back with more on this breaking story, so stick around. I'm Step Dancy, and this is FIX News—when the news is broken, you can count on us to FIX it!"

R ANCE PLEBEIUS TRIED NOT TO LOOK AT STRETCH BIGGERSTAFF, but he couldn't help sneaking a glance out of the corner of his eye as he quietly sipped his beer. The veins that crisscrossed Stretch's face like spidery lines on a roadmap were pronounced and redder than usual. His breath came in a wheezing whistle, like an old locomotive building up steam, and he kept ordering shots, even though he'd already downed enough to drop a bull. Rance had never seen anything quite like it, except maybe in the movies. But here

Stretch sat, tossing back shot after shot, and he didn't seem even slightly tipsy—indeed he looked sharper and edgier than ever. Like an elixir drawn from the urn of Vulcan, the drinks only appeared to fuel the tempest within . . . which, judging by Stretch's brooding gaze and lung-rattling breaths, would not be contained for long.

Stretch was grumbling now under his breath—something about taking them out, *all* of them—when Rance suggested they get some fresh air, take a stroll around the Mall.

Stretch didn't respond. He was focused on his tablet, which featured a live shot of the NCMSB broadcast in the lower right corner of the screen. The lefty freedom haters were in a feeding frenzy over the statements that had just been made to the press by the Senate Majority and Minority leaders. Stretch fumed at the sight of old McTory's sanctimonious puss.

Turncoat bastard, Stretch thought, with a bitter gleam in his eyes. *Every fucking one of them, a bunch of turncoat bastards.* Except maybe Reaper . . . but he was still a mealy-mouthed little bitch who reminded Stretch of that prissy cuck-fuck Latner. Both of them were little pretty boy princes who didn't know shit from Shinola, and neither was worthy of the keys to the kingdom.

Stretch downed another shot and wiped his chapped lips with the back of his hand as he continued to watch the circus of Liberal clowns in the corner of the screen. He scowled at Stan Schnetzer, who was currently sticking his nose as far up the pinko asses as he could. It was a disgusting sight.

"The one thing that is patently clear," Stan was saying, "is that the President is completely out of his depth."

"You think?" Chase Grimley replied, with a chuckle that made Stretch want to reach through the screen and throttle the old prick. Without taking his eyes off the tablet, Stretch tapped the bar top and held up two fingers, and the bartender refilled his glass.

The hits kept on coming, and Stretch's face grew redder with each one . . .

That smug suit O'Keefe, with his perfectly knotted tie and smarmy Irish eyes, kicked it off by quoting that dumb dago, ex-CIA Director Vito Pascale: "'I've never been so nervous in my lifetime about what may or may not happen in Washington. I don't know whether this White House is capable of responding in a thoughtful and careful way, should crisis erupt. You can do this hit and miss stuff over a period of time, but at some point, I don't give a damn what your particular sense of change is about, you cannot afford to have change become chaos.'"

Then that lousy dyke Meadow took her shot, quoting Walter Pederson, the kraut quack that Kingley should have sued within an inch of his life for libel: "'If we could construct a psychiatric Frankenstein monster, we could not create a leader more dangerously mentally ill than Royal Kingley. He is a paranoid psychopathic narcissist, who is divorced from reality and lashes out impulsively at his imagined enemies, and consequently the very last person who should be trusted with the nuclear codes.'"

Then the Shylock Hymie hack from that rag *The Pacific*, Davis Frome, tossed in his two cents worth: "The slow-motion train wreck that we're witnessing here is yet another example in a long list of examples of this president's inability to curb his self-destructive behavior. The only difference this time is that the self-inflicted wound may very well prove fatal."

Then Robertson chucked his spear at the target: "The President's conflict has been clear for quite some time now, with his former national-security adviser General Finch, campaign manager Phil Mangold, foreign-policy adviser Carlton Gage, political adviser and longtime associate Dodger Sloan, Attorney General Jasper Sassy, son-in-law Jacob Latner, and even his son Roy Jr., all under scrutiny in the FBI investigation into Russia's meddling in the election.

But this . . . I'm not sure there's a way out of this if it continues . . . if he goes back into the Oval Office . . . I can't see this ending well for him—"

"You mentioned Carlton Gage in there," Chase Grimley cut in, "and this is a guy that I find absolutely fascinating— I mean, in that train wreck sort of way you mentioned. I mean, what is it with that guy? I can't figure out if he's Verbal Kint or Keyser Söze! He's an enigma. He's like one of those fan dancers at a burlesque show—he wants you to focus on him, but he wants to tease you away from it the whole time, it's just plain *weird*."

Several of the Liberal pukes laughed. Stretch didn't find it funny in the slightest; he just grimaced and tossed back another shot.

"I mean, back in the election," Grimley went on, "Kingley is touting this guy Gage as one of his 'distinguished advisors,' but once the crap hits the fan, he's like 'Carlton who? Never heard of him.' It's like Kevin Spacey in Casino Jack: 'You're nobody in this town until you haven't met me.'"

More laughter. Stretch thumped the bar top, held up two fingers, and took the glass almost before the bartender finished pouring. It went down in a satisfying gulp but failed to dull his senses. The needling laughter of the lefty pricks came at him like a thousand knives stabbing at his every nerve ending, along with a barrage of arrows, aimed at the President but meant for Stretch as well . . .

O'Keefe: "The President is uneducable . . . "

Meadow: " . . . exactly what Secretary Crichton called him—Russia's puppet . . . "

Schnetzer: " . . . lacking any sense of control, discipline, or respect for the office he holds . . . "

Frome: " . . . self-destructive . . . "

Robertson: " . . . really shouldn't go back in there . . . "

Becklow: " . . . disturbing . . . "

Greenwood: " . . . far beyond Lincoln's depression . . . "

Wilton: " . . . batshit insane . . . "

O'Keefe: " . . . the most incompetent, most ignorant, most narcissistically self-absorbed president ever . . . "

Grimley: " . . . this guy in the mask, he's got the President's number, he's gunning for him, this is personal, and it ain't gonna end well . . . "

Stretch ran his fingers through his hair and expelled a wheezy sigh. He had to do something to control the situation. He had to do something to control the *President* before this thing went completely off the rails, and all that he'd fought for was lost. The country—*his* country, the United States of America—needed him now. The country needed him to step up and make the hero call. America needed a steady hand at the tiller to guide the ship to safety. America needed Stretch Biggerstaff to make the call that no one else could—or would—in this desperate hour.

America needed Stretch to take control, and there was only one way he could do it. If the President refused to listen to reason, Stretch would have to give him the proper *incentive* to listen to reason.

It was time for Plan B.

Rance Plebeius shot an odd side glance at the older man and said, "Your mood seems to have brightened."

With a queer smile, Stretch fished his mobile phone out of his pocket and said, "Maybe we'll take that walk around the Mall, after all."

"Really?"

Stretch shrugged as he typed a message on his phone and hit SEND. "Why not?"

Rance looked dubious, but he nodded with an awkward smile and said, "Well, OK then."

Stretch belted back one last shot, slapped the empty glass on the bar top, and turned to go.

With a tentative nod at Stretch's phone, Rance asked, "Who was that?"

Tucking the phone back into his pocket, Stretch said,

"Nobody. Just one of my guys at Beetlebart. Just letting them know I want to see any final copy on this before they post it."

The lie seemed to pacify the former chief of staff.

Stretch took the lead on their way out of the bar. As the brisk night air collided with his red face, he felt a surge of confidence . . . a confidence that was only bolstered by the image in his mind of the two words he'd typed into the message that he'd sent to his guy inside the White House. A simple command, yet loaded with far-reaching implications—and impossible to retract—the message read: "Do it."

B LAKE CRICHTON GAZED DOWN AT THE PRESIDENT FROM THE portrait in the ornate gilded frame that hung on the wall at the bottom of the grand staircase, just off the Entrance Hall. The former president looked impeccable in a tasteful dark suit and smartly knotted tie that kicked slightly to the left at the dimple and whose sky blue color matched his soul-probing gaze. Very solid-looking man, very presidential; the President could not deny this. But as he studied the portrait of the man who would have become the nation's first First Gentleman—had defeat not been snatched from the jaws of victory in a twist of fate that had stunned even the surprise winner himself—the President thought he detected the ghost of a smile at one corner of the former president's mouth. A sly smile, but not a cruel one—more like the sort of smile a good friend would give you as he steers you away from the cliff you're about to step off.

Careful what you wish for.

Blake Crichton had said that to him shortly after handing over the reins to the Texas bumpkin (*worst president ever—after Boyega, of course*, the President thought with a wistful sigh). They had run into each other, he and Crichton, at Shadow Creek, and over iced tea in the clubhouse, they had spoken about a possible future Kingley run for the White

House. Both of them had laughed about it, but Crichton had seemed to take it a bit more seriously, and offered a gentle caveat in his smooth Arkansas drawl: "Careful what you wish for . . . it may just come true."

Looking at that sly shadow of a smile now, the President couldn't help feeling that maybe he'd been had. Taken for a ride by the master himself—Bubba, The Big Dog, The Man From Hope, Black Blake (the first "black" president). Was it possible that he had been set up by the Crichtons? Could they have rigged up this whole thing from the very start? They were certainly spiteful enough, he knew that, without question, but had they actually set him up for this fall? Had they secretly wanted him to run for the presidency all along, egged him on, driven him to go for it, just so they could sit by and watch him fall flat on his face in front of the entire world? Was it possible that Hannah had entered the race with no intention of winning? Had it been her real goal all along to *let* him win, so that she and her perv husband could sit back and laugh at him as he floundered through the DC swamp and was dragged down by all the political sharks that they, the deceitful, nasty Crichtons, were so accustomed to swimming with? Could it be that all the while he'd thought *he* was playing *them*, it had, in fact, been the other way around?

The President's eyes narrowed as he contemplated the portrait of Blake Crichton. The Silver Fox—foxy, foxy man—with that hint of a smile curling at one corner of his duplicitous mouth, and that deceptively genial blue gaze.

Black Blake. The silver-tongued slickster had set him up cold. He and his crooked wife had *known* the presidency would prove an irresistible lure, and they had dangled it like a shiny object—a *golden* object—before his eyes, and he had pounced like a cat.

How could he have been so gullible? How could he have missed the signs? He had considered it a brilliant move to withhold his tax returns during the campaign, and despite the outcry from the media, he had still won. But now he could see the genius of the Crichtons' plan. Now he could see that this was precisely what the crooked Crichtons had *hoped* he would do. Unbelievably cunning, so like them; deceitful, sneaky, nasty people . . .

They had known all along that he would eventually be backed into this very corner and that all of his business dealings—which were *nobody's* business but his own—would be forced out into the open. What a devious web they'd spun to ensnare him—their vengeance knew no bounds. He could hardly believe that anyone could hate him so much that they would construct such an elaborate plot to take him down. And they'd had all the help they needed from the lying Liberal media, who had been in on the whole scheme from the start. They had set him up cold, and now they were all laughing at him.

The President's heart pounded like a great drum inside his chest as he continued to gaze at the portrait of Blake Crichton. He could scarcely believe that he'd ever counted this foxy false-faced man among his friends. How could he have ever trusted such a man? And he'd *voted* for him. *Twice.* What a terrible, terrible mistake that had been. The man was a disgrace, an absolute disgrace.

Blood thundered painfully—dizzyingly—at his temples, and his legs suddenly felt unsteady. The President sat down on the red-cushioned bench beneath Blake Crichton's portrait and dropped his face into his hands. He wanted so badly to rage, to tear down the portrait of Crichton and smash it to smithereens. He wanted to tear down *all* the former presidents' portraits and smash every last one of them because he was bigger and better and smarter than any of them. But he wasn't about to give them the satisfaction of another explosion. He was going to prove them wrong. All of them. He was going to be presidential. He was going to sit here under this fucking mocking portrait of Blake Crichton until he felt at least *equally* presidential to that lying, crooked, duplicitous perv.

The President's hands slid down his face, exposing a set of almost comically bulging eyes. He looked across the hall, at the iconic portrait of JFK with his arms folded under his chest, his head bowed in solitary contemplation.

That about sums it up, all right, he thought with a sigh.

He honestly couldn't recall a time he'd ever felt so alone. There had been so much support at the beginning—even when everyone was laughing at him for daring to enter the race and making fun of his descent on the escalator at Tower K. And that support had only grown with each knockout he'd scored in the primaries. What a happy time that had been—taking on Mini Mateo, Lyin' Tad, Lethargic Judd (boy, was he lethargic—they should've rented him out to insomniacs, he'd put them right to sleep), and Horse-face Corly (she really did have a terrible face—no one could look at that face and think, "Now, there's the face of a president!").

He smiled sadly. How he missed them all. Though he'd genuinely enjoyed knocking each and every one of them out of the race, he missed them now. They weren't really all that bad. Not really. They were just in his way. It was nothing personal, and he sincerely hoped they didn't hold it against him. He actually wouldn't mind hanging out with any one of them and sharing a few laughs over the whole thing. It was all in good fun, and they were all on the same side, anyway, right? Surely they weren't holding grudges. It would be nice to see them again. He would have to invite them for a little reunion in the rose garden some afternoon. They could all have a good laugh over the election. He'd show them that he was a good guy and that nothing he'd said during the heat of the campaign was meant to hurt any of them. He would even invite them to take a few jabs at him, and he would smile when they did it, to show them that he was a good sport and could take it as well as he could dish it out. It would be nice to be surrounded by friendly faces. It would be very nice.

But now it felt like he was all alone. The last man standing. Abandoned by those he'd trusted the most.

Faces flashed before his mind's eye, like shots popping up from an old slide projector: Jaden Chapins, Dustin Dumas, Moe Welsh—they'd all abandoned him. Weak men who could hardly be called men at all. Hell, even that obsequious little house elf, Jasper Sassy, hadn't run for cover. He'd turned tail when he'd recused himself from the Russia investigation, which he never should have done—what a terrible, disastrous move *that* was. But he hadn't run away— he'd threatened to, but he was still hanging in there. That little weasel knew which side his bread was buttered on, that was for sure. But the others—Chapins, Dumas, Welsh— they were pussies and traitors, every last one of them.

Not a single one of them had an ounce of the courage that mealy-mouthed little suckup Lúñez had, that was for sure. Lúñez had at least *tried*. His midnight run to the White House to dig up the dirt on that foul little Liberal slag, Sandra Price, had been a noble effort. National Security Advisor! Who the hell did *she* think she was kidding? She'd worked hand-in-fist with that duplicitous phony president, Boyega, to surveil Tower K during the election, and Lúñez proved it! And what did he get for his noble effort? They turned it all around on him and acted like *he* was the one who'd committed a crime, the pathetic bastard. Unbelievable.

The President sighed with a gleam in his eye. The memory of that night still gave him a tingle of pride. Lúñez had been like Paul Revere on his midnight ride, racing to save the day from tyranny and destruction. He'd failed, yes, but at least he'd tried. He'd even taken a crack at quashing that phony dossier—what a load *that* was! If the President had wanted to defile the Boyega's bed at the Ritz, he'd have whipped it out right there and taken the piss himself; he didn't need Russian hookers to do his dirty work for him.

The President shook his head. He supposed he could forgive Lúñez and Sassy both. They were weaklings—barely shadows of men, really—but they'd done pretty much all they could do, given their inherent limitations. Both would have made it pretty far on his old show, but neither would have made it to the final. He would have fired them gently, he supposed—no reason to kick a couple of lame mules that were already headed for the glue factory, anyway.

The real disappointment was Finch. He had been at the President's side right from the start, and he had turned on a dime the second things went south. That statement from his lawyer about having "a story to tell" and being "anxious to tell it"—just what the hell kind of loyalty was that? Finch had broken the President's heart with that little bombshell— broke it right in half and crushed the pieces under the heel of his jackbooted foot, the miserable old prick.

But Finch wasn't a worm, like Lúñez. Nor was he a jittery old maid, like Sassy. Finch didn't make idle threats. Finch *knew* things—more things than anyone else in the trusted inner circle knew, including Jake. Things that weren't bad, or illegal—at least not as far as he, the President, was concerned, they weren't—but things that could be twisted and warped to make him *look* bad, which is precisely what the dishonest media and his many, many enemies had wanted from the start. They were all such haters, riding the hate train, trying to topple him from the mountain. Unbelievable haters. Nasty—pathetic, really. And if push came to shove, Finch wouldn't hesitate to pick up a torch and pitchfork and join the angry mob of haters . . . and if *his* head ended up on the chopping block, Finch would bring down the whole house of cards with him. In a New York minute, he'd do it.

The President smiled a bitter smile of admiration. Love him or hate him, you had to respect that pinched-faced old bastard Monty Finch. The guy was a stone-cold, straight up, hard-core warrior with a real instinct for survival—his own. Finch knew the score. He wasn't the sort of player to take one for the team, and he certainly wasn't the sort to take one in the ass—for anybody. While the President admired these iron-fisted qualities, he could not deny that it would have made things much easier if Finch were more like Lúñez, or Sassy, or any of the countless other lemmings in his administration. But Finch was a powder keg on a short fuse, and as such, he needed to be handled with more than a modicum of caution.

If it came down to it, he would have to pardon Finch; that was a no-brainer. But there were others in the crosshairs—most notably, Jake and Roy Jr. were targets too, and the President sure as hell wasn't going to allow any member of his family to go to jail. Not with the power of the pardon at his disposal. Fuck that. The Liberal goon squad could do all the digging they wanted, but *nobody* from the Kingley family was going to prison, not while he still had the power of the pardon.

There was only one question. How many people could he get away with pardoning?

The power of the presidential pardon was absolute, he knew that much. But was it limitless? Could he just start pardoning people, left and right, and get away with it? Was there a magic number where somebody stepped in and cut you off like a drunk at a bar?

He had tried to look it up in the Constitution, but the stupid thing was written in that old-time double-talk that the founders wrote in to keep everybody guessing what they really meant. Just skimming the Constitution hurt his brain so badly that he'd actually considered calling the former president and asking him to decipher it—the guy had been a terrible president, possibly the worst ever, but no one could deny that he was really good at understanding all that Constitutional crap.

In the end, he hadn't called his predecessor for help. He'd gone online, and what he'd found had been just as confusing as the Constitution itself. *Everybody* had an opinion on the goddamn thing, and no two opinions agreed on anything—even Wikipedia couldn't give him a straight answer. Unbelievable!

The President sat forward now, his elbows on his knees, his fingers steepled beneath his chin, wondering how in hell he got into this mess. What had he done to deserve this? What could he *possibly* have done to deserve this complete and total mess? Could anyone tell him that?

The sensation of loneliness overtook him once again. And this time it threatened to suck him into the void . . . that dark, surreal place which hovered at the periphery of his subconscious during the few hours he spent each night when his mind and body became so exhausted that he had no choice but to cede control to the one thing he feared and loathed most. Sleep.

Pointless waste of time. Scientists should forget about all that climate change crap and come up with a pill to keep you awake twenty-four-seven, that's what they should do.

He closed his eyes and released a heavy sigh. He wasn't the sort of man who prayed, because prayer was for people too weak to make things happen on their own—no offense to any of them, and God bless them and all that, but praying just wasn't his thing. Never was. He never needed it.

But now things were different. Now maybe he *did* need a little help—maybe even more than a little. And so, with his eyes closed and his fingers laced beneath his chin, which seemed like the appropriate way to do it, he prayed.

Show me what to do, and I'll get it done. I'm a really smart guy, I've made a lot of money, built beautiful buildings all over the world—the best, the biggest, believe me, people come from all over to stay in my hotels and play golf on my courses, unbelievable courses, finest in the world, it's true—so just give me a sign, or even a nudge in the right direction, and I'll get it done. Just look at all I've achieved over the past three years, things that most presidents aren't capable of achieving in two whole terms! I'll get it done, I can get it done, just show me a sign, and I'll get it done.

He didn't know exactly how long it would take for an answer to come, but he figured it would be wise to wait at least a couple of minutes, so he silently counted the seconds by tapping the toe of one shoe on the marble floor.

He had reached nearly ninety seconds when a beautiful sound descended upon him, like music from heaven—not any of that flowery harp crap, either, but *real* music, the kind that sends a wave of tingles racing up your spine.

It took him a few seconds to realize that the music was not descending from someplace above but rather from the grand piano at the far end of the Cross Hall.

He sat still for a moment, listening to the haunting melody. Then he got up and headed down the hall.

When the piano came into view, the President halted and stepped behind one of the massive pillars, so that he could watch without being noticed.

Seated at the piano were his two youngest sons—Dane on the upper register, right-handed, and Barret on the lower, left-handed—working the keys in perfect tandem. They had gotten their hands from their respective mothers. Long, elegant fingers that moved with a fluidity that had always fascinated the President. None of his older children—not even Ilona—possessed an ounce of the natural grace that his two youngest boys did. Not one ounce.

The skillful movement of their fingers over the keys of the grand piano was so mesmerizing that the President stood frozen nearly a full minute before he reached for the mobile phone in his pocket.

The TuneSleuth app identified the piano piece as the "Main Title" of a film score: *The Usual Suspects*. The President vaguely remembered the movie. The non-pinko Baldwin brother was in it, but the rest of the cast was a bunch of Liberal losers. Especially that little rat bastard Spacey, who was good as the gimp in *Suspects* but sucked in that trashy little hatchet job on HBO. What a terrible show! Totally designed to undermine his presidency, that's all it was. Pathetic, really. They should have called it *House of Crap*. He should have sued HBO into bankruptcy for defamation, painting him out to be a psychotic homicidal narcissist with latent fag tendencies, repressed daddy issues, and an emotionally frigid, backstabbing wife. Well, maybe that was true of Iliana—God knew what a vengeful bitch she could be when the bug got up her ass—but the rest of his wives were all completely normal.

The President might have drifted off here and plunged into an internal rant about the low moral standards of HBO but for one thing: the evocative music echoing through the Cross Hall. That haunting theme from that so-so movie shifted his mood to a place where anger and frustration were subdued by an unfamiliar yet far more powerful emotion.

Though his first instinct was to recoil and resist this foreign emotion, he capitulated when a voice from deep within—one that he did not recognize as one of his own—beckoned him on with gentle persuasion. And soon, his vision was filled with the image of his boys, sitting side by side at the piano, striking chords so profoundly moving that for a terrifying series of seconds, the President actually feared for his next breath.

That breath finally came with a smooth exchange in the refrain, and as the President's lungs filled with fresh air, his sight shifted to Agent Hasney, who was standing nearby the piano, his deceptively calm eyes alert and ready for any eventuality.

The President had chosen well when he'd selected Hasney for this detail. He was a solid young man and a good influence. The President had been second-guessed for choosing someone so young to entrust with the safety of his youngest child, but he had picked the right guy for the job. Hasney would protect the kid with his life. He would protect both of them, Barret and Dane. The President had seen it in the young agent's eyes on that day in the Blue Room, and he could see it now. Agent Hasney was made of the stuff of heroes. A young man, not quite as experienced as the other agents, but a strong man, and he would protect the two boys sitting at the piano with his life. The President had never been more certain of anything. Never.

In his mind, the President could see the three of them, Hasney, Dane, and Barret, far away from the White House, someplace where no one could ever find them—including the President himself. A farm on some distant countryside with tons of land and a crystal clear lake and plenty of sunshine. Or maybe a tropical island, where the surrounding water was as clear and blue as the warm sky. He pictured the three of them, his two youngest boys and the agent who would guarantee their safety, living a life away from politics and industry and all the dirty things that are part and parcel of the "civilized" world. He pictured them carefree and happy and safe. He could set them up with new identities and more than enough money to last them a lifetime. *He* could be the hero in this one story. He could save these three young people, let the rest of the country fall into the shitter, but not these three. He could *save* them and keep them as pure and innocent as they were right now in this precious moment. He could do that. He was the most powerful man in the world. He could do it.

In a gentle flash, he could see them in this new life. His two boys, racing across the warm sand of the paradise he'd constructed in his mind, both of them laughing as their bare feet splashed through the incoming tide. Carefree and happy. He could not recall the last time he'd heard either of them laugh—certainly not Dane. But they *could* laugh again. They could laugh and play, as all boys should do, until they expended their seemingly endless supply of energy and collapsed on their beds for a long, restful sleep . . . with no bad dreams, no nightmares, no worries of what the next day would hold, because the next day would be filled with even more joy, more adventure, more *life*, the only way it can ever truly be experienced and appreciated: when you're young and healthy and free.

He could do it. He had the power to make it happen. It was the one accomplishment no one could deprive him of. The victory of his two youngest sons and their faithful young guardian and protector would be *his* victory. It would be his signature legislation, and he could do it without any approval from either of the do-nothing houses of Congress.

But not for glory. Not for accolades. Not even for the intoxicating thunder of applause from his base.

He would do it for posterity.

He would do it because someone had to survive and carry on, like Bergman in that movie about the Russian princess who'd survived the firing squad in the basement— what a brave girl, what a survivor. Unbelievable, but true.

The President's chest swelled with renewed purpose, and he raised his chin. But his moment of victory was cut short when he realized that he was no longer alone in the shadow of the pillar. He was flanked by the last two people he'd expected to find here in the Cross Hall on this night of national crisis.

To his right was his predecessor, President Boyega, and to his left was Hannah Crichton. Neither of them was here to gloat—a glance at their solemn faces told him that much— but they weren't here to wish him well on his plan to save his boys, either.

Boyega greeted the President in a warm yet formal manner: *Royal.*

The President hoisted his chin higher and turned his face away. "I'm not talking to you."

Hannah offered a sad smile and said, *Are you still talking to me?*

The President remained silent for a moment. Then he said, "Maybe. If you're willing to admit that I won."

With the expression of a weary yet indulgent mother, Hannah Crichton sighed. *Oh, Royal, is that what you really want?*

The President looked like a stubborn teenager who had no clue what he wanted.

Hannah eyed him for a moment. Then with a look at the boys across the hall, she rephrased the question: *What do you want for them?*

The hard edge of the President's gaze softened as he looked at his sons. "You know what I want. You're not really here—I'm not crazy, I know that much. You're just in my head, so you already know what I want. Don't play games with me."

Hannah shrugged. It was true—her appearance here was indeed merely in the President's mind. But as long as she was here, she might as well be honest. *While it's very noble, and I'm proud of you for putting your boys ahead of your own interests, it's not a very realistic option . . . but then, I'm guessing you already know that.*

The President knew it. He didn't like it—and he certainly didn't like having it confirmed, even if the person confirming it was only a figment of his imagination—but he knew it, all right.

Hannah waited a respectful moment before giving him a nudge: *They're young, Royal. And you know what the remarkable thing about young people is?*

The President didn't respond, but he was still listening.

The remarkable thing is their capacity to accept change, said Hannah. *They're not only open to it; they're eager for it. All they need is for someone to come along and offer them something new. Something special. They're so ready and eager for that change. And if you reach deep enough, you can find that kid that's still there inside of you, who's just as eager to make a change.*

The President looked at his boys with a hope in his heart

that he'd never felt so strongly before—not even back when he was a kid himself, filled with such longing and hope that he could scarcely breathe.

With his heart trying to pound a hole through his chest, he shook his head. If he reached out for that glimmer of hope only to have his hand slapped away . . . that was something he could not risk. To be rejected was one thing, but the humiliation of being rejected by someone who owed you his very life . . . that was something he could not abide.

Hannah smiled her sad motherly smile again. *Oh, Royal, that's the only risk truly worth taking. And it offers the greatest reward.*

The President's gaze remained locked on the boys who sat at the piano, playing that beautiful music. The little guy was still at the age where it was acceptable to get a hug from his old man, but the older boy wasn't. The President couldn't remember the last time he'd affectionately mussed that kid's hair and pulled him in for a hug. He couldn't remember the last time he'd seen the kid smile either. Probably years. As he recalled, it had been a somewhat sly and rather infectious smile, full of joy, with just a hint of mischief curling at the corners. But it had been ages since he'd last seen it. Something had changed when the boy reached his teens. The endearing smile had been replaced by a recalcitrant scowl; the bright light in the eyes had dimmed to a brooding gaze that bordered on defiance.

Of course, it had been the same with all of his children; they'd all loved him when they were little, hated him when they became teens, and then came back to loving him again once they'd grown up and got their heads screwed around straight.

But Dane was different. His older boys had feared him—he had seen it in their eyes whenever he'd threatened either physical or financial retribution. But Dane feared neither threat. You could knock him to the floor, and he'd get right up and spit in your face. You could lay a pile of money on the table, and he'd drop a lit match to it and give you his best "fuck you" glare over the flames. This wasn't hyperbole on the President's part either—he'd actually caught the kid burning a stack of cash, withdrawn from an ATM on the debit card the President had given him for his thirteenth birthday. It had taken both Roy Jr. and Merrick to pry his hands from the kid's throat. But even through the red rage of his blurred vision, Royal Kingley had clearly seen that there was no fear in the kid's eyes.

Thinking back on that moment, the President felt a grudging twinge of admiration. Not for the act of burning the money—any idiot with a loose screw could do that—but for the balls it had taken for the kid not to run away when he'd been caught. For the sheer brass balls it had taken for that skinny thirteen-year-old kid to stand there and give The Man that "fuck you and your money" glare. No matter how deeply it stung—and it still stung very deeply—the President could not deny that the kid had solid brass balls, that was for sure.

Standing in the shadow of the pillar now, with Hannah Crichton patiently waiting for his response, the President tried to imagine walking up to the piano and ruffling that shiny dark mop of hair, maybe even giving the boy a one-armed hug. But the image blurred in his mind, and he had to shake his head to clear his vision.

"You don't have boys," he said aloud. "You don't know what it's like . . . "

But suddenly he wasn't so sure about that. Maybe Hannah *did* know. After all, mothers had a connection with their children that fathers could never know or understand. It was a total mystery.

Hannah's eyes were smiling with a subtle yet knowing sparkle.

"Don't give me that look," the President said stubbornly.

And now her mouth was smiling too; that infectious smile that you couldn't help but return.

"What do you want me to do? What can I do? I'm not a mind reader. Tell me what to do, and I'll do it." He waved off her smile and turned to President Boyega. "I mean, can you believe this? I should have gone with you and given *her* the cold shoulder. Unbelievable."

He shook his head and looked back at Hannah. She didn't respond, but her eyes urged him on, gently so, toward the boys. But his feet were frozen to the spot; his hands hung useless at his sides.

You can do it. You just have to trust your heart.

The President didn't like that idea—he'd always had better luck with his gut than his heart. But when he turned his gaze back to the boys, he could feel the lock release on his frozen legs, and he could feel his heart hammering like a great drum, each thunderous beat driving him closer to the prize that both frightened and thrilled him. He *could* do it. He was strong enough to do it. This was his moment . . .

But before he got the chance to take that first crucial step forward, the phone in his hand buzzed with an incoming text message from Franco.

ARE YOU THERE, SIR?

The President replied: I'M BUSY.

YOU WANTED TO KNOW WHEN SPENCER GOT BACK.

The President hesitated and then typed: AND?

HE'S BACK. HE SAYS HE'S GOT SOMETHING YOU NEED TO HEAR.

WHAT IS IT?

I DON'T KNOW.

WELL, ASK HIM.

I CAN'T. HE'S INDISPOSED.

WHAT THE FUCK DOES THAT MEAN?

A few seconds passed before Franco's response.

HE'S IN THE TOILET.

The President rolled his eyes.

DO YOU WANT ME TO HAVE HIM CALL YOU WHEN HE COMES OUT?

The President paused and then typed: IS IT A NUMBER ONE OR TWO?

Franco's reply took a few more seconds.

HE'S BEEN IN THERE FOR A WHILE.

The President rolled his eyes again. It was like he'd hired a clown show to run his administration. Unbelievable.

Franco sent another message: SHOULD I HAVE HIM CALL YOU DIRECTLY WHEN HE'S DONE?

The President hesitated before sending his response: FORGET IT. I'LL BE RIGHT THERE.

He dropped the phone back into his pocket and took one last look at his boys. The tune had reached its final crescendo and was winding down to its mournful closing bars.

The President did not look to his left before leaving the Cross Hall. He couldn't bear seeing that sad motherly look of Hannah Crichton's again. He couldn't bear knowing that she was right, that what was happening here and now with his boys—this simple moment of perfection—was infinitely more important than anything that was waiting for him back in the Oval Office.

His mother used to say, *There are things a woman knows that no man should ever know.*

His father used to say, *Women reflect; men take action.*

And with those axioms in mind, the President did not look back as the final piano chord struck and echoed through the Cross Hall. He did not see the proud smile on Dane's face as the older boy pulled little Barret into a one-armed hug. He did not see their heads nodded together as they sat side by side on the piano bench. He did not see this tender moment of brotherly love between his two youngest sons.

He did not see them.

V ITALY TEPES SWIRLED HIS GLASS OF VODKA IN AN ARTFUL circle as he gazed at the television with a languid yet shrewd expression. There were those in the Kremlin who still found the outlandish behavior of the American president amusing, and they continued to refer to him as the *"Oranzhevaya Marionetka"* in the firm belief that President Tepes was pulling the strings from above. Tepes did not bother to correct them—the perception of his power, particularly through the eyes of his subordinates, only lent credence to the illusion; and like any prestidigitator worthy of his cape and wand, Vitaly Tepes was not about to pull back the curtain and reveal how the trick was done.

But watching what the American political strategist Mick Wilton so aptly referred to as the "shitshow" unfold on live television, Tepes felt anything *but* in control. Indeed he believed it may be time to cut the strings and let the *Oranzhevaya Marionetka* fall limp to the stage—and further, that it may be time to proffer a deal to cooler minds within the American political system. An irresistible quid pro quo. He could leak a small taste of what he had to offer them. And then, in exchange for the lifting of certain sanctions upon his country, he could present them with the head of the dragon who'd been scorching their land over the seemingly endless period of time following that fateful Election Day.

Of course, he would admit to nothing, and there would be no reprisals against him or any of his people. He would simply say that, through the diligence of his own investigation into the disruption of the American presidential election, his top agents in the FSB had uncovered information damning to the sitting President of the United States. There would be videos, of course; along with dossiers, complete with corroborating testimony from eyewitnesses, dates and times and names, financial transactions, all recorded in well-kept journals, with complementing photos and sound recordings, all completely verifiable. And of course, Russia would be credited for aiding the United States in its time of need—that would be nonnegotiable.

Vitaly Tepes sipped his vodka and thought it was a workable solution. Perhaps it was time for the curtain to fall on the shitshow.

Tepes was still looking at the television and working out the details in his mind when his mobile phone buzzed on the table beside him. It was a transatlantic call, with no name attached to it, but he recognized the number and picked up on the third ring. In his customary fashion, he put the phone to his ear without speaking.

The caller was young and spoke perfect Russian, even though he had lived in America since he was nine years old. His mother had been a devoted acolyte of Tepes; a beautiful girl with stunning hazel eyes named Olya, who had given birth to a beautiful baby boy with equally stunning hazel eyes. Tepes had sent both mother and son to live in America fifteen years ago and had personally paid their modest living expenses. The boy had been raised as an American but had privately been trained by a Russian operative Stateside. By the age of thirteen, the boy had not only become proficient enough in American English to blend in as one of their own; he had also developed into an expert at hand to hand combat, with a decided affinity for knives. Tepes's man Stateside had given the boy a backstory and put him into play shortly after Kingley had taken the Republican nomination.

Tepes hadn't known with one hundred percent certainty that the *Oranzhevaya Marionetka* would take a liking to the young man. But with the boy's clean-cut "all-American" good looks, tall frame, and deceptively gracious personality, the wily Russian president had fairly high confidence that his soon to be American counterpart would usher the trojan horse inside the gates without suspicion. After all, the boy looked like he'd come "straight out of central casting," as the Americans would say.

In the end, Tepes's bet had paid off. And now the nine-year-old boy he'd seen such promise in fifteen years earlier was calling him from inside the White House, where he was not only a member of the inner circle, he was one of the few the President truly trusted with all his heart.

The young man spoke in a casual manner, but the ominous undertone did not escape his mentor.

"Mr. Red has requested our assistance on a troubling board. If the white king is protected by one of his pawns, should the black knight retreat and regroup, or proceed to B-2?"

Tepes was silent for a long moment. The young man at the other end of the call waited patiently; he was neither impetuous nor impudent.

Tepes drew a short breath and queried, "Is the pawn protected?"

"Yes."

Tepes paused briefly. "By the queen or the knight?"

"The knight. The queen is out of play."

Tepes gave the scenario consideration. Taking out the queen was not an option—indeed it would be a prelude to war. But a knight was different. Americans, who foolishly valued icons over assets, would not only accept the sacrifice of their noble knight, they would *revel* in it. Tepes, who knew the value of a knight, wasn't so quixotic; he would sacrifice his own queen without hesitation.

Tepes gazed at his glass of vodka with a coolly thoughtful expression. A successful execution could rein in the problem quite nicely . . . and very likely give him far more than he could get out of any deal with the rational *Amerikanskiy politiki*.

Tepes swirled his drink again, watching with lazy eyes as the vodka licked the curved inner wall of the glass. It would be a stark message to send, but once it was received, the pawn would be returned, unharmed, of course—there was no reason to get overly theatrical. All that mattered was that the puppet understood how far-reaching the puppet master's grasp was. Once the master's dominance was established, the strings could be pulled with relative ease to make the *Oranzhevaya Marionetka* dance to a more pleasing tune.

Tepes took another breath, deeper this time, and said, "Does Mr. Red understand the implications of his request?"

"I don't think so," the young man replied.

Tepes almost smiled. The fat, red-faced American had always been his favorite—just enough sense to know when to keep his mouth shut, and not enough to know what was actually going on; it would have been so much easier had *he* been the candidate instead of the bolshy orange blowhard.

Tepes spoke clearly into the phone, "Then the black knight should take out the white knight and secure the pawn." When no response came, Tepes said, *"Da?"*

The response came immediately this time: *"Da, Papá."*

Vitaly Tepes smiled at the unexpected endearment. He'd lain with the boy's mother on more than one occasion, but other men had lain with her, too; he'd never had the test done, so he supposed it was a coin flip. Still, a part of him liked to believe that he saw a reflection of himself in that tall and handsome boy with those steely eyes.

In English, Tepes said, "OK. Bye-bye."

S PENCER MAHLER CAME FROM THE BATHROOM AT THE SAME moment the President entered the hallway. By the look of the little balding man, the President presumed it must have been a particularly grueling number two. Despite his sickly pallor, there was a fire in Mahler's lazy eyes that crackled with excitement. The President didn't like making physical contact with people who'd just been in the toilet, so he refrained from clapping Mahler on the shoulder and drawing him in for a handshake as was his custom when greeting confidants, especially ones bringing him information. Instead, he stopped a few paces shy of the smaller man and gazed down his nose at him with narrowed eyes.

Mahler was too fired up to notice. With a proud grin, he said, "Are you ready for this? The Deputy Director of the CIA—Hartman, you know him? Yeah, well, he's running a dark op out of that place—HiroBot—with some Middle Eastern kid, and a German, I think, running the whole thing." His eyes flared. "They've got a whole computer setup, with all these lines aimed at the White House. Like a targeting simulation or something. They've got like a mini tiger, or a bobcat or something—it was huge—guarding them." His eyes suddenly narrowed, and he lowered his voice to a conspiratorial whisper. "Hartman called me and told me to get out of there. He said that *he* was in charge and that if you had a problem with that, you could take it up with him. He said, 'The President knows where to reach me.' He said it just like that. Can you believe—"

The President cut him off. "Yeah, whatever. What about this viral game thing?"

"Virtual," Mahler corrected.

The President made a face and waved him off like an errant fly. "Virtual, viral, whatever. What did you find out about it?"

Mahler blinked in confusion. "I thought you said you didn't—"

"Yeah yeah yeah, forget what I said. Is this virtual-viral thing dangerous? Could it hurt Jake? Could it kill him?" The President snapped his fingers in front of Mahler's eyes. "Give me the straight dope. Can this freak in the mask fuck Jake up with his little toy, or not?"

Mahler stuttered for a second and then relayed everything Thackery had told him about the game unit.

"So, what you're telling me is, everything that's happening in there is all in Jake's head, like a movie?"

"A 3-D movie, yes."

"And when the game stops, this 'movie' stops, and Jake is fine—no damage, no pain, no nothing—he's good to go like it never happened, is that it?"

"Yes . . . according to the Middle Eastern kid. But don't you think we should—"

The President waved him off again. "That's good enough." He shot a hot breath out of his nose, and with his eyes teeming darkly, he released a mirthless chuckle and muttered, "I got this little prick, oh, I got him, all right. Wants to fuck with *me*? I got you, True Son. I *got* you, punk. You wanna play in the big boy sandbox? You got it."

Mahler said, "Yes, sir, but don't you think we should look into this dark op they're running? Maybe you should call the deputy director yourself—"

The President snapped his fingers, silencing Mahler, and turned to Franco to ask if he knew anything about a dark op being run out of the gaming company in Maryland, but he stopped short when he saw the guilty look in Franco's eyes. "*Et tu*, Franco?" he asked with a sad smile, then shook his head and sighed. "So much for front-stabbing, eh?"

Franco looked ashamed, but he did not avert his gaze.

The President rolled his eyes and expelled a heavy sigh. "First in line, last to know—what else is new?" He shook it off; he had bigger fish to fry. "Get in touch with Hartman. Whatever he knows, I want to know it the minute he knows it. Don't call. Text me. Can you manage that while you're pulling the knife out of my back, Franco?"

"Yes, Mr. President."

The President shook his head and sighed again. "Jesus, fuck me, I've got the weight of the entire world on my shoulders—is there anyone I can trust around here?"

Mahler raised his chin as he looked up at his boss with unflinching loyalty. Under normal circumstances, the

President would have been pleased by such an open display of fealty, but with everything that was going on, the best he could manage was a sickly half-smile that looked more like a grimace. Besides, he just couldn't shake the image his mind had conjured of Mahler in the john. Could there possibly be anything more disgusting, or pathetic, than a sweaty little balding guy squatting and squeezing one out in your private toilet? Honestly. Unbelievable.

MIRIAM RIVERS, THE DEMOCRATIC REPRESENTATIVE FROM California's 43rd district, had witnessed her fair share of crazy in her forty-six years of public service, but what she had witnessed so far tonight certainly took the cake. In her opinion, it was an abomination, and she wasn't about to sit idly by and watch Olympus burn. Somebody had to speak up, and more importantly, speak out against the man who was tearing the very fabric of the nation apart while shredding the Constitution. So, with a straight spine and an indignant glare, Miriam looked directly into the camera and spoke her mind.

"Let me be very clear, Rowan," she said. "This president does not represent me, and he certainly does not represent the majority of the American people, who *did not vote for him*. I've said over and over that he does not deserve the presidency, and I've said over and over that I do not honor him, I do not respect him. He is a morally bankrupt, reprehensible flimflam man who has zero respect for the rule of law and not one single iota of understanding when it comes to the Constitution of the United States of America. His disgraceful behavior toward women, minorities, the LGBTQ community, Latinos, Muslims, African Americans, is appalling. And now he's on TV, goading a terrorist into doing harm to an American citizen! His own *son-in-law*—a criminal, who, rightfully, should be sent to prison for his own criminal actions, but an American citizen, nonetheless. And the

President is in there goading this terrorist on like he's the caller at a Louisiana cockfight! It's a travesty—he's gonna get that young man killed!"

Rowan Meadow moved to respond, but Miriam scarcely took a breath before continuing with vigor.

"And I'll tell you something else, Rowan. I don't believe this president is in his right mind! There is something seriously wrong going on up there in his head! You can see it in his eyes. He's like a crazy man, carrying on about Hitler and little green men and whatnot. Now, some people may find that funny, but I *do not*. I find it disturbing and frightening. This is not the kind of talk you hear from a stable person! I have been saying it since the beginning that he needs to be removed from office and that he should be convicted and sent to prison, but now I seriously believe this man needs to see a psychiatrist! This is not the behavior of a normal person, and it is completely unbecoming to the presidency! We need to see this for what it is: the final straw. How much more of this insanity are we going to take? When are Republicans going to stand up, put partisan politics aside, and say, 'Enough is enough, it's time to take our government back from this crazy man!'—when is that going to happen, I ask you, when?"

Rowan Meadow was silent, along the others in both the New York and D.C. studios.

"We have children here," Miriam went on. "There are hundreds and hundreds of young people gathered in the cold on the Mall at our nation's Capitol. They've been gathered like a vigil out here in the cold, waiting and watching all night, if you haven't noticed, which I'm sure you have. But have we heard one word from this president? Does he even care? I think not! Something is happening in America. Right now. And this president is turning a blind eye to it. These children are out there watching right now. They are looking to the President of the United States, and he's turning a blind eye to them."

In the Pennsylvania local news studio, Ron Lybender smiled and said, "Well, he *is* in the middle of a crisis here—"

"That's poppycock, Ron Lybender," Miriam snapped, "and you know it! This president isn't doing anything that couldn't be done better and resolved quicker by far more experienced people than him. All he's doing is stirring the pot and spouting off crazy talk about things he knows nothing about like he's back on that ridiculous reality show of his. Well, let me tell you something: he's *not*. And this isn't a TV show. This is real life, with real lives hanging in the balance, and the last thing we need is some crazy man piping off about Hitler's brain being invaded by little green men! We need a leader, not some sideshow snake oil salesman, promising rain in the middle of a drought!"

Lybender's cheeks burned red.

Chase Grimley grinned. "Better to quit while you're ahead, Lybender." He turned a serious eye to the monitor that featured Congresswoman Rivers. "Miriam, I gotta tell you, I agree with you on this one. I've been telling these guys here, and I'm not sure they believe me, but I'm with you. There's something up with these kids out there on the Mall. They're out there for a reason. They *want* something from this president, and they ain't gonna leave until they get it. It's goddamn eerie—pardon my French, but it's true. Any thoughts?"

"Yes," Miriam said flatly. "It's time to end this presidency and get this crazy man out of the White House before he can do any more damage!"

Chase laughed, but not unkindly, and aside to Elwood Robertson, he said, "She's not gonna let that one go, is she?"

With a soft chuckle, Elwood said, "I don't think so."

Chase turn back to the monitor. "You're a tough lady, Miriam, and I say that with all respect. You have the courage of your convictions, which is more than I can say about most in either house of Congress. You speak from the heart, and you don't let anyone push you around, that's for sure . . . "

Leonard O'Keefe cut in suddenly. "My apologies to Congresswoman Rivers—and to you, as well, Chase—for interrupting, but I'm being told we've just received word from Kayley Tru at the White House that the President has returned to the Oval Office. I don't know if we have the live shot up yet—never mind, there it is. And as you can see, the President is back, and it looks like he's waiting. There's music coming from the speakers—I don't know if you can hear it—but the TV screen above the mantel is dark. It looks like someone has cleared away the remains of the television the President smashed earlier and replaced it with a new one. We don't know if this new television was delivered—though, I don't suppose any stores are open at this hour of the night—or brought in from another room in the White House. Perhaps they keep a supply on hand in the event of a presidential tantrum. Who knows? All we do know is that there's a new television in the Oval Office, and the President is there, waiting for round three to begin. For those of you who haven't been keeping score, so far the President is 'O for two' in this heads-up battle of the wits, and he looks to be headed for a complete shutout."

Chase barked a laugh. "You're brutal, Leonard! But it's the truth. The President—for whatever reason, his ego, his temperament, his complete and thorough lack of knowledge on even the most basic historical facts, call it whatever you like—the President is simply no match for this guy in the mask. He's like Mozart cringing in the shadows when Salieri shows up at the door dressed in his dead father's cloak and mask. This guy—and I don't even know if you can rightfully call him a terrorist, because he hasn't made a threat against us, the nation; all he's done so far is verbally slap the President's ears back—"

Lybender scoffed in disbelief. "He's kidnapped and tortured the President's son-in-law!"

"With a *toy*, Lybender," Chase nearly squealed. "With a virtual reality toy! I don't know, looks to me like the Latner kid needs to grow a pair, I don't know. I'm not saying I approve of this, I'm not saying that. But the fact is this 'terrorist' hasn't made a single threat against the country. He's made the President look like a stooge—as if the President needs any help in *that* department—and that's about it. If he wanted to do any real damage, he'd have already done it. This is not what it seems. Something is very fishy about this. Forgive me if I sound like a broken record—I know I've already said this, but I'm gonna say it again because it bears repeating: something is *off* here. I'm not saying it isn't serious—it's goddamned serious. But I've been around the block a few times, and I've picked up a thing or two along the way. Laugh all you want, but mark my words, before the curtain falls on the final act, jaws will be dropping on the floor, and *yours* will be one of them, Lybender."

Ron Lybender shook his head but remained silent.

Chase Grimley chewed at the corner of his mouth, a troubled look in his eye, as if he had the key but was still searching for the lock.

"I've got a bad feeling about this," he said, shaking his head. "Something isn't right, I can feel it in my gut. This guy in the mask *wants* something. He wants something he can only get from this president, and I don't think the President is either willing or able to give it to him. And when this guy figures that out—and he will, mark my words, he's a very smart cookie—that's when the floor's going to drop out of the room . . . and when *that* happens, you better be holding onto something because it's gonna be a hell of a drop, with no bottom in sight."

T RENT MICHAEL HAD SEEN SOME PRETTY FRIGHTENING IMAGES through the lens of his camera over the years—from the collapse of the World Trade Center to countless firefights in the Middle East that had followed in the aftermath of that tragedy. But with all due respect to those horrific events,

Trent believed the image he was recording right now was perhaps the most frightening of all.

Terrorist attacks occurred on a fairly regular basis all over the globe, and firefights in the Middle East were practically a mainstay. But this was different. This was something you didn't see every day. This was something no one had ever witnessed in the two hundred and forty-three-year history of the nation: the complete meltdown of a sitting president, broadcast on live television to the entire world. And every moment of it was being recorded by Trent's camera. It was, Trent thought as he pulled focus on the President gazing up at the widescreen TV above the mantel, a mind-blowing event.

The Oval Office was deathly silent now, save for the soft, steady sound of the grandfather clock against the west wall, its long golden pendulum ticking away the seconds while the press corps waited with expressions ranging from cautious anticipation to palpable apprehension. To the casual channel-surfer, particularly one with no knowledge of all that had transpired throughout the evening, the tableau of transfixed reporters in the Oval Office might have seemed a bit queer, even comical. But to the devoted viewers who had been watching from the very start, this surreal moment was the final act of a series finale that everyone, at home and abroad, would surely be talking about for many days, perhaps even years, to come.

The breathless silence continued as the President and True Son gazed at one another from their respective "corners" as if waiting for the bell to start round three of the match. Tracking in for a close-up of the President, Trent had the odd feeling that "round three" had already begun. With his chin held high and his narrowed eyes gazing stubbornly down the bridge of his nose, the President looked more like an obstinate child locked in a staring match with an adult than the most powerful leader in the world facing a foreign enemy. The moment went on so long that Trent began to believe these adversaries would turn to stone before giving in to each other.

From her place at the front of the press corps, Kayley Tru, who'd followed the President's rise more closely than any other reporter in the room, had no such illusion. She knew precisely which of the two opponents would crack and speak first, and silently in her head, she counted down the seconds. The damn broke a few beats ahead of her count, but the ensuing flood was just as she'd expected.

"You know what really gets to me?" said the President with an oddly wistful look in his eyes. "What gets to me is that when all of this is over, when I get you—and believe me, True Son, I'm gonna get you . . . sooner than you think, actually—when all of this is over, and you're in custody or dead, probably dead, you guys aren't really very good at being taken alive, you like that whole martyrdom thing with the forty virgins and all—" The President rolled his eyes, like the mere thought of dying for a cause was the silliest thing he'd ever heard. "—but what gets to me, and this is true, very-very true, is that after I take you out and prove to the entire world that I have what it takes, that I have both the power and the brains to get this job done, after I do that, when they see your corpse being hauled out of that rat hole you're hiding in, when they see you getting zipped up in a body bag . . . they'll go right back to this whole fake news Russia thing, or the Ukraine quid pro quo lie— terrible lie, there was *no quid pro quo*—I never even spoke to that Stravinski guy—or some other made-up bullshit. Unbelievable, eh?"

The President's gaze swept over the press corps before homing in on Kayley Tru. He shook his head with the sorrowful eyes of a disappointed father, and then looked away as if it hurt too much to see what she'd become.

To True Son, he said, "Can you believe these vultures? I'm gonna hand them your head on a plate—no offense, I know you're a patriot in your grubby little country and just doing your duty, and I respect that, believe me—but I'm gonna hand them your head on a plate, and your filthy black heart on a stick, and what are they gonna do in return? They're gonna rev up the old fake news machine and go right back to hammering me on this totally phony, completely made up Russian collusion thing."

The President switched gears abruptly, and spoke directly into Trent Michael's camera: "Russia, if you're listening, I don't know you, I don't *want* to know you, and I have no interest in colluding with you, OK? None whatsoever, OK? And as soon as I'm done dealing with this little terrorist dirtbag here, I'm gonna sign an executive order for more sanctions. Believe me, I'm gonna do it. Believe me."

He turned back to True Son and shook his head.

"Unbelievable. I can't win this rigged game. I came to drain the swamp, and they sucked me right into the muck. If it's not this Russia crap, it's the Senate—you see how that weasely turtle McTory turned on me? We were *that* close to repealing the disaster that is BoyegaCare, and that miserable old prick backs off, and now millions of decent Americans are going to die when BoyegaCare implodes. I wanted to prevent that. I could have done it too, if it wasn't for McTory and that pathetic old geezer, McQueen, with his grandstanding play on the Senate floor. Did you see him? Holding a hand up to stop the roll call as if *he* was the president! He had his chance and lost . . . to Boyega, of all people! War hero! He was captured—what's heroic about that? Yeah, I said it. I'm the only one in this town with the balls to say it. And he sure as hell ain't presidential, believe me, OK?"

The President shook his head again, while all looked on in silence.

"And if it's not Russia or the health care mess or that quid pro quo crap—none of which have anything to do with me—they'll jump onto one of the other nine hundred fake news stories. They've got a million of 'em, I'm telling you, these vultures feed on this stuff like rotten red meat, they can't get enough, nasty, vicious animals, every one of them . . . "

The President cast a shrewd eye up at the screen, where True Son stood stoically silent, and grinned.

"You're taking this silent treatment pretty far. What? You don't have any more wisdom for me? No more wiseass comebacks for me? Are you still upset because I blew off a little steam? Did that scare you when I got a little crazy with the TV? Or aren't you tuned in to the news? A smart guy like you probably has a whole bank of TVs there with all the news channels running—the fake news right alongside the real news. I only watch FIX; the rest are run by Liberal elites and pinko demigods. You remember that crazy socialist they had running against Shady Hannah in the primaries? A *socialist!* Can you believe that? He almost beat her too, and if she hadn't pulled her dirty sneaky crooked tactics on him—she's a very sneaky and crooked woman, nasty, really—he *would* have beat her, poor old loony bastard. I'd have beat him, anyway, of course—the electoral college loves me, absolutely loves me—but boy did Shady Hannah do a number on him! Crazy Benny, I call him, good old Crazy Benny—guy's like a thousand years old and still kicking, can you believe it? And he's back! And he's gunning for *me*, if you can believe that. They're all gunning for me: Crazy Benny, Sacheen Littlefeather, Sleepy Jocko Borden—talk about old, he was ancient when he was Boyega's VP! They even got a little token gay guy—Mayor Pat! Lil Mayor Pee Wee, I call him. He's a tiny guy but a tough one, looks like one of those Whos from that creepy Grinch movie—remember that movie? Creepy as shit, disturbing, really." He shook his head and released a sigh. "I don't know, after he loses, maybe they can make him Mayor of Whoville or something, he's *tiny*, you could put him in your pocket. Military guy—didn't see any action, probably didn't meet the height requirement, but whatever . . . yeah, they're all gunning for me, all the loonies, liars, and losers . . . "

The President waited for True Son's response, but nothing came from the man behind the mask.

The President's lips curled into a sly smile. "Don't you want to play anymore, True Son?"

True Son remained silent.

"Come on," the President coaxed with a chuckle, "I'm giving you gems here. Do your thing, spin it on me, I can take it, I'm a big boy. Come on, take your best shot, hit me right here." He thumped his chest. "Hit me with some more of your cool terrorist wisdom, blind me with all those facts, you walking thesaurus. Come on, I'm ready for round three and raring to go . . . "

Kayley Tru's eyes narrowed. With his predilection for obfuscation, it was often difficult to chart a path between the President's rhetoric and his intent. But with the not-so-subtle warning he'd already telegraphed—*believe me, True Son, I'm gonna get you . . . sooner than you think, actually*—Kayley got the distinct feeling that the President was not engaging in off-the-cuff hyperbole this time. And her read was correct. There was a real purpose in the President's gaze. He was deliberately attempting to provoke the terrorist into another dialogue. But why?

It didn't take long for the answer to come to her, and when it did, Kayley Tru felt a chill ascend her spine.

I'm gonna get you . . . sooner than you think, actually.

The CIA must have found a lead—a solid one—and the President was stalling, trying to goad the terrorist into another back and forth as a diversionary tactic, trying to distract him and give the cavalry enough time to move in. The thought both thrilled and frightened Kayley at once.

"Come on," said the President with a sweeping gesture to the press corps. "Tell me how to get these filthy vultures here, with their sick, twisted facts, off my back. Tell me that, Mr. Know-It-All-Smart-Guy."

The silence that followed seemed infinite, but in truth, it lasted only seconds.

.T. HOLDEN

Then True Son spoke.

"You can't," he said matter-of-factly.

The President's features shifted at the unexpected response. Then he regained his composure and smiled again. "Yeah, why's that?"

True Son said, "You've already triggered the dominoes, and there's no way to break the chain reaction."

The President pushed a sigh out of his nose. "What, when I fired Brushing?"

"No," True Son said simply.

"No?" the President asked with a faltering yet dangerous smile. "When did I trigger the dominoes then, smart guy?"

True Son waited a measured moment before replying.

"When you announced your candidacy."

The President's features froze. "Really?"

"You had the chance to break the chain over the course of the election, by bowing out. There was already an investigation into possible collusion between your campaign and the Russians, but you'd likely have skirted any charges stemming from that."

"You're goddamn right I would have. Because there's nothing there."

True Son continued as if he hadn't been interrupted. "But once you took the oath, your fate was sealed."

The President's eyes flashed darkly. "The hell it is. *I* control my fate. *I* got all the cards here. Nobody can touch me. The gate is secure."

"The gate has already been breached. You're in check right now. You have a few moves left, but eventually, it will be mate and game."

"I don't play chess."

"But your opponent does."

"Who? Tepes?"

True Son didn't respond, but a dim shaft of overhead

light glanced off the glossy surface of the left eye of his mask like a surreptitious wink.

The President scoffed. "Are we talking about Nervous Noreen and her clown car of House committees? She already had her shot at me with that bogus impeachment of hers, but she got shot down like a low-flying bird. Clipped her wings but good. Little Nervous Nasty Noreen ain't gonna be circling above my rain barrel anytime soon. She's still licking her wounds, believe me. Totally embarrassed in front of the entire world—she had it coming, that one, nasty woman . . . nasty-*nasty* woman . . . I took her out just like I took out that creepy old prick Boris Karloff—Special Counsel! What was so special about him? Digging into financial records that are nobody's business but mine—him and that laughable little grand jury of his. You see him testifying before that bogus committee? He's not all there, believe me, very unstable man . . .

"'A systematic and sweeping fashion!' he says—the only thing systematic and sweeping is the way he tried to railroad me out of the White House. And look at what it got him: I'm still here, and he's out on his ass with egg on his face, miserable old prick. Slid right across the Teflon coating of my frying pan and into the fire . . . after he completely and totally exonerated me, of course."

"Are you certain of that?" True Son inquired.

"Dead certain," said the President. "It's right there in his bloated report."

"Which, I gather you've read thoroughly."

The President pressed his lips together and pushed out a sigh of disgust through his nose. "Don't give me that 'I gather' crap. I read enough of it, OK? Believe me, more than enough. I read the summary by my AG, Bob Blerd—very smart guy, ingenious, really—and it states it clearly: the report fully exonerates me. Read it yourself."

"I have," True Son replied in that needling calm tone.

"Both the Blerd summary and the Manning Report, which on page two hundred and fourteen states: 'Accordingly, while this report does not conclude that the President committed a crime, it also does not exonerate him.'"

The President's features froze, and his eyes grew stormy. "You think that old spook scared me? You think I lost a wink of sleep over his phony little biased report? You think I gave a rat's ass what Karloff put in his trumped-up report?" He snorted indignantly. "I could've shut down Creepy Karloff's little special investigation any time I wanted, any time, believe me. But I didn't, because unlike the lyin' media and the deceitful Democrats, I'm not an obstructionist, OK? I don't obstruct, it's not my style, OK? No obstruction. No collusion. No quid pro quo. OK? It's not what I do. It's not me, OK? But let me tell you, with one snap of my fingers, I could have put that creepy old-timer and his whole team of lyin' investigators out to pasture. Could have done it at any time because I'm the president, OK? I got a little thing called Article Two—ever heard of it? Gives me total power and complete immunity. Total and complete. I can do anything I want, I can shoot somebody and nothing will happen, it's true, it's in the Constitution, beautiful document, magnificent document, the Constitution, you gotta love it—well, maybe not you, because you come from a shithole country, where they don't understand things like Constitutional rights, but believe me, Article Two is a beautiful thing, you should go back and tell your people about it, who knows, eh?" The President shot another breath through his nose. "Anytime, anytime I wanted, I could have shit-canned Special Counsel Karloff—not personally, of course, because the system's rigged, they rig everything around here, I'd have gotten so much done without all the rigging, believe me— but I could have gotten someone *else* to do it, at a moment's notice, believe me." The President shook his head. "Bank on it, that creepy old man's days of haunting this castle are over. Let 'em all play chess. I play Whack-A-Mole, and when old Karloff popped his head up too far, I crowned his king. And I did the same to Little Nasty Noreen, I crowned her *queen*. And if she wants to come back for seconds, I'll crown her little queen again, just like I did with all those federal judges—*non-elected* judges. Just ask them, ask any of them what happens when you push my buttons, they'll tell you, they know, all right, they know."

The President's face was getting red. Kayley could tell that he was trying to maintain control, but the more he spoke, the angrier he seemed to get. And all the while, the terrorist, True Son, held his composure—which only seemed to fire up the President all the more.

"*That's* who should be investigated here," the President seethed, "the crooked judges, defying their Commander in Chief. They should all be impeached. Impeached and jailed. They have no business questioning my authority. On anything."

"You believe the rescinding of your executive orders by the judges has undermined your authority."

"I believe the so-called judges have endangered this country by allowing terrorists like you to sneak over the borders and do what you're doing right now."

"In our previous conversation, you were fairly certain that I was already *in* this country—brought over as a child by my father . . . the goatherd."

The President sniffed dismissively. "Doesn't matter. The reckless actions of those judges only emboldened you and your kind."

"Some would say that *your* actions have emboldened me and my kind."

"They don't know what they're talking about."

"Some would say the same of you."

The President's gaze iced over. He sniffed again.

"The lyin' media," he said with a disdainful glance at the members of the press. "All lies. Very-very dishonest. Disgusting, really. They should be jailed, all of them."

"They fear your authority."

"They *should* fear it."

"You know what should be done, and they attempt to block you at every turn."

"You're goddamn right, they do."

"They use your words against you."

"They *twist* my words."

"They use them as a weapon, repeating them ad nauseam, refusing to see past your words and into your heart. They fear that they will see a reflection of themselves in you—the burden you carry so that they may enjoy the liberties and freedoms you provide, without the guilt."

The President shot a penetrating look at the TV screen. True Son gazed back at him. For a moment, the President felt as if he could see behind the mask, straight into the soul of the man himself. And though he knew that the man was dark and unlike him, the President could not deny the odd kindred sensation that crept over him like a stealthy thief in the night.

In the midst of his reverie, he sensed the former president at the periphery of his thoughts, reaching out with a cautioning hand, but he brushed it aside.

You had your chance. It's my *turn now. I'm* in *control here.*

For a second, he wondered if he'd said that out loud, but when he glanced at the press corps, none were looking at him strangely—or at least not anymore strangely than they usually did—so he assumed his rebuke of Boyega had only been spoken in his mind.

When he looked back at True Son, that odd kindred sensation swept over him again, and this time he drew it close, like a blanket, or a shield.

A cape, he thought distantly.

A red cape. Superman's cape. After all, weren't Batman and Superman kindred spirits? Even though one rose from darkness and the other from light, when it came down to the crux, weren't they both on the same side?

The President's eyes narrowed in contemplation. He was in charge here. He was the president. And when you're the president, you can do anything you please.

He looked up at True Son and said, "Gimme a second here—play some of your music or something. I'll be right back with you, OK?"

True Son did not respond. But momentarily, soft music rose from the speakers.

The President turned to the press corps and spoke in an oddly gentle tone. "All right, I'm gonna need some privacy here, so everybody out."

At first, they stood in stunned silence as if the President was joking. But there was no hint of humor in his eyes.

The President said, "Come on, let's go. Everybody out. There'll be refreshments in the hallway." He called out to the door, which had just been opened by his assistant. "Melanie, get some refreshments for these guys, bring up the Napoleons—you're gonna love 'em, guys, they're delicious—and some milk, Melanie. Milk and Napoleons for everybody—best Napoleons you've ever had . . . the very-very best, believe me."

As the reporters headed out of the Oval Office, Kayley found her courage and spoke up. "What about the cameras? Someone needs to stay to operate the cameras."

Members of the press who hadn't already left stood with hopeful expressions on their faces. The President looked at Kayley for a long moment, like an aging man trying to remember the face of a loved one. Recognition dawned slowly, and with it came a small, sad smile.

"OK," he said. "You can stay."

Kayley froze for a second. But her fear of incurring the President's wrath by pressing the limits of his generosity was overcome by her trepidation at being left alone in the room with him.

"But I'll need someone to operate the camera," she said.

The President gazed at her for a moment and then shot

a glance at Trent, who stood nearby with his camera still aimed and rolling. "OK. He can stay too. But the rest have to go."

As the other members of the press made their way into the hall, the President called out, "Melanie. Tell Franco to save two Napoleons, one for Lil Kayley, and one for . . . What's his name?"

"Trent," Kayley said.

"And one for Trent, you got that, Melanie?"

"Yes, Mr. President," said Melanie as she herded the last few reporters into the hall and closed the door.

The President turned back to Kayley and Trent with a look of appraisal. Then an odd smile broke at the corners of his mouth.

"You two make a cute couple . . . I don't know, maybe we'll make a match here tonight, eh? I don't know, we'll see, maybe. Anything can happen on TV, right?"

Trent, who was not only in a committed relationship but also gay, looked nonplussed. Kayley, who was accustomed to the President's enigmatic tangents, simply smiled.

"I thought so," said the President, his lips curling into a more natural-looking smile. "I got a sense about these things. I'm like Cupid. Anyway, trust me," he added with a wink, "you're gonna love these Napoleons . . . best you've ever had, trust me, they're unbelievable, you're gonna love 'em."

In the outer office, most of the press had gathered around the TV while Melanie and Franco passed out plates of Napoleons, along with napkins and plastic forks.

At the back of the pack, Josh Tanner of NCN stood beside E.G. Hephaestus of the *Post*. As both men sliced into their Napoleons, Tanner glanced up at the President on TV and, pitching his voice low, asked to the older man, "He *does* know that we can still see him, right?"

E.G. shook his head and chuckled softly, "I don't know."

ILIANA KINGLEY'S NAME POPPED UP ON HER DAUGHTER'S MOBILE phone, but Ilona was in no state of mind to take the call. She didn't have the strength to endure one of her mother's endless grilling sessions—not now, not with all that was going on—so she silenced the ringer and set her phone on the vanity.

The light switch in the small bathroom was adjustable; Ilona turned it down to its lowest setting and took a measured breath. She tried to block out all sound, but the newscast, muted by the distance of the short hall between the bathroom and the living room, still came through. Her father was back in the Oval Office, going at it with the terrorist once again, but she couldn't make out what they were saying. Her mind was still whirring with all the terrible things the TV pundits had said during the break—terrible, hurtful things that no daughter wanted to hear about her father, even if many of those things were true.

She pushed back against the voices of the pundits as she stood before the mirror above the sink, unable to look at her reflection. She just stood there with her eyes closed, willing her nerves to calm, willing herself to breathe. Jake was all that mattered. Jake and only Jake. She just wanted him back, safe and sound. She wanted her husband back home with her and the kids, and for all of this to be over. She wanted things to go back to the way they were before her father had decided to run for president. She wanted people to look at her the way they used to. She wanted her old life back. She wanted to click her heels and magically be transported back to that time when everything was normal and peaceful and good.

Life was good, she thought. *We had a good life, didn't we?*

No answer came, but she nodded, anyway, because she knew she was right. They'd had a very good life before getting sucked into this mess.

She didn't know how long she'd been standing there

at the sink in Marilyn's bathroom—it felt like a very long time—but something was different. Something *felt* different. So different, in fact, that for a moment, she wondered if her wish had actually been granted. She knew this wasn't the case; it was impossible to erase the present and go back in time. But it felt like she *had* gone back in time. For an odd moment, it felt as if all that had happened over the past four years—from the announcement of her father's candidacy to the moment he'd stepped into the Oval Office to confront the terrorist—had been swept away, and she'd been gently dropped into another place in time . . .

She could see herself now, as if in a movie or a vivid dream: sitting on her bed in Tower K, hugging a pillow tightly as tears brimmed in her eyes but did not fall. She'd had a terrible fight with Jake over something she couldn't even recall. And she had retreated to the only place she'd ever truly felt safe, the place that would always be her home.

The memory of that night flooded her consciousness with such force that for a second, she thought she could actually hear the song that had been playing on her iPod as she'd sat on her bed, fighting back tears.

The song was *The A Team* by Ed Sheeran.

She'd first heard it on the radio one night while driving with Jake to meet up with friends for dinner. Jake felt it was a maudlin tune and wanted to turn the station, but Ilona wouldn't let him. Despite Jake's eye-rolling and sighs, she'd believed that he secretly liked the song, and ever after, she'd thought of it as their song. It wasn't until that heartbreaking night that she realized she'd been wrong. Alone in her room with the mournful ballad set to repeat on her iPod, she'd understood that it wasn't *their* song; it was *her* song. And that's when the dam had finally broken, and the tears began to spill in earnest.

But that wasn't entirely true.

She hadn't been alone in the suite that night. The place

had appeared deserted when she'd arrived, but someone else had been there.

She remembered the soft footsteps on the carpet behind her, the gentle sinking of the mattress beside her, the comforting arm around her shoulder. No words, because words were not needed. Just that calming presence, that steadfast shoulder to lean on. That's when she'd felt safe enough to let down her guard and allow the tears to fall. Because someone had been there to catch her.

She opened her eyes now and looked into the mirror above the sink, fully expecting the song in her head to stop playing as she re-entered the present, where things were far more complicated and could not be resolved by a good long cry.

Only the song *didn't* stop.

She could still hear Ed Sheeran's sweet voice singing those familiar lyrics, faintly yet clearly.

It took a moment for her to realize that the song hadn't been coming from inside her head at all. It had been coming from the living room down the hallway, where Marilyn's husband, Kyle, reclined on the sofa watching the live broadcast from the Oval Office.

Ilona came from the bathroom like a sleepwalker whose every step brought her closer to consciousness; when she stopped behind the sofa, her gaze locked onto the TV screen, and she knew she was fully awake.

The Oval Office had been cleared. Only two people remained in the camera's view: the reporter, Kayley Tru, and the President. On the widescreen TV above the mantel, Ilona's husband sat bound to the chair and barely conscious.

But it wasn't Jake she was looking at. It was the tall figure, dressed in black, that drew her attention; it was the stillness and purpose behind the dark glass eyes of the mask that held her in thrall as wave upon wave of chilly tendrils raced her spine.

A box on the upper right corner of the TV screen featured a live shot of the children gathered on the lawn of the Capitol, and Ilona's legs buckled as Ed Sheeran sang: *"It's too cold outside for angels to fly . . . "*

Even as she shook her head in disbelief, the wall that had obstructed her view all night began to crumble, and blinding light poured in.

"Ilona . . . what is it?" Marilyn said with genuine concern in her voice.

But Ilona was focused on her phone now, dialing fast, waiting for an answer. But it just kept ringing. Ringing and ringing, and no one would pick up. No matter how many numbers she tried, no one would pick up. *Why wouldn't they pick up?*

"Ilona, tell me, what's going—"

"I've got to—" Ilona looked around desperately, her heart thundering, her head swimming. "I've got to get to my father, I've got to get to him right now, I've got to—"

Marilyn reached out, and her eyes went wide. "Jesus, Ilona, you're trembling all over!"

With tears standing in her terrified eyes, Ilona whispered, "You've got to get me to my father right now . . . you've got to . . . I've got to . . . "

Ilona reached out for support, but Marilyn wasn't there; she was down the hall, getting her coat and car keys while Ed Sheeran strummed his guitar and sang: *" . . . angels to fly . . . an angel will die, covered in white . . . "*

Andrew Jackson gazed down from his portrait with a glint of caution in his supercilious blue eyes, but the President, who could be just as hard-nosed as the seventh man to hold this office, wasn't going to be dissuaded from his present course. He'd already been mindfucked by one portrait of a former president, and he wasn't about to take any crap from another—not even Old Hickory, all due respect.

The only ex-president that mattered right now was the one who'd been haunting him ever since he'd set foot in this office. He had removed every reminder of the guy—every stick of furniture, every knickknack (except for that bust of MLK, which he'd been forced to keep because of the whiny NAACP mouthpieces accusing him of being a racist—*him*, a racist, as if anyone could believe that!). But he hadn't been able to remove his predecessor's *essence*. It lingered, like perfume, or the scent of rain after a spring downpour. It invaded his senses like burning leaves, acrid yet somehow pleasant, even comforting at times. Always there, in every corner, every crevice—watching and waiting, *expecting* him to stumble.

Without looking up at the TV above the fireplace mantel, the President said, "Sometimes I see him in here."

Dim light glinted off of the black eyes of True Son's mask in a questioning flicker.

"I see him right there," the President said, pointing at the leather chair behind his desk, "sitting right there, as if he's still the president . . . judging me with that high and mighty look of his . . .

"I mean, I know he's not really there, because he's off on some island somewhere with that monkey fuck Brantley— *Sir* Brantley!" The President expelled a short, contemptuous laugh. "In what Mickey Mouse army would *that* deranged limey ape qualify for being a knight is beyond me, unbelievable, the Queen should strip him of his title, seriously, don't you think?"

The President didn't wait for a response; he just shook his head in disbelief that such a ridiculous clown of a man as Robert Brantley could hold a title of such importance.

"Anyway," he went on, "I know he's not really here— Boyega—because he's off with that British freak, windsurfing, or jet-skiing, or whatever the hell it is British freaks do on their private islands. And he's laughing it up over what a complete mess he left me with—he's an unbelievably vengeful man, mean-spirited, spiteful, hateful, really. People don't know this—*I* know this, but people don't—they don't know what an incredibly spiteful and mean-spirited man he is. He hates me so much, he really does—can't get over the fact that I beat him. Because it really wasn't *her* I was running against—well, it *was* her, and I beat her, badly, as everyone knows—but it was really *him* that I beat, and it kills him, Boyega, totally kills him. He's a very jealous man—tremendous jealousy, unbelievable jealousy. He thinks about it all the time, night and day, he can't get over it. And he harbors so much hate for me—people don't know this, but it's true, ask anyone, they'll tell you, he's a hater."

True Son waited, and when it was clear the President was finished, or at least taking a breather, he said, "You still think about him."

"I can't get him out of my mind. I mean, look at this place. He's everywhere. I replaced all of his crap, but you can't get rid of his *essence*—they have that, his people, 'essence.' It's everywhere. You can still feel him, like a yuge, looming shadow, casting itself over everything . . . everything I do, everything I think, he's always there, I can feel him. I can see him in the glass panes of the doors at night, like a reflection of him, like a ghost, you know what I mean? Like he's standing outside on the patio. Just standing there, looking in at me. But not with that shit-eating grin of his— you know, that grin that makes you want to kick his fucking teeth in?"

The President released a sigh, and with it, his anger. He shook his head, deflated.

"But he doesn't have that grin," he went on. "It's almost like . . . it's almost like he's worried about me . . . concerned, you know? And it's really sincere, his concern is—he can be very sincere when he wants to be. I know that sounds crazy, considering what a merciless, conniving, two-faced bastard he is, but it's true."

The President paused and acquired an oddly pained expression. Then he looked at the TV above the mantel, where the shiny black eyes of True Son's mask peered back at him—like the eyes of a dark angel whose black wings, once spread, could shield him from any attack.

"I wouldn't tell this to a lot of people," said the President in a confidential tone, "mostly because they'd think I was nuts or something, but sometimes I have dreams about him . . . Boyega . . . nothing weird, just dreams. Usually, we're just sitting here and talking. Sometimes we're walking around the halls, checking out the paintings of the past presidents, laughing about some of them, looking up at others like 'wow, that guy was something else, eh?' And all the while he's like the nicest guy, really concerned, like he genuinely wants to help me, like he knows that I . . . like he knows that I can be a great president, maybe even the greatest, and he wants to help me, like a mentor. It's true . . . "

The President's eyes suddenly went dark.

"But then things shift. Just when we're having a good time, laughing it up and chatting, things shift and turn ugly. The walls start peeling, like the paint and the wallpaper start peeling, and the faces on the paintings don't look like faces anymore . . . and there's no ceiling. It's just an open space above, where you can see the clouds swirling in the sky, just swirling and swirling, because it's like a storm up there. It's like a tsunami in the sky, nothing but black swirling clouds that look like they'll suck you right up into space or something . . .

"And then it's like there *is* a ceiling, but only . . . only it's made of glass—you can tell because it's rumbling and shaking, you know, the way that glass does that? Because of the clouds . . . they're like swirling like crazy now. And just before that glass shatters, I can hear her . . . I can hear that vindictive nasty woman cackling up there in the clouds. You know that cackle of hers? I can hear it. And then I can see her, up there on a broom, and she looks just like that witch from *The Wizard of Oz*. Boy, did that scare the shit out of me when I was a kid—you know, with the flying monkeys and all? Gave me nightmares, unbelievable nightmares, unbelievable, believe me . . .

"And so in my dream, there's old Hannah on her broom, cackling away while that crazy rattling ceiling shatters and rains all these jagged razor-sharp slivers of glass down on me, like knives, and she's just loving it, I tell you, she's just *loving* it."

The President shook his head.

"It's a wonder I can get any sleep at all, I'm telling you, with those two creeping around in my dreams."

True Son waited for a moment. Then he quoted, "'I could be bounded in a nutshell and count myself a king of infinite space, were it not that I have bad dreams.'"

The President shot a hard sidelong glance at True Son, but his eyes looked haunted.

"*Hamlet*, Act Two, Scene Two," said True Son. Then he shifted gears. "Have you considered reaching out to him?"

"Who?"

"Your predecessor."

The President rolled his eyes like it was the stupidest suggestion he'd ever heard.

"Perhaps you'd fare better with some outside advice," True Son suggested.

The President's eyes narrowed.

"You've been an outspoken critic of many within your administration," True Son went on. "Most notably your former AG, Jasper Sassy—"

"Don't even get me started on that malicious little turncoat Hobbit. If he had just stood his ground instead of turning tail and recusing himself, we could have shut down that whole phony Russia investigation before it got legs. Believe me." He sniffed deeply and shifted back to the issue of his predecessor. "And even if I *wanted* his advice, he wouldn't take the call. Not from me."

"And if he did take the call," True Son prompted, "what do you suppose he would say to you?"

"I don't know, some fancy Harvard bullshit—he's a smooth talker, like you—thinks he's got all the answers to every question ever invented. A real smart guy—he'd like you, the two of you would probably be besties."

True Son responded with another quote: "'The man of knowledge must be able not only to love his enemies but also to hate his friends.'"

The President shot another sidelong glance at the TV screen and smiled darkly. Then suddenly, his gaze turned stormy, and words spilled forth in an explosive burst.

"Well, if he's so goddamn smart, how come he couldn't stop me from getting here? Ask him that. He worked his skinny black ass off to get Shady Hannah inside this office and behind that desk. If he's such a goddamn genius, how come his little master plan to knock me out of the running didn't work? Ask him *that*, see what smart answer he comes up with.

"He leaves this place—the whole *country*—in a complete and total mess, and *I* should put on the begging bag and go crawling to *him*? *I* should drop to my knees and open wide? Is that it?"

True Son stood silent.

The President shot a hard breath through his nose and glared up at the screen. "This is what you do to me? I take you into my confidence, tell you things I've never told any-body, and you turn on me like a little cheese-eating rat? You think you could do better with that skinny lying Harvard prick? He'd be running for the hills by now. *I'm* here. *I'm* talking. *I'm* the one you deal with. *I'm* the President. Not him. *Me*. You got that, you little smartass punk? *I'm* the smart guy here. I can handle you, I'm handling you. That's what I do. I handle things, OK, smart guy?"

True Son remained silent, waiting for the wave to crash and recede from the shore, and within moments, it did.

The President released a labored sigh, and when he spoke again, the fire was gone.

"I'm working with you here, OK? We're working on this together, OK? We don't need him. I'm a really smart guy, ask anyone. I can do this . . . "

He took True Son's continued silence as a sign that they were back on the same page. Then his eyes drifted to the mullioned door, where he could see the outline of President Boyega in the darkened panes of glass. As he gazed at his predecessor, the President's eyes grew introspective, almost dreamy, and he muttered, "You're not so smart . . . you *wish* you were smart . . . believe me . . . you're not so smart . . . *I'm* smarter . . . *way* smarter . . . I've got this . . . "

At the same moment the President drifted into his dreamy state of introspection, three events occurred that he would only come to comprehend after it was too late.

The first event happened outside on the National Mall, where the army of children gathered before the Capitol Building began to move. Not to advance on the Capitol, nor to retreat from it, but rather to shift their positions on the lawn, allowing them to spread out into several separate clusters, each lined in perfect formation and facing toward the White House. To Dayton Hammersmith and Nero González, who stood side by side on the steps of the Capitol, along with the rest of the police force, the assembly of children suddenly looked more like a battalion, formally presenting itself—but to what purpose, neither man could tell.

The second event took place in the deathly quiet hallways of the White House residence, where the bodies of three secret service agents, each silently removed from play by the same blade, lay slumped in pools of blood while the assassin continued down the hall with catlike precision, toward his primary target.

The third event occurred just across the Potomac, in the

loft headquarters of HiroBot, LLC, where Thackery Ansara had finally caught up with the girl of his dreams—the elusive blip on his computer's screen, which he'd affectionately named after his first crush, a sweet girl with curly red pigtails who'd always dashed away with a bashful smile whenever Thackery had looked her way on the playground at Sequoia Middle School in Fresno.

But unlike the real Daisy, whose speed and dexterity had made her impossible to catch, her namesake wasn't running away. Indeed she was flashing at the center of Thackery's screen like a heartbeat, waiting for his embrace.

And she was in the last place he, or anyone else, would have expected to find her.

Thackery dialed Melville Noyce's number at once. It took only two rings for Melville to pick up.

"Are you sitting down?" Thackery asked, but he didn't wait for a response. "I found Daisy—and you're never gonna believe where old girl is."

Within minutes of Thackery's phone call, two other calls were made: the first was from Melville Noyce to the acting director of the CIA; the second was from the CIA to the White House. The latter was forwarded directly to Franco Scaramanga, and the caller didn't waste time with small talk.

"This is Deputy Director of the CIA Buzz Hartman calling," the gruff voice said. "Am I speaking to the top dog's top dog?"

Franco hesitated only a moment before responding. "Yes . . . yes, sir, you are."

"Well, listen up, Number Two, because I'm as serious as a heart attack here. We've got a positive lock on the terrorist's signal. It's coming from 1600 Pennsylvania Avenue. He's transmitting from inside the White House. Olympus has been breached. Scramble every available agent you've got. I repeat: *He's inside the goddamn White House.*"

Barret Kingley stirred in his sleep, opened his eyes briefly, and then rolled onto his side. As his cheek sank comfortably into the pillow, a soft sigh escaped his lips.

Agent Hasney looked up from the chair across the room, where he sat in silent vigil. The chair was built for show rather than comfort, but that didn't matter to Hasney. His sole concern was the safety of the sleeping boy in the regal four-poster bed.

On any other night, Agent Hasney would be at home getting sleep so that he would be fully rested and ready for duty the following morning.

But this wasn't any other night.

Something was off at the White House—more off than usual. Something was in the air, like a scent on a not so distant breeze, drifting closer with each passing tick of the clock. Hasney couldn't shake the feeling that something was happening—was *about* to happen—something that had little if anything to do with the drama presently unfolding in the West Wing.

With his eyes still on the sleeping boy across the room, Hasney recalled something his field instructor had said to the class on their first day of training at FLETC in Glynco.

Regret mates for life, ladies and gentleman—you will never encounter a more possessive paramour. If the situation doesn't feel right, listen to your gut and take the appropriate action.

The boy had fallen asleep at the piano in the Cross Hall, shortly after the departure of his older brother. Hasney hadn't bothered to wake him; he'd just lifted the boy into his arms and carried him up to the residence. With his head resting on Hasney's shoulder, Barret had stirred and clung briefly before allowing the Secret Service agent to lower him onto the bed. By the time he'd got Barret changed into his pyjamas and tucked under the covers, where the boy promptly drifted off to sleep, Hasney had made up his mind to keep watch through the night.

Regret mates for life.

As the warning of his former instructor echoed in his mind, Hasney's eyelids became heavy, and he reclined in the chair that was built for show and not comfort, thinking, *Just for tonight, just until the crisis passes . . .*

Hasney drifted into a light slumber, where the sound of a pulsing heartbeat that at first he'd thought was his own drummed at his ears like distant cannon fire, getting closer with each boom. Then out of the darkness, a shadowy mist rose, from which there emerged a lone figure. Hasney stood before the mist, instinctively understanding that he was dreaming. Normally, he would be able to wake himself with little effort, but there was something about this dream, an underlying urgency, that pressed him to remain; to confront the approaching figure from the mist.

The sound of the heartbeat slowed to a staggered throbbing, yet the volume did not diminish. Indeed, it grew louder as the figure stepped from the shadows of the mist and into the light. Hasney stood frozen in his dream, gazing into the eyes of his younger brother Marc, who'd been killed by a stray bullet at the age of ten. The boy looked the same as he had on that warm spring day in their living room, just before the bullet had pierced the front window.

Hasney pushed back against the sudden wave of emotion that threatened to impede his ability to react to imminent danger. But it was already too late. Before he could break his paralysis, the booming heartbeat stopped, and a small circle opened at the left side of Marc's chest—a tiny black bud that scarcely seemed alarming until it bloomed into a deep crimson stain across the front of his younger brother's white T-shirt.

Marc didn't notice the bullet hole; nor the rapidly spreading blood. He continued to gaze into his older brother's eyes as he spoke two words in a chillingly calm whisper: *Wake up.*

Agent Hasney woke instantly—though, not with a gasping jolt, as most would from a scary dream. He simply opened his eyes and peered into the surrounding shadows. The room was silent, save for the steady rhythm of Barret Kingley's breathing. But it wasn't the sound *inside* the room that concerned the Special Agent.

Hasney rose from the chair and moved soundlessly to the door, where he stood and listened for a brief moment. He took one last glance at the sleeping boy before he opened the door and stepped into the hallway.

Had it been a stranger approaching from the opposite end of the hall, Agent Hasney would have most certainly drawn his firearm. But the young man with the sharp features and intense hazel eyes was not only familiar to Hasney but someone who'd been granted free access to the residence by the President himself.

As he made his way down the hall, Bart Benedict knew not to engage his disarming smile—the charm that worked so beautifully on the President, as well as his sycophantic entourage of *vernyye idioty,* would not have the same effect on a skilled Secret Service agent. He knew not to stop or slow his gait, either . . . at least not until he was within range. No one was faster with a blade than he, but Bart had studied Agent Hasney's dossier as thoroughly as he'd studied the dossiers of every other agent on the President's protective detail, and he knew that Hasney was not only a quick draw but also a crack shot. Like himself, Hasney never missed, and Bart liked that. He liked facing an opponent of equal strength and skill.

Halfway down the hall, Bart tilted his head back in greeting, and, in doing so, exposed his face to the dim circle of overhead light. Hasney noticed the tiny red flecks on Bart's cheek below the left eye, and something inside him shifted. Bart's eyes shined with detached malice. It was nothing personal; in another place and time, he and Hasney might have been good friends.

The knife slid from Bart's sleeve and into his waiting hand like a smoothly executed magic trick.

Hasney sensed the movement before the knife was released, and in that split second he understood three things simultaneously: one, the target wasn't him—it was the ten-year-old boy who'd just stepped into the hallway behind him; two, in order to save the boy, he would need to block the knife with his own body; and three, this was precisely what Bart expected him to do—there just wasn't enough time to draw his weapon, take out the threat, and protect the boy from the imminent danger of the speeding knife.

It happened so fast that the sting of the blade scarcely registered as Hasney turned and crouched to shield the boy. The knife penetrated his back below the left shoulder blade, but it didn't stop him. He had just enough time to shove the boy back into the room and reach for his firearm before another blade struck—this one in the meaty flesh of his right leg.

Two more blades followed fast.

The first struck Hasney in the side, just above his left hip; the second penetrated his chest. Still, Hasney managed to draw his weapon, but before he could get off a shot, Bart was upon him. Quick as a whip, Bart grasped Hasney's wrist and slammed it against the wall, and as Hasney's grip on the firearm loosened, Bart drove the blade of a fifth knife into Hasney's stomach.

For a moment, time appeared to stand still, and everything seemed very clear.

Then the gun fell to the carpet, and Bart kicked it away as Agent Hasney slumped to the floor with his back against the jam of the open doorway. He could see Barret in the shadow-streaked room. The boy's eyes were brimming with tears, and his little heart was racing, but he did not turn and run in fear.

Brave kid, Hasney thought as his vision began to blur.

Bart Benedict squatted down to face Hasney and said, "You're an exceptional knight. But, personally, I would have sacrificed the pawn and taken the shot."

Hasney gazed into Bart's eyes but did not respond.

In one swift movement, Bart pulled the knife from Hasney's chest; though the pain was excruciating, Hasney did not cry out.

Bart leaned in close, his nose almost touching Hasney's, and said, "Because you are *istinnyy voin*—a true warrior—I'll make this quick, bro."

Hasney took a pained breath through clenched teeth, and with his glassy eyes still focused on his opponent, he spoke in a gentle tone to the boy: "Close your eyes, Barret."

Bart smiled at the gallant gesture of the brave Secret Service agent—but then he made the critical error of glancing into the moonlit room, where Barret Kingley knelt with his eyes closed like an obedient little soldier.

Bart's lips peeled back from his shiny white teeth in a crooked grin. He was about to tell the boy "no peeking" when Hasney's hands suddenly sprang from the floor, grasped the sides of Bart's head, and twisted in one powerful and lightning-fast movement. The accompanying sound was brutally flat, like a bundle of dry branches snapping.

For a seemingly endless series of seconds, time appeared to stand still once again.

And then Bart Benedict's lifeless body tumbled like a rag doll onto the hallway carpet.

Upon hearing the thud, Barret opened his eyes and scrambled over to Hasney, who was bleeding freely now from the open wound in his chest. Hasney took a staggered breath, which most certainly would have been one of his last had it not been for the timely appearance of an unlikely rescuer at the far end of the hall . . .

Press Secretary Skip Spinner had been ringing the phones in the residence since the news came in from the CIA that the White House had been breached. When he'd asked one of the scrambling agents if anyone had been sent up to the residence to check on Barret, the guy had briskly brushed him off.

"Negative. The Egg is out of the nest, along with Venus, back in New York. Golden Eagle is the sole priority."

But Skippy knew that couldn't be right. He had been there when the President had told the First Lady that she could "jump ship" whenever she liked, "but the kid stays here."

With no one to turn to, Skippy had taken it upon himself to check on Barret.

Upon discovering the bodies of the three fallen agents on the landing at the top of the stairs, Skippy feared the worst. But when he'd soldiered on and spotted young Barret halfway down the residence hallway, he breathed an audible sigh. His sudden relief at finding the boy alive and unharmed was quickly replaced by horror when he got close enough to see the carnage.

Nothing could be done for the President's aide, Bart Benedict—Skippy could see that much at a glance—but Agent Hasney was still alive.

Skippy didn't stop to wonder if the perpetrator of all this carnage might still be around and waiting to pounce. His instincts as a Navy Reservist immediately kicked in. He wasn't a medic and had no formal training beyond basic CPR and the Heimlich maneuver—he currently held the rank of "commander," which was more ceremonial than practical—but it didn't take a medic or a commander to assess the immediate danger.

He took off his suit jacket and quickly folded it into a square, which he pressed against the wound in Agent Hasney's chest. Then he turned to the boy and said, "Are you injured?"

Barret shook his head.

Skippy had the eyes of a Basset hound; even when he smiled at you, his eyes looked sad. People on TV, as well as people in his father's administration—including his father himself—often said mean things about Skippy and called him a liar. But Barret had always liked the man with the sad Basset hound eyes because he knew that the man wasn't making up the stories that made people say mean things about him. He knew that Skippy was only repeating the stories because that was his job, and if he didn't do his job, he would get fired. Indeed, he had already been fired once for not doing his job (Barret's father had been particularly angry one time when Skippy laughed with the people from the press because he felt that the press secretary was laughing at him, and no one should ever laugh at the president). But Barret's father had rehired Skippy and made him promise to "just stick to the script from now on." Barret had felt bad for Skippy and secretly wished that he could find another job—one where he wouldn't have to tell stories that weren't true—because when Skippy was just talking to you, without the cameras and the press people there, he never told stories or pretended to be interested in things that weren't interesting. He looked right into your eyes, and you could tell that he was honestly interested in what you had to say, and he never told you things that weren't true.

Barret liked the sad-eyed press secretary for that. But more importantly, he trusted him. So when Skippy instructed him to press his hands against the jacket to keep pressure on Agent Hasney's wound, Barret did as he was told. And when Skippy told Agent Hasney to hang in there, that help was on the way, and that he was going to make it, Barret believed him.

When the medics arrived and started working to save Agent Hasney's life, Barret stood next to Skippy, holding onto his hand tightly, and Skippy didn't pull his hand away, not even when Barret's palm became sweaty. He just held the boy's hand and stood by his side, gently reassuring him that all would be well, that Agent Hasney was going to pull through.

And Barret believed him . . . or at least he believed the

part about Agent Hasney pulling through. The other part—
the part about "all being well"—he was pretty sure that
wasn't really true. But he reckoned it was a forgivable lie.

K AYLEY TRU REACHED INTO THE POCKET OF HER BLAZER TO
silence her buzzing phone. She did so with more than
a modicum of trepidation and without taking her eyes off
the President. Though his focus was currently locked on
the terrorist, Kayley, who understood just how mutable
the President's focus could be, didn't want to give him any
reason to turn that steely gaze in her direction. So with a
steady hand, she found the tiny button on the side of her
phone and switched it off.

At the same time Kayley was silencing her phone in
the Oval Office, Ilona Kingley was pleading for her to pick
up. In the passenger seat of Marilyn's speeding Prius, Ilona
groaned in frustration. "She's not picking up. Are you sure
this is her number?"

"Yes," said Marilyn as she weaved through traffic,
regretting that she hadn't grabbed her own phone from
the kitchen counter before they had headed out. Of course,
Marilyn knew that the odds of Kayley answering her phone
in the middle of an international crisis that she happened
to be covering on live TV were slim to none. Still, those
odds would have been better if the call were coming from a
number that Kayley recognized.

Ilona hung up before it went to voice mail and dialed
another number. And then another, and another, but no one
at the White House was picking up—not even Kori-Lynne,
and Kori-Lynne *always* picked up when Ilona called.

Ilona pounded the heel of her hand against the dash-
board and cried out, "Why won't they pick up? *Why won't
anyone pick up?*"

Marilyn knew better than to offer meaningless words
of comfort; she just kept her eyes on the road ahead and

concentrated on getting to the White House as quickly as possible.

As the Prius weaved through the DC traffic, Ilona tried calling her father's mobile again.

In the heart-stopping beats between the endless series of rings, she could hear that song, *The A Team*, still playing in her mind. And farther back in the recesses of her memory, she could hear a tiny voice—tiny yet confident . . .

No no no . . . that's me!

She could see the greeting card—a fine ivory stock with tasteful gold lettering embossed on its cover—and recalled all the time and thought that had gone into picking out that card because it had to be just the right one. She could see the card, open on the desk . . . the message written inside . . . and the signature at the bottom.

That's me. That's me!

If the pronouncement hadn't been so earnest, she might have laughed. But she hadn't laughed; indeed, she'd felt a lump rise to her throat as the tiny forefinger pointed at the signature on the card once again and those intense grey eyes looked up at her with such grave sincerity.

That's me!

The sudden blaring of a car horn pulled Ilona back to the present just as her father's voice came through her phone. But it was only his recorded greeting. She hung up without leaving a message and dialed again.

At the same time, just a few miles southeast of Ilona's location, another call was about to go unanswered. The mobile phone the President had been using all night—the one he'd borrowed from a staffer after his own had gone missing—began to buzz in his pocket.

The President ignored it. He was in the middle of a hot debate with True Son over the issue of nukes and North Korea, and he finally had the little smart-mouth pecker on the ropes, because if there was one undeniable success of his presidency, it was, without question, his handling of the North Korean nuclear threat. He had that shifty-eyed little psycho slope right where he wanted him. So what if the crazy little yellow bastard was testing long-range missiles on a regular basis? And so what if his techs had finally managed to miniaturize nuclear warheads? With the President's full-throated promise that any threat from North Korea would be met with "fire and fury, the likes of which the world has never seen," that fat little Shih Tzu was put on notice. He could bark and yip all he wanted, but if he decided to take a bite, the President would be right there to show him how the *big* dogs bite.

"I'll take that bad haircut out in one chomp," the President said, "and he knows it, believe me, he knows it."

True Son said, "You're prepared for nuclear war then."

"You bet your little muffin ass, I am. And anybody who isn't ready for action best steer clear. I'm cocked and loaded, believe it. All hellfire will be unleashed if that stubby little panda even blinks in my direction—tremendous hellfire and fury, the likes of which this world has never seen before."

True Son considered for a moment. Then he said, "In the Bhagavad Gita when Prince Arjuna is called upon to take up arms against his cousins, he refuses to fight."

"The Baghdad of what? What the hell is that? Some Muslim story?"

True Son ignored the slight. "The Bhagavad Gita is the Hindu scripture."

The President rolled his eyes. "Muslim, Hindu, it's all the same. So, what's the moral of the story? I'm sure it's a good one. What's the deal with this Prince Juno—he sounds like a real loser, but I'll bite. What happens when he refuses to fight his cousins? You got me hanging on the edge of my seat here."

True Son went on, unfazed by the President's flippancy. "When the prince recognizes the combatants on both sides as kith and kin, he orders Krishna, his charioteer, to convey him onto the battlefield and to bring the chariot to a halt between the two armies, certain that neither side will fire, for fear of striking their favorite."

The President shook his head. "So, he's a moron *and* a loser. Lemme guess. He gets himself killed, but he dies nobly, right?"

"No," True Son replied like a patient teacher instructing an impulsive pupil. "When Arjuna throws down his weapons, making clear to all that he will not fight, Krishna casts aside His guise of 'charioteer,' revealing that He is, in fact, Vishnu, the Supreme Being. He commands the prince that it is His divine will the battle take place, and when the prince hesitates, the Blessed Lord takes on His fierce multi-armed form, and proclaims, 'Time I am, and I have come to engage all mankind. And with the exception of you, the sons of Pandu, all soldiers here on both sides will be slain. Now I am Death, the mighty destroyer of the world.'"

The President stood frozen for a moment. Then, without a hint of sarcasm, he asked, "What happened?"

"The prince did his duty," True Son replied flatly.

"He killed his cousins?"

True Son remained silent.

The President pondered.

Then slowly, a light dawned in his eyes, and the ghost of a smile touched his lips.

"So," said the President, "in this little whatchacallit . . . analogy of yours . . . I'm the prince, is that it?"

"No," True Son replied in an even tone. "I am."

The President's lips parted, but before he could come up with a response, the mobile phone in his pocket began to buzz again.

True Son said, "You can take it. I'll wait."

It wasn't a call this time.

It was a text message from Franco, which read: KEEP HIM

TALKING. THEY'VE GOT A LOCK ON HIS LOCATION. THEY ARE CLOS-
ING IN ON HIM RIGHT NOW.

The President gazed at the message for what seemed like eons. Then he looked up at True Son on the big screen.

For a moment, time seemed to stand still as the two gazed at one another like lone warriors at opposing ends of a silent and bloody field . . . or like poker players, heads-up at the final table, each secure in the belief that he is holding the winning hand. Of course, only one of them had the absolute stone-cold nuts. With his tactical team currently moving in on True Son's location, the President was confident that *he* would be the one raking in the final pot.

The sudden urge to shove all-in was nearly irresistible, but Franco's message had said to stall, and so the President worked to contain his impulsive id . . . at least for a while.

He smiled slyly and said, "You think I'm a monster, don't you."

"No," True Son replied plainly. "Just a loser."

The President's features tightened briefly. Then his smile returned, slyly. "You haven't seen my cards yet. They're very good. I might even have the nuts, I probably have the nuts, I don't know, who knows? Maybe you've got the nuts, and I just *think* I've got the nuts. Who knows? I don't know, but I probably do . . . "

True Son didn't take the bait.

The President shifted gears.

"You don't fear me."

"Should I?"

"A lot of people do. Many-many people. Believe me."

"And yet they rise up to repel you at every turn."

The President shook his head in stupefied wonder. "Hard to believe, eh?"

"Not really."

The President raised a curious brow.

True Son expounded. "You force them to recognize

the fragility of precious things, and in turn, they rise up to defeat you every time. And with each defeat, your grip on your base weakens."

The President flinched as if he'd been slapped.

Then his lips curled into an ugly grin and his eyes shined darkly.

"This is gonna be my comeback," he said. "I've been down before, but they've never taken me out—and when I take *you* out, they'll all come home, like good little sheep . . . "

"And you're the shepherd."

"I *am* the fuckin' shepherd," said the President with cold conviction. Then, on a dime, he shifted gears and smiled again, a pleasant yet sickly smile. "And like a good shepherd, I'll welcome them back into the fold with open arms—even the ones who worked so hard to turn the others against me, because that's the kind of leader I am. Oh, I'll make them grovel at my feet—there has to be some sort of punishment—but eventually, I'll forgive them and accept them back into the fold."

He shook his head with a sad smile, but his eyes still shone with bitterness and resentment. True Son waited patiently for the obligatory exposition, and in short order, the President obliged.

"You think you've caused all this trouble for me, turned things upside down and inside out, but what you've *really* done is given me a gift. A wonderful-wonderful gift, with a big shiny red bow on top. I'll tell you something a lot of people don't know: People love me. Especially the weak ones—the strong ones love me too, but the weak ones *really* love me. You wanna know why? Because they see me as their champion. They've been getting their asses kicked by the big bully on the block, and so they went out and got themselves a *bigger* bully to defend them. They love me because I say all the things they only *wish* they had the balls to say, and I say it all in public. Nothing can touch me. *Nothing.* I'm

Elliot Fucking Ness to these people. I'm untouchable. Ask anyone, they'll tell you."

"And yet your sinking numbers appear to indicate the opposite," said True Son in that maddeningly calm tone. "And as more and more pieces of the façade you've so clumsily constructed are chipped away, your acolytes recoil in greater numbers. Because they can see what lies beneath the bravado."

"Yeah? What's that, smart guy?"

"A frail and frightened child, lashing out with the only weapons he possesses—anger, resentment, frustration—desperate for the approbation he was denied by the only person that ever mattered to him."

The President raised a brow. "You think I've got daddy issues?"

"It doesn't matter what I think," True Son replied smoothly.

"I'm the fucking president of the *United fucking States* here!" the President snapped. "The old man ain't got *nothing* on me. *I* run this shit. *I* call the shots. *I'm* king of the hill now."

"A fool capering about in the king's crown is yet a fool, regardless of the applause that echoes in his memory."

"They're still applauding," countered the President, dismissively. But his face was reddening now, and his gaze was stormy. "I've got my base, trust me, they ain't going anywhere, believe me. I got 'em right here in my hip pocket. They don't give a flyin' rat's ass what I did with Russia— they'd tell me to do it again, they'd back me up one hundred and ten percent just to see that lousy crooked nasty woman get hers, believe me. They're with me for the long haul, and nothing is going to change that. Believe me. I'm nobody's fool. You got that? *Nobody's* fool."

True Son quoted: "'A nation can survive its fools, and even the ambitious. But it cannot survive treason from within. An enemy at the gates is less formidable, for he is known and carries his banner openly. But the traitor moves amongst those within the gate freely, his sly whispers rustling through all the alleys, heard in the very halls of government itself—'"

"I'm *their* bully!" the President shouted at the screen in a sudden burst of anger. "*They* know who I am—I kick the ass of the bully who's been kicking *their* ass!"

True Son calmly continued quoting as if he hadn't been interrupted: "'—For the traitor appears not as a traitor; he speaks in accents familiar to his victims; he wears their face and their arguments, he appeals to the baseness that lies deep in the hearts of all men—'"

"I'll tell you who the traitor is—that slippery fuck Boyega—where the hell was *he* when all this Russia shit was going on?"

"'—He rots the soul of a nation—'"

"*I'm* the only one who can *save* this fucking nation!"

"'—he works secretly and unknown in the night to undermine the pillars of the city—'"

"This country is *screwed* without me!"

"'—he infects the body politic so that it can no longer resist—'"

"They *need* me!"

"'—A murderer is less to fear.'"

True Son halted, the darkened eyes of his mask fixed on the President; then he tilted his head and acknowledged the author of the quote: "Marcus Tullius Cicero."

The President stood frozen for a second, his chest rising and falling with staggered breaths; then he stabbed a finger at the screen. "You want to play hardball with me, you little bitch? Is that what you want? You want to lock horns with the big bull, is that it? You think you can come in here—into *my* office, *my* country—and *humiliate* me . . . in front of the world . . . on *TV* . . . and get away with it? You little punkass pinko night-fighter foreign piece of shit! You think you can stick one up *my* ass and get away with it? You think that, you dirty little hadji *fuck? I will end you, motherfucker! I will fucking end you!* You think you're dealing with that arugula-eating eggplant Boyega here? Or that skeezy little crook Hannah Crichton? *Fuck you, and your goat-herding old man! I will fucking E N D you, you filthy little cocksucking goat-herding terrorist bitch!"*

At some point during the President's tirade, True Son had cued a new piece of music, which started low and incrementally grew louder. With each upturn of the dial on True Son's remote control, the old man's rant got louder and more aggressive. It went on like this until the sound pouring from the speakers became so loud that the President was reduced to nothing more than a manic mime, stabbing his finger at the TV screen while his eyes bulged with fury and his face bloomed purple with rage, like a plum in a vice on the verge of exploding.

Adding insult to injury, the overpowering music wasn't the dramatic Batman/Superman theme, with its sweeping grandeur, or the catchy pop tune by that boy band, FIYM, or even one of those nasty, insinuating *Hamilton* songs, which at least sounded like real music. It was that screaming rap filth—a real ear-blaster, called *Hit the Floor* by Linkin Park, according to the TuneSleuth app. And it just kept driving at the President, scraping at his brain like broken glass on a chalkboard. Driving and cutting, so deep he couldn't think straight.

Then the President was pointing at the screen again and shouting at the top of his lungs: *"TURN IT DOWN! DO YOU HEAR ME? TURN THAT FUCKING SHIT DOWN RIGHT NOW!"*

But no matter how loud he yelled, he couldn't make himself heard over the bile spilling from the speakers.

For a moment, he thought of attacking the speakers,

ripping them down and trashing them, as he'd done with the TV. But then he wouldn't be able to hear True Son's screams when the troops arrived and took him down, and the President very much wanted to hear those screams. More than anything he'd ever wanted in his entire life, he wanted to hear True Son cry out in agony.

He stopped shouting and ran his fingers through his sweat-drenched hair, sweeping it back. His body was trembling with rage, but somehow he managed to push back against it. *He* had the upper hand here. *He* had the stone-cold nuts. He was the fucking president! Of the United Fucking States! And nobody but *nobody* was going to push him around. Not on TV. Not with the entire fucking world watching on *live TV!*

This was going to end right here, right now. And everyone was going to see just how goddamn presidential he could be. Tomorrow they'd be throwing celebrations for him all over the country. They'd be marching, all right. They'd be marching *in* his honor, not against him. The gays, the blacks, the Hispanics, the women in their little pink pussy hats—all of them would be marching for him. The hugest crowds ever, bigger and better than any inauguration—*way* better, *far* bigger. Even his many enemies would be joining the marches, and they would love him—even the ones who hated him the most would love him and praise him. And he would forgive each and every one of them for ever doubting him because he was, if nothing else, a gracious and forgiving man.

It was going to be a sight to see, a wonderful, wonderful sight to see. All he had to do was plug this leak and right the ship.

I'm the president! I AM the president! The fuckin' buck stops right here, right now, with me!

With a trembling hand, he typed three words into the message box on the mobile phone—SHOOT TO KILL—and pressed send.

With the trashy music still pounding in his ears, he typed another message: I'M SERIOUS. I WANT THIS FUCKER DEAD. THAT'S AN ORDER!

The moment he pressed SEND on the second message, the music stopped.

The silence came like blissful relief. When the President looked up from the phone, Kayley Tru took a step backward, while Trent Michael moved in for a close-up.

The President looked up at the TV above the mantel. Blood still thundered at his temples, his breath came in ragged, noisy waves through his nose, but he looked calmer, almost serene. He even managed a crooked smile.

"I'm going to get you, True Son."

"So you've indicated."

"I mean, I'm really, *really* gonna get you. And you wanna know why, tough guy? Because I'm *smarter* than you. Because, while you were wasting your time learning all that useless crap from books, I've been out there in the *real* world *making* history, not *reading* about it. I'm smarter than you, and I'm gonna get you because I never lose, no matter what, I always come out on top. People go down all around me— big people, little people, doesn't matter, they all go down— while I stay right here, right where I'll always be: on top of the world. *Nobody* can knock me off this mountain—not you, not those weak little pricks in Congress, not Karloff and his entire team of so-called special investigators, *nobody*. I walk between the raindrops, buddy boy, and I never lose. Because I'm a *winner*, and I'm *so* much smarter, *so* much more smarter than anyone can imagine. I've got you right where I want you, and you don't even know it. Because I'm smarter than you, True Son. I'm *smarter* than you, and I'm gonna get you, and you can't even see it coming—"

The President halted abruptly, gritting his teeth, wanting so badly to tell the little bastard just *how* he was going to get him, but he held the secret in and reiterated the core truth: "I mean I'm really, *really* going to get you."

"I'm counting on it," came the calm reply.

The President uttered a strange half-laugh, despite the painful throbbing in his head.

"You got some Kryptonite hiding behind that mask, Batman? You gonna take out the Man of Steel? You ready for the dawn of justice?"

He chuckled again, that same strange half-laugh. But before he could say any more, music rose from the speakers once again. Not more of that nasty rap rubbish, but *real* music. A smooth, nearly hypnotic ballad that the TuneSleuth app identified as *Demons* by Imagine Dragons.

But the President couldn't avert his gaze from the widescreen TV, even when the phone hummed in his hand to alert him that TuneSleuth had fetched the title of the new song for him.

He couldn't take his eyes off the screen for the very same reason that every other person watching the live broadcast around the world couldn't take their eyes off their television screens . . .

Because True Son had set down the remote control and was now reaching up with both hands to remove his mask.

Dane Kingley looked up from the greeting card on his father's desk and with bright yet grave eyes cried out, "That's me!"

Ilona smiled indulgently at her five-year-old brother and said, "I know, honey, but that's not what you think it means. It's supposed to say—"

"No no no," Dane interrupted, emphatically. He had never been a wilfully stubborn child, but when he felt misunderstood, he could be incredibly rigid. He pointed resolutely with a tiny finger at his signature on the Father's Day card and nearly squealed, "That's *me!*"

The memory of that moment from ten years ago kept

rolling in Ilona's mind, like a film clip caught in a loop, and she pressed the heels of her trembling hands against her temples in a vain effort to push back against it.

That's me!

But even as Marilyn's car screeched to a halt before the North Portico of the White House, the memory loomed large, like a towering wave, threatening to crash down and plunge Ilona into the depths of a bottomless black sea.

That's me! Right there, that's me!

Ilona broke from the car, raced through the throng of reporters—those who hadn't made the cut to join their peers in the Oval Office—and was immediately stopped by a security detail. She didn't recognize any of the officers blocking the entrance to the White House, but she pleaded with them to let her pass, anyway. When the officers stood firm, she turned and looked around desperately for a familiar face.

Please, please, please, she screamed inside her head, *somebody, anybody, please!*

Just when she thought all hope was lost, someone called out her name and waved her over to a group of staffers across the driveway. She ran to the group and addressed them in a breathless voice: "I need to speak with my father! I need to get inside and speak to him right now!"

A young staffer with rimless glasses and tousled dark hair said, "You can't. The whole place is on lockdown. Four people are dead, and the terrorist is still on the loose inside. He's been transmitting from somewhere in there the entire night! I heard it from Mary in the Veep's office. She overheard some Secret Service guys in the hallway. They said the President gave the order for them to take out the terrorist—'shoot to kill,' that's what Mary said."

Ilona, who'd scarcely heard anything the young guy had said—beyond "four people are dead" and "shoot to kill"—turned to the female staffer who'd called her over, and said, "I've been trying to reach my father, but he's not answering his phone. I've got to reach him, I've got to speak to him right now—*why isn't he answering my calls?*"

The young guy with the messy hair and rimless glasses said, "He doesn't have his phone. Kori-Lynne took it away from him so he wouldn't tweet."

"But I *saw* him with his phone on TV!" Ilona nearly shrieked.

The young guy said, "That's my phone. Your dad borrowed it after Kori-Lynne took his phone. He told me not to tell anyone, but I guess it doesn't matter anymore, with all that's—"

Ilona pulled out her phone and said, "What's your number?"

The staffer looked confused.

Ilona spoke sharply and clearly. "Give me your number right now!"

At the same moment Ilona was getting the young staffer's phone number, the President stood transfixed, his gaze locked on the TV screen above the fireplace in the Oval Office.

In the background of the frame, Jacob groaned, but the President wasn't concerned with his son-in-law right now. He was focused solely on the tall figure dressed in black. The song *Demons* (which the President had quickly realized wasn't about real demons but rather the sort of demons that people carry in their minds) had kicked into high gear and was closing in on what Skip Spinner referred to as the "money line."

But this didn't concern the President, either. The only thing that mattered to him was the scene playing out on the wide screen above the mantel: Batman was about to reveal himself to Superman, and *that* was an event worthy of his undivided attention.

The gears inside the helmet whirred as the magnetic lock was released, and the faceplate of the mask disengaged itself from the helmet, allowing the entire apparatus to be removed from True Son's head in a single piece.

A breathless moment passed.

Then the mask and helmet hit the carpeted floor with a thud whose echo sounded in the hearts of every person watching the live broadcast.

On the driveway outside, Ilona, who was not watching TV but already knew what lay behind that mask, listened to the endless ringing from the phone pressed close to her ear and whispered, *"Please, please, please, Daddy, pick up, please pick up . . . "* As a chilly breeze passed along the North Portico like Death's final whisper, the memory Ilona could not repress continued to play out in its endless loop . . .

That's me!

I know, sweetie, but that's not how you're supposed to sign it. That's not what it means. You're supposed to sign it Your son— Your son, Dane.

No no no. TRUE Son. That's me! TRUE Son, Dane!

A sudden wave of emotion had swept over her at that moment, and as she'd looked into those earnest grey eyes, she could see that the boy had overheard their father speaking with her and Roy Jr. a few nights before.

I don't know. He's probably the gardener's kid, maybe the pool boy's—he kinda looks like the pool boy—who knows?

Their father had only been joking, of course. He'd just had a terrible fight with Daniella and had made a bad joke, Ilona knew that. But she also knew that the flip comment would have sounded like anything *but* a joke to a five-year-old boy.

I'm True Son, the boy had said declaratively, pointing to the signature on the Father's Day card he'd chosen with such care. *I'M True Son!*

In the Oval Office, the President stood in trancelike fixation before the image on the screen, which he could scarcely credit. The numbness that had washed over him when the mask and helmet hit the floor was so complete that he didn't even notice when his thumb swiped across the screen of the ringing phone in his limp right hand and tapped the SPEAKER icon. And suddenly Ilona's voice sounded off, loud and clear.

"*Daddy?*" Ilona cried. "*Daddy, can you hear me? Daddy, call the agents off . . . it's Dane! . . . Daddy, call them off! It's Dane! Daddy, please call them off! Call them off now! It's Dane! Daddy, it's Dane!*"

But her plea could not compete with the mesmerizing lyrics that spilled from the speakers now, penetrating her father's defenses, probing his soul, like an accusation concealed in a confession . . .

> *Curtain's call*
> *Is the last of all*
> *When the lights fade out*
> *All the sinners crawl*
>
> *So they dug your grave*
> *And the masquerade*
> *Will come calling out*
> *At the mess you've made*

"*Daddy, can you hear me? Can you hear me? Daddy, please, call them off . . .*"

But the President stood paralyzed, mesmerized, as he gazed at the unmasked face on the TV screen . . . the careless falling of shiny, dark hair over those brooding grey eyes; the determined set of that defiant chin; the posture of a man in a teenager's body; the stoical stance of a worthy opponent.

True Son.

His son.

Dane.

With the force of a hurricane, words came raining down on the President, flooding his senses, seemingly from all directions at once . . .

You are the father, are you not?

I am the father.

You're overwrought.

I'm just getting started, little man.

The prince refused to fight.

And I'm this prince, is that it?

No. I am.

This is about your old man.

I am True Son.

Sold you on that load of crap.

Second to the Last.

Ever since you were yay high.

Diviner of Secrets.

Do it!

Destroyer of Demagogues.

Do it for Daddy!

And you are?

                              I am the father.

It is not my intention
to break him.

                              Do it, you pansy-ass
                              little Daddy's boy!

The prince did his duty.

                              I'm gonna get you, True Son.

I'm counting on it.

                    TURN THAT FUCKING SHIT
                    DOWN RIGHT NOW!

. . . while, from the speakers, the lyrics kept coming at him, like razor-sharp blades, carving into his skull . . .

            Don't wanna let you down
            But I am hell bound
            Though this is all for you
            Don't wanna hide the truth

. . . and from the phone, Ilona crying out: "*Daddy . . . Daddy, can you hear me?*"

            No matter what we breed
            We still are made of greed
            This is my kingdom come
            This is my kingdom come

Dane Kingley's eyes shimmered under the dim lights

of the First Family's private cinema in the East Wing, which had provided him with all he needed to carry out his plan: a quiet location for his base of operation, with easy access to the rest of the White House, so that he could come and go without arousing suspicion—and more important, the last place anyone would expect to find True Son . . . until he was ready to be found.

On the bank of security monitors he'd set up below the huge projection screen, Dane could see his father's assault team moving down the corridor of the East Colonnade, just like they did in training drills. Only, this wasn't a drill. In seconds they would come crashing through the doors, their weapons drawn, ready for action.

Dane turned his gaze back to the big screen, where his father, the President, stood frozen, powerless, impotent, under the onslaught of the carefully selected song . . .

> *They say it's what you make*
> *I say it's up to fate*
> *It's woven in my soul*
> *I need to let you go*
>
> *Your eyes, they shine so bright*
> *I wanna save that light*

Gazing into his son's eyes, where tears brimmed but did not fall (the kid was hard as nails—you had to give him that), the President felt a facile icy finger touch his spine . . . right at the moment the money line hit:

> *I can't escape this now*
> *Unless you show me how*

Then the chorus came raining down:

> *Look into my eyes*

> It's where my demons hide
> Don't get too close
> It's dark inside
> It's where my demons hide

But this was drowned out by the sound of Ilona scream-ing, "Daddy, it's Dane! Daddy, please, call them off! Call them off! It's Dane!"

But by then, it was too late.

The doors at the back of the cinema crashed open, and the sound of men shouting was followed fast by an ear-split-ting burst of gunfire (later, one of the shooters would swear that he saw a weapon in the teenage boy's hand, but a thor-ough scrub of the scene would reveal that Dane Kingley, aka True Son, was armed only with a remote control, which was still clasped in his left hand when his body hit the floor).

The moment the shots rang out from inside the White House, Ilona broke through the startled security ranks and raced inside. She was immediately stopped by another security detail in the East Colonnade and would have been escorted out of the hall if not for the timely appearance of Kori-Lynne Carpwell.

One of the security guards was still holding Ilona back when Kori-Lynne shouted, "She's the President's daughter! Let her through!"

Ilona rushed past Kori-Lynne to the open doors of the cinema and raced down the aisle. She did not stop to see if Jake was all right. She ran straight to her younger brother, fell to her knees in the pool of blood that was rapidly bloom-ing around the boy's body, and lifted his head onto her lap.

Dane looked up at her with glassy eyes, and his lips parted. Ilona stroked his hair with trembling fingers and spoke softly, gently. "It's all right now . . . someone is coming . . . someone is coming to help you. Lie still now."

Dane swallowed, his eyes fading under the soft glow of the spotlight. His lips moved, but no words came out.

Kori-Lynne stood behind Ilona now, her eyes wide at the sight of all the blood. She placed a hand on Ilona's shoulder, but Ilona scarcely felt it. With tears spilling down her cheeks, Ilona leaned in closer to hear what her brother was trying to say.

Dane spoke in a gurgling whisper as blood leaked into his lungs, but this time Ilona heard him. He said: "He . . . can . . . see me . . . can . . . see me . . . "

Tears spilled from her eyes as Ilona recalled that day in her room at Tower K when Dane had come in and sat next to her on the bed to comfort her while *The A-Team* played over and over. That had been six years ago. Dane had only been nine at the time, but even at that young age, he possessed a calm and quiet strength. He had stayed with her and comforted her until all the tears were gone and she could think clearly again.

That's what she needed to do now. She needed to think clearly and be strong. She needed to comfort her younger brother the way he had always done for her.

"Yes, baby," she said. "Daddy can see you . . . he sees you, and he loves you, he loves you so much, so very much . . . "

Dane swallowed and with effort moved his head ever so slightly, once to the right and then to the left. "He . . . can . . . see . . . he . . . can . . . see . . . me . . . "

Ilona stroked her brother's damp hair gently and cooed soothingly, "Daddy sees you, and he loves you, my angel, he loves you so very much . . . "

Dane closed his eyes and tried to muster the strength to speak again, but there was nothing left in him. When he looked up one last time, he could see Kori-Lynne standing above with a comforting hand on Ilona's shoulder. In Kori-Lynne's eyes, he could see that she understood exactly what he'd been struggling to tell his sister. He held his gaze on Kori-Lynne as a single tear spilled down his cheek.

And then he was gone.

Though the tragic ending of Dane Kingley's short life had been broadcast to the entire world on live TV, no one noticed that he'd pressed the button on his remote control one last time before releasing his final breath.

And so, when the exit music rose—not only in the Oval Office but all around the White House, where Dane had placed a series of speakers for the finale—some were surprised, some were moved to tears, some were too numb to notice. But only one had his phone out to identify the music.

THE PRESIDENT HAD STEPPED OUT OF THE OVAL OFFICE shortly after the Secret Service had cut the live feed in the cinema. By then, the jackals at the news stations had come back on to parse what had just happened for their hungry viewers, and he didn't have the stomach for it. He didn't begrudge them the spoils of their victory, but he wasn't about to stay and watch them pick at the remains of the corpse.

At first, the President thought the music drifting down from the high ceiling of the deserted Cross Hall was only in his mind, perhaps conjured by some distant memory of which he was only vaguely aware. But when the mobile phone in his hand buzzed with a new alert from TuneSleuth, he realized the music was real. TuneSleuth identified the song as *Que Sera, Sera*. But the singer didn't sound like Doris Day. And the instrumentation was all wrong. It sounded dissonant and twisted, like one of those nightmarish tunes they play for babies in nurseries—sweet but kind of creepy. TuneSleuth identified the artist as Pink Martini. Whether that was the name of a singer or a group, the President did not know; all he knew was that Pink Martini was no Doris Day, that was for sure.

He bridged the distance between the west and east ends of the Cross Hall in hazy, dreamlike steps, and eventually found himself in the open doorway of the East Room, where his youngest child, Barret, had spent most of the past two weeks working on a surprise for him.

Someone had said something to him about Barret as he'd passed through the hallway outside the Oval Office a few minutes ago, something that he couldn't quite recall now. Something about Barret being safe. Something about Agent Hasney too. The President had just nodded and continued on his way in silence. It was good to hear that Barret was safe, and he really liked that Hasney kid—good kid, solid young man. It had been the best decision he'd ever made, hiring Hasney. Let them say what they would about his other decisions, but none could pooh-pooh him about his decision to hire Agent Hasney.

Without realizing just how correct he was, he muttered, "At least I got that one right . . . "

The President was startled out of his trancelike state when he took a step into the East Room and the toe of his shoe bumped the wooden block on the floor.

The chain reaction that followed was at once both fascinating and frightful. The wooden block he'd accidentally knocked over was the trigger for a long and winding string of white tumbling tiles, which wrapped around the perimeter of the East Room and wove into the base of the structures. The snaking pattern of tiles fell in perfect succession, like a burning fuse racing toward an explosive charge, as the President stood by, powerless to stop that which his misstep had set in motion.

The culmination came in the stunning collapse of the structures Barret had worked so tirelessly throughout the past two weeks to construct. They went down, one by one, in spectacular fashion—the Lincoln Memorial, the Washington Monument, the Pentagon, the Capitol Building, and finally the White House itself, which appeared to disintegrate, in slow-motion, from within.

As the President stood like a sleepwalker, gazing upon the rubble that spread the length of the East Room, the music swelled in an unexpected dramatic wave, its discordant notes sounding more like a funeral waltz than the sweet ballad he recalled from his youth.

And there at the center of the floor, he could see Hannah and Boyega, dancing between the rows of spilt tiles. Waltzing gracefully through the destruction as if they hadn't a care in the world.

The music swelled even higher as a parade of stretchers was wheeled out of the North Entrance of the White House by EMTs. The first five stretchers carried sealed black body bags. The EMTs loaded these stretchers into the backs of large white coroner's vans.

The other stretchers carried two young men, who both appeared to be alive.

Watching the scene on the television in the executive suite of Tower K in New York, Roy Jr. recognized Jake at once. He might not have recognized the other young man at all, if not for the boy walking alongside the stretcher. The injured man was a Secret Service agent, Hasney, and the boy was Roy Jr.'s youngest brother, Barret.

Skip Spinner was there too, and when the stretcher stopped at the back of the waiting ambulance, Skip lifted Barret so that he could speak to the Secret Service agent. Roy Jr. was surprised when Barret hugged the agent and kissed him on the cheek. The agent looked dazed and weakened, but he reached up and gently squeezed the back of Barret's neck while the boy clung to him. When they finally separated, the agent said something to Skip Spinner, and Skip, who stood behind Barret with his hands on the boy's shoulders, nodded reassuringly in response.

It wasn't until the Breaking News banner at the bottom of the TV screen changed from "Crisis At The White House" to "Courageous Secret Service Agent Risks Own

Life To Protect Youngest Son of POTUS" that Roy Jr. became aware of the tightening in his chest and the rising lump in his throat. He tried to fight the emotion, but when his sister Tabby came from behind and wrapped her arms around him, his resistance broke, and the images on TV were suddenly no more than a blur through his tears.

In Ben Stiverson's DC apartment, Merrick Kingley lay curled into a fetal position on the sofa, his body trembling, tears spilling down his cheeks. He choked back a desperate sob when his older sister, Ilona, appeared on the TV screen.

She came from the White House and was immediately rushed by a gaggle of reporters, all of them shoving microphones at her and demanding a statement. To her credit, she did not respond. She just kept moving, with the aid of Kori-Lynne and her old college friend whose name Merrick could not recall. When they reached the Ambulance that Jake had been loaded into, one of the EMTs took Ilona's hand and helped her inside. Then the doors closed, and Ilona's face, drained and numb, peered out the back window with unseeing eyes.

It wasn't the pallor of her skin or the vacant look in her eyes that had tipped the scales for Merrick. It was the flecks of Dane's blood on her cheeks and in her hair that had done it. Just tiny flecks, scarcely noticeable, but when Merrick saw them, he began to scream . . . while from the speakers his younger brother had set up outside the White House, that eerie song played on and on . . .

"*Que sera, sera. Whatever will be, will be . . .* "

As they approached the entrance to the North drive of the White House, Rance Plebeius and Stretch Biggerstaff were greeted by Deputy National Security Advisor Marshal Berenger, who was accompanied by two uniformed marines; all three men wore grave expressions.

Berenger addressed the former chief of staff in a formal tone. "Would you excuse us for a moment, sir. We'd like to have a word with Mr. Biggerstaff."

Rance looked confused, but he nodded and headed up toward the White House to see what was going on.

Stretch squared his jaw and gave Berenger a stern look. Berenger, who'd stood toe to toe with his fair share of tough guys, didn't blink. He studied the older man's eyes, and in them, he found what he was looking for.

Stretch stared down his nose at the major. "So, what do you need?"

Berenger said, "Just a moment of your time, sir."

The major led the way up the drive, and Stretch followed, flanked by the marines. They stopped at one of the big white coroner's vans, and Major Berenger gave a nod to the attendant. The EMT opened the back doors, rolled out the stretcher, and unzipped the body bag. Stretch recognized the young man inside the black bag at once—with his purplish-blue face and his neck twisted at a brutal angle, Bart Benedict didn't look so pretty anymore.

Berenger produced a mobile phone from his pocket. Then he reached inside the body bag, pulled out Bart's left hand, and pressed the thumb against the phone's home button. The screen glowed into life instantly. Berenger brought up the last text message thread and held the phone so that Stretch could see it.

The last message displayed on the screen read: "Do it."

Berenger looked into Stretch's eyes, and calmly asked, "Can you explain what this message is in reference to, sir?"

Stretch gazed at the mobile phone's screen for what seemed an eternity, and only when the Deputy National Security Advisor repeated the question did he respond. With his gaze still locked on the phone's screen, where the damning message glowed like a neon sign pointing straight down the crapper, Stretch Biggerstaff replied in an uncharacteristically soft tone of voice, "I think I'd like to speak with my attorney now."

At the same time his former chief strategist was being taken into custody, the President found his way back into the Oval Office—he just couldn't take Hannah and Boyega's victory waltz anymore. They'd set him up beautifully, and he had fallen right into their trap. He didn't begrudge them their victory, but he couldn't stay and watch the celebration. Not now. There had to be a mourning period. He would never kick somebody when they were down; it just wasn't his style. Sure, he'd taken a few shots at Hannah after her humiliating defeat, but she'd really had it coming—and at least he'd waited a few days to stick it to her, when the wound wasn't quite so fresh. At least he'd done that. But to celebrate on the spot, before the body was even cold . . . it was tasteless, really.

The corrupted version of the Doris Day song was still playing, but he tuned it out as he watched what was going on outside. Having lost the fresh meat of his distraught daughter, the media vultures had descended on the nearest roadkill they could find.

Poor Kori-Lynne, he thought distantly. *She looks like hell, but she's still kicking . . . those media shrews won't stop until they've used up every last one of her nine lives.*

He felt for her, truly—at least as much as the numbing cloud around his mind would allow—but he had to admit, she looked terrible. Her hair was a mess, and her face was even worse—no woman should look like that: lipstick faded, rouge all smeared across her cheeks, mascara running in black streaks—like the face of a tragic clown at a circus that had long since shut down without anybody bothering to tell her. It was pathetic. Heartbreaking, really.

The insatiable press was still shouting questions at Kori-Lynne as she headed for her car.

"Kori-Lynne, can you confirm that Dane Kingley's last

words were 'Can he see me?'—and, if so, was he speaking about his father when he asked that question?"

Kori-Lynne stopped and looked the reporter in the eye. "No, Margaret, that's not what he said . . . that's not what he said at all."

"Can you tell us what he did say? And was he speaking of his father?"

Kori-Lynne's mouth opened and closed. A tear spilled down her cheek. Her lips trembled, but she managed to hold it together, despite the wave of emotion that threatened to pull her under.

"You know what—" she began in a shaky voice. "You know what he was . . . he was a very sweet boy, and he . . . he was . . . he was kind and gentle, and he didn't deserve this . . . he was just a kid, and he didn't deserve any of this . . . and . . . "

The tears began to fall in earnest, but she did not give in to them. In her mind's eye, she could see Dane Kingley in that final moment, gazing up at her, knowing that she knew.

" . . . and he was better than this . . . us . . . all of this . . . he was better than . . . "

She swiped at her eyes, but the tears kept coming.

"You want to know what he said, Margaret? You want to know what he said about his father . . . ?"

She was visibly trembling now. She swiped at her eyes again and looked off into the night, where hundreds of lights began to flicker in the nearby darkness. Though she couldn't see it clearly yet, she understood what it meant. In her mind, she could see Dane's eyes looking up at her, and she smiled sadly with an understanding that was solely her own for the moment. But soon that would change. Soon that understanding would reach every person watching the live news broadcast around the world.

She turned back to the reporter and said, "He was a good kid . . . people need . . . people need to know that . . .

people need to know the truth. They need to know. He was a really good kid . . . a really good kid, and don't let anybody tell you different. Don't you dare let them do that."

Kori-Lynne shot a hard glance at the White House, shook her head, swiped away tears, and went to her car without another word.

The emotion in Kori-Lynne's voice, along with that last glance she'd pitched in his direction, might have broken through to the President—Kori-Lynne was, after all, one of the very few who possessed the ability to penetrate his defenses with a single glance. But by the time she'd hit him with that glance on this night, he had already begun to recede . . . back to that place in his mind where things were infinitely more controllable than they were in the real world; where visions sprouted and grew without the stifling constraints of rules and regulations that never failed to muddy the waters; where words, and sometimes even actions, weren't afforded nearly as much weight as the contents of the heart, because, as the President firmly believed, the heart knew no boundaries, and by that token, could not be faulted for its many and varied excesses.

He understood this intuitively. Just as he understood that you couldn't possibly measure the greatness of any man—regardless of the consequences of his actions, good or bad, right or wrong—without factoring in the content of his heart.

The President turned away from the TV now and took his rightful seat behind the desk in the deserted Oval Office. With his back to the window and all voices tuned out—save for the only voice that mattered: the one that came from within—he did not hear the revelation on the live news broadcast.

He did not hear Rowan Meadow covering the story that was currently unfolding on the West Lawn of the Capitol.

He did not see the kids who had patiently stood vigil

throughout the cold night to fulfill their promise to True Son, who had reached out to them on his website and guided them to this moment in history.

Now against the backdrop of the cold dark night, hundreds of lights shimmered from the mobile phones the young followers of True Son held above their heads—all angled in the direction of the White House and properly spaced to form a single message . . . the last words True Son had spoken before expelling his final breath:

HE CAN'T SEE ME

On the TV above the mantel in the Oval Office, an aerial shot appeared of the children's message, still glowing in the night. And as newscasters around the world translated and repeated those four words, which would become a mantra over the remainder of his presidency, the man with the weight of the world on his shoulders retreated to the only place he had ever truly found solace—that simple and comforting twilit corner of his mind, where nothing and no one could reach him.